TRENCH

W

E

S

Kenton
Hill

Hoaklin

Trent

Dunnitch

Dorser

Scurry

Hesson

A
FORBIDDEN
ALCHEMY

A
FORBIDDEN
ALCHEMY

STACEY McEWAN

SAGA PRESS

LONDON **NEW YORK** TORONTO
AMSTERDAM/ANTWERP NEW DELHI SYDNEY/MELBOURNE

SAGA PRESS

AN IMPRINT OF SIMON & SCHUSTER, LLC

1230 AVENUE OF THE AMERICAS, NEW YORK, NEW YORK 10020

First Saga Press hardcover edition July 2025

SAGA PRESS and colophon are trademarks of Simon & Schuster, LLC

Interior design by Erika R. Genova

Manufactured in the United States of America

1 3 5 7 9 10 8 6 4 2

Library of Congress Cataloging-in-Publication Data is available.

ISBN 978-1-6680-7618-7
ISBN 978-1-6680-7620-0 (ebook)

To my children, Zoe and Dean.
You'll choose your own magic.

PROLOGUE

NINA

I took the name of a dead canary.

My birth coincided with the collapse of a nearby mine—the most catastrophic collapse the continent of Belavere Trench had ever known. All 104 men within those tunnels were buried alive that day, with the exception of one—my father—who miraculously emerged from the dust, suffocated canary in hand.

My father liked to retell that story whenever whiskey persuaded him to, which was often. "Heard the blasted thing fall right off 'is perch, I swear it! She was always bloody squawkin', you see? Never fuckin' let up. Named it Caranina after that singer lady, you know the one? Moment she went quiet, I knew somethin' weren't right. Next I knew, the whole fuckin' place was cavin' underfoot. Barely reached daylight." Fletcher Harrow would gesture to me then. "Came home to find me girl were born! It were fate, you see? God snuffed that canary so that I could see Nina with me own eyes!"

He'd smile for a moment, remembering a newborn version of me, and then he'd remember those 103 men buried and grow solemn. The solemnness would turn to anger. Anger meant whiskey.

"Fuckin' mines," he'd mutter. Then, "Fuckin' *swanks* in their fuckin' fancy robes," and as though the words were combustible, other craftsmen, whatever their trade, would ignite.

Together, they'd cradle their cups and curse their poor fortune. They would blame the Head of House first, then all the Lords, then all Artisans for their luck in life.

There were only two kinds of people in the world, and I'd known it before I could talk. There were the people like my father, who worked honestly. Craftsmen who were paid far too little for their long days in the mines, the factories, the farms. And then there were Artisans: the fortunate. The high-society swanks with their magic.

"Who says they've got more to offer than us, aye?" This, from some other drunkard. "Sittin' in their fine houses, butlers and all."

"God's whores," someone would say. "If Idia appeared before me, I'd wrap me hands 'round her holy throat."

But the Holy daughter, Idia, was likely somewhere high above laughing. The Artisans were in Belavere City, miles and miles away. And as for these men, their fortunes would never change. Their fate had been determined for them in childhood when they had been put on a train to that fancy city, prayed to Idia, and swallowed a solution that would determine if magic lived within them, or if they were of better service out in the brink of the continent, sweating and moaning and occasionally being buried alive.

Eventually one would speak too brashly or throw his glass, and the coppers would drag him out and jail him a night or two, but this was the extent of their rebellion. There was no one out here to fight but each other.

And anyway, who could raise a hand against those Artisans, whose blood was imbued with magic? Surely not this sorry lot.

I chuffed from my barstool, imagining these bloated clucks stumbling toward a blue-robed, Belavere-branded Artisan. They wouldn't stand a chance.

"Nina," my father said, just now remembering I was there. "Go on home, now. Tell your ma to heat some supper. I won't be far behind."

Ma wouldn't be at home. Hadn't been home in several years now. But whiskey was a magic all its own. Nothing to do but nod.

I ran barefoot down dirt roads the entire way, skipping over reeking drains and spilled coal dust. I didn't stop until I was safely through the door of our two-room lodging. Then I exhaled the Scurry stench and took my tingling hands over to the Scribbler's cranny.

A Scribbler's cranny usually consisted of a writer's desk with piles of waiting parchment. Artisan Scribblers were the source of all correspondence in Belavere Trench. A continent of Artisan magic had no need for boats and trains or birds to send messages, not when Scribblers could ink a page from many, many miles away with their mind alone.

There was a special sound associated with a Scribbler's message. The parchment in the Scribbler's cranny would crinkle just slightly, a gentle scratch would ensue, the insides of your stomach would clench. Who was sending word? What news would the ink bring?

Ma, I'd think. *This time it will be from Ma.*

It never was.

Our Scribbler's cranny was not so much a cranny as the space between boiler and bench. And there wasn't so much a writing desk as there was an old chopping block balanced atop a stool. The pile of waiting parchment curled at the corners.

I had been aching all day to sit by it, and not because I anticipated a missive from my mother. I was older now. It had been a long time since I'd bawled for her. No, this night, I awaited a letter of much more importance.

I imagined every child of twelve to be sitting just as I was, hovering over a parchment, waiting on a Scribbler who sat hundreds of miles away, curling their names and addresses in order. Over and over, I convinced myself the parchment was moving, that a spot of ink was beginning to appear, but hours passed, and the parchment remained obstinately plain.

At midnight, a clock tower chimed its warning, my father stumbled through the door and landed face-first on his cot. No ink. No cursive.

But I stayed by the boiler, blanket around my shoulders and eyelids back. And in the very early hours, the first rustles bolted through the chamber of my chest.

The parchment cracked, awakened.

I leapt from my stool.

Words unfurled from nothing.

BY ORDER OF BELAVERE TRENCH NATIONAL COUNCIL

To the attention of Miss Nina Harrow
of
348 Cobbler and Brum, Row 5, Scurry.

On the 23rd of September, 1892, all children who were born twelve years prior are henceforth summoned to Belavere City and the National Artisan House to enact the 535th Siphoning Ceremony, as per the below articles 2, 3, 6, & 18 of the National Constitution of Belavere Trench.

Long live Belavere.

2. Idium Quantum

To incite the birthright of magics, male children upon the age of twelve years are mandated to consume one ounce of idium dilution. The effects thereafter will constitute the legal status of the individual's magics, and they shall be irrevocably designated Artisan or Craftsman.

3. Idium Quota

A citizen with official Artisan branding is eligible to an allotment of one ounce of idium dilution twice annually.

6. Education

Every child will be offered approved curriculum. Those deemed Artisan will attend the National Artisan School. Those deemed Craftsman will thereafter seek education at their guardians' volition.

18. As of the 469th year of siphoning, female children upon the age of twelve years may also rightfully consume one ounce of idium dilution. The effects thereafter will constitute the legal status of the individual's magics.

CHAPTER 1

NINA

In late September, I boarded a train.

The smokestack left plumes in our wake, dirtying the carriage windows, and I wondered if the smoke hadn't followed us from home. I pressed my nose to the glass and made out the silhouette of Scurry in the distance, then saluted the town with my middle finger and turned away from it forever.

The carriage was filled to the brim with children: twelve years of age, fraying socks, soot on their eyelashes and mush in their heads, I imagined. Lady chaperones in long woolen skirts and slickened faces stumbled down the aisle against inertia. One leaned across the seat and flattened the lace trim collar of my blouse without looking me in the eye.

They yelled ineffectually at those who hung over their seats, at the boys who dared take off their caps, at the girls who bunched their dresses above the knee. *Sit proper! Wipe your nose! Roll down your sleeves!* The pleas went unnoticed. The children of Scurry bickered and caterwauled. We were teeming and swelling and spilling over with adventure. Something new was upon us. Something vast and frightening and intoxicatingly possible.

Possible.

I clung to that word. I wasn't swept away by the same vicious thrill as the rest. I sat quiet and still. I gripped a badly bound wad of parchment, its pages filled with profile sketches and plant anatomy. I looked dead ahead and saw the possibilities my brain conjured. It drew me pictures of white marble walls and clean canvas. Of starched white blouses and badly stained aprons, imbued with years of paints and clay and charcoal. A landscape stretched in my mind of never-ending rooftops, where the church steeples and bell towers stretched high enough that one could see all the way to the edge of the continent from their rafters.

Soon, the pictures turned to dreams. The chaos aboard ebbed and flowed. The steam chest coughed. The floor rattled atop the cranks. We were carried farther and farther away from all we'd ever known.

I journeyed all the way to the Artisan capital city without a single thought for home. There were only dreams of brilliant crimson blood that turned inky blue.

CHAPTER 2

PATRICK

Farther north, a different train with an asthmatic whistle pulled to a stop at Kenton Hill.

A boy named Patrick Colson boarded with his breath held, wiping sweat from his hands onto the seats. He waved once to his brothers, to his mother, and silently vowed he'd return tomorrow.

The train pulled away with a jolt, and the boy sighed and pressed his back into the wooden bench, swore quietly, curled his nails into his thighs until they bit.

He watched home slip sideways through the window and felt the distance like a slow amputation. A simmer of dread that emerged at breakfast now boiled over.

Beyond the clatter of the tracks, he heard the train's farewell whistle, and it sounded like the signal of shifts changing in the mines. His dad and older brother always worked the second shift, never the first. When Patrick returned to Kenton Hill tomorrow, he would join them.

Miner's blood, through and through—black with soot, like his father, and all the fathers that came before. And therein, this journey was redundant for Patrick. He didn't need the Artisans in their capital city to tell his fortune. What he needed, very badly, was to return to his mother, who waited at the bay windows of a black brick building. He needed to be among those close walls and low ceilings. Back to the yellow grass hills. To the mills and canals and the great gaping holes in the earth that swallowed men and spat them back out. He needed to be waiting by the whistle in the morning when the night shift ended and ensure his father and brother were spat out with the rest. He needed to be there if (God have mercy) none came back up at all.

At that moment, the worker's whistle was sounding all over the continent, in dozens of different towns, while dozens of different trains battered across tracks toward the nation's center.

Much like Nina of Scurry, Patrick ignored the frenzy of children. But the Kenton boy did not sleep. He rubbed his nose subtly to catch tears before they fell over his lip. He stifled the sick in his belly with anger, jutted his chin, stared straight ahead. He dared the bloody Artisans to try and take him away to their fucking school.

They had everything in the world already.

They couldn't have him.

CHAPTER 3

NINA

The chaperones herded us on foot into the heart of Belavere Trench, and I became suddenly, brutally aware that I was a speck on an ever-expanding map.

Scurry had always seemed half collapsed. Even as a younger girl, when the world was supposed to seem made of giants, it had never been big enough for me. Ma used to say that my mind was big and it made the outside small. "Girls like us," she'd say. "We're made for bigger places, you hear me?"

I'd heard her.

I'd heard everything.

Heard all the parts she didn't say, too. Heard the door shut when she'd left. Heard Dad crying in the night. Heard all the neighbors and their snide speculations of where she'd run off to.

I thought she was likely in a place like this—somewhere big. If she wasn't, then she was in hell, and I didn't care much to visit her in either place.

Belavere City—a place for dreamers and innovators. For artists. For creation. This city was *the* seat of creation—the very center of it, and I now stood in its heart.

I'd stolen my uncle's *Anthology of Belavere* and studied every mural and fresco and blueprint and diagram. I had bothered my father with incessant questions since I'd had a mind to ask them. *Are the boilers Artisan-made,*

9

or *Crafter? What about the shaft pulleys? The conveyors? Surely the conveyors were invented by the Artisans?* It seemed that everything of value, everything worth something, was conceived here.

The towns out in the brink were only the clogged arteries that led to the heart.

I had never seen buildings so tall, so clustered. Their red-tiled roofs and off-white facades matched perfectly with their neighbors'. The doorways were framed in arches, alcoves, steep steps to tiled landings. A girl ahead of me pointed and exclaimed at the domed roof in the distance, its fine sculpted stone decorated with gold. A man stood precariously on its top, and before him, the gold filigree morphed and changed, creating new patterns.

Flowering vines spilled from windows and off balconies. Fat-chested pigeons preened on the gutters. Wagons of coal trundled by with no one behind to push them. The women wore wide-hooped skirts, and the men wore neckties and long coats. They looked up and smiled knowingly as we children passed through. Smaller kids pulled on their mothers' hands and pointed, lamenting the long wait until they too came of age. A man blew into his closed fist, and light appeared. It burst through the cracks between fingers. When his hand unfurled, the light flew from his palm like a dozen released doves and was captured by the lanterns that lined the street.

"Fire Charmer," we whispered.

Here, clean water flowed streetside in tiny trenches no wider than a bucket. The residents need only step beyond their stoop to access it. I wondered at the team of water Charmers it must take to move so much water through the city.

There were Craftsmen here, too, and they were easy to spot, for their wagons and carts did not move for them unless pushed. Their clothes were hardly so fine, their brows already beaded in sweat. I supposed even a city that thrived from the minds of the most brilliant Artisans must still require manual labor, and Crafters were gifted with what the Artisans were not—superior vigor, strength, endurance.

On and on we walked, and I looked in every direction, seeking out the fine details. Every Belaverian book and sketch and testament I'd ever swallowed was spilling from me, unfolding into perfect replicas. Everything glistened. No precariously hung shutters, no puddles in the alleys. The exactness of it all, the cleanliness, was all painfully beautiful.

The National Artisan House was ahead. Its marble columns reminded me of ancient ruins. I knew from my readings that the sculptor had had them in mind when he'd crafted the building's facade.

The crowds of children funneled through the narrow cobblestone pathways and bloomed again into an expansive courtyard behind the building. Here, things were not quite as opulent, and I frowned despite myself. The stone walls were stained with limescale; the ground was not bricked or cobbled, but compacted with dirt. The tall perimeter walls were not lined in the same neatly trimmed hedges at the building's front.

But the air smelled like a million known and unknown things—coffee, kerosene, pastry, tobacco, horse shit. I heard bells and carts and voices upon voices—the cogs of a city perfectly churning, and my excitement returned.

Possibility. The sounds and smells and gleam of it.

It was, despite my father's beliefs, possible that I would become a student of the Artisan School. Didn't the teachers in Scurry say I had a remarkable capacity for the arts? "Natural aptitude," one had called it.

If it wasn't the Artisan School for me, then I would find a way to live among these tightly packed buildings and winding roads. If I couldn't imbue magic, then I would ensure I was surrounded by it. It was still preferable to Scurry.

I would not be boarding another train.

Shoulders bumped into mine. Children continued pouring into the courtyard until we were pushed to its very edges. When it seemed the square surely could not fit one more body, another surge of entrants arrived, hustled in by the calls of chaperones.

We pressed together like cattle in an abattoir, shifting nervously. The smell of so many bodies soon became intolerable.

Finally, someone in navy blue lapels stepped out from the National Artisan House and onto the steps. He held a shiny brass microphone in front of his mouth. It screeched as he pressed its receiving button, and the sea of twelve-year-olds fell silent.

"Good morning," the man said. He had small teeth and thin lips, a bulbous nose, large jowls, sparse hairs plastered over his forehead. There were posters of this man in all the taverns of Scurry. The first-shift miners threw darts at it in the evening.

"Welcome to the National Artisan House, children," said Lord Tanner, the Head of House. A small smattering of awkward applause. Another of my pictures unfolding into reality.

The Lord Tanner. I beamed. What an incredible sight! And what extraordinary invention, to throw one's voice so widely.

I was not alone in my wonder. A girl tugged my sleeve unconsciously and stood on tiptoe to see him better, and another cupped her hands to her mouth. But there were those who were not so taken. One mean-faced boy stood behind my right shoulder and spat on the ground right between his feet.

I, however, knew more than he did about the governing leader of Belavere Trench. I had studied his art. Lord Tanner had crafted marble statues around the city that depicted weeping angels and dying saints. He'd sculpted a granite bridge that scaled over three hundred feet across the Gyser River. He'd created these things with his mind alone. He was a stone Mason of the highest order, and the sight of him turned my skin to gooseflesh.

"To see so many of you is to feel immensely proud of this nation, and its people. People from all walks of life, coming together to celebrate community, prosperity, and . . ." But whatever else it was we were celebrating was impossible to hear. From behind, a low voice laughed derisively, then muttered, "Fuck off."

It was the spitter. Of course it was. A boy with dirty brown hair and an extremely clean shirt, standing too close for my liking. He smiled like he didn't mean it, stood still like he wanted to bolt, stared at the man with the microphone like he'd knock the tiny teeth from his mouth, given the chance. The boy shook his head, shifted his weight to his left leg, then looked me right in the eye.

I was taken aback by their color. Pale blue. Crystal clear. Completely at odds with the rest of him—cracked fingernails, wrinkled trousers, the sole of his shoes gently peeled at the toes. A suntan that circled the bottom of his neck, a starched button-down shirt that made him fidget. He adjusted the collar and the sleeves like he'd found himself in someone else's clothes by mistake. He was too skinny for his height. The belt around his trousers looped over itself.

I wrinkled my nose, mouthed the word *pig,* and turned back to Lord Tanner. Praise God.

". . . and the Almighty sent to us His greatest creation, His daughter, who was not deity nor goddess, but a human who walked on this land as one of us."

Idia, I thought, staring wide-eyed at the book Lord Tanner now held: the Book of Belavere. He read from it in a voice adults use when they believe what they're saying is gravely important. I straightened my shoulders, determined to remember every word.

"Through Idia, the Lord spoke, and He told us this land was a Holy place. He bade us protect it, and when others came to sully its sacred ground, Idia led our armies, and she bled when we bled . . . and her blood was ink." And here, Tanner held high a familiar stone.

It could have been a lump of coal if it weren't for the sun that shone through it, filling it all the way up with light, revealing its true color. Blue like the deepest part of the sea, like slow-falling night.

"Terranium," Tanner stated. "The most important ore our land bestows. For only within this particular stone do we find the crystallized blood of Idia, mined from the land, and given back to its people, even thousands of years after She was returned to God."

Murmurs stirred. I shifted restlessly.

"Through idium, we are made better. We become the person God intended. Through Idia's teachings, we know that creation comes from the body and the mind. Craftsman and creator. Both are equally vital in the turning of the world, for who will shift the Earth on its axis, once the idea has been conceived?" Then, Tanner's free hand lifted.

Awe stilled the crowd. The children fell still and silent and reverent, for who could deny the miracle before them? I gaped at Lord Tanner's empty hand, the way his fingers flexed and relaxed. Hovering above it was a small but perfect sphere of granite stone, spinning in the air by Tanner's will alone.

Tanner watched the stone intently, just as we children did, and it began to change shape. Pieces broke away, crumbling to dust at his feet. I heard the minute cracks as it was carved into something new by no visible force. It became the model of a church, then a hammer, a clock tower. When he needed it, the discarded fragments at Tanner's feet rose again to rejoin his sculpture, and soon the stone crumpled inward, and became a solitary planet once more, smooth and unblemished, rotating in the hand of its sun.

I had never seen a thing so beautiful.

Amid the exclamations, Tanner replaced his stone with a vial of dark liquid. Idium. The purported blood of Idia, siphoned from stone.

"Today, children, you have the very great privilege of learning what God plans for you, whether it be pursuits of the mind, or that of the limbs. When you welcome Idia into your bloodstream today, you become an important part of Belavere's body, and you will begin to aid in its many necessary functions." His tiny teeth flashed in a smile. "So welcome once more to all of you. Today, you have arrived on the threshold of adulthood, and you will leave knowing your purpose."

There was short applause, and I led it. It was tempered with nervous anticipation for that gleaming vial of inky blood—the precious substance we were all about to consume.

Lord Tanner stepped away from the microphone with a politician's wave and disappeared back into the building, and the crowd broke into a violent, frenzied chatter.

I did not join in the conversation. Emblazoned in my mind was that piece of granite transforming into ideas, again and again, and a smile crept in.

I looked skyward to the highest story of the House, where Tanner's office likely was. I would wager it was the size of my entire home back in Scurry. Bigger, even. Filled with oil paintings and sculptures and busts and ornately carved furniture from the finest everything, and I longed to be in the presence of it all.

Would the Artisan School be like this? Austere and bright and towering?

The double doors opened out to the courtyard again, and a dark-haired woman with narrow features and heeled shoes approached the microphone and said, "Residents of Belavere City and Baymouth will queue first for siphoning. Five lines at the door, please. No fighting." And that was that.

While the summoned twelve-year-olds moved forward to queue before those double doors, the rest of us hung back. Some moved to find friends. Some tried to find a place to sit while they waited. I, however, was too filled with absolution to sit. Too evangelized to chat. I simply stood there, beaming from the inside out, filled to the brim with that same light that had impregnated the lump of idium.

I suddenly felt sure, though I couldn't explain why, that I would be deemed an Artisan this day.

A person destined to the pursuits of the mind—that was me.

Inside the waist of my skirt was the parchment I'd saved, but back in Scurry was the pile I'd discarded, strewn with sketches and landscapes and dried flowers and all my thoughts painted into shapes. I'd always had "natural aptitude." I was made for bigger places, meant to be surrounded by creation spun from the loom of one's mind.

I relinquished a smile.

"There's a pin stickin' out of your arse," said a voice.

I turned to find the spitter frowning, arms crossed, staring at the waist of my skirt. When he saw my obvious disgust, he merely shrugged. "Just thought you should know."

I adjusted the pin at the small of my back, poking it securely into the folds of my skirt. "Keep your eyes elsewhere," I bit out.

He frowned. "I think if I were likely to sit on a pin in the near future, I'd want someone to tell me."

"Weren't goin' to sit on it," I muttered, hoping he'd say no more.

Instead, the boy stuck his hands in his pockets. He rose his sun-bleached eyebrows. "What's your name?"

I didn't answer, didn't want the spitter to know me, but the pig ploughed on. "Mine is Patrick Colson. Patty, if you like."

I continued to glare.

"I'm from Kenton Hill." He persevered. "Reckon I'm headed back there, too. Where're you from?"

"Scurry" came the answer. It flew past my lips without my permission. I clamped my mouth shut.

Patrick nodded knowingly. "By the river."

I hesitated, then nodded. I was surprised, perhaps by the idea that anyone outside of Scurry knew of its existence, perhaps that this boy knew anything at all.

"I'll call you Scurry girl, then," he said, expression suddenly serious. "Why's there a pin in your arse, Scurry girl?"

My nose wrinkled. "Don't call me that."

"Gotta call you somethin'. I don't know your name."

"It's Nina." I sighed, annoyed. "And the pin is keepin' this skirt from fallin' round my ankles."

He gave a low whistle. "That'd ruin the occasion, eh?"

I rolled my eyes and turned away again, looking for somewhere, anywhere to escape to.

"I, on the other hand, would *love* to see this whole fuckin' ceremony ruined." He said it in a voice made of razors.

I couldn't help but turn back to peer at him again, to watch the gentleness in his features harden. "I'd gathered," I said. "You spit like a miner."

"Ah," his eyes sparked, as though I'd revealed something important. "So, your daddy's a miner, then?"

"And just as bitter."

"Not much to be pleased about when you're stuck in a hole all day."

"Then it should please you to be here, shouldn't it? Maybe you'll be destined for a different line of work." I didn't quite know why I bothered arguing. The woman at the microphone called for the children of Brimshire and Bunderly to queue next, and there was more shifting of bodies, more space as children went in through those double doors and didn't return, and yet Patrick Colson and I stood in place, steadfast and immovable amid the tide.

I could only assert that his face was hugely annoying, that his tone was superior, and that I very much wanted to prove him wrong.

He also reeked of the same hatred that frothed from the mouths of men in Scurry, and it rankled to hear it here in the city, so far from the soot.

"Nah," Patrick said nonchalantly. "Not me. Son of Craftsman who was the son of Craftsman and so on. I'll be back on that train by nightfall, just you watch." His smile waned a little, as though he was suddenly not so sure. "And if the idium *does* take, then I'll refuse to ever take another dose. They'll have to send me home eventually." He seemed comforted by the idea. I nearly envied him that.

Then I remembered those bigger things I was meant for.

"What about you?" he continued. "You're prayin' to be at that swank school, I take it?"

I didn't like the way he said it, like it was a myth only gullible kids still believed in. I lifted my chin. "Why wouldn't I?"

He grinned knowingly. "You look like the type. Bow in your hair. Pin up your arse. No interest in an honest day's work." They sounded like someone else's words. Words he'd learned by heart.

It was common vitriol in towns like ours. My father thought Artisans lazy, indulgent. He commented on their houses and decor and running water and woodless stoves and lamented them, that they would let their bodies waste away while their minds did all the labor. Weak men. Brittle women. An entire class afraid of dirty hands and exertion. All this he said as he dabbed bluff into the abrasions on his skin, then plundered his gut with liquor.

I thought of all those working facets of the body that Tanner had mentioned, specifically the ones the Artisans were responsible for: architecture, engineering, innovation, design, beauty. How could such things exist if there was not a mind to think them up? There was more to this world than what could be achieved through blunt manual labor. I had heard about the plight of the "honest man's work" enough times to recognize the same pinched expression, the same hateful tone, even if it was borrowed. Which meant I had already heard every version of what Patrick Colson might say next: that the Artisan government was a corrupt one that undervalued the Crafters, that the pay was blatant robbery, the conditions downright deadly, the sway of wealth completely one-sided.

It wasn't that I disagreed. I was just tired of hearing it said and seeing nothing done. I found it difficult to sympathize with those who seemed to take twisted pleasure in their own misery. Ma used to say it was one thing to be down, and quite another to dig yourself a grave.

"I sewed this skirt myself," I told Patrick Colson. "Made it too big. Do you know why?"

Patrick stared at me dumbly. Waited.

I lifted my hand to my tailbone and pulled the pin out. I let the skirt fall over my hips, revealing trousers beneath. Hardier fabric, cuffed up to my knees. Then I gathered the skirt and unfastened the back, sweeping it over my shoulders and putting my arms through the pocket holes until the inbuilt sleeves turned inside out. Finally, I stuck the pin in my hair. So there.

Patrick gulped, his cheeks pinkening slightly. I would have bet my last penny that he didn't have any sisters, and he'd never seen a girl drop her skirt before.

"I'm not goin' back on that train, whether I'm Artisan or not," I told him outright. "I've got plenty of my own complaints about what it's like out in the brink. I just don't see the use in whinin'. I'd rather think up grand ideas and create things. And if I can't be an Artisan, then I'll use the mind I've got." I raised my eyebrows at him pointedly. "I won't be goin' home."

Patrick stared at me without blinking. He watched as I slowly dragged the makeshift coat from my arms and constructed it back into a skirt around my waist. Lord, but it was heavy. Heavy enough for cold nights out in the open. Heavy with everything I was able to stitch into the hem.

He shook himself from his reverie. "Well," he said. "That fuckin' showed me, didn't it?"

Patrick Colson liked to say *fuck* a lot.

CHAPTER 4

PATRICK

A Smith."

"Why would you want to be a Smith and not a Mason? Or a Charmer?"

"One fuckin' word, Nina Harrow," Patrick said, arms stretched wide. *"Gold."*

Nina flattened her lips in that way girls did when they thought you stupid. "I think you'll find that diamond is more valuable than gold."

"Is not."

"Sure it is."

"Oh yeah?" he remarked, flicking a pebble at her. She barely flinched. "How would you know, Scurry girl?"

"Because I *read*," she said simply, and she had him there. Patrick could barely read more than the newspaper headlines. The schoolroom bored him.

She was smart, that much was clear. Not smarter than Patrick, he was sure. But a different kind. A blistering kind. "What do you want to be, then, since you have all the answers?"

"Somethin' that matters," she said, pulling her knees up to her chest.

He raised one eyebrow. "You mean terranium?"

Her flat expression told him he was right. She surprised him once more. It was true that many of their peers probably hoped to be a famed terranium Alchemist. After all, what could be more vital to the continent then the careful extraction of idium—a job only a medium of terranium could do. And rumor had it the number of terranium Alchemists was dwindling quickly—few knew how many were left. But still, Nina didn't seem to Patrick like a person vying for fame or glory.

She seemed like a person who was running away.

"Hmm," Patrick murmured. "I thought you might say a Scribbler."

She gave him a look of disbelief. "The lowliest of Artisans?"

He shrugged. "Seems more excitin' than drawin' blood from a stone. Scribblers travel all over." It was true. There was a Scribbler in every town and parish of the Trench, sending and receiving missives from the capital and collecting payment from anyone who could afford to send notes to a distant loved one.

Nina shook her head. "If I'm gonna be an Artisan, I don't want to sit around all day sendin' notes with my mind. I want to do something more important."

"And you want terranium to be your medium?"

"I want anythin' but pen and paper to be my medium."

"And yet, you've got a bindin' of parchment shoved down the waist of your trousers," he grinned. "Saw it when you dropped your skirt."

Her cheeks pinkened, a small victory. He chucked his chin at the place near her hip. "Can I see what you wrote?"

"No," she said immediately. Patrick thought of animals with their legs caught in traps and decided it was best not to press her. He rolled his eyes and didn't ask again.

Around them, conversations of similar nature were happening simultaneously. Boys and girls sitting or standing and waiting as the crowds thinned. Waiting for the name of their birthplace to be called through the crackling microphone. In the meantime, they debated the hierarchy of the Artisans.

Mediums known as the lesser arts: painting, drawing, writing, composing, were the pastimes of swanks. Most Artisans excelled at doing one or more of these. Some showed aptitude in all. And then there were the more highly ranked classifications . . .

A Scribbler's medium was, quite simply, ink. They could make it appear from half a world away.

Cutters specialized in precious stones: diamond, quartz, amethyst, and the like. They were the pretty decorators, the designers of finer things. Cutters could mold gems into any shape a rich mistress pleased. Patrick thought them rather useless.

Smiths molded copper, iron, nickel, gold, and silver. Patrick admitted the intricacies of their work could be admired.

Masons were a higher order of Artisan. Wood and stone were vital resources in a world made from little else.

Alchemy was most important, of course. Only an Alchemist could crack open a lump of terranium. Without them, there was no idium. No siphoning ceremonies. No Artisans. There was only one other order that might match the class of an Alchemist.

"What if you were a Charmer?" Patrick asked her now, this girl who wasn't going home.

Her answer was instant, as were all her answers, as though she'd already thought of every question the world might demand and banked her thoughts on the matter. "Earth," she said.

"Why not fire or water?" Patrick liked quizzing her. Liked hearing the sureness in her voice.

"Not hard to guess why."

"I suppose it's the glory?" he guessed. "You'd be the only earth Charmer in a hundred years or more."

She frowned, reproaching him. "More earth Charmers means fewer mine collapses," she explained, rather like she were teaching a bug to count. "Imagine if each mine had a Charmer to keep the tunnels from folding in."

He didn't care to imagine it. To imagine it was to think of his dad and brother back in Kenton Hill, readying themselves for passage down the shaft. He didn't want to think of tunnels that closed in like card houses.

Instead, Patrick peered at her, trying to pick off the peculiarities one by one. There were scratches on her throat. Her fingers kept finding their way back there, worrying absently at nothing. He'd never seen a person itch for something so much it found its way onto their skin. But Nina itched. Lord, did she.

She pointed to the spired roofs of the buildings over the courtyard ramparts and named each one of them as though they were well acquainted. She crossed and uncrossed her legs in different directions, sometimes remembering to be proper, and sometimes reverting back to a kid from a town like Scurry who sat like sitting was meant for comfort. She had blond curls spiraling in every direction, flushed skin, a thousand freckles, and widely spaced teeth. She had dancing fingers and dark brows that rose and fell with each word. Her hazel eyes seemed to see everything. Nina pointed to the clock tower and told him it was crafted by a blind Artisan named Jeffrey Waltzer. This made him smile widely.

"Me brother Donny don't see too well," he told her. "Bet he'd like that story."

"It chimes a different tone at every hour," Nina continued, "so that one needn't look to tell the time. They can hear it."

"*Hear* time," Patrick scoffed. "Artisan bullshit."

Nina sighed. Her shoulders fell dramatically, and Patrick suddenly became worried that she'd had enough of him. "It is clever, though," he added hastily.

"Liar."

He grinned. "I just don't understand it, is all."

"Don't understand what?"

He fumbled for an answer that didn't sound like an insult. "All that artsy stuff . . . hearin' time and feelin' colors and whatever else. Artisans talk like the wind blows just for them. But wind is just wind. There's no meanin' to it."

"You're wrong," she said, not angry, but animated, sparkling eyes big as planets. "There's meanin' in everythin' if you look hard enough. There's joy in it, too. That's the problem with Crafters," she sniffed, drawing her knees up to her chest. "Too worn out to feel anythin' other than angry. Do you know what my dad hates most?"

Patrick shrugged warily.

"Music," she said. "Dancin', too. Says it turns people into clowns. Imagine being so . . . so . . . ."

"Constipated?"

She smiled reluctantly. "Miserable. Every one of them's the same. Miserable and tired. Too uptight to dance."

Her lips had thinned as she spoke, sourness curling them inward. *Every one of them's the same.*

"Maybe in Scurry." Patrick frowned. "But not everywhere. Not in Kenton Hill."

Nina rolled her eyes.

"We dance." A strange desire to impress her had come over him. "*I* am an excellent dancer. Just 'cause we ain't Artisan, don't mean we're no fun."

She laughed once, then turned her head away, dismissive.

Lord, but she was annoying. Huffy. Edgy. He thought it was likely time she had someone show her up, take her off that high horse. For a Crafter's daughter, she sure had the opinions of an Artisan.

Patrick stood abruptly, towering over her. When she looked back, confused, he flattened his expression into one of severe concentration.

Then Patrick danced. Nothing too ambitious, just a folk jig. His feet kicked up the dust and a group of nearby girls giggled and backed away. When Nina's cheeks flamed, he spun on the spot, lifted his arms, jumped. He heard others clapping in time, hooting insults.

Then he was yanked back down to the dirt, Nina's hand gripping his belt.

"Bloody *hell*," Nina cursed, only releasing Patrick once his arse had firmly hit the ground. She looked about her with rising embarrassment. "You got gas in your head?"

He sniggered. "Got music in me feet, Nina Harrow, or whatever Artisan bullshit you'd prefer."

A smile broke free, then a burst of laughter. Then he was laughing, too. Both of them falling about in fits.

He wanted to ask her a thousand other questions. He was acutely aware of the time ticking by, though he'd forgotten all about the train he was so desperate to return to.

"If you don't get into the school," he asked cautiously, "Where will you go?"

She shrugged like it didn't much matter. "I'll find a place."

"In the city? You gonna work in a factory? That's all the Crafters do here, you know. My dad says it's worse than prison."

"Won't matter much when I become an Artisan, will it?" She stared pointedly back at him, daring him to contradict her, and he wanted to. If it wasn't for the knowledge that she might stab him with that pin in her skirt, Patrick would've called her daft.

"What makes you so sure?" He was leaning closer, not wanting to miss the answer. He stared at her lips, just in case.

It took a moment. She rolled those lips around like she needed to chew the words first. She looked over Patrick's head to the endless rows of red rooftops, and her hands danced in her lap. Finally, she looked back at him, grinned, and said, "Just feel it. In here." And she didn't point to her head, where the Artisans believed creativity lived. She pointed to her chest, and Patrick knew that if she could show him directly beneath the skin and sinew and bone, there would lie her beating heart.

He wanted quite desperately to know what it was back in Scurry that would make her so eager to live on unfamiliar streets. He wanted to know what made her itch.

Whatever drove her, it was sprinting through her mind as they sat there, a foot apart, in fancier clothes than they ought to be in. It ran wild in her blood, chasing her away. For one horrifying moment, her eyes went glassy and she gulped in a fragile way. Patrick had the urge to touch her cheek.

In the end, he didn't.

"If the idium doesn't work, you could come back to Kenton Hill with me instead," Patrick heard himself say. Didn't know why he'd said it, except that his chest was surging and Nina hadn't blinked.

She didn't answer. She only dried her eyes on her sleeve and looked to the woman waiting by the microphone. "How long do you think we'll wait?"

"A while yet," Patrick said, relieved. "They're not past Dorser and Dunnitch."

She deflated. Her stomach grumbled and Patrick's responded in kind. Neither of them had eaten since their respective train rides, and the food carts on board had only offered bread with vinegar or biscuits that turned to dust in your hand.

Patrick chewed his lip and glanced around the courtyard. At the side of the National Artisan House, servants used a side door to enter and exit with crate upon crate of goods. A man with a bald head bellowed at the wagons that trundled to a stop before him. Capped drivers with sweaty faces alighted from their seats and unloaded their wares.

Normally, Patrick wasn't one for stealing. His older brother Gunner had almost had his hand cut off over a ten-ounce bag of sugared orange— one of their more foolish conquests. But when Patrick looked at Nina, saw the loosened bow in her hair, the scratches on her throat, the eyes that saw everything, he felt the feverish urge to do something foolish.

So he snatched up her hand. "Come on, Scurry girl."

CHAPTER 5

NINA

Patrick pulled me through the courtyard, around the groups of children resorting to schoolyard games in their boredom. I went without protest.

It was hot. I was tired and hungry and sick of waiting. I was fizzling with an anticipation I couldn't bury. It was a relief to move.

I realized too late where he was leading me. His fingers curled tightly into the back of my hand and pulled me down the side of the building where several children sought shade and the servants of the National House smoked. There was nothing here but more sandstone perimeter, more ivy climbing the limescale walls, more dust and dirt underfoot. The lane was filled with horses and carts and wagons of all sizes. Drivers bellowed at one another to make way as they came and went, trying to barrel through and around to make their next delivery. Craftsmen, every one of them.

"We're not s'posed to be down here," I hissed, pulling back at Patrick's hand.

He turned, winked one of those startling eyes and smirked. "You're not scared, are you?"

I gave him the most derisive look I could muster. "What are we doin'?"

"Gettin' somethin' to eat. I'm starvin'."

I was, too. "If we're caught, they'll throw us out!"

Patrick stopped as a door to our left opened, and we dropped to the ground, protected from view by the crates stacked precariously along the exterior wall. The servant who exited did not look our way. They whistled to the driver. "You next!"

I breathed a sigh of relief. "Lord, that was close."

But Patrick's eyes were plastered to that open door, the servant with his back turned, the space between. His face took on a frenzied gleam.

My eyes widened. "Patrick. Don't even think it."

"Chicken," he whispered on a grin.

"I'm not a *chicken*."

"Then get your wits about you, Scurry girl. On the count of three. One—"

"Don't you dare."

"Two."

"You honestly think I'll follow you, don't you? Do I look stupid?"

"Three." Patrick dropped my hand, saluted me, then hurdled the crates and sprinted through the open door, disappearing within.

"Shit," I breathed. There was absolutely no sense in following. So many people came and went, Patrick was bound to be caught. Boys were truly idiots. He'd likely smacked straight into the chest of a copper when he stepped inside. His wrists were probably in irons. He'd be taken back to the train any moment.

It was very well for *him*. Patrick *wanted* to be sent back out into the brink. What did he care if the House rejected his right to a siphoning? Perhaps it was what he sought—a way to avoid the gamble altogether.

It occurred to me then that perhaps Patrick was afraid. What if he took to the idium and it revealed him as an Artisan? He did not speak of home with a stiff jaw the way I did. No, he spoke of home as a place he belonged. What if the idium revealed he didn't?

Perhaps I'd leave him to this poorly hatched plan, to his train and bad fortune. What did I care, after all?

The moments passed, and he did not reemerge. The door hung open, and the servant who'd exited it seemed engaged in a heated argument with a driver. No police officer hauled Patrick back out into the dust.

Go back to the courtyard, I told myself. *Before someone sees.* But I stayed and I waited. My heart galloped.

Suddenly, his head reappeared. Patrick's eyes peered around the door-jamb and spied me in the hollows between crates.

The smug bastard raised an eyebrow.

Get back here! I mouthed to him, gesturing frantically. My eyes darted to the servants and drivers, all of whom were so harried that none spared a glance for the children playing cat and mouse by the door.

Hurry! I mouthed.

But Patrick Colson did not budge. Instead, he rolled his eyes, as though he'd never met a girl quite as hysterical as me, then disappeared once more.

The servants and drivers carried on with their scrimmage, and truly it seemed no one took notice of a damn thing besides. I imagined what else Patrick would call me, should I stay safely outside. *Wimp. Wuss. Coward.* I could already see the smirk on his face.

There was that other niggle, too. The one that longed to see the inside of this building.

Suddenly, there was an earsplitting crash as two drivers ran their wagons into each other. Horses whinnied. Men swore. The rabble intensified.

A switch inside me flipped.

Over the bleating and braying of the traffic, I bolted from my hiding place, bounded over a slew of fallen potatoes, and slipped inside the National Artisan House.

A long hallway stretched ahead, and at its end, I saw the oak desktops stretch within an open hall. Five men with bored faces sat along its length, vials in their hands, queues of children before them.

The siphoning ceremony.

Only it wasn't so ceremonious. The officials called "Name?" as new children approached them. They ran a focusing glass down long, long lists. They retrieved a tiny vial from the crates stacked haphazardly at their sides and put it down again on the desk in front of them. "Drink," they said.

The children did. I watched entranced as they uncorked the vial and brought it to their lips with shaky hands. They drank the solution and cinched their eyes closed as it went down. Then the officials pointed to a box of lumpy items that sat on the desk before them. "Hold each one in your hand."

The children did as they were asked, questions in their eyes, wondering if there was something they should be feeling. They picked up and replaced each item in the box like they were shopping for ripe fruit. When nothing happened, the officials barely looked up from their lists. "Crafter," they said. And the children's eyes either fell or widened with relief.

There was only one child who earned a different reaction. A boy, well dressed and well groomed. He stood with his back straight and his chin high. He looked so thoroughly highborn that I couldn't help but stare. "Theodore Shop," he told the woman behind the desk. He drank his idium, and when he put his hand toward the box, a drinking glass filled with water quaked threateningly.

Both child and official reared back, eyes wide.

"Easy, boy," the official told him. "Let it come to you."

Theodore Shop frowned in concentration. Instead of lifting his hand, he simply stared at that glass.

The water within rippled with increasing intensity, swirling in violent circles, until finally the glass tipped, and water dashed across the tabletop and seeped over its sides.

Quickly, a servant approached with a rag, sopping up the mess before it dampened swaths of lists.

"Artisan. Charmer!" the official said, clapping, smiling—the first smile of any. "Medium: water!"

Theodore Shop merely stared at the mess he'd created with his mind, and a small, rose-cheeked grin emerged.

In the next moment, a hand closed over my mouth and dragged me sideways into a dark room. A door closed and smothered all light. I was pressed abruptly to a wall, and some instinct bid me to bite down.

"Ouch!" Patrick's breath washed over my face. His fingers disappeared. "Fuck!"

The sound of footsteps in the hall approached, and we both froze. But they didn't slow or stop, didn't open the door to inspect. They passed by, the sound softening, and Patrick and I sagged and stifled laughter in our cuffs.

I put a hand against my thundering heart. "Holy shit."

"Yeah," there was a grin in his voice. "Holy shit."

There was a click. A flicker. A flame spluttered to life in Patrick's hand, illuminating his face.

For a moment, I gawked at it. It came from a tiny silver tin. "What is that?" I hated how awestruck I sounded.

Patrick watched me curiously. "A lighter. You don't have none in Scurry?"

"If we did, would I bother askin' about it?"

Patrick smirked. "This particular one is me father's invention. Here," and he held it up for closer inspection. "This wheel here, it sparks the flint. The oil in the canister keeps the flame burnin'."

I eyed it warily. "Your dad, you say?"

Patrick winked at her. The flame danced in his irises. "Not all genius belongs to the swanks."

My eyes fell to his lips as he spoke. He was quite a bit taller than me but as close as he'd yet been, and my stomach came alive, networks of sputtering bursts erupting from my gut up into my chest. I felt suddenly shy. My cheeks heated. "We should leave," I whispered to him. *"Now."*

He was far from panicked. In fact, his smile widened. "You followed me in," he stated. "Didn't think you would."

"What?" I spluttered, the reverie broken. "You gave me no *choice.*"

"Nah," he shook his head. "There were plenty of choices." The lighter flickered as he held it higher, as though to see me better. "You chose to come in with me."

My stomach twisted once more, and he seemed to see it.

His eyes glinted. "You like me, don't you?"

Heat flooded my face. "What?" I blustered. "*Ugh!* You're disgust—"

Patrick threw something at me then. I only just saw it before it hit my stomach. Something round and heavy.

A little cake sat cradled in my hands.

"Eat up," Patrick said. "Then we'd better go. You're a bad influence on me, Nina Harrow."

I hesitated, but the rumble of my stomach soon silenced any other thought.

I said nothing as I ate, but I found myself smiling around the pieces of cake in my mouth and wondered whether the pounding of blood behind my eyes was fear or furious excitement. The two seemed tightly braided.

Patrick paced around the shelves that lined the walls, illuminating small patches as he went with his lighter. It appeared we were in a storage space of some kind. It stunk of moisture and fouling vegetables. There was movement in the corners: Patrick's light sending rats back into the walls. Stack after stack of crates were organized in aisles. All were identical except for the brands burned into the wood, marking their contents: BRUNDLE'S CANNERY; TIMPTON AND SONS CO.; LIPSHORE LINENS.

He almost didn't see where the floor fell away. His lighter caught on the edges of the hole before his feet did.

"Stop!" I hissed, my hands outstretched, and I pointed down. His foot hovered over the abyss.

He held the lighter into its depths. Shallow steps led to a cellar's hatch. An *open* cellar hatch.

"What do you s'pose they keep in here?" he asked, and I saw that manic stupidity in his eyes return.

"Don't even think of it."

But Patrick had already begun to descend the steps. He lowered himself carefully onto the ladder. "We've come this far," he said. "Might as well look around."

I dithered for a moment, then followed him in.

The cellar was cold, with a floor of compacted dirt. But as for what it contained, I couldn't tell. Patrick stood with his lighter held high, blocking all else from view. I had to shunt him aside to see.

Shelves and shelves of shallow crates stacked against one wall. The very same crates I'd seen discarded by the siphoning officials' feet.

"*Fuck me,*" Patrick intoned. He held his lighter to the brand singed into the wood grain of one of the crates. PROPERTY OF BELAVERE TRENCH, it said. "You don't think—?"

"Of course I bloody *think*," I rasped, my throat suddenly closing. "Don't touch it!"

Patrick lifted the lid of one of the crates immediately. He pulled a small vial from its insides, dark viscous liquid sloshing within. "Holy shit," Patrick said. Then louder. "Holy *shit!*"

I'd clapped my hand firmly over his mouth in an instant. "Shut up, you idiot!"

Patrick slipped my grasp. "It's *ink.*"

"We're in a storage room next to a *siphon' ceremony*, half-wit. What did you think you'd find?"

A clatter above announced the arrival of another, and my blood turned cold.

Yellow light descended into the cellar through the open hatch. "In here" ordered a bodiless voice.

In the space between breaths, Patrick extinguished his lighter. His fingers made a fist in the front of my blouse and he pulled me sideways. We tucked into a far, dark corner, where damp-smelling linens hung out of overflowing boxes and concealed the top halves of our bodies. I prayed the shadows would obscure our legs.

Sounds of movement and harsh breathing came, though I saw nothing beyond the browning cloth. Deliverymen, I assumed, carrying supplies overhead and dumping it where directed. An assertive voice instructed them. "Not there! Over *there.*"

The interminable thumping of my heart. The shuffle of Patrick's feet. The feel of his breaths on the crown of my head. My fingers shaking in his. *Surely*, I thought. *If they come down here, we'll be heard. We'll be found.*

Patrick squeezed my fingers. *Hush.*

"Idium, sir?" a gruff voice asked.

"In the cellar" came the answer.

My heart seized.

I heard the grunts of a man clambering down into the dark, the dull thud of his feet finding the ground. "Pass it down," he called.

I didn't dare look. I sealed my eyes shut and prayed. There was the sound of wood against wood and the music of shifting glass. "These ones got wax seals on 'em." The man heaved on each word as though he'd run several miles. "Never seen 'em bother with wax. What do you—?"

"Be on your way" was the only response. Footsteps sounded on the ladder and then receded, but the yellow light remained. Was the room above empty? Was it safe to emerge?

Another voice suddenly joined the last, and I jumped. I stepped on Patrick's foot and felt him wince.

This time, the voice was high-pitched and lilting. It bounced off the walls. A woman's heeled footsteps slapped the tiles above as she spoke. "Thomas, have someone come and collect the clutter out in the hall, the crates are piling up again and we're not yet halfway through the siphon-ings. Where on *earth* are your staff?"

"Bringing in the deliveries, ma'am."

"Then do it yourself. And bring more vials, if you please."

The male voice seemed to hesitate. I heard him shift his feet nervously. "Ma'am . . . the, er . . . the *wax seals*, or?"

"No," said the woman. "We've got just about all the Artisan children needed this year, the water Charmer was one of the last. Only brink towns are left." A pause, perhaps only half a second. Enough time, though, for my heart to collapse in its cage, for Patrick's hand to turn limp, for both of our frames to shudder, rocked at the foundation.

"Bring the Crafter-marked vials. With any luck, we'll be finished ahead of schedule," said the woman.

The man seemed to start a sentence, then think better. "There's a girl in the courtyard," he said. "Small, ginger hair. Thin as a reed. It doesn't seem like she's eaten in a good while."

The woman sighed deeply but not unkindly. "She was fed on the train," she said. "And she'll be fed again before she returns to her family."

"Just seems like one or two of the poorer ones could be spared that life," the man continued. "It'd be easy enough to swap the vial—"

"Speak wisely," hissed the woman, her voice dropping to a whisper. "Such thoughts will have you swinging from the gallows, sir. Do you understand me?"

A shuffle. "Yes, ma'am."

"Only a handful are trusted with this knowledge, and you are paid handsomely for your remit, are you not?"

"Yes, ma'am." It sounded more defeated this time.

A gentle sigh came, and then, "There have always been those more fortunate than others, Thomas. It is the way of the world, however unkind. Not all can be trusted with power. It must be meted out *carefully*."

"Of course, ma'am. I only thought . . ." His voice trailed off. And whatever Thomas thought was never voiced.

I wished I could see the woman's face. I wanted to see if it was sympathetic or wretched or uncaring. I wanted to see what flashed in her eyes when she said, "The only thing we may do for those children is pray for them."

There was the sound of crates shifting, the harsh heeled tap of the woman's shoes receding. The man named Thomas sighed from somewhere near the hatch. And then his feet came down the ladder again.

I peeked out from behind the musty linens to see him stare forlornly at the crate in his hands, and I realized that he was much older than I'd imagined. He gripped the sides of the box as though he might crush it, but instead he set it down with the others and turned away. He climbed up the ladder and closed the hatch. The yellow light evaporated.

Patrick and I were alone again. Stiff-kneed and limp-tongued.

It took several moments for Patrick to lift the linens and step out. Longer before he remembered to come back for me. He untangled me from sheets in the dark, and I did not have the presence of mind to help him.

The lighter flickered, and a flare appeared in the space between his chin and mine, turning us both blood orange.

"What did she mean?" I asked him, much in the way a child asks an elder.

His lips looked white, even in the glow. "I don't know."

"Crafter-marked." I looked to the crates branded PROPERTY OF BELA-VERE TRENCH. "She said 'Crafter-marked.'"

Patrick held aloft the vial he'd plucked earlier. Atop its cork was a red wax seal that barely coated the vial's neck.

I thought of those children I'd seen in the hall, uncorking their waxless vials of idium and being declared Crafters.

We've got just about all the Artisan children needed this year.

"What does it mean?" I asked again, desperation leaking through. My stomach bowled. The lighter sputtered out.

"Patrick . . . what does it mean?"

Somewhere inside me, a screw wound tighter and tighter.

CHAPTER 6

PATRICK

Nina's bottom lip shook.

We should leave, Patrick thought. *Before they come back.*

But his feet wouldn't—or couldn't—move. His head clawed at those crates on their shelves, scratched at the wood in need of answers.

"What does it mean?" Nina whispered over and over, like a fading prayer. The words belting around inside him.

I don't know what it means.

He couldn't leave. Not until he could make some meaning.

Patrick placed three crates on the ground and cursed them for rattling. He lifted their lids and cringed at the groan and squeak of the timber. He ran his thumb down the flint wheel of the lighter he'd stolen from his father and held the flame next to his knees.

Two crates of twenty-four vials, all corked, all missing wax seals. One smaller crate—twelve vials only, all of them lightly coated in thin red wax, as though the administer did not much care if the glass was sealed or not. Patrick reached for one vial and pulled the wax away easily. Without its marker, he could not identify the difference between this vial and that of its counterpart. They both glistened with inky dilution.

"They're marked," Nina said, her breaths shallow. "They're marked for Artisans. For the ones . . . the ones they've already picked out."

Patrick found he could not answer while his blood was so laced with heat. Pounding in his head was a growing litany. A cumulative din of every vitriolic word he'd heard since he was small. Every drunk and sober spray in the direction of the Artisan government. A flood of it bloomed within him now. It set him on fire. He was in danger of crushing the vial in his trembling hand.

But while Patrick burned, Nina seemed to extinguish. "I never had a chance, did I?" she asked him. Her voice was so very small. "I never had a chance."

Nina's eyes glistened. Her sideways bow slipped another inch.

Without deciding to do it, without really thinking on it at all, he wrapped his arms around her shoulders and pulled her to him.

And perhaps she found him dumb and foolish, but she buried her forehead into his chest just the same, gripping the back of his shirt with both hands.

He felt her warm breath permeate his shirt and shivered. He felt inexplicably reluctant to let her go. "We need to leave, Nina."

"I know."

"*Now.*"

"I know."

But before they slipped back up the ladder and through the hatch, out into the hall, the lane, the courtyard, Patrick plucked four vials of idium from their resting places and shoved them deep into his pockets.

Two with wax seals, and two without.

CHAPTER 7

NINA

"Scurry, Sommerland," called the Artisan woman at the microphone. Her voice was bored.

In the pockets of my skirt were two differing vials of Idia's blood. I gripped them tightly as I moved forward toward those wide-open doors.

Patrick was gone. Kenton Hill had been called along with Lavnonshire already. Hours ago, it seemed.

What do we do? I had begged.

Nothin', he'd said, pulling me back from the alley into the rabble of waiting children. *Nothin' to be done.*

It's all pretend. All decided!

Yeah. He'd looked as though I'd taken the words and beat him over the head with it.

I'd stomped my foot. *There's always somethin' to be done. Always. We cannot simply do nothin'.*

And for a moment, Patrick had stirred there in the courtyard, filling with something. But then he let out a long breath, and his head fell forward. He had wiped his nose on his shirtsleeve and looked away. He said, *I was gonna be on that train home, one way or another.* Then, *Fuckin' dictators.* And, with more venom, *I could kill every last one of 'em.*

For a frightening moment, I'd believed him.

I'll never . . . I'll never be an Artisan, I'd whispered. The hidden parchment jabbed into my stomach. He looked at me with so much pity that I wanted the earth to swallow me.

I thought he might invite me back to Kenton Hill again.

I thought I might say yes.

"Kenton Hill!" came the call. "Lavnonshire!"

Patrick cursed. He picked up the hands laying limply by my sides, and I felt cool glass press against either palm. His blue eyes, now afraid, were still astonishing. *You've got a mind of your own*, he reminded me. *Don't let those fuckers take it.*

Then he leaned down, pressed his lips briefly against my cheek, then walked through those double doors the way a man walks to the gallows.

He turned to look back at me once, mouth quirking upward awkwardly and then falling. He looked brimming with things to say but pressed his lips tightly closed. All the weight of Belavere Trench held in the mouth of a miner's boy.

Thus, Patrick Colson was gone, and I believed I would never see him again.

· · · · · •

The children of Scurry and Sommerland pressed through the doors to the National Artisan House to find out how they would spend the rest of their lives.

I felt a deepening pity for them all. I wondered if there were any like me, who had been banking on a life better than the one they'd left.

"Five lines," the Artisan woman called and I heard the familiar clacking of heels on the tile. *We've got just about all the Artisan children needed this year.*

The hall inside was splendid and overly decorative. Ornate paintings hung from the walls, none of them smaller than me. The vaulted ceiling unbalanced me, every inch of it artfully reticulated in gold. But nothing glistened anymore. It didn't swallow me the way I always imagined it would; the way it might have, if it weren't a lie.

The children of Scurry formed queues in front of the oak tables waiting at the hall's far side. A kid shoved me from behind in my hesitation to move toward one.

Voices rose to the high ceilings and bounced around the open space so that one hundred people sounded like a thousand. Ahead, a boy strained to see better. A girl kept turning to grasp the arms of a friend and proclaim her need to be sick.

"You think it'll taste bad?"

"What if I can't drink it?"

"I heard that a boy dropped dead last year."

"Me sister said it were like swallowin' lightnin'."

"Next!"

They shuffled up their lines in their handed-down church clothing, in their barely contained hairdos and cracked lips. When was the last time a child from Scurry had become an Artisan?

I couldn't think of a single one.

Happens less and less these days. Dad had told me. *It's all about the blood-lines, you see? And you ain't got the genes for absorbing idium. You got no chance.*

"Next!"

I kept my hands in my pockets as I shuffled forward, my thumb sweeping over their tops and feeling the wax and cork alternately. Artisan and Crafter. Not a destiny, but a choice. It seemed an easy one to make.

But it seemed a dangerous one, too.

"Next!"

I wished I could see Patrick nodding at me. I wished my mother had never left.

"Next!"

Each child said their name, pulled the cork out, swallowed, waited. Nothing. Down the halls they left in single file. Back to a train that would take them northeast to little futures.

"Next!"

Inside my skirt pocket, I used my thumb and forefinger to peel the wax away from the cork. It only took a second.

"Next!"

I walked forward.

Behind the glistening oak tabletop, a man no older than twenty perused a lengthy piece of parchment. He did not look up as I approached.

"Name?"

"Harrow. Nina."

He checked off the name with a quill and ink. I wondered vaguely how the man knew which names were Artisan and which were Crafter.

"Is this one for me?" I asked, lifting the vial for his examination.

The man squinted at it a second. "Ah . . ." he said. "Where—?"

"It was on the floor," I said blankly. "Must have fallen from the crates."

The man spared a glance sideways at the precarious stack of discarded boxes.

"Idium is finite. Thank God it didn't smash on the tiles," I said with a pointed look to the woman in the obnoxious heels. She watched the officials like a hawk.

"That is . . . I need to ensure the dosage is correct." Beads of sweat emerged over his brow.

"They're all the same," I said then. "Aren't they?"

I had the sudden, vicious desire to hear him say it. To contradict me out loud. Then I could point and scream red-faced to everyone in the hall that they were, each of them, liars.

And then I'd return to Scurry, and nothing would change.

The administer cleared his throat, shot a furtive look at the high-heeled woman. "Yes. Well . . . if you please," he said ruefully.

I swallowed back the bile climbing up from my insides. I had the sense that I was doing something catastrophic. But there was that teeming ocean in my mind, swelling and crashing in color and sound and a constant desire to seek, and I pulled the cork out. I wasn't going home.

I tipped the vial to my lips and drank it all.

Then I waited.

The dilution tasted of metal against my tongue. It was oily. Cold. It slipped down my throat reluctantly, clinging to the sides.

At first, there was nothing. A small tingling in my chest, maybe. A clenching of my stomach.

Then, there was everything.

I felt dust particles touch my cheeks as they fell. Light rays that separated into singular photons and pierced the air, pierced my skin. I felt every mechanism of my body at once, in perfect harmony. And the color.

Color bloomed everywhere. It deepened and lightened and shone. I could dissect the minute differences of blues in the canvas painted into oceans on the far wall. I could hear music in the city sounds and the way they were interwoven.

I felt how easy it would be for my hands to mimic *life*: on parchment, on walls, in stone and wood and dirt.

I felt, for a sheer fleeting moment, absolutely, incontestably filled with answers.

And then the feeling was gone.

I shuddered. Blinked.

"Hold each one in your hand," said the administer, pushing forward a small wooden box with a brass clasp. He ran a finger down his list of names without further regard, clearly ignorant that the person before him had just been irrevocably morphed by something holy.

My breaths rattled. I could hear nothing else as I reached forward. I had the sudden impression that it would sting to hold anything against my skin.

The official sighed and looked up at me impatiently. "Go on," he ushered.

I swallowed. My fingers neared the box.

Nothing happened. The wood did not rattle in place or tip over. An object from within did not tumble toward me—another planet falling into the orbit of its sun. The glass of water at its side didn't quake.

But there *was* a tremor within *me*. A pulse in my fingertips. Even more prominent was the sensation of my mind expanding, clawing, searching.

"Pick them up, miss," the official said. Pushing the box even closer. It clattered noisily across the desk.

And with the movement came a small cloud of dust. The unbrushed particles of the stones and gems within.

I saw each particle as they rose, and watched as they spun in the stagnant air, and so did the administer. He froze in place, pen leaking ink onto the page before him.

More dirt rose, but not from the box this time. It wormed out from the tile crevices, from the soles of shoes, from creases of skin. It swept in from the doors, curling over the steps and stealing inside. A squall rose, dust swirling in every direction. The children shrieked and covered their eyes. The officials stood, their chairs knocking, falling. Voices were swallowed in the storm.

And I felt like a giant. A god. All around me, the universe pulsed.

Something in my chest recoiled—the snap of elastic stretched too far, and abruptly, the surge died. Dirt rained to the floor. Silence blanketed us all.

In the palm of my hand, a small mound of dust collected, no larger than an anthill.

I smiled at it, forgetting for a moment where I was or from where I'd come. I was only aware of the small weight in my hand, its exact texture.

How many times had I felt dirt at my fingertips, and yet none of it had made my mind burst into a kaleidoscope?

Around me, I heard the delayed feedback of hurried footsteps. The click-clack of heels seemed far away, then abruptly beside me. It took several moments to notice the eyes stabbing me from every corner of the room, down the entire length of the table.

It took longer for the shapes of their lips to form coherent sound. Words I understood, though never, even in my wildest imaginings, in reference to me.

Earth Charmer.

Earth Charmer.

"Earth Charmer!"

CHAPTER 8

NINA

E arth Charmer," uttered the man behind the desk.

He stared at the vial in my hand as though it were a grenade with its pin pulled. "Artisan," he called out hesitantly.

The word catapulted around the room. It thrummed inside me.

And I smiled.

I was only twelve.

Later, it would be a litany. A lullaby. *You were only twelve. You couldn't have known.*

A hand gripped my upper arm, and not gently. The high-heeled Artisan woman stood beside me. I tried to pull my arm from her grasp, but her fingers were a vise. She smiled tightly. "How wonderful," she uttered, loud enough for all to hear, and then she began towing me away.

I stumbled over my own skirt, dropping granules of dirt in my wake. She marched me around the desks, down a long hallway, past a series of paintings. We took a left turn, and only then did she release my arm, having caged me adequately in an empty hall with no exit.

We were alone.

"Give me your name."

She was severe in every facet. Precisely combed black hair, neatly painted lips, peaked chin, narrow-nosed. Tall and slender with hands roped in veins. She stared at me, awaiting an answer.

"Nina Harrow." I was sure I'd never felt so afraid.

The woman seemed to be completing some immense calculation. Her eyes marked me by inches, totaling the sum of my parts. Frayed socks, scuffed shoes, blouse buttoned at the wrists and throat. I hoped my bow was on straight. I hoped I met the score of an acceptable candidate.

Of course, I didn't. Dread settled over me. This woman would tell me it was all a mistake. She'd put me on a train home. Without another dose of idium, none of it would matter, would it?

But when she spoke next, her voice did not match the shell of her. "God help you," she said, then rubbed her forehead with her fingers. She turned away, placed her hands on her hips and tipped her head back. She whispered questions to herself for a moment. Wisps of them made it back to me, and they all started with "How . . . ?"

I did not dare interrupt this private consult. It seemed the woman was still devising her equations.

The sum of a Scurry girl turned Charmer.

When she finally faced me again, the shell had hardened once more. "I'm Francis Leisel," she said. "And you are Nina Clarke."

I frowned. "I'm—"

Francis Leisel stepped closer, towered over me. "From this moment onward, you are Nina Clarke. *Clarke.* Nina Harrow has ceased to exist. You were born in Sommerland, *not* Scurry. Your mother was my sister, and she was an Artisan wood Mason. Her name was Greta Leisel. Your father was Frederick Clarke—a Craftsman from Sommerland. Both are dead." Her words overlapped. She glanced over her shoulder repeatedly as she spoke. "Repeat it back to me, girl."

"But I—"

"Listen to me, now," she pressed, bending until her nose almost touched mine and her voice became little more than hot breath. Her eyes flittered across my face with alarming fervor. "It is most important. Do you understand? You must do as I say."

I understood enough, even then. A sense of danger crept out of the woman's pores and drenched the hall we stood in.

"There's been a mistake," she said. "One that cannot be undone."

I was relieved. The hawk-woman did not think the mistake was mine. I wasn't in trouble.

"You . . . you will be all right. But only if you remember to do as I say. Only if you *never* breathe a word of this conversation to another."

"Yes," I said. I tilted. The hallway tilted.

"You are Nina Clarke. *Say it.*"

"I am Nina Clarke." My lip trembled. The feeling of catastrophe returned.

"You were born in Sommerland."

"I'm from Sommerland."

"Your mother was Greta Leisel."

"My mother was . . . was . . ."

"You are my ward."

"I am your ward."

Francis Leisel placed a long-fingered hand on my shoulder. "When I call on you, you will refer to me as Aunt Francis. It is crucial that you remember."

"Aunt Francis." I was nodding mechanically. "Yes."

"Promise me."

"I promise."

"Should you forget, Nina Clarke," Aunt Francis warned, "we will both be thrown from this city forever, or worse. Is that what you want?"

Lord help me, it wasn't.

· · · · · ·

I was first pulled into a secondary room for something Francis Leisel called processing. I'd pictured the moment to be more ceremonial in my mind. In reality, there was only a flushed woman with a sweaty upper lip holding an iron brand in the coals of the open fireplace, then pressing it into the underside of my wrist for four excruciating seconds.

I screamed and bit into a leather strap. Aunt Francis held on to me.

The burnt skin showed a bubbling depiction of the Artisan emblem—the profile of Idia, her eyes closed in death, her hair sweeping around to form a near circle.

That was that.

The Artisan children had boarded carriages that waited before the National Artisan House, but all had departed, save one.

Here, the building facade was luminescent and clear of limescale. The street beyond the drive and the rampart were filled with onlookers, waving and fluttering kerchiefs as I was hustled out the grand doors. They cheered good-naturedly. Wished me success. Long live Belavere.

The coach was black. The horses were sabino. The driver was a Craftsman who tipped his hat to me. These were the only details I could recall later as I sat alone in the National Artisan School dormitory, clutching my bandaged forearm, barely believing I was there on that narrow bed, in that unfamiliar room.

In the morning, I would dress in the apprentice's uniform waiting in the wardrobe. I would blindly follow the other freshly branded first-year students to the refectory, then to the orientation. I would sit in a curved room with vaulted windows and oak desks. The professor would take us through the school rules, schedules, classes, and then point to a large charcoal sketch affixed to the paneled walls—an elaborate diagram of terranium ore.

The professor would say, "We will start at the beginning."

I would sit among my peers, whose eyes would slither in my direction, and wish for the first time in my life that I were home in Scurry.

In the evenings, I would lay awake in that small characterless room, unable to sleep. I'd summon dust from the candelabra, from the narrow windowsill, from the floorboards beneath my bed, and watch it dance in my hand.

In the pocket of an old skirt hanging in the armoire was a vial that pretended to be idium but wasn't.

Meanwhile, in a forgotten mining town far away in the North, rumors of fixed siphoning ceremonies would begin to spread.

HONORABLE HEADMASTER OF THE NATIONAL ARTISAN SCHOOL
Professor H. Dumley
To
RIGHT HONORABLE MASTER OF THE NATIONAL ARTISAN HOUSE
Lord G. Tanner

My Lord,

On this 535th year of siphoning, our great Belavere welcomes two hundred and sixty-six inductions to our academy of the finest arts. Most exciting, of course, is the inclusion of a genuine earth Charmer!

Nina Clarke, an unexpected presence among the mix, appeared on our registry as the daughter of Mr. and Mrs. Frederick Clarke of Sommerland. Regrettably, both are deceased.

Nina Clarke is joined by a water Charmer, Theodore Shop, whose father resides in your House of Lords. What a blessing it is, to welcome two Charmers into our hallowed classrooms in the same year!

This year's siphoning also accrued a healthy number of Masons and Smiths. Unfortunately, I must report that there were no new Alchemists among the lot.

While you may find this news distressing, I am hopeful that the coming years will see a resurgence in Alchemists and their ancient art form.

Long live Belavere,
Prof. H. Dumley

RIGHT HONORABLE MASTER OF THE NATIONAL ARTISAN HOUSE
Lord G. Tanner
To
Miss Nina Clarke

Miss Clarke,

It was with utmost joy that I learned a new earth Charmer was added to our esteemed school of arts. I write to you now to formally welcome you into the fold. I do hope your years under the tutelage of our masters are as rewarding as they are fruitful.

It has been some time since a Charmer of your medium has blessed this country, and though your journey has only begun henceforth, I grow elated to think of all you might do for your countrymen.

I must admit that I was greatly interested to hear of your parentage, Miss Clarke. I knew your mother and father quite well. Well enough, I think, to have remembered the blessing of a child while they lived.

Please accept my belated condolences.

I am most pleased that you have emerged from the shadows. After all, Miss Clarke, an earth Charmer is a wonder to behold. As for a child of false breeding, who is of no great benefit to me? Well, a child such as this is better placed in Scurry.

I will be kept informed of your progress.

Long live Belavere.

Yours faithfully,
Lord Geoffry Tanner

CHAPTER 9

NINA

I sat in the last row of my minerals class. It was more difficult for anyone to watch me back there.

A sat beside a girl named Polly Prescott. She was a Scribbler from Lavnonshire with beautiful warm eyes, dark hair and skin, and a weak, trembling chin. I'd opted to sit beside her whenever space allowed; us being the only two brink children in our year.

The professor, a Mrs. Cromley, described the properties of different metals while we took notes.

"Most regard terranium as the most significant of the metals, and it certainly deserves considerable study. Terranium deposits alone encase the idium we seek. Terranium also contains bluff—from the outside, both kinds of terranium look nearly identical, but while idium is detected by its blueish hue, bluff is of the blackest ink, with no magic-enhancing properties. It does, however, accelerate healing when carefully diluted, and act as a powerful sedative when not."

This description of bluff was rather wanting in my opinion. While medicinal bluff was, indeed, almost miraculous in its healing properties, it was also highly toxic in large doses. Artisans with the money to do so could purchase recreational bluff and consequently be separated from their mind for a time. In the brink, pure bluff was a luxury the average Crafter could not indulge in. Small amounts of bluff were mixed with laudanum and meadowsweet instead. The miners in Scurry sometimes spent a week's wages to dose themselves with badly mixed bluff. You could find them lying in the street with ink-stained lips and glassy eyes.

"More curiously, terranium ore is the most brittle of the metals. When tampered with inexpertly, it crumbles, and when mixed with liquid idium, becomes putrefied. Of course, our Book of Belavere states that the Goddess constructed the ore this way *on purpose*—to protect idium from unrighteous hands. Only Alchemists can siphon both idium and bluff."

Billy Holloway beckoned from the front row: "But Alchemists are rare. What happens if the existing ones pass before more appear? Do we run out of idium?"

The rest of the class sat up straighter, young eyes widening in Mrs. Cromley's direction.

Mrs. Cromley was a kindly woman. She smiled gently. "We needn't concern ourselves with what we cannot control. God will give what is needed, when it's needed."

The class settled, mollified, and I was jealous that they could believe her.

In my pocket, a letter burned between sheets of parchment. A letter written by a hand that I believed had usurped God's. I was too afraid to leave it in my dorm, lest someone find it. Too afraid to burn it, in case someone were to interrupt me or find the remnants. It stayed on my person at all times. Every time I sat or bent forward, the parchment crackled, and I was reminded of Lord Tanner with his tiny teeth and hanging jowls. Had it only been weeks ago that I'd beamed up at him from the crowd? Now, his name sickened me.

Beside me, a boy snickered. When I turned to look, he and his friend averted their eyes, smothered their laughter. One held his hand up in my direction. In the center of his palm, marred by sweat and creases, was the word *worm*.

That's what they had taken to calling me. Never to my face, but I heard it still in the halls and bathrooms. On several occasions, I'd found live worms in my bed, in my shoes, mixed in with my dinner. Each time, a scream ravaged my throat but never breached my lips. I'd forsworn tears. I got rid of the creatures in stony silence.

Polly was monikered "squid," an unimpressive interpretation of her medium. Her punishment for being born to Crafter parents was to have her clothes, sheets, and parchment constantly ink stained. It seemed she could hardly survive a class without some little shit "accidentally" knocking an inkwell into her lap or over her desk.

If it were Scurry, I'd have caved in their faces and stomped on their chests. But this was the National Artisan School, where children carried out their torments in passive, secretive ways. So, I imagined cracking their teeth, but never did it. Polly only sat silently in quiet refrain, her small chin ever quaking.

I ignored the sneers. Instead of mashing their brains in I was counting in my head, waiting for my body to unwind when the classroom door thrashed open, none other than Professor Dumley appearing in its frame.

Until that moment, I'd never seen him: the headmaster of the Artisan School. Even at our orientation, he had not appeared. But here he was now, in my minerals class, and his eyes caught on to mine immediately.

He was a man with overlapping chins and a peculiar complexion, blotched and spotted with age. I guessed he was seventy, but he could have been a hundred. He could have been as old as the school itself. He certainly commanded the room that way, as though the bricks and mortar had been built around him, for him.

I do not mean to say that he was menacing. In fact, his eyes twinkled kindly when he found me, and he wagged a finger in my direction as though I'd been intentionally hiding from him. "Just the young lady I'd hoped to catch," he said.

The letter by my waist may as well have burst into flames. I felt it sear my flesh. Surely, he'd see it, wouldn't he? Burning a hole into my middle?

But Dumley only turned to Mrs. Cromley. "I'm also looking for a Theodore Shop?"

"Here, sir," said a boy. He stood from the front row, nodding his head politely.

The other Charmer. The same boy I'd seen at the siphoning ceremony. I'd noticed him in several classes, in the halls and common rooms. A water Charmer, yet not scorned for his singularity. Instead, he was a magnet, and it wasn't difficult to see why.

He was dark haired, brown eyed, and light-skinned, a beacon even in the shade. Some people, I knew, were simply born with that kind of light. It seeped out and lured in those closest. Even his smile—closed and polite—was charismatic, difficult to ignore.

The other students were just as well-groomed, straight-backed and proper. But while they seemed to walk with an air of affectedness, Theodore Shop made his station seem a humble accident of birth, which it was.

"Ah, yes! Well, Mrs. Cromley, I apologize for the interruption, but might I steal these two away for the rest of the lesson?"

I doubted there was a single person in the room who saw it as a real question.

Dumley led the two of us through the vaulted halls and their oil paintings, up a spiraling case of stairs to a floor I hadn't yet been. We passed bay windows that overlooked the gardens and courtyard, past busts of other headmasters and to a set of double doors so intricately carved, I thought the wood Mason responsible must have blinded himself in its creation.

It was the Battle of Belavere, captured in woodgrain. A hundred mounted soldiers and swords and fire, all rushing the center of the trench. "Good God," I uttered, noticing the engravings on sword handles, the slope of Idia's eyebrows, the fury in her static cry.

"It's quite something, isn't it?" Dumley said happily, reaching to take hold of a handle. "Carved three hundred years ago by a man named Valino Ferdinand. He died the day after this work was completed. Threw himself off a bell tower, if you can believe it. Such a *waste*." He pushed the doors inward and beckoned us inside.

Theodore waited with his hands behind his back. He nodded to me. "After you."

I went in ahead of him warily, half expecting that he might drop worms down my collar. "The Artisan killed himself? But why?" What on earth did an Artisan want for?

"Well," said Dumley, approaching a lush pair of upholstered settees. "His last recorded journal entry stated that he believed nothing could surpass the work, that he'd reached the summit of his ability, and the thought of descent was intolerable. His last missive said, '*If the best of my creations has come to pass, then for what do I live now?*'"

Dumley sat on one settee and gestured for Theodore and me to take the other. In the space between, there was a thin-legged table with a waiting china tea set.

"Surely there's more to a life than the sum of one's creations," Theodore said easily. He sat a polite distance from me. I wondered who had taught him to speak like that. Articulate and confident. Without a drag in his vowels or a hitch in his consonants. His posture, too, was perfect. He did not stare at the china or the portraits or the fresco on the ceiling like I did. I felt suddenly horribly deficient.

"Ah, but is that not what all of us seek, young Theodore? To reach the heights of our abilities?"

Yes, I thought. Even now I felt that itch, the one that clawed for bigger, better. I scratched my neck to rid the urge.

"Even if it might kill us," Dumley continued, "would we not want it still?"

I'd never thought of desire that way—that it was the wanting that consumed a person, not the object they sought.

"Seems a high price for a pair of pretty doors," Theodore replied, but his eyes were star bright and it softened the mockery. "However exquisite they may be."

"Indeed, son, indeed. And yet, any poet would bid you to find passion as bright and burning as our friend Valino." He didn't look at Theo. He watched the fingers I raked against my neck.

"You know," he said. "I once painted a mural for a boy I was deeply in love with. I'll admit I'm not the most precise with a brush, but I labored night and day over that piece, and in the end, I considered it a triumph! Of course, it is those moments of triumph that lift us to cliff's edge, isn't it? I was so very proud of it. Which made it all the more grisly when I shredded it to pieces with my bare hands."

I was too stunned to temper my expression. "What? *Why?*"

"My dear muse didn't like it." Dumley shrugged absently. "Said it was stilted and lacked movement."

I looked over at Theodore, he at me, and we shared a private confoundment.

"In any case," the professor continued as he took the teapot from its tray, "we should speak of things less bleak for our first meeting."

"First, sir?" asked Theodore.

"Ah, of course! I ought to explain myself." The teapot clattered back down. His arms widened as though a grand tale were poised to unspool. "I have taken it upon myself to tutor you privately!" He slapped his knees and smiled broadly.

Theodore cleared his throat. "Privately?" he pressed. Again, we shared a mystified glance. "Is that . . . er, usual?"

"Not at all," Dumley chortled. "And I'll admit, it's been a while since I've presided over a class, but with two new Charmers in one cohort, I can't help but want a hand in your tutelage."

His smile was still kind. There was nothing at all to suggest the meeting was anything but what he said. And yet . . .

I will be kept informed of your progress.

"Professor?" I asked cautiously, wondering if I ought to shut up, but if I were to sleep tonight, or any night, I needed to know. I tried to mimic Theodore's inflection. "Does this have anything to do with . . . Lord Tanner?"

I felt Theodore's stare swivel between Dumley and myself, but I did not look away from the professor. I wanted to catch the flicker of a reaction, if it were to come.

But Dumley's smile only widened. "But how did you guess, Miss Clarke?" He chuckled again. "It was Lord Tanner's very idea! And you both should feel honored that he's already taken such a keen interest in you. We've had many a water Charmer pass through, Mr. Shop, but I've never seen the House of Lords so excited!"

For some reason, Theodore's smile fell slightly. "My father is a minister there, Professor," he explained. "Likely Lord Tanner saw the relation."

Dumley waved the assumption aside. "Lord Tanner sees *potential*, Mr. Shop. You ought not diminish yourself. A Charmer is a prize to be coveted. I should know." With that, Dumley waved his hand toward the waiting hearth, and a fire blazed to life, unaided by wood or tinder. It simply floated there, several inches from the clean tile base. He laughed merrily at it, his chins stretching. "Of course, we're not the most humble of creatures, are we? And as for the lovely young lady who stopped us all in our tracks!" He held his arms out as though he expected me to run into them. I did not.

"A Charmer of *earth*! The first of your kind in more than a century. Where, oh where, did you come from, young Nina?"

"Sommerland," I answered immediately, too loudly. It took several seconds to realize the question was rhetorical.

"Of all places!" he chortled. "A farming town, if I'm not mistaken?"

"Sheep," I said. I'd been sure to research my "hometown" the second I'd found the school's expansive library. "And cattle. For the wool and leather and meat."

Professor Dumley nodded politely, feigning interest, as though I were an infant pointing to something entirely base. I wondered vaguely what he'd have to say of the terranium mines of Scurry.

Theodore and I sat on the settee, drinking tea, listening to Professor Dumley chatter about the exploration of learning we would embark upon together. He told us stories of his own years as an apprentice and his assent to headmaster. His hands danced to the stories with ever-intensifying flourish, and the room grew hotter and hotter until I was desiccating, desperate for escape.

"And now, we should really turn our attention to today's lesson," he said with gentle reproach, as though Theodore and I had been a grievous distraction. "Tell me, Mr. Shop, have you yet experimented with your medium?"

Theo blushed. It was somewhat endearing. "We aren't permitted to use our mediums unsupervised in our first year, professor."

"Oh ho!" Dumley laughed. "Yet no one's the wiser when those dormitory doors close, are they? I was once an apprentice, too, you forget."

Theo grinned, then said, "I can levitate small amounts, but I've yet to make it take shape."

"But levitation is quite advanced!" Dumley said. "Would you show me?" And he opened the lid of the teapot, gestured for Theo to do as he may.

Theo hesitated for a single moment, then, with a glance in my direction, he slid to the edge of his seat, wiping his hands on his trousers. "Should I just . . . ?"

"Don't be bothered by any mess," Dumley assured him.

Theo cleared his throat, then, with a certain measure of awkwardness, he brought his palms up.

The teapot trembled delicately, threatened to tip sideways, but then a speck of liquid floated from the spout, another from the opening. Theo's hands trembled.

A shifting orb of tea slowly appeared, its shape morphing in the air. It held for a moment, suspended above the tea set, to the resounding cheer of Professor Dumley, and then it shuddered and fell, the tea splashing off the spoons and saucers.

And Dumley laughed and clapped.

After a moment, I clapped, too. It seemed bad manners not to.

Theo panted slightly and sat back in his chair, a smile spreading from ear to ear.

"Quite amazing, isn't it?" Dumley said, watching Theo closely. "That sensation?"

Theo nodded, his hands trembling. "There's nothing like it."

Dumley winked. "Worth dying for, some would say." He clapped once more, shaking his head in a show of amazement. "What a talent you'll be."

Then he turned to me.

"But I haven't forgotten you, my dear." He wagged a finger at me, then stood and consulted a dusty credenza, lifting from its top a large clay urn.

He dropped it on the tea table with a clatter, and Theodore and I jumped.

He said, "Here we are!" as though he'd just proffered a gift. "Just dug it from the rose garden myself."

The urn had been half filled with dark, damp earth. I could smell it from here. Feel its texture already, as though my mind had fingers, soil building up beneath the nails.

"How about you, Miss Clarke? Have you yet dabbled?"

I twisted my fingers together. "A little."

"Well, do not be intimidated by young Theodore here. We must all start from the beginning." He looked upon me kindly, already sitting back in his chair, already sympathetic. "Why, it takes many students some time to learn to levitate their medium at all. When *I* was a lad—"

But his sentence was cut short.

The earth rose from the urn, and Dumley's mouth went slack.

What I had learned so far in my "dabbling" was that my mind was an extension of my hands. I now felt that familiar expansion, my mind unfolding until it tripled. I felt the dirt in my palms as though I cradled it. I felt it sift and crumble. It was wet, heavy. Malleable. My hands twitched at my sides.

I compacted it first, made it into a planet hovering before me, smoothing out its edges until it was near perfect, then I made it spin.

I'd yet to try charming earth so pliable. I made the sphere into a cube next, then a funnel, a small windstorm, and finally I lifted all those specks of dirt higher, higher, until they were suspended in that vaulted ceiling like a thousand muddy stars.

I knew Dumley and Theo were on their feet, as I was, staring up at the galaxy I had made. And then my mind shuddered, the pressure grew insurmountable—elastic stretched to the furthest extent.

Then it snapped.

Dirt rained to the floor, onto the settee, into the teacups. It plinked off Dumley's head, clung to his whiskers.

His eyes remained on me.

"Well," was all he said. "Well, well, well." It seemed he was coming to some grand summation. He looked around his drawing room, at his sullied rug.

I suddenly felt foolish. "S-sorry," I said, gesturing lamely to the tea table. "For the mess."

A grin dawned slowly over Dumley's face.

I heard Theodore mutter a curse. Quite unlike him.

Then Dumley walked over to me. He gripped either side of my face in his papery hands. "My word," he uttered. A laugh escaped him. "Idia has blessed us." And I thought I saw tears in his eyes as he took my hands and patted them. "What a blessing you'll be." His chest ballooned. He turned to Theo. "What fine assets you will *both* be."

· · · · · ·

An hour later, Theodore closed those ornately carved doors behind him, the ringing trills of Dumley's goodbye following us.

"Well," Theodore uttered. And from his pocket, he drew out two handkerchiefs. "Our headmaster is insane."

Perhaps it was the heat trapped in my skin, or the absurdity of the meeting, but a laugh escaped, then more of it.

"Here," Theodore said, waving a handkerchief toward me. I took it gladly, mopping the sweat from my throat and the back of my neck. The-odore did the same with his own.

I giggled again, half relieved that I'd not been thrown from the school, half feverish. "Do you think the rest of the class will notice us drenched in sweat?"

Theodore took a moment to respond, and when I looked back at him, his eyes had stuck to me. They narrowed with interest. "Where did you say you were from?" he asked.

I realized then that I'd allowed my tongue to slacken. A drawl had snuck free. "Sommerland," I said, tightening the consonants. The letter at my hip burned.

"Huh," he said. "Not far into the brink, then?"

"Near enough." I hoped my voice had morphed smoothly into some-thing less graveled.

"You sound almost Northern," he stated, smiling easily.

Eastern, I wanted to say.

"I've always wanted to travel out to the brink," he continued, and somehow he managed to loosen the knots in my stomach, if only slightly. "Do you have many friends there?"

"No."

He frowned at me, gesturing that I go first down the stairs. "Have you met any new ones here? It seemed like you were sitting alone at breakfast this morning."

He would have seen me blush if my cheeks weren't already mottled with heat. "Not many." I had the strange urge to tell him about the taunts in the hallways and the worms in my bed, but I saw pity in the way he averted his eyes, and I was suddenly sure he already knew about them.

"Sit by me," he said. "Whenever you'd like."

My answering smile was grim. "You don't mind worms in your food?"

He turned a brilliant crimson, and it was as good as a confirmation.

"Thank you, Theodore," I muttered. "But I'm all right."

The halls were filling with students, all identical to the next in their deep Artisan blue. Theodore paid them no mind at all. "I insist," he said. "As long as you stop calling me Theodore. Just Theo will do."

"Theo, I really—"

"Come on," he said, and he took my hand in his, just like that, and as though he'd magicked it, some of his light trickling onto me.

That's how it was from that moment onward: Theo leading me through runnels of apprentices, me basking in his glow. Hot drawing rooms and mad headmasters and the promise of passions big enough to consume.

Big enough to kill you.

CHAPTER 10

THE TRENCH TRIBUNE

MURMURS OF STRIKE ACTION IN THE BRINK

Speculation has arisen from the Northern mining towns that a strike may be forthcoming after a third mine collapse across the continent in as many consecutive days, as well as a gas explosion in Kenton Hill, tolling hundreds dead. The information was offered by an anonymous Scribbler who allegedly wrote to the House of Lords, informing them of a number of unsanctioned meetings and even suspicions of a union for Crafter's rights.

This coincides with other rumors of unknown origin spreading in the Northern and Eastern provinces, casting aspersions as to the legitimacy of Belavere's siphoning ceremonies. Whispers suggest a possible link between such accusations and the rousing of a so-called union.

The Right Honorable Lord Tanner, however, assured this reporter that the racket is, in his words, "nonsensical."

"The siphoning ceremony is a sacred religious ritual upheld for hundreds of years in our nation's history. The idea that the siphoning of idium has been somehow corrupted is impossible, and quite frankly, an illusion of the desperate. Only Idia may bestow a man [or woman] with a faculty for magic, and idium cannot unlock what is not present."

The Right Honorable Lord also offered his sincerest sorrows to those in mourning after the recent catastrophes. "Long live those souls lost to us. And long live Belavere."

The words *Kenton Hill* seemed to leap from the page. They racketed around my head all the way through my classes, where I performed averagely aside from Headmaster Dumley's private lessons.

I was in the first dregs of my second year at the Artisan school. I now spoke without my Scurry dialect without much thinking.

I'd never heard from my father. He must have assumed I'd become an Artisan when I didn't return home that day. I wondered if he'd tried to pay a Scribbler to send me a note, only for them to fail to find a Nina Harrow.

It had been Theo who had handed me the newsprint at breakfast.

I was headed to Aunt Francis's house before curfew, clutching the newsprint in my hand. She lived only a short way from the school, just beyond the National House, where she worked in the treasury, making coins from nickel alongside a slew of other Smiths.

At this time of night, the streets were slower, filled with music. It floated out of windows and traveled on the breeze. Insects chirped along, the water trickled by in its troughs, the city of Belavere always in complete harmony with all its working parts. Whenever I ventured out on the weekends, I was reminded of why I'd so badly sought it in the first place. Such things weren't always so clear from inside the school's walls.

Aunt Francis opened the door to receive me herself. Her station as a Smith was not so high that she could afford servants, yet her terrace home was lovely. It was humbly decorated with fine furnishings she proclaimed were family heirlooms. Her being the last real remaining Leisel made Aunt Francis's home an exhibition of artifacts that I did not feel comfortable sitting on or eating off.

She was not the sort of woman who embraced another or even smiled too widely. She never seemed particularly thrilled to see me, and yet there was evidence to the contrary. There was always a plate of cake waiting and a teapot steaming when I visited. She looked over my face and person before remembering to invite me over the threshold, as if searching for signs of harm. She always, always asked a thousand questions about my classes, about my interactions with others, about any correspondence I might have received from Lord Tanner. I never told her about the letter.

I walked across her trim carpeted floors to the kitchen when she bid me to come inside.

"You no longer run to get to the cake," she said. "Thank the heavens."

I smiled a little for her benefit. I did not tell her it was because I no longer feared a skipped meal, or that somewhere between twelve and thirteen, I'd departed childhood.

We sat. She looked at me squarely. I looked at my fingers.

"How are your classes?" she asked first, then sat up a little straighter, if it were possible. "Are you progressing well with Professor Dumley?"

"Yes."

Earth Charming, I'd learned, was a matter of weight and scale. The more there was to be moved, the harder it became. Professor Dumley said the magic was a muscle that would grow stronger with practice. But I was making fine progress—more progress, I thought, than he could quite believe.

Overall, I feared I was only a novelty. If it weren't for the fact that I was the only living person who could charm earth, I would probably be of no consequence at all.

But I *was* an earth Charmer, and the title lent itself to higher praise than I was worth.

"Have you made any new friends?" Aunt Francis asked, and her eyes tightened.

"A few," I lied.

"And . . . Mr. Shop?"

"Is one of them."

She shook her head slightly with a deep breath. "I see his father often, you know. In the papers. Most believe he will be next in line if Lord Tanner ever relinquishes his position."

I nodded. Swallowed. I had a sudden ridiculous fear that she might forbid me from speaking with Theodore anymore. "He doesn't know anything," I told her. "I swear it."

Aunt Francis blanched. We usually obeyed an unspoken rule that we would not mention the ruse, even to each other, as though Lord Tanner himself were pressing his ears to the windows. "In any case, it seems the House of Lords needs an earth Charmer more than it needs to right the order of things," she said.

"Then it shouldn't matter who my friends are."

Aunt Francis's cheeks flushed. She stood abruptly. For one wild moment I imagined her launching across the table and grabbing me by the collar, and my body curled in on itself.

But she did neither.

"Listen to me, Nina," she said, her voice still low, if tremulous. "Theodore seems like a nice boy. I know he has been . . . kind to you. But it remains that his father is a man in a very powerful position, and men like that don't take kindly to frauds. Particularly when they are found consorting with their children."

A fraud, I thought. Was that what I was? The word needled. "If I am a fraud, then aren't we all? I only siphoned what the rest of you did."

Silence, and this time, Aunt Francis was the one to avert her eyes.

We waded in dangerous waters. But I took my chances. "We are taught that all have the right to consume idium, but that only some are capable of truly siphoning its magic into their bodies. I know now it wasn't true. But was *all* of it a lie?"

Aunt Francis's chest had begun to heave, her eyes flitting to the windows and doors.

"Please," I said. "I only want to understand, and then I won't ever ask another thing." I scooted so close to the edge of my chair that it teetered.

She clenched her fists, closed her eyes, then finally sat. She seemed older.

"I don't know the answers, Nina," she said. "And in truth, I do not wish to. I only know what they told us when I took that position." She sighed. "The rest, I put together of my own accord. I think once, perhaps long ago, out of memory, every citizen was permitted the chance to consume idium . . . and it went very badly."

I frowned. "How?"

Aunt Francis shook her head. "You are very young. Perhaps too young to imagine what happens when the means for destruction is placed in the wrong hands. But I believe it once led our nation to war."

I frowned. "The Battle of Belavere is the only war in our history," I said. "And it was fought against invaders. Outside nations."

Aunt Francis shrugged. "We only know of history what is recorded. And records are easily lost or rewritten. I can't know for sure. But the fact remains that at some point, our leaders thought it better that power be meted out only to those who could be trusted with it."

I wondered how they decided who that should be. By what criteria were we judged? What lord had ever ventured east to Scurry, for instance, to scout these paragons of moral virtue?

Then, I thought of what they might find—a horde of vitriolic miners. What would a person like that do with the power to charm fire, for instance?

Aunt Francis continued. "Most children of Artisans become Artisans as well, as we all know. The lie is in letting the population believe this is the fault of bloodlines, much in the way a child of brown-haired parents will likely be born the same, but might also be blond. Genealogy is difficult to predict. It provides a reliable loophole, you see? When highborn parents have committed a crime or some other disgrace, their child tends to become a Crafter, despite generations of supposed Artisan breeding. The reverse happens for those Crafters whose families serve the House of Lords well. Their children are deemed Artisan, even if they are the first of their family to possess magic ability. If the intake of Artisan children runs low one year, then the next will see an upswing of brink children miraculously turned Artisan."

"Do you think it's right?" I asked her, something burning the sides of my throat. "That only the lucky few, the trusted few, should get to live this life?" I wondered if she'd ever stepped foot in the brink. I wondered if she had any inkling at all as to the streets and houses she'd find in Scurry.

Aunt Francis wavered. Her answer seemed to weigh on her chest.

"No," she finally said in a quiet voice. "I am sure it isn't fair. But . . ." She looked at me earnestly. "The House of Lords is charged with protecting this Nation, from outside adversaries and from itself. I wonder if that isn't of higher import than what is right and fair."

I felt us at opposite edges of a chasm; I dithered on the edge, wishing to cross it, but couldn't.

I held up the newspaper still tightly rolled in my hand and unfurled it on the table. "Theo gave me this," I said, pointing to the front-page article.

Aunt Francis stared at it with distaste. "Yes," she said. "I read about it."

"There was a boy at my siphoning ceremony. He came from the North."

Her head tilted curiously.

"He . . . well . . . he was with me that day. When we found the vials. Except he—"

"He went home," Aunt Francis guessed. "To the North, you said?"

I nodded glumly. I thought of Patrick Colson's face, of his gentle hands and tormented eyes. There was rarely a day where I didn't. I'd taken to drawing his face obsessively, scared I would forget it. I remembered him slipping those vials into my pocket, kissing my cheek, whispering in my ear that I had a mind of my own.

"Do you think . . ." I stumbled, my heart pounding. "Is it possible that *he* started these rumors?"

Aunt Francis had her thumb between her teeth. She chewed on it subconsciously as she stared out at her kitchen, drawn into her own turbulent thoughts.

"This boy," she said eventually. "What was his name?"

There was something about the way she said it. The forced casualness of it. It made me lock away the name in my middle. "I didn't know his name." I was a better actress than Aunt Francis, it seemed. I frowned, modulated my voice.

She looked slightly mollified, as though I'd just taken a task out of her hands. "Well, even if it was this boy, he is just a boy. Rumors pass."

But these rumors are true, I thought. *Doesn't truth find its foothold eventually?*

"As for a union," Aunt Francis continued. She said the word *union* as though it were absurd. "No such group unsanctioned by the House of Lords will make much headway. If one exists, I'm sure the culprits will be quickly flushed out."

I said nothing. Patrick Colson's face swam around my mind, refusing to fade.

CHAPTER 11

THE TRENCH TRIBUNE

TANNER REFUSES MINERS UNION DEMANDS

A demonstration in Baymouth last month leaves little doubt of dissenters in the Northeastern provinces who dub themselves the "Miners Union." This, after the House of Lords flagrantly denied the existence of such a movement for more than a year.

Crafters of all trades lined the streets of Baymouth, halting all works for several hours in the town, marking the first promised strike from the Miners Union in a long list provided to this esteemed reporter.

The police house in Baymouth did not submit to questioning, with speculation arising that the officers in charge willingly stepped aside for the demonstration.

"All actions taken in aid of or aligned with any criminal organization will be met with the fullest penalty from Belavere's High House," said the Right Honorable Lord Tanner in his latest address.

When asked of the allegations of idium corruption, Lord Tanner made no statement except to remind this reporter that accusations against the House were considered an act of treason. No doubt, the strikes come at a grave time for the governing lord, with the sourcing of terranium at record lows.

Lord Tanner made no statement regarding the ongoing terranium scarcity.

The Miners Union promises more strikes ahead of the House's re-
fusal of their demands, which included salary increases and a referen-
dum on the siphoning ceremonies.

As to the time and place of these strikes, they remain as elusive as
the Miners Union itself, whose leaders and headquarters are still yet to
be discovered.

TRIBUTE TO FALLEN ALCHEMIST

Famed Alchemist Lester Brickem died peacefully in his sleep late last
week, report his wife and five children, who farewelled their beloved in
a funeral attended by the full House of Lords.

Brickem, aged 78, was one of three surviving Alchemists in Bela-
vere Trench. His death has sent a ripple of concern across the nation,
as the House reports that no new Alchemists have arisen in the latest
siphoning.

The newspaper was left strewn across the table of Professor Dumley's drawing room. The fire was roaring. Sweat was collecting in my collar. The headmaster was humming to himself as he poured out barely steeped tea.

"I imagine the House of Lords must be becoming anxious," I said out loud, and when Dumley looked at me questioningly, I gestured toward the newspaper.

Theo cleared his throat beside me, then gave me a look of warning. I resisted the urge to stick out my tongue.

Our third year had brought about a change in him. He was much taller, his shoulders broader. Hair was beginning to spout along his chin and upper lip. I enjoyed teasing him about it whenever I could, which was often. Thanks to Professor Dumley's continued interest in us, we were regularly together in this drawing room, or on excursions out into the wider city to seek our mediums.

Dumley's eyes slipped to the newspaper for the briefest of moments.

"Oh, not at all," he muttered, collecting the pages and then setting them aflame in his hand. The fire never seemed to burn him.

I watched the cinders with a frown. "But surely, they must be taking the Miners Union seriously now?"

Theo scoffed. "You worry too much, Clarke. Father says Tanner will eventually throw a bunch of money their way, and they'll wander back to their pits and dig up more terranium." He made it sound as though they were rats rummaging for crumbs.

"In any case," he continued, "there'll be no need for unions unless they find more Alchemists. Soon, we'll all be a bunch of Crafters."

"Now, now," Professor Dumley interjected. "This is hardly talk for the classroom, is it?" Never mind that his classroom consisted of a tea set and a life-size painting of a naked woman.

"I have a surprise for you both today," Dumley went on. "You see, I received a small scribble this morning from someone most esteemed!"

A knock came, and before Professor Dumley could move toward the doors, they opened, and in strode Lord Tanner himself, smile widening, jowls quivering.

My lunch made itself known, bubbling into my throat.

"My lord," Theo said, bowing his head in the proper way.

The man was taller than I remembered him. More robust. Less a receptacle of power and more a mountain of it. The drawing room seemed somehow smaller, less grand.

He said, "Dumley. How are you?" without looking at him. He bared his teeth in a grin, staring at me with a pincerlike gaze as he shook Theo's hand.

He knows what you are, I thought, and I had the urge to bolt from the room.

"Please excuse Miss Clarke," Professor Dumley said now, eyeing me pleadingly. "I quite underprepared her for your arrival, my lord. She forgets herself."

It was only then that I remembered I should be standing, curtsying, chiming a greeting.

"Apologies," I muttered, tripping on my skirt as I stood and curtsying awkwardly for the first time in my life.

"Probably the heat," Lord Tanner said, nodding his head to me. "Lord almighty, but it is *stifling* in here, Dumley. I'm sure the devil keeps his drawing room cooler than this."

Dumley snapped his fingers with a flourish, and the fire in the hearth extinguished. "I barely feel it anymore," he said gaily. "I fear I've become rather cold-blooded with age. Tea, my lord?"

"Milk and sugar, if you don't mind." And he took Dumley's usual seat, opposite my own. He seemed to envelop its frame. As Dumley hummed serenely, making the tea, Tanner crossed his legs and leaned back with a strange grace, continuing to stare.

I felt horridly peculiar.

"You'll be pleased to hear, my lord, that Miss Clarke and Mr. Shop have made tremendous progress this past month alone," Dumley offered, passing Tanner a teacup without minding the slosh of its insides. "We have great fun, don't we, children? Why, Nina and I just yesterday ventured to the wheat farms just outside the city and tilled an entire field within an hour!"

Lord Tanner said, "Well, now. That's something." But his interest was clearly feigned.

"And Mr. Shop's abilities already supersede those of our sixth-year water Charmers!"

"His father will be rapturous," Lord Tanner said. "Not a day goes by that Lord Shop does not remind me of his brilliant son."

Theo smiled weakly. "That's very kind, sir."

"I suppose you'd like to see it for yourself!" Dumley exclaimed, bouncing off his seat. "We could—"

But Lord Tanner held up a hand. "In a moment, Dumley. My visit today shall be a short one. I don't wish to steal these two from their studies." He drained his absurdly small cup and placed it down, smacking his lips. I felt as though his eyes were peeling back my skin.

"I'm sure, given all the chatter about town, that the two of you have heard mentioned the founding of a union, led by a mob of angry Crafts-men."

I went still. I'd never heard any professor or even Aunt Francis bring up the strike action in the brink. Indeed, it seemed they were determined to ignore it altogether. As though admitting its existence would make it so.

Theo and I shared a momentary glance. We'd spoken about little else in the past months. Heads almost touching over lunch, hunching over newspapers in his room after dark. Speculating about the implications if further strikes ensued.

"So . . . it is true, then?" Theo asked, once again far braver than me.

Lord Tanner turned pensive. "That's the question, isn't it? Does a union truly exist if it hides itself away? I'm afraid that despite whatever this little group of thugs calls itself, it has yet to come into the open be-fore the House of Lords, or indeed, name its leader. And until it does, it will only ever be something in the shadows, stirring trouble among good people. Good people who will suffer the consequences of their crimes, if they indeed strike."

I swallowed, hoping my voice would not betray my nerves. "Is . . . is another strike likely?"

"That's the difficult thing about my position, Miss Clarke," he said. "One must always *prepare* for eventualities, no matter how improbable they are."

I hardly knew what he meant.

"Now, rest assured, the House of Lords believes wholly that the mob will disappear shortly, but I'd be a fool not to ensure I have all my knives sharpened, now wouldn't I?" he spread his arms wide toward Theo and me, as though we were the prized blades in his collection.

Theo frowned. "Us, sir?"

"All of us, Mr. Shop," Tanner said with a laugh. "All Artisans would need to come together, if the situation arose. And the two of you are in possession of some of Idia's greatest gifts. No doubt she saw you fit to use them for the sake of our great Belavere."

"I don't understand," I said.

"Then let me speak plainly, Miss Clarke." I thought he put rather a lot of emphasis on the name *Clarke*. "Sometimes the Craftsmen, when they're feeling disgruntled, stop doing their jobs and make a little noise. A little noise is easily stifled. But sometimes a squeak turns into a deafening roar that drowns sense. Part of my duty is ensuring peace and quiet, Miss Clarke. Do you follow me now?"

Nod, I thought, then did so.

"I will do whatever I can to quash that noise, if need be. And as a good leader, I must ensure I have the means to do so. Artisans have the means. *You* have the means."

"Me, sir?"

"Our nation of Belavere Trench has the advantage of being . . . well, a trench. A nation surrounded by mountains. Rich, dense earth. Do you understand my meaning, Miss Clarke?"

"I . . . yes."

"Should certain conditions come to pass"—and here, his eyes swept to Theo as well—"the Capital will require your assistance."

Theo frowned, jaw tight. "Of course, my lord," he said.

Tanner turned to me. "You would do what is necessary to protect this city, would you not?"

I swallowed. I tried to mimic Theo's tone. "Of course."

Lord Tanner smiled. "Wonderful. Now, why don't you two show me what you can do?"

Theo and I became Dumley's theater performers after that. We charmed until our palms grew slick and our eyelids fluttered.

Tanner did not utter a word until the demonstration was over. "Quite advanced," he offered. "As you said, Dumley."

Despite the bland praise, Dumley seemed elated.

Tanner stood, pulling from his breast pocket two envelopes. He passed one each to Theodore and me. "This is special writ, allowing each of you to obtain a quarterly dose of idium from the dispensaries."

Theodore and I looked warily at each other. Theodore cleared his throat. "Quarterly, my lord? By law, we are only allowed to consume idium every half year."

"Unless ordered otherwise by sanctioned writ," Tanner said, smiling thinly. "I know the law, Mr. Shop. Better than most people, I would think."

"Why?" I asked. It slipped out before I could blanket it, soften it. But I sealed my lips shut and waited for the answer.

Tanner donned his jacket. "To sharpen the knives, Miss Clarke."

And he left.

CHAPTER 12

NINA

In my fourth year at the Artisan school, I sat in the dark theater grandstand alone, covertly watching a stage play rehearsal.

I couldn't sleep. For three nights it had eluded me. I was tired of lying still and waiting for my body to settle when it wouldn't. My head would not quiet when I bid it, either. It replayed the clinking glasses and muttered conversations of Lord Shop's dinner party. Eventually the echoes of those ambling monotones grew intolerable. I found myself high in the red-back seats instead, watching these fine performers be berated.

Tomorrow, I would be sixteen.

Every year it grew easier to believe that I'd been born Artisan, and that Scurry was a fading dream. It disturbed me that I could not conjure the exact colors I would use to paint the place I'd come from.

Tumultuous thoughts plagued me. They swam round and round and round.

"Clarke?"

I jumped. At the end of the aisle, a silhouette stood—another phantom in the dark.

"Theo?"

I knew his shape and voice better than most. He sidled toward me, bent double like a porter, though no one looked up.

"Can't sleep?" he whispered, the stage lights reflecting off his dark eyes. He settled into the seat beside mine.

"No."

"Nor can I." He smoothed his hair—a newer habit. I caught him looking at his hair in every reflection he passed to ensure its exactness.

We fell immediately into a companiable silence. It was easy to do. I spent more time with Theo than I did with any other. We were The Charmers. People suspected we were dating, even our closest friends.

He was much taller than me now, and if you looked closely, he resembled a man. His modest politeness had turned to self-assurance, sometimes even boisterousness. He would gladly charm water to put on a show for friends, making models in the air from the remnants of their drinking glasses to cheery applause.

I, meanwhile, remained quiet, though I'd grown in my own ways. My lips were fuller and my two front teeth didn't seem so far apart. My chest and hips had swollen outward, my waist inward, and my legs were no longer thin knobby-kneed stalks. I was wholly a different shape.

Theo's arm sometimes dangled over my shoulder in the refectory, where we shared a table with others, and I was ashamed by how starved I felt when it lifted.

Theo bumped my shoulder with his. "What's keeping you from sleep, Clarke?" he asked. His tone was light, but there was real worry there as well.

I grimaced. "Same as always," I lied. "Volcanic sediment."

He smirked. It made a dimple appear deep in his left cheek. It was hard not to notice how handsome he was.

"Why are you awake?" I asked, folding my arms across my chest. I'd donned a woolen jumper before I'd left the dormitory, but I was suddenly very aware that beneath, I was only in bedclothes.

"My father visited today," he said with a sigh. "Wanted to discuss a proposition—an opportunity, he called it. To work in the cabinet, then in the House of Lords come our fellowship."

My eyebrows rose. "Theo! That's fantastic."

"It is," he said. "I just wished it felt as fantastic as it sounds."

"Why doesn't it?" I asked gently. "Your father is a Lord of the House. You're a Charmer. It makes sense that you'd be offered a position."

He was quiet for a moment. And then, "He said *you'd* been offered the same position."

I went still. I hadn't been ready to voice such an admission. I hadn't yet made sense of it.

"Were you?" he asked, waiting patiently for an answer.

I relented, nodding. "At the dinner," I said. "By Lord Tanner." The dinners with the Lords and ladies of the National House had become something of a regular occurrence this past year.

Neither Theo nor I particularly enjoyed them.

"The first woman in history," he uttered reverently. "It's remarkable."

"It's all I ever hear," I grumble. "I'm remarkable, outstanding, perfection incarnate."

He grinned. "Most people would be happy for the praise."

"Except that I'm not any of those things," I said hurriedly. "I'm a fair painter, a good dancer. I can draw a decent likeness, make an excellent sandcastle—"

He snorted.

"It wouldn't matter how good I was, even at charming earth—they'd praise me the same."

Theo was quiet for a moment, then sighed. "Will you accept the position?" he asked. He seemed desperate for my answer, like it might inform his own.

I only scowled. "It wasn't presented to me as a choice."

He seemed surprised by my reaction, and there, again, lay the difference between Theodore Shop and me.

He shifted, nervous. "You know, being a lord wouldn't be so bad if *you* were a lady." He looked down at my lips. "We could help. We could *change things*. What Belavere needs is progressive thinking," he said, touching my cheek gently, hesitantly, with the very tips of his fingers. A current traveled from his skin to mine. "Ministers who work with the Craftsmen. Ministers who aren't *one hundred years old.*"

I laughed through my nose, allowed my face to surrender to his cradle.

"We could do it, Nina," he said. "We could change things."

I liked the way he packaged us together. But Theo was merely a sympathizer of the working class; he didn't know what I knew.

"I don't want to say yes unless you're saying yes with me."

My heart sprinted. I almost said yes right then and there. Instead, I stared into his beautiful eyes and stopped breathing, and he closed that final, infinitesimal gap. His lips were on mine, his fingers were in my hair, and I thought that he was right, and wonderful, and everything a person like me could hope for. And for a moment, I believed him. Together, we could tip the great scales of Belavere Trench.

Midnight struck.

I turned sixteen.

CHAPTER 13

NINA

The same Scribble appeared simultaneously at all households in Belavere City:

Attacks on Belavere City imminent.
Depart to open country immediately.
By order of the Miners Union.

It had caused the exact stir the House of Lords had, up until that point, so successfully prevented.

But the House denied any need for action. It had been eight days since the warnings had appeared in every Scribbler's cranny, and now the city thrummed on, seemingly unfazed. Just a scare tactic of the Miners Union, people believed. What lowlife thugs. An infection to be cut out.

I held *The Trench Tribune* in my hands, a skillfully sketched caricature glaring up at me amid the print.

It had the face of a man with a wide nose, mottled in sores and moles. His eyes were beady, belly protruding at the belt. His lips were parted and revealed missing teeth. The artist had even added droplets of spit spraying from the man's lips. There was not a single hair added to his head, just a worker's cap, patched and falling sideways. In his hand was the severed head of Lord Tanner, a lit stick of dynamite protruding from his mouth.

The modern-day Craftsman, said the caption.

A cruel depiction, but perhaps not so far from the truth. The sketch could have been my father, Scurry's mill foreman, the mine's timekeeper, the pub's landlord. That is to say, if the gut were not overflowing and the cheeks weren't so plump. The implication that a Craftsman be so grossly overfed made me scoff.

But my father's forehead had strained just like that when he was loaded. He'd threatened things worse than decapitation of the nation's leader. In Scurry, they all had.

The symptoms of craftsmanship were accurate enough, but what most Artisans ignored was the cause. Crafters were born to parents without means. Often, those parents died young. The children worked at an early age for little pay, subject to occupational hazards an Artisan would never face. They medicated themselves against the trauma, the injuries, the knowledge that the next day would bring them nothing better, and if they survived to the right age, they eventually raised their own hungry children. It was a cascading line of falling bricks that built the brink.

I scrunched the newspaper into a ball and threw it aside, though it did little to quell my trembling. The headlines still appeared before me when I blinked.

MINERS UNION TAKES STRIKE INTO SIXTH WEEK
TERRANIUM FAMINE FEARED
CLAIMS OF IDIUM CORRUPTION NOW RAMPANT
FAMED ALCHEMIST MIRANDA MILANY TAKEN BY INFLUENZA
THE LAST ALCHEMIST, DOMELIUS BECKER, MOVES INTO HIDING, SAYS SOURCES

But no mentions of any specific names or places. Just vague references to the Northeast or the brink towns, or miners in general.

I swallowed thickly. Clenched my hands.

In a few hours, I would graduate from the National Artisan School, and just as I had on the fated day of my siphoning ceremony, I felt a shiver of catastrophe travel up my spine. I was suddenly twelve years old again, awash in terror as Aunt Francis gripped my arm.

She would be in the audience today as I read my fellowship oath and received a scroll from a tower of identical scrolls that prescribed my status as a Charmer, my medium of earth, and my academic ranking of high order.

And then I would officially be an Artisan. Someone who existed outside these walls. Perhaps this was the source of all my terror.

I wondered, and not for the first time, whether I still would have slipped that vial from my pocket six years ago had I known then what I did now.

Had I known that the stories of corruption would leak down the rivers and canals into towns spilling over with Crafters; had I known the country was on the knife-edge of revolution. If I'd known then that my reserved part in a likely civil war was to be its artillery, perhaps I would have unstoppered my given Crafter's vial after all, for that little din that Lord Tanner once spoke of was now a roar, even if he pretended to be obtuse about it.

I tied the ceremony cape at my throat—it perfectly matched the blue of my skirt, my stockings, the fake idium in the bottom of my trunk. It billowed out just past my elbows and no lower, leaving the Artisan brand uncovered on my forearm—a stark, blister-red Idia with her fanning hair.

The accumulation of my life was packed inside the bulging case next to me. A meager sum of clothing, shoes, journals, sketches. It would be packed into a coach and taken to an undisclosed location. A location I would soon be transported to, just as soon as I'd received my fellowship assignment.

The safe house will only be for a short while, Lord Tanner had told me in Dumley's drawing room. *An earth Charmer is quite a valuable thing, Miss Clarke. One that many would covet. We wouldn't want these rebels getting their hands on you, now, would we? Best to err on the side of caution and wait for all the dust to settle.*

I wondered if Domelius Becker, the last surviving Alchemist in the trench, would be waiting in this "safe house" with me, both of us now the only one of our medium. How long would it take for the "dust to settle"? It seemed to me that dust was a growing storm.

The city was riddled with the effects of the strikes. The refectory meals had grown sparser as farmers left fields untended and didn't return. Deliveries weren't made. The coal supply was being rationed carefully. Even bluff was hard to come by, with only a single Alchemist left to siphon it.

It was rumored that the next siphoning ceremony would be postponed—that there wasn't enough idium left in reserve.

To me, it seemed even the exterior of the city was showing its first cracks before its inevitable fall, and yet the Lords went about their business as though its foundation weren't quaking.

Just a precaution. These dark times will come to an end soon enough, Professor Dumley had assured me just yesterday. *And with you assisting in the House of Lords—an earth Charmer!—why, the Miners Union might as well lay down their banners now.*

I thought of those Lords with their polished tabletops and fine china cups, and wondered if they truly needed my assistance.

I thought of those miners, so desperate to escape the life I had narrowly escaped.

I thought of this school, which I'd come to love, each corner of it intricately beautiful.

I thought of collapsing mines and children left to scour the streets for food.

I thought of a boy from Kenton Hill with blue eyes, and I wondered if he'd survived these past years or suffered the same fate as most men born in the brink.

I thought of disappearing. I dreamed of it almost every night, in fact.

I deliberated until the voices and faces and headlines pendulumed, and cracks spread on either side of my skull, and then I pushed a pin through my hat and left my room behind, biting the inside of my cheek until it bled.

· · · · · ·

The theater was full to bursting, and I was saddened by the idea of leaving it for good. The stucco-plastered ceiling was carefully embellished in cherubs, rose gardens, the gates of paradise. I'd heard the finest opera singers cast their voices into the ether here, seen ballerinas thrown through space and land on the tips of their toes. I'd heard compositions and poetry and the cries of a boy in a costume simulating grief.

In the velvet-walled staging hall, I listened to the rising voices of the audience beyond the curtain. The noise climbed over the rigs and lights and found us waiting apprentices, soon-to-be fellows. It raised gooseflesh on my skin.

Young men and women were separated for their graduation. It was tradition, they said, for the gentlemen to go first. I suspected the separation was more an afterthought. Women hadn't always been welcomed here.

"Nina?"

I jumped, heart clanging against my ribs.

Theo appeared at my side, his fingers already wrapping around mine. "Shh," he warned, eyes darting to a custodian checking names off a list. "Come with me."

Theo pulled me out of the line into the corridor, and like a fool, I followed him, swelling with hope.

We only went as far as the corner, where the L-bend of the hall became a series of doors for backstage preparations. He leaned his shoulder against the wall and kept his grip on my hand. My fingers tingled in his.

"I wanted the chance to . . . to wish you luck," he said, hurriedly. "And to say goodbye, I suppose."

Hope fled. Theo could see it leak out of me, I was sure. His eyes tracked the way my shoulders fell. I didn't have the fortitude to hide my disappointment.

I ached all over.

It had been weeks since he'd cornered me in a garden and told me that circumstances had changed. That he'd changed his mind. That he was so very sorry.

I didn't understand how he wasn't aching. It had been weeks, and I ached still.

"Well," I uttered. I did not recognize my voice. "Goodbye, then."

He sighed and looked away, and finally, finally, he showed some of the torment I felt. He squeezed my hand, his eyes pinched. "It's for the best, Clarke."

"Is it?"

He grinned sadly. "I'm afraid so."

"Is that what your father told you? Your mother?" I dared to ask. The words had crouched and readied themselves each time I'd passed Theo in the halls.

He frowned. "We're only eighteen," he said. "If . . . in two years' time we still feel the same way for each other—"

"What do you want, Theo?" I cut him short, for surely he wanted something other than to say good luck and goodbye.

His stare softened. "Clarke, I—I only wanted to check that you were well."

"I am."

"And that there were no hard feelings."

A cheerless laugh bubbled up from me. "There are no feelings at all. You made that clear."

He groaned and scrubbed his face with his hand. "You don't play fair, Clarke. I never said that. You're my best friend. I . . ." Whatever he wished to say seemed stuck in his throat. "You know what my father expects of me. What I've been working toward. I'll be leaving for Thornton next week and won't return for two years. I don't want to keep you waiting." This much was true. Lord Tanner himself had insisted that Theo spend time in the channels of the South with the nation's most renowned water

Charmers. A huge honor, though I suspected Lord Shop simply wished to remove his only child from the city while it was under threat and had struck a deal with someone.

Theo groaned quietly, then came closer. Somehow, he'd grown even more handsome in the past few weeks. Every girl in this hall would agree. "You know that I care for you, Nina." His hand came to my cheek, then slid into the snarls of my hair. "Whatever you may think of me," he whispered in my ear, "you must know that this isn't what I wanted."

I felt the slow unspooling of my restraint as he spoke, but I did not completely thaw. There were rumors that already he'd replaced me with someone else.

"If you want me to come for you when I return," he said softly, angling my face to his. "Then say it, and I will come."

And wasn't this exactly what I'd wished for?

He watched as my mind stumbled, and in the absence of an answer, his lips descended.

They pressed against mine, just as achingly sweet as I feared they'd be.

My hands found his chest, then the lapels of his jacket. His arms gathered around my waist and pulled me in.

"Nina!" The hiss came from behind me, and it sounded dreadfully like Aunt Francis.

I turned to find her looking down her nose in fury at Theo, who now stood with his hands clasped behind his back. "Hello, Ms. Leisel," he said, a casual grin affixed.

"Back to your *place*, Mr. Shop," she said sharply. She watched Theo as he left, his hand resting a second longer than necessary on my shoulder before he went.

Aunt Francis closed the distance between us, her severe expression exaggerated in the dim light. "That boy," she said tersely, her fingers rising to tease loose curls behind my ear, "has his claws in you."

I shook my head. "Not anymore."

"Good," she uttered dryly. "Boys are fond of treating hearts like toys. Particularly the boys of Lords. I've told you this."

The reminder was not so much to point out the importance of the title, but to point out the illegitimacy of my own. Fake parentage. Fake name. "I know."

"Right, then," Aunt Francis said, the words slipping past her teeth in a tumble. "That's that. The boy will be shipped to Thornton, and you'll be expected in the House of Lords as they . . . prepare."

This, after she'd blanketed me in reassurances that sounded like lies.

Those so-called renegades in the brink haven't a hope, she'd told me. *What could they accomplish against those of our ability? They would be fools to try.*

I grimaced. I knew those in the brink to be fools, and they had little to lose.

Aunt Francis saw my expression and sighed. "There is no turning back now, Nina. This is your side." She did not smile. "You are an exceptional talent—you've surprised even me. There is nothing to fear."

It was only then that I saw the sheen on her forehead, the ropes of tension peeking out beneath her lace collar.

Suddenly, projected all around us were the words of Professor Dumley, speaking of loyalty and serving one's countrymen.

"Come," she said, swallowing thickly. "They'll call on you any moment."

I nodded, though the dread returned, churning slowly from my center into an all-engulfing spiral. "Aunt Francis—"

"We've no time," she said, and she marched me around the corner.

The queue trickled closer to the curtain openings as the boys were called, then the girls. I grew sicker with every inch gained.

"Nina Clarke. Charmer; Earth. Fellowship of High Order." It boomed in my ears.

Light applause sounded, followed by a hushed curiosity. I took a seismic breath, pushed the curtains aside, and was transported into the light.

The stage was wide and oval-shaped, cascading onto pearly steps already filled with graduates. They waited with their heads turned to watch me. The spotlights glared down, golden and blinding. They warmed my skin and made the audience nothing but a dark abyss.

The clapping died as I moved across the stage, eyes pinched as I tried to see past the glare to the podium where Professor Dumley stood. He smiled kindly, his eyes glinting with a spark of pride. He proffered his hand as I came near and looked back out at the audience as though he were presenting an art piece. *Look*, he seemed to say. *Look what I have created.*

I shook his hot hand and took the scroll. I bowed my head as I was told to do, and felt sheer panic. The audience applauded once more, unaware that I was an epicenter.

And as though the feeling had leaked from my pores and burrowed into the varnished wood beneath me, the stage trembled.

At first, I thought I only imagined it. But the quaking persisted. Grew. The building was humming. A quick, muted crescendo into a monstrous roar. The audience stood and screamed. They barreled over one another down the aisles.

Then, the earth beneath us concussed.

Like houses of cards, we fell. The ground seemed to rise beneath them, swelling like the belly of a giant and then caving, the sound pitched to the point of pain. I screamed as I saw the graduates on the steps tumbling, and Theo looked back at me with his hands over his ears, his eyes bulging in terror. The curtains and lights and rigs splintered and dropped, one by one.

Attacks on Belavere City imminent.

The Miners Union had come.

The stage lamps popped and erupted.

Aunt Francis was before me, scrambling amid a sea of the flailing. Swarms of crabs scuttling over one another's backs.

"Nina!" she shouted, her face bloody.

She was sideways, or I was. She reached me on hands and knees and bid me to stand. Dust rained down in a cloud above her. "Hurry!" she said. "Hurry!"

An alarm was sounding, distant and sleepy. It whirred in one long drone, barely discernible above the screams.

I clambered over fallen rafters with Aunt Francis, tripped on blasted pieces of furbished timber. I fell across the body of a man with part of his head caved in.

Smoke was thick on the air. It joined the dust and made it impossible to see ahead. A Mason tried to persuade fallen bricks from an exit, but she was already out of breath and the stone moved slowly, sluggishly. Others joined her, lifting their hands before them and grunting until the stone gave. They tumbled away, clearing a path.

A flood of Artisans barreled through. The earth continued to quake. Boom after boom shook the walls, cracked the ceilings. Great plates of plaster detached and fell from above. The entrance hall was littered with it. Marble tiles lifted and danced in place. Walls buckled, the entire frame of the school growling its last before it gave in.

And I ran.

It never once occurred to me that I might try to stop the earth from breaking apart. There was only fear.

I was young.

I was not the weapon they thought me.

I gripped Aunt Francis's hand. I propelled myself headfirst down the entrance hall toward the open doors. A gentleman groaned against a wall, his calf bent at a sickening angle, his eyes wide with shock. I grabbed his elbow, but Aunt Francis wrenched my arm away and screamed in my ear.

I heard nothing above the titanic groan that rose and rose as the walls fell. I spilled down the front steps, Aunt Francis's hands at my back pushing me forward.

I felt it when her arms fell away, turned in time to see a splay of her limbs, a whip of her black hair as the rubble crashed atop her, and I screamed.

And then I was swallowed, too, buried in the marble and sandstone.

CHAPTER 14

NINA

Sound was muted there, beneath the debris of the Artisan school.

A five-hundred-year-old institute, now imprisoning its students beneath its weight, crushing air from our lungs.

There were burdens upon my arm and leg, too. Timber. Stone. Things I could not hope to shift. My head was bent awkwardly so that I looked sideways, up the steps to a building that once housed me but was now a crumpled burning ruin.

I was trapped. In a moment of desperation, I put my mind to the ground beneath me and bid it to concave, but the rubble only sank and took me with it.

I do not know how long I lay there, in a bowl of the earth, blanketed in wreckage, but it was time enough to believe I would die. To consider who exactly had killed me.

Rebels. Crafters. The Miners Union. All one amorphous entity.

What could they accomplish against those of our ability? When I'd first heard the words, they had sounded like derision. Now they sounded like a terrible realization.

What *could* they accomplish?

What damage could be rendered?

My ears were so clogged I did not hear the grating stone, but I felt the crushing weights on my limbs lift free, followed by a sudden onslaught of pain. I cried out.

"Nina!" A voice graveled, choked by dust. "Thank *God*. Thank God."

Theo—his arms winding behind my shoulders and knees. He pulled me against his chest and I screamed. I pulled my damaged arm into the cradle of my body.

I was surprised to look up and see that the sky still existed, still bogged in fat gray clouds. Cries not my own rent the air; they intensified when I pulled my ear away from Theo's shoulder.

"Are you hurt?"

All over, I thought. "My arm."

"You're bleeding."

I could feel that, too. The warm, slow drip from jaw to collarbone. Blood flowing from a cut on my cheek. I thought my arm might be broken.

I turned my face inward again and hoped Theo would carry me for longer. *Take me away*, I thought. *Take me anywhere*. I was sickeningly dizzy. I wanted to go home. Home to Scurry.

"Can you stand?" He didn't await an answer. Gingerly, my feet were guided to the ground, and the rest of me quickly followed, crumpling there on the warm cobbles.

"Whoa!" Theo said, his hands on my shoulder, my wrist. "Just sit. Catch your breath."

I blinked furiously until the vision before me solidified into one un-fractured picture. The Academy in pieces, its roof inverted, fire scampering among the heap and consuming morsels. Artisans everywhere. Bleeding. Crying. Working to unbury the buried. Injured Masons struggled to free people from all that stone.

"Aunt Francis—"

"You can't help her," Theo said brokenly, leaning in to fill my vision. "I'm sorry. I tried to get her out, but . . ." Here his words failed him. "She's gone."

I knew already. I had meant to say, *Aunt Francis is dead*. My lips shook. My chest heaved.

"We need to go somewhere safe. The Union might attack again," he said, panicked.

A cold, cruel dread swept through me.

"We'll go to the House of Lords," Theo gripped my chin, commanding me to focus with a pleading look. "My father will help us. Help *you*. Nina. *Nina?*"

But the House of Lords intended to hide me away, to keep me safely locked up until they needed a weapon. The very same Lords who had bid us to stay, to ignore the warnings.

I'd be a fool not to ensure I have all my knives sharpened.

"We need to hurry," Theo said, eyes darting around the dust. "Let's leave. Now."

To the House of Lords. To Lord Tanner. To be those knives they wanted us to be.

An earth Charmer is quite a valuable thing.

You would do what is necessary, would you not?

You've got a mind of your own. Don't let those fuckers take it.

"Come on," Theo said, pulling me to my feet. "I'll carry you."

"No. Wait."

"My father will know what to do—"

"I can't," I shook my head, and the world spun. "I won't."

A pause, and then: "What?"

"I can't go to the House," I said. "I . . ." People around us screamed and wept, and I thought, *This is what it is to bury people alive.* Then I thought, *This is what they'll ask of you. To bury the Union in return. Bury the Crafters. Bury the brink.*

I couldn't.

Lord. I couldn't.

"We should run."

Theo's mouth fell. I noticed a graze on his chin, a scrape on his neck.

"Run away with me," I said, this time more forcefully. I took the lapel of his jacket with my good hand and clutched it tightly. "We'll leave the city. We can go anywhere."

But Theo's face had taken on a look of panic, of confusion. "What are you talking about?"

"Please," I said. I was twelve. I was thirteen and fourteen and fifteen. I'd only wanted to paint and dance and see what else life could be. "Please. Come with me."

His hands dropped away. His confusion turned to alarm. "You're not thinking clearly," he said. "The Miners Union . . . if they find you, they'll kill you. The House of Lords will keep us safe."

But they hadn't.

"These fucking *Crafters* will get what's coming to them." He spat the words through gritted teeth. His jaw shook. He looked around at the chaos, and a choked sob sprang free. "We can help," he said with a nod, as though convincing himself. "We have to help, Nina. We can fight back. The House needs us." Theo grabbed both sides of my face. Pain splintered down my neck. "You're the most powerful Artisan I know, Nina Clarke. You can *bury* these fuckers."

And I saw clearly the world divided in two: him on one side and me lost in the middle.

"Aunt Francis," I said, the words springing from my lips half-formed, half-thought. "I need to see her. I need to know."

"They've already started clearing away the bodies—"

"*Please, Theo!*" I shouted, my voice cracking. "At least let me see her one last time. Then we'll—we'll go to the House," I said. "We'll find your father."

I watched his expression falter, then give way. "Wait here," he told me. Then he wiped the blood from my cheek with his cuff and disappeared into the rainstorm of dust.

I watched him go.

Then I mustered all that was left of me, and dragged myself off the ground.

And I vanished.

RIGHT HONORABLE MASTER OF THE NATIONAL ARTISAN HOUSE
Lord G. Tanner
To
HONORABLE HEADMASTER OF THE NATIONAL ARTISAN SCHOOL
Professor H. Dumley

Professor,

My most sincere condolences in the wake of the attack on our national academy. It was with great sorrow I felt the ground shake seven nights afore. My sorrow only grew when the scale of destruction and loss of life was relayed.

I write this letter in hopes of bringing you comfort. The House of Lords meets today, wherein we shall condemn the rebels who sought to bring down the womb of our great state. War will be declared.

This calls to question the location of the earth Charmer, whose faculties will be sorely needed in the days to come. With the dust settled, I had hoped she would have appeared before us by now. Make no mistake, Professor. If she should not avail herself to her state, the renegades will surely take advantage where we cannot. I do not need to explain the implications of such an event.

Our police search as I write this letter, and should they find an individual harboring Miss Clarke, such a party will be penalized most severely.

This uprising shall soon come to pass, and with the Artisan school rebuilt from the rubble with the greatest minds at your disposal, I know your ministry shall reign once more.

Yours faithfully,
Lord Geoffry Tanner

CHAPTER 15

NINA

THE TRENCH TRIBUNE

REBELS RUMORED TO HAVE CAPTURED THE LAST ALCHEMIST

Following an attempt to seize the National Artisan House last week, a group of Crafter rebels have been taken into custody, including a man rumored to be the leader of the Miners Union, sparking citizens to wonder if this could be the end of the conflict. The Right Honorable Lord himself reassured the press that the incident had been contained, and the terrorists apprehended. And yet, other whispers suggest that perhaps the rebels' ploy had not been entirely fruitless.

Despite the placation of Lord Tanner, sources close to the House report that the last living Alchemist, Domelius Becker, is now missing, and rumored to be in the possession of the union.

While the nation awaits good news from the House that the union leader has, indeed, been arrested, Belavere suffers resounding silence. It seems that still, five years into this enduring conflict, the House of Lords has no names and no pins on the map. The Miners Union remains as mysterious as it has always been, and the Lords' Army fight a masked adversary.

This reporter can only assume the silence purports an adversary still very much at large. And if the rumors of the missing Alchemist are true, then surely the House of Lords ought to proclaim this day the darkest in

Belavere history.

I discarded the newspaper with the others. This issue was two years old, and the street was littered with copies of it. The print factory I walked by had timber nailed over its windows. I imagined this had been *The Trench Tribune's* last before the factory was choked off by strikes, and still the headline lingered, crawling up my spine.

I shivered. I thought of those shadows the Lords' Army was fighting, scratching for a center they couldn't find. In my opinion, it was not so difficult to remain elusive in a country split apart. After all, I'd managed it for seven years.

It was easy to take up a different name while so many died and left theirs behind. Simple enough to burn away the brand on my arm until it was just an old wound. There were a thousand different towns to lose yourself in, to move on to when the fighting started, and it always did.

Hiding, I'd learned, was simple. Gunfire made for good distraction. Running on foot was far from out of place. Stealing was expected. Desperation was normal. Women were often alone. On the outside, I certainly didn't look like the world's only earth Charmer. I looked like the thousands of other women fleeing a conflict in which we were collateral.

At first, I'd run to Aunt Francis's home. My toes were bloody before I'd arrived. I'd waited there for a short while, hoping Aunt Francis would walk through the door and tell me what to do, pluck a new identity from the air as she had when I was a girl then send me to bed.

Before anyone could come to look for me, I'd slipped my broken arm into one of Aunt Francis's cloaks, slipped out the back door, and fled.

I wouldn't belong to the House, couldn't belong to the Union. Nothing to do but hide in the middle.

I'd tried for Sommerland first, boarding a train that was derailed by dynamite halfway along. The second explosion in the span of two days. I believed then that the world was on fire.

I soon discovered that there were worse things than bombs and guns.

Sommerland was filled with police. So were Baymouth and Trent and Lavnonshire. Infantries of Craftsmen sworn to obey the command of the National Artisan House, with steep rewards for loyalty and even steeper punishments if they fled. They turned their eyes on me when I walked by, scanning my features and wondering if I was her: the missing Nina Clarke. I imagined whoever found me alive would be showered in riches and promotion.

It did not take long for sketches to appear on shopwindows: WANTED, they said, BY ORDER OF THE NATIONAL ARTISAN HOUSE. The likeness was, unfortunately, precise. I wondered which Scribbler had drawn it. Perhaps one of my own classmates.

I wasn't the only face plastered on windows across the country. There were other Artisans who had abandoned their posts when the revolution began, refusing to side with either party, or else sympathizing with the Crafters in their war against the capital. *Deserters*, the National House declared them. *Terrorists*.

The lampposts and bulletin boards became so saturated in wanted posters that people walked right by and paid them little mind. My face was lost in the slew.

I worked as a Crafter when I could. I sewed uniforms in a Dorser factory for the Artisan command, sorted parcels in Dunnitch before the factory walkout, painted china in a small shop in Hesson. When waves of Artisan infantrymen rolled in off their trains, I disappeared. By the time a finger pointed in my direction, I was already gone. I became proficient in watching, in listening, in spotting a glint of recognition in one's eye. I did not stay long enough for whispers to catch me.

And yet, catch me they did.

It must have been near my birthday. This was what distracted me as I walked down a dark street in Gilmore, a large industrial wasteland of a town just outside Belavere City, now mostly abandoned.

I grimaced at the muck wetting my shoes with each step and imagined charming it away. But it had been years since my last dose of idium. Years since I'd melted away the brand needed to enter a dispensary. And now I couldn't charm a speck of it. Before I graduated, I'd been proficient, even talented. I'd easily dammed rivers, dug trenches a mile long within moments. Now I shook mud off the bottom of my shoes.

I pulled my coat around me. I did not know the precise date, but I thought it must be September. The air was growing colder. In the days to come or perhaps in the days already past, I would be twenty-five.

I felt both older and younger.

Too young to have seen so many terrible and grand things—tree branches artfully bent to shelter a courtyard; a horseless carriage trundling down the lane; a cannery on fire with its workers trapped inside; a flying sparrow made of glass; a man with a grenade, its pin pulled; a woman dragging her screaming children onto a boat; centuries-old architecture; a thousand soulless, sunken faces, queueing to board a train.

But I felt old, too. Much older than I ought to. I was tired. So tired that I stopped in the middle of the street beneath a flickering lamp and I found myself praying to God that I would not meet the age of twenty-six.

And then, as though my prayer were answered, the night disappeared.

Something was thrust over my head. Arms constricted around my stomach. My feet left the ground, and instinctually, I kicked and thrashed.

A sharp crack, and then sickening, liquid pain seeped through my head. I thought it a kind mercy for one such as me, too much of a coward to do anything but hide and pray.

Seven years I'd eluded them all. Now one side or the other had me.

· · · · · ·

I awoke to labored panting, cussing, a pitching sensation. The man whose back I was draped over held my wrists at a painful angle. I feared the bones of my arm were snapping by minute degrees.

"God almighty, she's heavy!"

"She's half your size, Scottie."

"Aye, but she's wringin' wet and dead asleep."

The pain must have escaped through my teeth then, because the rocking stopped. The men fell silent.

The shuffle of feet, and then the sack that covered my face lifted slightly. The glow of a lantern blinded me.

"Mornin', swank," said the unknown voice. I couldn't see his face beyond the light. He lowered the burlap over my eyes again.

I was dropped unceremoniously, and my arse hit water.

"Me fuckin' back is screamin'," groaned the one called Scottie.

"Yet all I can hear is your whinin'."

The pair bickered, but I heard very little. Pins lanced every inch of my skin where the water breached my trousers and blouse. Pain surged so intensely behind my eyes it made them bulge. My wrists ached beneath their bindings.

Rope, it seemed. The scratch was familiar, so was the smell of damp earth. The air was thick with it. Somewhere nearby, a canary sang.

While the men argued, I lifted my bound hands and rid my face of the blindfold.

Weak lantern light. Rotting wooden frames. The intermittent drip of water through the ceiling. The ceiling was so low.

Tunnels, I thought, and a wave of nausea followed.

"It's a quarter till, Scottie. He told us to be back by noon!"

"All I'm sayin' is, we catch our breath a moment 'fore we keep movin'. Maybe have ourselves a li'l pickup?"

The sound of liquid swilling in a glass bottle found me.

"You take a single hit, and I'll sing like a fuckin' bird."

"All right, Otto. All right. Stand down."

More splintering pain as I sat upright, and I whimpered.

"Oy! Put that sack back over her head!"

Mud spattered my face as one of them stomped over, but I'd already caught a glimpse of them both. One burly, one wiry, both too covered in grime to make much of their features other than the stark white of their eyes. Ghosts. Craftsmen. The miners of my childhood.

The one named Scottie bent to peer at me. "All right there, swank?"

I spat at his boots in answer, and he swiftly took my sight away once more.

"Not too ladylike, is she? Ain't she high-ranking?" said Otto.

"Come on, princess," Scottie grunted, hauling me upright by the front of my blouse. I felt two of the buttons rip free. My arm scraped against something solid: a wall. "Walk on, now. Mind your step."

But I refused to yield. I shivered violently.

"Move, swank," Otto intoned. "You ain't got much choice." With that came the click of a pistol's hammer and the press of cool steel on the back of my neck. "No tunnel can kill the likes of *you*, can it?"

If only.

"Fancy an earth Charmer, scared of bein' underground," muttered Scottie. "Maybe . . . maybe we got the wrong one?"

"Nah. I tailed her a good long while. She's the spittin' image of them posters. Look, she's burned away her brand, see?"

"I dunno, Otto. Might be all for nothin' if she can't—"

"Shut up, Scottie."

We walked interminably with our heads bowed and our backs hunched. With each passing second, I grew colder. The ceiling dripped constantly, sending rivulets past my collar. The tunnel floor lay beneath an inch of water, and the walls cracked and groaned every so often, a monster awakening as we slunk through its veins.

Scottie and Otto spoke as though they weren't enclosed on all sides by the earth's mantle.

I breathed in shallow bursts. I counted. I felt my heart squeeze and release in painful thrums as fear spiked and ebbed. I was plagued with images of who I'd be met with on the other side of this tunnel and what they might do. I reasoned these Craftsmen would not go to all this effort only to torture and kill me. Better the Miners Union than the Artisan government. *Just do as they say*, I told myself.

I ignored the way the earth crept into my nostrils, past my lips, into my eyes.

"I just don't like the way she was lookin' at him," Otto was saying. He had a Northern drawl, a boyish levity.

"Well, you ain't a proper pair yet, are you? The girl can look as much as she pleases, at whomever she pleases."

"She *kissed me*, though. Why's she lookin' at bloody *Hank Shawley* if she's kissin' me?"

"Perhaps she got tired of waitin' on you to grow some hair on your bullocks and knock on her door?"

"I'm tryin' to time it right."

"She bloody kissed you, Otto. A month ago. A bigger window I can't foresee."

"I've got a plan in mind."

"Yeah? That plan involve Hank between your lady's legs?"

"Shut up."

"Take it from me, kid. You don't want to settle down just yet. The day I married was me last day o' peace."

"Ha, you're startin' to sound like the boss."

My ears pricked.

"You could stand to be a little more like him."

"Yeah? Alone and angry?"

Images of my father swirled to mind, a bloated face and bloodied eyes.

"Nah," Scottie grunted. "Boss ain't lonely, he just don't want a woman. No longer than a night's worth, anyway."

Otto chortled. "Can't blame a fella. He's got plenty who're willin'."

"Like I said, you could stand to be a little more like him."

Finally, mercifully, the ground seemed to slope upward. The floor became slowly emptied of water. I slipped often, and Scottie's hands pulled me upright each time.

"Easy, princess."

I pulled my arm from his grasp. "Get off me."

"Ah! She speaks! You hear that, Otto?"

"Good. She'll be doing a whole lot of talkin' in a few minutes."

A few minutes. Just a few minutes between me and my captor.

A hand suddenly pushed down on my head. "Duck, princess. We're goin' up."

My scalp glanced against a timber frame as I lowered it, and I collided with Otto.

I heard the machinations then. The sound of iron squealing together, of metal chains clinking along their tracks. The floor beneath my boots shuddered, and I pitched forward as we moved. Upward, upward.

The groan of timber and the strain of metal wheels rebounded around us, but after a short time, they disappeared altogether.

Silence fell, and a hand prodded me from behind. "Out you get," Otto said.

My boots met uneven ground once more. It felt drier here, compacted. The light was muted but certainly brighter. I could see the fine fiber of the burlap.

And then a voice called to us from ahead.

I jumped at its sound, shrank against the reverberations.

"Mornin', boys," it said. "You're late."

It was heavily accented. Northern, like the other men's, and not at all familiar. It was like smoke. Smooth and deep and gut-churning.

"Yeah, well, Scottie knocked her out for a good long while, and we carried her most of the way here," Otto blithered. I heard Scottie grumble at the accusation.

"How were I to know she'd drop like that?"

"She's *Artisan*, you idiot. They *all* drop like that."

The other voice interrupted them then, and Otto and Scottie fell quiet. "Take off her blindfold. Untie her hands."

Perhaps its tenor had the same effect on them as it did me, because Scottie cleared his throat, swallowing whatever rebuttal he'd readied, and I felt the rope fall free of my wrists. The burlap pulled back over my face.

I took one long, sweet breath. Still cloying. Still earth-rich and damp, but it filled my lungs.

I blinked rapidly, trying to dispel the sudden light that poured through an aperture at the end of the passage. I looked over to my captors in the light and found that Otto was short, dark-skinned, and wiry. He had close-cropped black hair and a miner's uniform. Scottie was distractingly huge, pale, with no hair and a bulging neck.

We were still underground, still enclosed by walls made of dirt. But the passage was short. There were rough timber steps leading to our escape, and on the bottom rungs sat a large man in black boots, a black expression, and a worn brown coat.

He was younger than I'd figured, certainly more handsome. He had defined cheekbones and jaw, wavy chestnut hair, the chain of a pocket watch against his chest. From the inside of his coat, he pulled a tin lighter and lit a cigarette between his lips.

"Hello, Miss Clarke," he said in that same drawl, as though every word dragged from his lips was one too many. He studied me openly, his eyes gliding over my feet, legs, waist, chest, neck, and then, finally, his eyes found mine.

Prismatic blue.

A shock bolted through me.

"I've been lookin' for you," he said.

Then there was nothing but a weighted silence.

I stared at him, and he at me.

Eventually, Otto interjected. "She's definitely the one, boss. We tailed her for a good long while, didn't we, Scottie?"

"Are you the earth Charmer?" the man asked me. Though it seemed he knew.

I could only hesitate, lips agape, and after a moment he smirked.

I shifted my eyes away and cleared my throat, cheeks flaming.

There was little to be gained from lying. In any case, I did not seem to have a mind to do anything but nod. I was fitting pieces together, locking keys into nooks.

"Nina Clarke," he said. Another pull on the cigarette, his stare held, and it was inescapable. I feared I would become entranced by it. "Do you know who I am?"

I did. Only it was not a title that came to mind, but a twelve-year-old boy with dirty hair and a double-looped belt. *Don't be*, I thought. *Please be anyone else.*

"I'm Patrick Colson," he said, and the memories collapsed and unfolded before me, recreating a man better dressed and fully grown. A man I both knew and didn't.

He stood. Watched me carefully. "Welcome to Kenton Hill."

I looked around as though the walls might fall away to reveal the town, but there was only him.

He was tall. Tall enough that his hair scraped the dirt ceiling. His eyebrows were thicker, darker, his chin more pronounced. Dark lashes framed those eyes, and I was as startled by them as I had been in a courtyard thirteen years ago. I'd realized him handsome as a boy, but as a man, he was shocking.

There were things missing now, however. A sense of ease, that glint of mischief. In their place was an expression that remained unsettlingly dark.

It wasn't clear if the recognition was reciprocated. He only stared. Was he lingering over the parts of my face he remembered, the way I was?

My heart stuttered.

"She don't say much," Scottie offered, wiping his forehead on his sleeve.

"Hmm," Patrick mused darkly. "Perhaps you knocked the sense from her." At that, his eyes turned on Scottie, cold and reproachful. "I told you to use a light hand."

Scottie, far burlier than any man I'd seen, looked chided. "Aye," he said. "Nerves got the better of me. Apologies, miss." He slapped me gently on the back.

I raised my eyebrows at him.

"I should offer my apologies, too," Patrick said, and I found myself disarmed once more when his gaze fell over me. "I ordered these men to bring you to me. The cautionary measures," he gestured to the sack, the rope in Scottie's hands, "were needed. At least until we get to know one another."

I almost laughed. I stood with my shirt plastered to my skin and un-buttoned to near indecency. My legs shook in an effort to keep me stand-ing. I was covered in mud. There was a lump swelling at the back of my head, and these men were offering their regrets now?

My teeth gritted with the cold. "I know enough." Exhaustion made me brave. Careless. If Patrick Colson didn't recognize me, then it would be more prudent to leave it that way.

He nodded, discarded his cigarette. "And what do you know?" His voice seemed to swarm in my chest. "That we're animals and criminals who go around blowin' everything to holy hell, I'd bet."

That was the most common rhetoric on the Miners Union, though it wasn't mine. To me, all of them were animals. Artisans and Crafters alike.

I lifted my chin. "I know the skinny one hasn't any hair on his balls." I said it with perfect Belavere inflection. "I know the round one doesn't love his wife. I know that *you* are lonely and angry, or so say your men here." I waited a beat, enough time for the beginnings of a grin to slip briefly onto Patrick Colson's lips. "I know that you're not stupid enough to capture a Charmer without realizing the hazard you've brought to your town. So why don't you tell me what it is you want, Mr. Colson, and what you'll give me in return as payment for not burying us alive?"

Silence. Just that small smile on Patrick Colson's lips.

Scottie and Otto shifted about uncomfortably, as though considering for the first time that I might be a threat to them. "Ah, she's all bluster, Patty," Scottie said warily. "This one's scared of the tunnels, ain't you, miss? Barely kept herself together—"

"Do you know what all the little Artisan boys and girls are taught to do in that school, Scottie?" Patrick asked casually.

The man hesitated. "They—"

"They're taught to paint and write poems and sing very prettily," Patrick was pulling a new cigarette between his lips. "And they're taught how to put on a character, to act." The sound of struck flint, a burst of orange. His face was illuminated, then doused in shadow again. He played with the lighter haphazardly but stared at me. "She ain't afraid of the tunnels, lads."

Scottie was momentarily struck dumb, or at least dumber. His gaze swiveled toward me with fresh appraisal. "But she were whimperin'," he said weakly.

"She were *actin'*," Patrick corrected. He eyed me blankly. "In the hopes you'd think she weren't the earth Charmer."

Patrick watched me, waiting for me to deny it, perhaps, but I shrugged indifferently. He wasn't exactly correct, it was true I'd hoped to fool them, but it hadn't been difficult to fake fear so far beneath the surface. If those tunnels had collapsed, I wouldn't have been able to charm a damn thing, though I had no intention of telling Patrick that.

"She hasn't got any idium on board, lads," Patrick said then, seemingly amused as he watched me. "Hasn't had a hit in a while, I'd bet."

So he was an arrogant prick, then. "Idium is in terribly short supply, Mr. Colson. Rumor has it the Union has the last Alchemist chained to a wall somewhere."

Scottie spat on the ground in faux outrage, and Otto gave the canary cage an incensed shake. "Those ruddy bastards," he said theatrically.

"Fuckin' thieves, the lot of them."

Patrick's slight smile didn't break. "I've never much cared for rumors."

I sighed. "And am I to believe that you lot are the Miners Union welcoming party?"

Patrick blew out an achingly slow cloud of smoke, and in the silence, I squirmed. He had a way of stealing the air, leaving you vulnerable. "I've been searchin' for you, Miss Clarke," he drawled. "Me and everyone else, it seems."

I squared my shoulders, though my knees shook. "Well, here I am."

"There you are." I thought there was a speck of wonderment in his voice. "And right lucky it is that I'd be the one to find you. I imagine you've earned yourself quite the prison sentence by now. They're jailing rebels and deserters alike these days."

"Is that your deal then?" I asked, eyes narrowing. "Do as you say, or you'll throw me to the House of Lords?"

He pretended that I hadn't spoken. "I've come to the assumption you've only remained neutral all this time because there's some morsel of sympathy you can't rid yourself of. For Crafters, I mean. For the Miners Union."

"For terrorists?" I asked. "No, sir. My sympathy is reserved for civilians—the ones who never asked to be a part of *your* war."

"Hmm," he graveled, the sound cinching my stomach. "Then we'll need to change your mind. Redeem ourselves."

I wanted to laugh at him. How could all that blood possibly be redeemed? "What do you want from me?"

He waited a beat. Considered his words carefully. "Partnership."

"And if I refuse?"

"There's a train leaving Kenton Hill in a half hour," he said easily. "I'll take you there myself."

"And tie me to the tracks, most likely."

The men chortled. Patrick's eyebrows rose. "Do you think us gangsters, miss?"

I did. It was written in the way he stood, in the pistol strapped to his side beneath his coat. "I think you're murderers," I said coldly.

He nodded sagely, stubbed out his cigarette. "Not all of us can be daughters of aristocrats, I suppose." Then his eyes bore into mine again, and there was that missing glint, that shiver of trouble. We were twelve once more, daring each other to steal cakes.

He doesn't know who you are, I thought, trying to ease my thrumming pulse.

"If you don't want me for a partner, then I'll let you be on your way, miss. You can go back to sleepin' in the slums and tellin' your lies and scrapin' for a meal, awaitin' the day Tanner catches up with you."

I didn't bother to argue. It wasn't so far from the mark.

"Or, you could agree, and in a few short months, when our business is done, I'll ensure your safe passage off this continent."

I stilled. My heart galloped.

"Ah, you see?" His eyes trailed over me, raised gooseflesh over my skin. "There's something you want. A one-way ticket on a big old steamer headed anywhere but here. To the islands, maybe, where there's no idium to fight over, and no one's ever heard of the renowned Nina Clarke."

I narrowed my eyes. "How long have your men followed me?"

Otto chuckled. "Long enough to know that you prefer the seaside towns, the ports and harbors. I watched you try and bribe your way onto one of them cargo ships."

I shivered at the thought of this man tailing me for that long, just out of sight.

"But they're all jammed up and anchored," Otto rambled. "Tanner won't let anyone in or out, will he? I figure there ain't much a woman on the run wouldn't do for escape."

"A tale as old as Idia," I said darkly. "Men have always believed the way to win a war is to hold a woman hostage."

Patrick shook his head. "Then you misunderstand me. You're no hostage. Partner with me, and I'll get you on a ship out of Hoaklin by the end of spring."

My entire being coiled at the thought of that ship headed away, headed anywhere. But it was impossible. As Otto said, I'd tried every port, every fisherman, every vessel manned by a Crafter.

But no one could leave, and certainly not someone who looked strikingly like a wanted bulletin.

The canary screeched. I shivered. Somewhere above us all, a distant bell rang.

Seven years I'd avoided this. Avoided these impossible choices in a fight that would likely never end.

I didn't believe Patrick Colson. No one had a way out of the Trench.

And as for running, if I were to leave Kenton Hill now, I'd find myself in shackles soon after, I was sure. "What is it that you want me to do?" Not an acceptance, but not a denial, either.

"Talk," Patrick said. "I need information. Things you might know about the House."

"And?"

"And, I need your tunnelin' expertise."

"A miner asking an Artisan to build a tunnel?" I muttered, shaking my head. "Where will the tunnels lead?"

"That depends," Patrick answered, voice snaking into my insides once more, "on how much you talk. Do we have a deal?"

He waited. Otto and Scottie were silent. Even the canary paused its tirade.

I wavered. "I need to know that you'll fulfill your end of the bargain. There are no ships in or out of Belavere Trench. How will you get me out?"

"There is one ship that continues its passage. It won't be stopped at port."

"How do you know?"

"Because it won't make port at all," Patrick said. "The ship will hold some supplies I've purchased from far-off lands. It will anchor briefly for one hour in late June, east of Hoaklin. You'll be ferried to it."

I chewed on my tongue, shifted my feet. Hoaklin was a fishing village. Its boats still trundled over lazy waves a short way south. If it were true, if he could get me out, then it would all be over. No more war. No more running.

I'd been running for too long. "I won't kill anyone."

"I won't ask you to," he stated. There was no humor in his voice now.

"And I won't blow anything up." I thought of Aunt Francis.

He nodded. "Just tunnels. You have my word."

I sighed deeply, reigned in a shiver that went bone deep, and glared at Patrick Colson. "Then find me somewhere to sleep and something to wear," I said, wrapping my arms around my torso. "Maybe something to drink."

I thought I saw his shoulders sag some. "After you." He gestured to the ladder behind him.

I felt his gaze on me as I climbed, rung after rung, and it made me clumsy. My foot slipped on the iron, and my pulse sprinted as his hand enveloped my ankle.

He doesn't know who you are.

I clambered out into warmth and light, and Patrick followed.

"Welcome to Kenton Hill," he said again as he rose to his feet. Together we stood on a knoll where the setting sun above burned the clouds and made titanic shadows over rolling hills, chestnut trees, and the silhouette of a town in the distance. "Hope your swank legs have strength enough for a short stroll."

I tore my eyes from the town in the distance, looking back over my shoulder. Otto and Scottie did not emerge.

"They'll be along," Patrick answered before I could ask. He put his hands in his pockets and walked on. "Come."

"And what if I were to attack you while it's just the two of us? Don't men like you need lackeys?"

He chuckled dully. Lit another cigarette. Released the smoke into the sky.

"You wouldn't hurt me, Nina Harrow," he said. "We know too much about each other. Don't we?"

CHAPTER 16

PATRICK

Nina's eyes flared, likely ignited by the instinct to run.

She still had that coiled look, her body tensed to spring. Years on the run had left marks everywhere on her. "You don't look so different," Patrick lied. "Wetter, perhaps. Should've cut your hair. Ain't it the thing to do in hidin'?"

The flares went out. Her expression flattened, exactly as it had when she was twelve and she'd thought him an imbecile.

Her eyes flitted to the west.

"You won't have much luck out that way," he told her. "These hills aren't safe. Trigger mines everywhere. You ever seen a mine blow a person apart?" He hollowed his cheeks to mimic detonation. "Not a pleasin' sight."

The shattered stare Nina gave him indicated she'd seen quite a few mines. Only war gave a person that look. "You buried mines around your own town?" She sounded disgusted.

"It's wartime, darlin'. Never know what's comin' round those bends." Patrick pointed to the place where the train tracks bent into the hills and disappeared. From this height, at this distance, all of Kenton Hill was just visible, fading into the encumbering night.

Small. Unassuming. Weak. That was likely how the town looked to her, how it looked to anyone from the outside.

Patrick turned to Nina once more. "Shall we?"

"When did you figure out I was the earth Charmer?" She didn't move an inch, didn't avoid his stare the way others did. Her glare burrowed deep and clung on, and Patrick was glad. It gave him permission to stare back.

So he stared for as long as he liked.

A smatter of remaining freckles. No yellow left in her ringlets. Her hair was limp and wet but still tightly curled, the color of spun gold. Her hands were clenched, her legs now long and distractingly feminine. All of her now shaped and carved into the valleys of a woman.

But some things she'd brought with her; the same discerning eyes, hazel-flecked and heavily shadowed in lashes. Her lips were fuller, but pressed into a familiar line when she scowled. She still spoke like bullets were loaded on her tongue, even if she'd learned to speak like a proper swank.

Patrick decided to tell her the truth. "I knew the day of our siphoning."

And it was true. The second word got out that an earth Charmer had been siphoned, he'd been sure it was her. "No one spoke of anythin' else on the train home—a Crafter girl turned into an Artisan?" He whistled. "As you and I both know, that almost never happens. And an earth Charmer, no less."

She exhaled and looked back to the township below. "And what did people say when you told them?" she asked. "I bet you sung like a canary, didn't you?"

There seemed little point in arguing. If she wanted to think of him in such a way, Patrick would let her. He buried his hands in his pockets. "Not many people take the word of a twelve-year-old seriously," he said.

Nina scoffed, eyes wide. "You know, for the first few days in that school, I couldn't eat. Couldn't sleep. I was terrified someone would figure me out, someone would talk. But I never worried it would be you."

Lord, those hazel eyes sank deep into a man's skin.

"I had complete faith in you." Her arms loosened a little, her shoulders fell. "Naïve of me, wasn't it?"

It wasn't, but Patrick nodded anyway. "It was clever, changin' your name."

"It wasn't my doing," she said bluntly, though Patrick had figured this much on his own. It wasn't a ruse a twelve-year-old alone could uphold.

There were endless things Patrick and Nina hadn't considered in that courtyard, many of which he had since come to know. He didn't question her further. He was all too aware of the tightening springs in her legs, the grit on her cheeks.

"You look a fuckin' sight," he said casually, then began down the hill without her, if only to drag his eyes away. "Come on. I got a place for you to wash yourself. There's even a bed."

"No dungeon?"

"Havin' them remodeled," he answered, grinning at the sound of her feet following. "The chains are all rusted up."

The grass whispered around her footfalls as she walked, her breaths shortened. "What of the land mines?"

"No need to worry." Patrick turned to walk backward. He tapped his temple twice. "Got them all memorized. Just walk where I walk and stay close."

Her cheeks turned sallow and she quickened her pace.

Day waned, and weak sunlight turned the grass stalks flaxen. Patrick led a complex and winding path through the deadly maze, unmarked by anything discernible. They passed a sole apple tree, rounded a broken wagon. He heard her breaths hitch with the decline of the slope, and for a moment he thought he felt her exhales hit the back of his neck. A lump rose in his throat.

"You've changed much more than I imagined," she said without warning, the dirt paths just ahead.

Patrick thought it the most understated thing he'd ever heard. "That I have."

"I read the papers," she said. "Every week. When the rumors about the idium popped up, I wondered if you'd started them."

Patrick scoffed quietly, darkly, though when he looked at Nina, her face was stricken. "Me?" he questioned. "No, Nina. *We* started them. You and me, the day we broke into that fuckin' cellar."

She blanched. "Those rumors started the first ripples of war."

"That they did."

"Yet I'm supposed to trust that you'll see me safely out of the Trench?"

"You should trust no one, Nina" was his answer. "Not a single soul."

In the distance, from the muddied alley of two brick town houses, came a swift-moving silhouette. It bounded, barking madly, over a low-bearing fence and out in the fields toward us. For a moment, it became sidetracked by a scent to the west. Only when Patrick whistled once, short and sharp, did the creature turn and resume its course.

Nina watched the dog leaping happily over grass stalks in every direction. She scowled as it circled Patrick's feet manically.

"Hello, Isaiah," Patrick said. The animal panted up at him a moment, then bounded away, running freely over the open land.

"There aren't any land mines," Nina said. "Are there?"

"There are." Patrick grinned. "Nowhere nearby, though. That wouldn't be safe, now, would it?" He found a stick in the grass and threw it toward Isaiah. "No dungeons, either."

She made a noise of exasperation or sheer annoyance. It was difficult to tell. "Trust no one," she muttered.

Lord, he'd hoped she hadn't grown to be beautiful.

"We're not villains, Nina," Patrick said. "Just simple Crafters."

"Simple Crafters who blow up schools," she spat.

He sighed bitterly. "In our defense," he said, "we told you we were comin'."

CHAPTER 17

NINA

The dog led the way into town, his brown tail swinging side to side and nose to the ground. He turned every so often to spy Patrick, who paid him no mind. Patrick only watched the ground as he walked, kicking stones away from his boots, hands in pockets. He did not slow his pace for me.

For days after the bombing of the Artisan School, I'd been shell-shocked, my skeleton rattling inside me long after the fact. On occasion, my head still swam, my vision blurred unexpectedly.

I felt that way now, like I'd been thrown in opposite directions.

I wanted to hurl something vitriolic at him. Accuse him of killing my friends, my aunt. But in truth, there'd never been many friends, and my aunt wasn't truly my aunt. So instead, I said, "You murdered children in that school, you know."

He didn't turn. "Did we? Or did our Right Honorable Lord ignore the dozens of messages we sent in warnin', directin' him to evacuate the city?"

"But he didn't," I said. "And you blew it up anyway."

He spun on his heel. He didn't seem as self-important as before, only intimidating. "All right, then we're villains," he said darkly, eyes piercing. "And we burned down your castle, if that's what you need to believe. But if we're villains, then Lord Tanner is the fuckin' devil."

I ignored the tremble in my core. I looked him up and down. "Patrick

Colson," I said in a voice I hoped was derisive. "Leader of the Miners Union."

The House of Lords should have accounted for an angry boy who might one day stumble onto a crate of fake idium, might board a train back to the brink and divulge.

Might one day lead an army of revolutionaries.

Patrick clicked his tongue. "Son of the chairman."

I peered at him, saw again that boyish glint beneath the veneer of a man. "Your father?"

His jaw ticked. "My father is—"

"Detained." The pieces fell together. I saw the light in his eyes deaden and continued anyway. "In a clink somewhere in the city, I'd imagine." The papers had been vague in their headlines. They never published a single name. Not the leader's, not the town whence he'd come. Perhaps the writers didn't know.

Two years since his father's arrest was made.

"John Colson," Patrick said. I felt that overwhelming heaviness return. His voice was shadows. "When he returns, he'll resume his seat, and my brothers and I will do as sons do."

I scoffed. "What their fathers tell them?"

"What their fathers *taught* 'em," he corrected. "If they were fortunate enough to be taught."

We entered what I assumed was the main street, and I halted. Whatever quip I'd prepared abruptly fled.

From afar, Kenton Hill had seemed not so far removed from Scurry. Hillier, smaller, but the same—lines of chimneys that coughed smoke and the rhythmic clinking of the mills; blackened roof tiles atop clay-brick town houses. Row after row, curving to its middle like a snail shell. A mining parish. A town in the brink, identical to the next.

And unrecognizable in its middle.

I turned in every direction, scanning the street from road to rooftop, from doorway to doorway as far as I could see, my mouth agape.

I'd drawn a picture as a child in a Scurry schoolroom—something of fantasy that didn't exist outside my mind and I'd known so even then, at the age of six. A crooked street with building facades decorated in an assortment of instruments. Bells and horns and birdcages hanging from shingles. Perhaps it hadn't been my imagination at all. Perhaps I'd glimpsed the future and seen Kenton Hill.

It was a normal main street of brick facades, except that it was not normal at all. It was decorated and embellished. Mismatched and absurd. The walls were crawling in bizarre networks of pipes. The copper glinting beneath . . . lanterns? A thousand of them, hanging from lines that spanned the eaves along the street, as though someone had reached into the sky and pulled the galaxy closer. Meanwhile, the light posts had no lanterns. They were topped in large steel bowls. I couldn't fathom their purpose. Nor the purpose of the large basins that teetered on the edges of shingles, the grates lining either side of the street, the steel tracks that ran straight down its center. Surely they weren't for a train? The question was answered when a shrill whistle sounded and a machine the likes of which I'd never seen trundled up the lane.

It was a mutation of several recognizable things. A steam train smokebox without its stack, six wheels that resembled that of a coach and a black carriage to match. But the inside was elongated, hollow. It held only standing passengers, and all ten of them grasped belts that hung from the ceiling and leaned out the sides. The locomotive moved along the steel tracks slowly, without pistons or steam. There was no driver, just an incessant, low clanking that I realized came from cables above. Isaiah ran along beside the vehicle, barking merrily. The passengers onboard did not wait for the machine to stop before alighting; they jumped from the rear of the carriage when they pleased.

"It's called a trolley," Patrick said suddenly, and I jumped.

He stood a distance from me, looking where I looked.

I laughed despite myself. A few of its passengers tipped their caps to me, or perhaps to Patrick. "Where is it going?"

"Only from one end of town to the other. It will head back in a moment."

"But . . ." I teemed with questions, none of them forming a sensible line.

Patrick looked about with indifference, as though we weren't standing on a jerry-built jumble of thought. A patchwork paper town. "We've made some . . . modifications these past years."

"How . . ." Again, words alluded me. I'd seen many towns in the past seven years, walked through their main streets, and most were littered by remnants of conflict—walls buckling, orphans sitting among the bricks, shop owners patching their windows and carrying on. Business as usual. The stench of despondency thicker than smoke.

Those other towns were depictions of Scurry, or how I remembered it, untouched and unchanged. The Crafters worked and worked with the turning of the earth and transported their goods out of town. There was time for little else.

The only other places in the Trench that had made me marvel were the mountains, the ruins, the seaside, and of course, Belavere City, where the Artisans were the machines that turned the cogs.

Kenton Hill matched none of this.

"How?" I uttered. "How is this possible?"

Patrick walked ahead, his coat billowing out behind him. "It's amazin' how much time and resources can be made available when you no longer work for Belavere City."

I followed hurriedly, trying to keep pace to hear him. It had been a long time since the first strikes at the mines, at the mills, the factories, the docks, but some labor had resumed under the pressure of the Artisan government. Only where there wasn't a choice. Towns already impoverished could not afford to go without the capital's support for long. "You held your strike?"

"We did," Patrick said easily. "Been a long time since we turned over a single dime to Tanner. We're completely independent."

I skirted puddles at the last moment, sputtering, "But how? How have you—"

"Survived?" Patrick offered. "Without the House of Lords blowin' us to pieces, you mean."

I pressed my lips together. It was exactly what I meant.

He sniffed knowingly. "You won't speak ill of 'em," he noted. "Suppose I wouldn't, either, if they'd fed me from their silver cutlery and dressed me in silk."

I ignored the gibe. "How?"

"Oh, just some luck," he said, drawing a pocket watch from his coat. He glanced at it and said no more.

A few residents still remained on the streets. They seemed familiar with Patrick, nodding or making way for him as he passed. Those who looked at me averted their eyes quickly. I imagined I resembled a beggar of sorts, but I cared very little. I had forgotten the dirty clothes sticking to my skin, the ache of my legs. My neck craned as I tried to discern more of the buildings and their strange facades. "What do the pipes carry?"

"Gas," he said. "Water."

I shook my head in wonder. "Simple Crafters, you said."

He only nodded.

"What of your police?" I asked, for every town had government-instated police. "Or the Scribblers?"

"We're a small town, miss. We've only ever had the one Scribbler. A handful of police."

"And you aren't worried someone will recognize me? That they might turn me in to authorities? There's a price on my head, Mr. Colson."

"Patrick," he corrected. "And no, I'm not worried."

"No." I grimaced. "Because you run this town."

A huff of mirth escaped his lips. He clicked his tongue as he looked over at me with those unnaturally clear crystal-blue eyes. "No one *runs* us. You don't listen much, do you?"

He crossed the street then, whistling to Isaiah. He walked purposefully toward a tall, teetering building, its many windows alight. The sign hanging above the door read COLSON & SONS. Patrons spilled out onto the street, wobbling as they walked. A cat slipped through the swinging door and disappeared inside. Above, floors of windows wavered higher than the other town houses.

I panted as I reached Patrick's side again. Lord, but my head pounded. "Surely you're not an innkeeper as well as a gangster?"

He caught the door as it swung open once more, two women holding fast to each other stumbling out. He waited for them to pass, then said to me, "In you get."

I scowled, then peered beyond him. A tall, polished counter stretched along one side, lined with occupied stools. A man in a peaked cap spat thickly into a waiting bucket at his feet. Round tables crowded the floor, bustling with yet more patrons and their drinks. The volume was like a blast of hot air. Laughter, shouting, music—a piano. A man stood atop a wooden chair and tried to tap dance but abruptly fell sideways.

Isaiah suddenly appeared at my thigh, panting for attention.

"On your bed, Isaiah," Patrick said firmly, and the great dog lumbered off to a waiting nest of blankets by the wall. "Nina, go on in."

My nose wrinkled. "I'm not a dog." But I strode into the fray regardless. I thought I heard him inhale sharply as I passed.

The noise grew impossibly louder.

"Oh ho!" came a throaty call. A man alighted his stool awkwardly, spilling half his pint on the floor as he did so. He had a pockmarked face and hair sprouting from his jaw in uneven patches. He was before me in two large strides. "And who've we here?"

He smelled of sweat and grease. The black smeared on his gums explained the watery look in his eyes. *Bluff*, I thought. The bad sort. I remembered the look from Scurry, where the men would trade for and swallow a dose of it before their shift in the mines. They went down the shafts smiling and bleary-eyed, then came back with shaking hands, dry tongues, and a penchant for throwing bottles.

I backed away a step.

"Look at this, lads! A lady in trousers." He hooted, grabbing a belt loop at my waist. I shoved his fingers away. "You're soaked through, miss," he said, undeterred, and his eyes lingered on my chest, where too much cleavage showed. "Lemme warm you." He reached for me.

A chill swept through me. Fear. Every muscle in my body became taut.

"Hello, Bernie" came Patrick's smoke-hazed voice. He stood over my shoulder, a head taller than me, close enough to put a hand on my waist. I felt the heat of his fingertips through my clothes.

Something strange happened then, a reaction. Not just from the man named Bernie, whose eyes had left my face and become afraid. Not just in the energy that left Patrick's fingertips and imprinted on my skin, but in the entire establishment.

The music stuttered, then softened. The patrons closest immediately quieted, alerted that something was imminent—a sizzle of danger. Whatever silent warning had been sent through the air quickly found the broader crowd. Conversation died. Laughter was smothered. A charge lingered. Each patron stared over my shoulder to where Patrick stood.

I looked back at him to see eyes I did not recognize. Cold as glaciers.

"Patty," the man named Bernie said, pulling his cap from his head. "I . . . I meant no harm, Pat. Apol-gees." But the bluff made the consonants blend where they shouldn't. He tried again. "*Apologies*, miss. I thought you were alone."

Silence. For a moment, Patrick only stared at the man, but the effect was haunting.

Then he looked across the room. Smiled thinly. "No trouble," he said, eyes finding Bernie again. "A misunderstanding."

Shoulders relaxed, breaths were exhaled. The piano man picked up in the middle of the melody, right where he'd left off.

I, too, drew a breath as the tension broke, and all eyes turned away once more. But Patrick stepped closer to Bernie. He patted the man's shoulder amenably and leaned down to his ear: "You don't want to do that again, Bernie, or I'd have to cut a piece out of you. You know that."

"Pat, I—"

"Go home to your missus," Patrick said, straightening. "Wash your fuckin' mouth out before you get there."

I watched, entranced, as Bernie nodded fervently, eyes rolling in his great head. He donned his cap and skirted around us with his nose down, then fled. There was no other word for it.

Around us, festivities continued.

Patrick grimaced. "This way." He took my wrist as he passed, fingers pressing firmly into the flesh, and the sounds, the smells, the feel of his calloused palm on my skin—it sent a roar of memory shuddering through me.

My father's hands had been the same, skin thickened and worn.

He threaded us through the crowd with a sense of urgency, to the side of the bar where a door waited. Before he pulled me through it, I caught sight of a woman glowering at the two of us. She stood by a large keg, a dishcloth tucked into the apron around her waist, jaw taut, mousy hair tied back, eyes as blue as Patrick's.

Then the door swung shut, and we were in a claustrophobic spiral stairwell.

"Let go of me." I said immediately, pulling my hand free.

Patrick shook his head, then began taking the stairs two at a time. "Thought that school might've taught you better manners."

I cursed beneath my breath, hurrying to keep up once more.

He tsked. "You can take the girl out of Scurry, but you can't—"

"Fucking hell, Patrick, slow *down!*"

He gave a low whistle but didn't slow at all. "Still got a pin in your arse, I see."

I stumbled as the echoes of his quiet laughter spiraled up to the distant ceiling.

We climbed to the very top, finally arriving on the last landing. A narrow hallway with three doors, brass numbers screwed into the wood: *13, 14, 15.*

A young man no older than eighteen or so sat on a stool at the end of the skinny hall. He stood at the sight of us. "Pat," he greeted, shifting his weight from foot to foot.

Patrick nodded to him, then pulled a key from his pocket. He ignored the door to the left and the right and unlocked the last one, number fifteen. "As you were, Sam," Patrick told the boy, and I looked back to see Sam nod eagerly, sitting straight-backed on the stool and looking dead ahead, except for the furtive glance he spared for me.

Patrick had to duck his head to enter the room. I followed him, and the door shut with a weak thud.

The ceiling was bowed in its middle, like it might split at any moment. The four walls were papered in faded cherry blossoms, the only break in the pattern coming from a crack along one wall and the window fitted with a bench. The bed was made of timber, the mattress lumpy, even with its neat coverings. It was a room redrawn from a hundred other rooms I'd occupied before. Sparse. Small. Dark.

But pipes fed through the plaster and hung over a large basin, and there were valves on the sides. A chute wedged beneath the other side of the windowsill, disappearing over the roof tiles. By the bed was a cord that hung from a sconce, and I could not fathom its use.

A large bleached rug covered the floorboards, and a squat wardrobe sat beside the door.

"There are some clothes and linen in there," Patrick said, watching me closely. "If you need anything else, ask for Mrs. Colson."

I spun. "Your wife?" *But of course he should have a wife. He's not twelve anymore.*

"My *mother*," he corrected. "And the innkeeper."

The bar maiden with blue eyes flashed through my mind again. *Colson & Sons.* I exhaled and nodded. "You didn't strike me as an innkeeper."

He smiled thinly. It did not reach his eyes. "It will be less complicated if I don't strike you as anythin'."

My pulse quickened. It suddenly seemed entirely improper that we should be standing in this room together, door pressed shut at my back.

I shifted uncomfortably. Why did it have to be him?

He looked down at my legs, then back to my eyes. "You're nervous," he accused softly.

My face heated. "Shouldn't I be? I was knocked unconscious and brought here blindfolded."

He tsked. "Scottie lets his nerves get the better of him sometimes. He'll be properly scolded, I assure you."

I chewed over something I wanted to say but wasn't sure how to. "Those people downstairs. They seem . . . *afraid* of you."

He was slow to answer. "Do they?"

"You threatened to cut that man." I pressed, my fingers trembling. "And I'm supposed to believe you won't lay a hand on me?"

He went still then. Pensive. His hands moved to his pockets, and he buried them. I found myself unable to look elsewhere, though every instinct suggested I should.

"It's not wise to trust anyone at all, Nina Harrow, though it might ease your mind to know that we won't be seein' much of each other after tonight. You needn't be nervous."

I raised my eyebrows skeptically.

"Earth charmin'," he said, by way of explanation. "That's all I need from you. When it's time, you'll go to the tunnels and move the earth so that we can get where we need to go undetected. Our diggers will help you where they can. Until then, you won't be bothered."

"That's how you've stayed hidden all this time?" I asked. "You move about in tunnels?"

"We're miners," he said, and I hated the smirk in his voice. "It ain't so mysterious."

"And what of the information you mentioned?" I asked. I wondered what intel I could possibly have that he wanted.

"I'll have someone collect you when there's somethin' we need to know."

I frowned. "We?"

"Colson and Sons." False grandeur colored his tone. He gestured to the room around him as though it were a showpiece. "In the meantime, you'll rest. Sam will wait outside your door, should you need somethin'."

I glanced back at the door in question. "He'll wait there all night?"

"He's paid handsomely to do so."

"And if I should wish to explore Kenton Hill? I'd like to see the land-scape. Perhaps visit Idia's Canal." A small eagerness kindled in the pit of my stomach. I thought of the main street of Kenton Hill and its many oddities.

Patrick sighed, pulled a cigarette from the inside of his coat. "You know Idia's Canal, do you?"

"I read a lot."

"I remember." He said nothing more for a moment, tapping the unlit cigarette against his thigh. "This here is a fine window." He gestured to the pane. "One can see for miles."

I felt each muscle in my body tighten. It took colossal effort to unlock my jaw. "And if I should grow tired of the view?"

"Then you'll need to break down the door and hope Sam is feelin' generous enough to let you pass. Though I wouldn't wager it if I were you. I've paid him to drag you back in, should you try it. *Don't try it*, miss, for my sake. One knock on the head is regrettable, two would begin to make me question my honor."

So I was a prisoner, then, as I'd suspected. My lip curled. "I thought I was free to take the next train out?"

"Ah," he said. "I'm afraid I lied about that, too. We've repurposed the trains and their tracks."

My mouth fell open.

He didn't smile as he spoke. "We can both act, Nina, only I didn't need a fancy school to teach me."

"Fuck you."

He twirled the cigarette in his fingers and looked out the window once more, thinking. It was a while before he spoke again.

My head pounded. I wished he would leave.

"You speak different," he said into the small space. "Stand different." There was no inflection to it. I couldn't tell if it was an insult or something else. "You've got that high-society swagger now. Nose in the air." He allowed his eyes to travel openly over me. They stuck to that place on the inside of my forearm, where an ugly, shapeless scar contorted the skin. "But you didn't join 'em, did you?"

I wondered if he spoke to himself or to me. We held that gaze for an interminable time, trying to peel back the layers of each other and find something recognizable beneath. Trying to make sense of our paths that had diverted so wildly and yet somehow rejoined.

Bellowing inside me was the insistence to run while I still could.

He said, "I need you to stay inside this room, in this buildin'. It's important that you don't go farther, miss. Do you understand?"

"I understand plenty," I said between clenched teeth. The effect was dampened by my sudden swaying. It seemed my legs were finally beginning to give out.

Patrick took two short strides toward me, his hands reaching my shoulders before I teetered over. "Whoa there," he grunted, then cursed softly.

I found myself sitting on the bed, dizzy now.

"Someone will bring up a plate of food," said a voice, its direction unclear to me. "Rest, Nina. I'll have a doctor visit you in the morning."

"Don't need a doctor," I murmured, words blending.

"Nevertheless, one will be sent. For now, take this." He handed me a corked amber bottle. Its glass was emblazoned with the words INK TINCTURE. Bluff.

My eyes closed of their own accord. I unstoppered the bottle and brought it to my lips, grateful for the medicine.

But the liquid, I realized with aching slowness, did not taste of bluff. It was metallic. Icy cold.

Idium.

My eyes opened, and I found Patrick watching me warily.

"So then, you have the Alchemist." I said, only it came out slurred. "The rumors are true."

I fell back onto the covers, the bowed ceiling sinking closer and closer.

"Rest." His voice was deeper, hypnotic even. "I need you ready for what's comin'. You're safe here, I promise."

Nowhere was safe.

A sigh, and then a hand swept tangles of damp hair from my forehead, and I could not tell if it was my own or that of another. Darkness smothered sensation, and I gladly curled into its embrace.

CHAPTER 18

PATRICK

Patrick closed the door behind him, took the key from his pocket, and locked it.

Sam had already sprung to his feet, and he caught the key when Patrick threw it to him.

Patrick needed badly to find a drink.

"Don't let anyone pass you by, Sam," he said in a far-off voice.

"Yessir."

"Good man."

The piano music and raised voices crept up the stairwell, muffling the sounds of a rhythmic moaning on the third floor, a drunken argument on the second. Patrick paused on the last step, pinching the bridge of his noise, forcing his racing mind to shut up.

Then he cursed lowly, pulled his collar higher and pushed the door open.

The volume swallowed him. Clarence was belting the piano keys to the poor accompaniment of "Ol' Digger Come," sung by a small crowd with closed eyes, arms banded about one another's shoulders. The pastor sat in the corner, puce-faced as he arm wrestled a boy half his age. Beneath a framed portrait of Patrick's grandmother, two women pressed into the wall, mouths and hands and hips joined.

A drum beat incessantly behind Patrick's right eye.

"Pat!" trilled Marie-Laure. She wore a blouse pulled low over her breasts with the first button undone. "Join us!" Her teeth were wine-tinged. It made her look cannibalistic. The man whose lap she sat upon had turned at the sound of Patrick's name and grinned drunkenly in his direction. "Brother!" Donny shouted, almost dislodging Marie-Laure. "You're back already? Weren't so hard to get her here then, eh?"

Patrick's little brother felt around the stained table for his drink, almost knocking over several others in the process.

"Lord, kill me," Patrick groaned, then took the glass of whiskey before Donny could reach it, swallowing the remnants. For a brief moment, he shut his eyes in pleasure, then turned to Marie-Laure. "Excuse us, darlin'."

She pouted and demurred but stood all the same. She made sure to touch a discreet finger to Patrick's belt as she passed. An invitation.

When she had melted into the crowd, Patrick grabbed Donny's coat from the floor and threw it to him. "Get up," he said. "We've got business."

Donny groaned, then slumped onto the tabletop. "Please, Patty. Not tonight."

"Get up," Patrick told him once more, and started for the exit.

Patrick made it three paces before he was stopped. This time, a different woman blocked his way. She wore an apron and carried several empty pints, a furious expression souring her fair looks.

She glared up at Patrick with eyes he'd inherited, though hers were harder, more cutting. Deep lines sprouted from their corners.

"Ma," Patrick greeted her, resisting the urge to scrub a hand over his face. *Let this fuckin' night end.*

Tess Colson had a stare that could gouge out a man's insides. If someone cut Patrick and his brothers open, they'd find empty husks.

"Where've you come from?" she asked shrewdly. Her voice reminded him of cracked leather, the heavy Northern accent born from her marrow.

"Runnin' errands," Patrick answered, smiling in a way he hoped was genial. "I'll say goodnight, then—"

"Who was that wringin' wet girl you brought back with you?" She eyed the door to the stairwell. "Never seen her before."

"Just a guest," he said bluntly. "Sam's lookin' in on her."

Her jaw ticked. "Another?" She was not fooled by the evasion. "You plannin' to fill up the entire buildin' with Artisans, Patrick?"

"If I see fit." He suppressed harsher words. "Tell the cook to send up somethin' for her, would you?"

Tess Colson shook her head in resigned reproach. "Who is she?"

Patrick didn't answer the question. He often found he didn't need to where his mother was concerned. Tess Colson had the ability to weigh her sons' breaths and read the morphing valleys of their expressions.

"*Her?*" she blustered, shaking her head in exasperation. "It's *her*, ain't it?"

Her. It meant many things at once. "It is."

She nodded. It was not a gesture of support. "My, my," she said. "You've gone and fucked it all up now, son. Haven't you? You're gonna bring the whole world down upon us."

Patrick stared at a spot above her head and tempered himself. "She's on our side now," he said firmly.

"Is she?"

"She will be."

Tess closed her eyes, and when she opened them, Patrick felt her exhaustion, her worry—a mother's worry. "Be careful, son," she said. "Please, for all our sakes. Promise me."

Before he could nod, a hand took Patrick's shoulder from behind. He did not bother looking back to see who it was, but Tess Colson did.

Her expression turned disapproving. She looked expectantly back at Patrick. "What's this? You ain't takin' your brother nowhere in his state."

Donny chose that moment to lean his chin on Patrick's shoulder. "What state?" he drawled.

"He's drunk," Tess said. Donny was now pursing his lips around an invisible cigarette and attempting to light it. "Get him upstairs. Now."

"We've got a small matter of business first," Patrick said. "Won't take long."

Tess sighed, eyeing her sons as though God had given her a small reservoir of strength and they'd stolen it all at birth. "I don't want to hear nothin' about it in the mornin'," she said. "You hear me?"

"Night, Ma," Patrick said, stepping around her. He left her seething in place and pushed the door open. Isaiah lumbered over from his spot by the fireplace and followed them out.

Once over the threshold, Patrick didn't keep moving right away. Instead, he lifted his face to the night sky, sucked breath into his lungs. *God help me*, he thought.

Donny had followed close, his hand still pressed to Patrick's shoulder, releasing it once they'd cleared the stoop. "I was about to take that girl to bed, Patty. This'd better be important," he said, eyes staring somewhere beyond. They never stilled. His pupils were the same hue as Patrick's own, but they twitched minutely, even under the weight of whiskey.

"Which girl?" Patrick scoffed. "The whore?" Isaiah nosed his hand, eager to get moving.

"She weren't a whore," Donny staggered, overbalancing. "Said she were a traveler girl from Dorser."

"Well," Patrick exhaled, beginning down the street. He tugged on Donny's sleeve until he fell into pace. "Unless I'm mistaken, I seem to remember Marie-Laure growing up in her daddy's scrapyard on Rutting Way."

Donny gasped. "Fuck me. Was that *Marie-Laure*?"

"It were," Patrick said. "You need to stop drinkin' like that, Donny."

He sniffed. "Couldn't see straight before I started drinkin'. Ain't gettin' any blinder, am I?"

Patrick supposed he was right. Donny had never seen well as a kid, and it had only worsened with the years, his sight fading until there was nothing at all. Blind before he could find the first hair on his chin.

Patrick sighed. "Blindness ain't ever hindered you so much before."

"Come to think of it, her tits did feel familiar," Donny muttered. "Hey, wait a minute. Where's me wallet?"

"Long gone, I'll bet."

Donny dropped his hand to Patrick's coat sleeve, gripping the fabric behind his elbow between two fingers. "Women," he bleated. "Takin' your money whether you bed 'em or not. A boyfriend would at least spend the night with me."

Patrick lit a cigarette and put it in his brother's hand, then lit another for himself. "Marie gets more done in a day than you do in a week, little brother," he said. "Cost me a lot fuckin' less, too, mind you."

"I earn my keep," Donny protested. "I'm out here with you now, ain't I? You plannin' on tellin' me where the fuck we're goin'?"

Patrick's jaw flexed, the irritation he'd stemmed earlier returning. "We're off to old Bernie's place," he said. "I need a quick word."

Donny slowed a moment, then hurried to catch up. "Bernie? What'd he do?"

Patrick tried to frame the words carefully, though they fell flat no matter their shape. "He insulted a friend."

"A friend?" Donny scoffed. "Who? *Otto?* Probably deserved it."

"Not Otto."

"Then who? Bernie is a dolt, but he's no threat, Patty. We ought to leave him be. People will think—"

"I need a word with the man," Patrick placated. "That's all."

He could feel Donny frowning behind him. "No cuttin'?"

"No," he said. "No cuttin'." Though the idea had merit.

"This *friend*," Donny continued. "Who is he then?"

Patrick didn't answer, and Donny only sighed. The youngest Colson brother pulled a pistol from the inside of his coat as they walked, feeling for the bullets within the barrel. He blew smoke over his shoulder and did not ask further questions. He rarely did.

The Colson boys did what was asked of them. Just as they had for their father.

"Just give the man a scare, Donny," Patrick told him. "And we'll be on our way."

CHAPTER 19

NINA

I awoke in the same clothes I'd traveled in.

The fabric had dried and creased in odd places. My boots and socks had been removed. I stared, confused, at the cherry blossom walls, the concave ceiling, and the light seeping in from the window.

Kenton Hill.

I groaned, sat upright. To my surprise, I did not ache all over the way I'd expected I would. There was a muted throb from the bump at the back of my head, but otherwise, the only sensation came from my fingertips. They tingled.

I raised them to eye level, inspected them curiously, and then recalled the taste of metal on my tongue.

Idium.

My eyes widened. I smiled.

On the floorboards by the door, three plates of food sat waiting, untouched. The mashed potatoes had browned and a thick skin clotted the gravy. A bowl of oats was sweating. I wondered how long I'd slept.

There was a note by my feet, folded unevenly.

Miss Harrow,

The left pipe releases heated water. Don't burn yourself.

It wasn't signed.

I stared at the lettering for a long while, tracing the elongated tails of the *P*'s and *F*'s. I looked at the name, *my* name, with a sort of removal, as though I was spying on someone else's mail.

The pipes were indeed different temperatures. I turned them on one at a time, watching the steam rise slowly from the first. I filled a large copper basin halfway and turned the valve until the flow of water subsided.

Then I laughed. *Genius.* I wondered how the water was heated, if it was by fire or gas or some other invention I hadn't yet seen. How did it arrive at the turn of a lever?

I followed the paths of the pipes out the window and couldn't find where they led.

But I resolved that I would.

First, though, I needed a bath.

I undressed and retrieved a cloth from the wardrobe, then doused it and sighed as I ran it over my body. I was shocked to look down and find I wasn't covered in bruises. I ached, but apart from the mottling on my left wrist, my skin was mostly unblemished, only paler than I'd remembered, even against the blond of my hair. Just beneath the surface, the idium hummed softly.

I'd lost some weight in hiding—gone were the days of the banquets. The swell of my hips and breasts had diminished some, and I sighed. I thought I looked much like a bird—flimsy bones, easily broken. I resolved to eat until Patrick's hotel was in arrears.

I found clean clothes and shoes to dress in—a blended green skirt and a sallow-colored blouse with loose cuffs. I buttoned the top to the hollow of my throat and lamented the way it billowed at the sides. The leather shoes were old and cracked but fit well enough. I combed through my curls as best I could, though there was often little point. I resorted to pinning them back instead until they collected at the base of my neck. Without oil, there was little else to be done.

Then I ate everything. The potatoes and leeks and onions and sausages.

I ate the cold porridge and scraped the sides with a spoon. I drained the glass of water in one go and felt achingly, gratifyingly full. I laid back on the faded rug and let my belly distend, then closed my eyes again, wondering if I ought to go back to sleep.

I was good at entertaining myself inside small spaces. The past seven years had taught me to. Proficiency in hiding was proficiency in being alone, in being bored. I opened my eyes now and looked for those same silly games I'd used to while away hours, days. I could trace the wallpaper in the air, count the cracks in the building, name the exact hue of everything my eyes touched and think of how to replicate them in paint combinations.

How long would I be here for?

The sun spilled in through the window and highlighted the waltzing dust motes, but still the room was dark.

I turned to find a lantern, but though there was a sconce, no candle sat in its hold. Instead, there was a wire spring and a small brass opening. I eyed the cord that hung from its bottom, then gently pulled on it.

A flame appeared. Small, but real. It flickered to life with a small click, and I staggered back. Laughed. *Magic.*

I thought of the street below with its many winding and twisting oddities, parts welded together to create things I'd never seen. Then I stared at the wallpaper once more and considered counting its flowers.

But I was tired of hiding.

I went to the door and knocked on it, called out the name Patrick had used last night . . . or was it the night before?

Footsteps, and then the door cracked open. A scrawny, tan-skinned boy filled the space. "Miss?"

I smiled genially at him. "I'd like a walk about town," I said. "If you'll just step aside."

The boy gaped at me. "But . . . Pat . . ." he looked behind him, as though Patrick might appear over his shoulder. "I'm sorry, miss. You gotta stay in there. Boss's orders." He straightened as he spoke, galvanized. "I ain't lettin' you pass." He was steadfast, juvenility notwithstanding.

But I had an advantage now that I'd not been allowed these past seven years, and it surely counted for something. "Do you know me, Sam? Did Patrick give you my name?"

Sam jutted his chin, staring me down. "He tells me lots of things," he said proudly. "He's trustin' me to keep you safe."

I smiled. "He must see great potential in you."

I saw the twinkle in his eyes, the eagerness. "He says you're the earth Charmer," Sam continued. "Says we gotta keep a close eye on you. Keep everyone else out. There's a lot of people lookin' for you, miss. Lots of people who'd pay to find you."

I sighed. "He's an honorable man, then?"

"He is," Sam said with a smile, chest inflating.

"And what do you think he'd say if I brought the entire building down around us?"

Sam's expression was wiped clean and replaced with fear. He took a reflexive step back but quickly regained himself. I heard his hand grip the doorknob. "You—you wouldn't do that," he stammered. "You'd only bury yourself with it."

I shrugged slowly. "That's quite a gamble, Sam," I said. "I only wish to walk a short while. I'll be back within the hour."

Sam's brow furrowed; his eyes darted to the stairwell.

I sighed impatiently. "You could accompany me. Ensure I came to no harm?"

He wavered; I saw it in the twist of his hands. "I can't let you pass, miss. Patty will be furious."

Sam warred with indecision; I could see this was about more than just money. When he spoke of Patrick, there was not only a deep tenor of admiration, but also fear.

Sam would do what he was told, and not for the pay. Had there ever been a greater motivator than approval?

I could think of only one.

I planted my feet more firmly and made a show of closing my eyes in concentration. I could feel Sam watching me through the crack in the door as I raised my hands from my sides like some storybook sorceress. I drew every grain of dust and dirt from the room until it swirled in a storm in front of me, and when I opened my eyes, I saw Sam watching it in horror, as though granules were more than just dust.

"S-stop!" he said. Then louder, more panicked. I made the dust storm spin faster. "Damn it! I said stop!"

"Are you going to walk with me, Sam?"

"Yes! Yes, all right! You don't need to—"

"Perfect," I said, and my hands dropped. The dirt rained down onto the floorboards. "Someone should sweep up in here."

CHAPTER 20

PATRICK

The inn had never been his mother's dream, but his father's.

It was his pa's before him, named Colson & Sons for close to a century, and for most of Patrick's childhood, it was a source of constant strain between his parents—a slowly fraying string holding them over boiling water.

Patrick imagined John Colson had painted quite the pretty picture for his mother when they first married. A thriving inn—the staple of the town, resurrected from dilapidation back to its original state. He likely spun tales of the profits it would reap, the status it would grant, to be the proprietors of such a large establishment in a shrunken town. Tess Colson said she had been stupid in her youth, but Patrick thought she had probably just been in love.

The inn had been a sad, rotting shell when the newlyweds inherited it. Patrick's grandfather had fancied himself a gambler. Before he'd died, collectors had strolled in and taken what moth-eaten furniture remained. The walls were impregnated with mites; the town chancellor had cordoned it off with paper notices that read DANGER. UNSTABLE FOUNDATION.

But John Colson was a dreamer. What he envisioned tended to come to life between his hands. He could whittle dry root into game pieces. He could fix all that was broken: shoes, windowpanes, creaking doors, axles, wheel spokes, and saddles. He had enough ideas to fill three men's skulls and they'd still overflow.

But he was a Craftsman of Kenton Hill, so he went to the mines.

They mined coal in Kenton Hill. Always had. The low-bearing hills hid the largest coal seam on the continent. Patrick had seen miners slam their pints together and salute the enduring role this town had played in the great mechanism of the Trench since he could walk. *But do those fuckin' swanks deign to thank us? To share any of the profit of our labor?*

No! the rest would shout, and resentment would brew among them until it was thick enough to turn a softer man violent. Those men, blackened by soot, addled by liquor, would take that violence home to their families.

In the brink, nary a Crafter town differed.

John Colson had been determined to set a different course. His miner's pay funneled into the refurbishing of the inn, and he spent his nights working instead of drinking. Eventually, the inn reopened, and it fell to his wife to manage its books and fill its rooms, serve its patrons and stock the bar. Eventually, it became the establishment John Colson dreamed it would be, though he barely saw the inside of it. His days were spent down the shafts, in the dark, earning the wage necessary to keep Colson & Sons open despite Tess's protests.

The inn is bleedin' us dry, John. The repairs, the heatin'. We've barely turned a profit since it opened. It's been years, John. Years! And you're still down that blasted mine every bloody day.

It'll turn around yet, love, you'll see, John would say. For years he said it. By the time Patrick returned from his siphoning, he'd stopped believing it.

By then, Patrick knew the truth. He and his brothers would all mine coal with their father until they keeled over. He knew his mother would climb that fucking staircase every hour of the day until her legs gave out, and he knew that the money his father had promised would never arrive. Even with the addition of his wage and Gunner's, there was always a bill to pay, always a repair to be made, always a shift the next day, the bell for the nightmen ringing out at dusk.

And yet, it had been a future Patrick was willing to bear. There was nothing else for him if there was not that staircase, that bell, the obstinate resolution of John Colson's dream. Patrick's life then was a warm accumulation of smoke and his mother's rare smiles and the bedroom he shared with his brothers. There was nothing else to miss as much as home.

That was what he'd told himself when he returned from Belavere City, all the way down the platform, right to the back door he now stood before, wiping his boots on the same straw mat he had back then.

The house was hidden behind the pub. Three rooms for five people, turned four. John's portrait still sat in its silver frame on a sideboard. The kitchen smelled, as it always did, of pastry and onions and rendering fat.

The oldest Colson brother sat at a round table with mismatched legs, leaning back on a chair their father had once occupied in a time before his capture. It still rankled Patrick to see someone else in his place.

Gunner turned his weary head to Patrick and watched him remove his coat. The two brothers were alike in many ways. Both dressed in a fashion that did not match their surroundings: finely tailored pants, a brass-buttoned waistcoat, a starched shirt, shoes shined like a lord's. But the contrast between them was stark. Gunner's beard now reached his chest and was streaked in early grays. On a reddened visage, his dark eyes floated, unable to anchor themselves. He slumped in the chair, hair in disarray, one hand shaking on their mother's kitchen table, the other holding a bottleneck in his lap.

"The boss man is here," Gunner muttered darkly. His eyes rolled to the counter where Tess slapped pastry onto a butcher block. "Better hide your sherry, Ma, 'fore he confiscates it."

"Shut up, Gunner," Tess said, taking a rolling pin to the pastry with unspent fury.

"You here to lecture me, Patty?" Gunner said now, leering over the tabletop. He pointed to a place on his chin. "Come to smack some sense into me?"

Tess slammed the rolling pin on the counter. "I said, shut up!" She turned to Gunner with all the fierceness of a warden. "Do you want a place to sleep off that fuckin' bottle you took from my shelf, son? Or should I send your sorry arse home to Emily? Eh? Which will it be?"

At the mention of his wife, Gunner sobered, relaxing back into his chair, averting his eyes like a petulant child.

"As I thought," Tess muttered. She turned to Patrick. "You want breakfast?"

He nodded but didn't take his gaze from Gunner. He wondered how long his brother had been here, taking up space in Tess's kitchen. How long would the bender last this time? "I went to see Emily," Patrick said. "Knocked on her door."

Gunner shrunk, the great hulking brute of a man collapsing in on himself. "What'd she say?"

"Says she'll take you back, so long as the whiskey and bluff stay behind." Patrick stared a hole right through his brother's head.

Gunner swallowed thickly, ran his tongue over his dry lips, probably tasting the final remnants of bluff. A glimmer of hope sparked his muddy eyes. Their father's eyes. "She'll have me home?" he asked, words wobbling. He leaned forward to hear the answer, bottle slipping sideways.

Patrick took it from him, then emptied it into the sink. "It took some convincin', but yes. God help her."

"Thank you, brother," Gunner said quietly, somewhat brokenly. He rubbed his eyes with the heel of his hands and Patrick saw something pitiful in him. A kicked dog. "Clean yourself up, Gun. She ain't givin' you more chances after this one. You hear me?"

He nodded, wiping his hands on his pants. "I'll straighten out," he said, to himself more than anyone else. "Tell her for me, will you? And tell her . . . tell her I love her."

"Tell her yourself," Patrick said, disgust in his voice. "She's a good woman."

"I know."

"You ain't gonna trick another into marrying you."

"I know."

"Do you?" Patrick said, louder than before. Heat rose from his collar and Gunner could see it. He pressed his lips together.

Patrick stepped close, then knelt until their eyes were level. "Then don't fuck up again," he ordered. "Next time she kicks your arse to the street, I won't darken her doorstep on your behalf."

Gone was the big brother who'd have clocked Patrick in the chin for daring to speak down to him. The man who would sooner die than let another man stand over him.

Gunner Colson was nearly a husk now, carrying around the wet weight of someone barely recognizable. He nodded, sniffing and wiping his nose on his cuff. "This'll be the last time, Pat. I swear it."

He hadn't always been so pitiful. The Gunner of their childhood had been strong. Impenetrable. Admired. He had taught Patrick how to re-light discarded cigarette stubs, how to throw a punch, which schoolbooks had the nude models sketched onto the pages. He had pulled Charlie Fawcett by the collar all the way to the old quarry and threatened to throw him over the side after he'd taken Donny's lunch.

He'd been a force to be reckoned with until he'd been sucked down those mines. He had come back up much like the rest—hollow, afraid, in desperate need of some relief.

"It's just the walls, Pat," Gunner said, his voice whisper-thin now. Patrick knew he was moments from losing consciousness. "The walls keep fuckin' fallin' in on me."

Patrick was familiar with the sensation—the weight of the tunnels pressing inward, puncturing organs, skull cracking beneath the pressure, the whole world dark and desperate. Calamitous panic. Fear. Sometimes Patrick woke with his blood screaming in his ears.

"You're aboveground now, Gun," Patrick told him, taking his brother's slack head in his hands. "Look around you. No dirt. No struts."

"No fuckin' canaries," he said, smiling wetly.

"No canaries," Patrick agreed. "You're a man who wears a nice suit now." He patted Gunner's shoulder once, then stood straight again. "I need you on your feet again soon. There's business."

"There's always business," muttered Tess from behind them. She was stirring something that smelled like a stew. "All this bloody business, and never any peace."

She wasn't referring to Colson & Sons, of course. These days they had housekeepers, cooks, barkeeps. No, it wasn't the inn that kept that bitter lament on Tess Colson's tongue. It was the Miners Union. Yet another thing their father had burdened her with.

Patrick sighed, turning back toward the door. "There's a community meeting tonight," he reminded her.

"Don't I know it," she murmured. "You're not stayin' for breakfast?"

He shook his head. He didn't want to stay here another minute looking at his dosed brother in the chair of his missing father. "It's a busy day," he said. He donned his coat again, then jutted a finger in Gunner's direction. "He can't have hard liquor at the bar anymore, Ma. Tell the keeps."

She looked for a moment as though she might argue. But she glanced at her eldest son and bit the inside of her cheek again. Nodded.

Gunner had dozed off.

"If I hear he's fallin' off your barstools, I'll be handling him myself."

Tess's eyes darkened, but again she nodded, swallowing warily. She looked Patrick up and down like she barely recognized him. "You sound like *him*," she said, and Patrick didn't need to ask whom she referred to.

He turned his back on her.

The air outside was colder this morning. The seasons were turning. Soon, the hills would turn brown and frostbitten, the gas would run low again. The water heaters would groan ominously.

But no one in Kenton Hill would grow cold in their homes. No one would go hungry. No coal would be spared for Belavere City or anyone else. Not anymore.

Patrick entered the narrow alley that ran down the side of Colson & Sons. He was due to meet Otto and Scottie, see what news they'd heard along the tunnels, then the Miller family about the produce distribution at the marketplace. There were problems to be solved. Always fucking problems. Running a town was a succession of crises—there was no bottom to the barrel.

"Pat!"

He'd barely set foot into Main Street.

Sam jogged toward him, the boy's face shiny and harrowed. "Pat . . . I'm sorry . . ." The boy looked over his shoulder frantically. Patrick half expected a cavalry on his tail. "She's gone."

"What?" Patrick's stomach hollowed. "How long ago?" *How far could she have gotten?* His feet turned to the south, to the old train tracks.

Sam panted heavily. "She said we'd walk together, that she wanted to explore . . . then she was just gone—"

Patrick whirled again, his skin prickling. Sam took a purposeful step back.

It always seemed to Patrick that there was something on his face or in his voice that unsettled people. Warned them. Perhaps it was the mere fact that his last name was Colson.

"A *walk?*" Patrick repeated, voice deadened. He decided it was not a good idea to grab the boy by the collar. He was just a kid. "You took her on a fuckin' *walk*, Sam?"

"I told her no," he said, gripping his cap in his hands. "But she threatened to break apart the buildin'! And you weren't in the pub. And she promised it were just a walk—"

Patrick shook his head. Cursed at his feet. "Where did you lose her?"

"By the candlemaker's," he answered in a hurry. "Turned around and she were gone." He made a gesture with his hands, as though Nina had turned to smoke before his eyes.

Patrick looked up Main Street, filled now with merchants and Crafters of every trade completing their day's work. The trolley rattled by, filled with ruddy-faced children dressed for school. Nina was nowhere.

"I think . . . I think she's gone, Pat. She's made a run for it."

"No, she hasn't," Patrick said, already walking, feet falling hard against the cobbles. "I'll find her."

Sam hurried to catch up. "But . . . where?" he asked, exasperated. "I searched everywhere."

"Go home," Patrick told him. He did not spare the boy a glance as he took off. Patrick ignored the nods of those he passed and took a left turn at the end of the road, where the streets turned to canals and funneled out into the hills.

You're still here, he thought, quickening to a jog. *And if you're not, I'll be bringin' you right back.*

CHAPTER 21

NINA

The canals were soupy and pungent through the industrial buildings, but when they spilled out into the hills, they transformed. The brick coping became rocks. The water cleared a little. The farther I followed, the more color I could discern. Moss, cobalt, rust. Eventually, when the town was behind me and the vein of water wove through shallow valleys between knolls, I caught the upsets of small fish disturbing the surface. Away from the grime of humans, water was just water.

The land was beautifully devoid. There were barely any trees, just wave after wave of hills and their dancing grass, all shades of gold. No wildflowers. No blue sky. Just ghostly green mountains in the far distance, and the ribbons of water running through hand-hewn troughs.

These canals were Artisan-made, I knew. Trenched by an earth Charmer, no doubt, who knew the ways to curb the possibility of erosion. Miles upon miles of canal networks, all intersecting and diverting to every corner of the continent. They were the channels of most Belavere trade.

But this canal, the one whose edge I toed with bare feet, this was Idia's Canal. The very first carved into the earth, by the daughter of God herself. I wondered why Idia had chosen Kenton Hill, of all places, to bestow this first gift.

I wondered if she peered down on this place now and regretted it.

Idia's Canal, to my horror, had been intentionally dammed. Tons of rock and dirt blocked the water's exit. No boats. No tracks or trains. No way into Kenton Hill except on foot. It was no wonder the House of Lords had never come looking here. It was an impossible trek.

Unless, I supposed, you knew where the tunnels were.

I walked a narrow path to the top of a hill, where it seemed many had come to contemplate. The grass made way for me, well acquainted with visitors.

The earth felt different in this place. I could feel a subtle shift beneath my feet. It was minute—a warning of something bigger. Greater. I wondered if there were tunnels beneath this exact place, if the disturbance I felt was not intuitive but mechanical, man-made.

In my schooling, I'd learned that earth differed wherever one walked. Sometimes it slid underfoot where one couldn't see it, the silt beneath the surface forever rearranging where the seawater and wind persuaded it. In the city, the earth hummed, magnetic and pulsing. Here, though, in the brink, the trench bowled out into widespread land, and the earth was ravenous. Every now and then, it opened its jaw and swallowed men whole.

I sat on the hill's peak, but I did not look out into the wide-open spaces and marvel at the trench. Instead, I turned my body toward the town of Kenton proper and shook my head in disbelief. I wondered what my professors would say to this.

The wind responded, colder than I'd expected, harsher, blowing through the stalks and sending ripples over the ground. The seasons were colliding. I closed my eyes, tipped my head back.

How I hated the quiet. The solitude. Seven years, and it clung to me still. I wanted volume and laughter and the tinkling of many voices talking at once. I wanted meals in the company of others whose elbows rested alongside mine. I wanted to reclaim familiarity with someone who knew who I was. I wanted and wanted and wanted but had learned to ignore it.

Hiding was safe.

I was made of both parts that were logical, careful, and parts that clamored to be something loud and brilliant, and even after all this time, I hadn't learned to reconcile them. The two sides parried in my mind in an endless loop.

No one can be trusted. Don't get close. Run.

Listen to the ground. Can you hear it? Why does it tremble?

Heavy panting mercifully broke the quiet. A great shaggy head appeared over the cusp of the hill.

And I smiled, despite myself. "Hello, Isaiah," I said.

The great dog bounded to me, his tongue dripping into my hand as he sniffed. He galloped away again just as fast, returning to the man who appeared ten paces behind, his peaked cap hiding his face.

I didn't bother to stand. I squinted at him instead. "Patrick," I said evenly. It was difficult to restrain inflection. I wanted so badly to be indifferent to him, unintimidated. Unafraid. Once, he'd only been a brash boy with a double-looped belt.

The scowl failed to mar his features. Cold eyes and all, he'd grown to be as finely carved as a sculpture. Tall, imposing, and wholly masculine.

He came to a standstill, breathing heavily, then raised his eyebrows as though I should be the one to speak next. The sun broke through and kissed his tanned skin, the two of them old friends.

"A walk?" he asked. It was that same flat tenor he'd used in the tunnel, the one that resonated all the way to my bones. "You wanted to take a walk?"

"I did," I smiled sweetly. If it irritated him more, then good. He'd tried to lock me up by myself inside a dark room, after all.

"Your lodgings not to your likin'?" he asked. Isaiah begged at his feet.

"They're lovely," I said. "But I do like to walk."

"Alone, apparently."

"Ah." I nodded. "I did *want* to stay with the boy, but he's awfully skittish. Kept insisting we return."

Patrick hissed something through his teeth, then took a flask from his waistcoat and unscrewed the top. He seemed irritable. Heated. It amused me, though I couldn't explain why. "Seems a little early for liquor."

"No it fuckin' ain't," he murmured, and brought the flask to his lips.

Patrick had a long swig, then took his time stashing it away. All the while, he stared at me with a puzzling expression. It was not a friendly one.

He clicked his tongue, then said, "Well, shall I throw you over my shoulder and drag you back? I'll confess, it's what I fantasized doing on the way over here."

Confidence fled. I swallowed.

"Your cheeks have gone red," he said blandly, shaking his head. "God. That school turn you chaste?"

"It's resentment." I quickly turned my eyes away, tried to banish the heat in my face. "I don't take well to kidnapping." I wasn't sure that he wouldn't, in fact, drag me back to that room with its damned cherry blossom walls. I curled my fingers into the grass.

He stalked toward me then, curved over me, eclipsing the sky, and a thrill fluttered through me. But instead of hauling me upward, he gave a resigned sigh and took the space next to me on the ground, resting an arm on one knee. Isaiah settled in front of him with his head on Patrick's shoe.

He stared out over the town's rooftops. "You can relax," he said. "Wouldn't be wise of me to put hands on a woman who could bury me alive, would it?"

"I suppose I should thank you for the idium," I said slowly.

He gave no reply.

I wet my lips and spoke again. "It was quite a risk. Who knows what I might've done?"

He leaned back on one hand. "Call it a show of good faith. As I said, I need you ready." He closed his eyes for a moment, lifted his face to the sun. The pinch in his expression seemed to melt away.

And I stared at the column of his throat, the stubble that darkened his jaw, the shadows beneath his eyes.

"Was it everythin' you expected?" he asked.

There were lines that joined the corners of his mouth to his nose, more between his eyebrows. It was easy to be lost in the pathways of his face. "No. It's nothing like I expected."

He nodded, opened his eyes. "We filled it in when Tanner declared war."

I blinked. "What?"

"Idia's Canal." Patrick nodded downhill, where the water met the dam. "It's why you gave Sam the slip, ain't it? Why I had to chase you all the way out here."

I shifted uncomfortably, trying not to look at him. "You needn't have chased me at all. I'm not running."

"No," he said, stroking Isaiah's head but looking at me. "You're not." It seemed as though he wanted to say more but didn't. The silence stretched.

I couldn't help but let my eyes stray over him. "You look wretched," I lied. "Tired."

"Didn't sleep. Had some things to tend to."

Something about the way his tongue flicked made it sound ominous. "What kinds of things need tending in the middle of the night?"

He waited a beat before answering. "There's always a problem to fix around here."

"Like what?"

I knew immediately that I would not be privy to whatever "problems" he saw to in the late hours. Not yet. "Leaky pipes," he said.

I wondered how much he controlled, how many people he was responsible for in this town he'd barricaded from the rest of the world.

The skin under Patrick's eyes was purple and heavy. Perhaps it was exhaustion that stopped him from hauling me back to Colson & Sons. In any case, he seemed content for now to settle into the grass, leaning back on his elbows.

A wordless tension fell.

I twisted my fingers in my lap, fumbling for something to say. "How does the water reach the pipes?"

Patrick raised his eyebrows. "It collects in tanks on the roof. The pipes connect to the tank."

"But how does it heat?"

"Roof tiles heat it in the summer. In the winter it passes through a boiler." He went quiet again, in no hurry to say anything, to go anywhere. He only watched me, absentmindedly petting Isaiah.

"What of the light—"

"You don't like the quiet, do you?" he interrupted, his voice swallowing mine whole. There was a grin to his tone, though it did not materialize on his face. "You prattle even more than I remember."

My mouth snapped shut. I scowled.

That grin broke across his face, though he seemed reluctant to let it. "The glare is just the same, though. About as dangerous as a loaded fuckin' pistol."

That smile, the one he tried to hide, made him startlingly new, changed the hue of his eyes. I tried not to pay too much attention to his lips. "You don't like women who speak?"

"Can't fuckin' stand them, truth be told," he said. "They have a way of talking over the stuff they don't want you to hear."

I bristled, my face heating. "Maybe you're just a lousy conversationalist," I said. "Or an arrogant prick. Either one."

He broke out in laughter then. True laughter. "Oh, it's definitely both, but I was just pulling your leg. I don't mind your prattlin'. I just wanted to see that scowl again."

So, we both liked to get beneath each other's skin.

"Why am I here, Patrick?" I asked stiffly. I didn't like the way he made me feel off-kilter. Like he might pull a mask from his face at any moment. "You offered false promises of freedom, and then locked me in a room. We knew each other once. Why not just ask me for whatever you needed? I might've said yes."

He breathed deeply out of his nose and took his time to respond. He had a coin between his fingers, though I didn't see where he'd drawn it from; he simply flipped it from knuckle to knuckle. "You know how long it took me to find you, Nina?" he asked, voice quiet. "Six months. Six whole bloody months."

The answer surprised me and didn't. It surprised me that he'd been so intent on finding me. It didn't because I'd been a ghost. "I move often."

"You do," he agreed. "And you're smart about it. Careful. Don't use the same name twice. Don't use the same clothes, neither. Find new work wherever you go. Never leave your apartment unless you need to. Never talk to anyone." He looked up at me through his eyelashes. "You were a difficult find, Nina." That same weariness seemed to shroud him again. "For better or worse, you're the only one with your particular skillset. I wasn't banking on a few hours of childhood kinship to see the deal through. I need you, Nina."

"To help you win the war?" I asked, my eyes rolling.

His jaw flexed. "You don't think we can do it," he guessed.

"I don't think anyone wins."

"I disagree," Patrick said. "The winner in the end is the one with the most idium."

"Then what do you need me for?" I implored, my heart thudding viciously in my chest. "I'm no Alchemist. Tell me why you brought me here, what you'll have me do. And don't just say 'tunnels and secrets.'"

He caught my stare. "Here it is, then. I need a route into the capital where they won't see us coming. I need your help to free my father, and I need to know where Lord Tanner sleeps at night, so that I can sink a bullet between his eyes before anyone knows I'm there."

If only it were so easy.

I shook my head and looked away. I wasn't a fool. There was more, and he didn't intend to disclose it. "You want my help digging a tunnel into the city," I repeated.

"For now," he said. "You have a good understanding of the National House and its layout. I'll need your help with that, too."

"And how do I know you aren't planning on gunning down every Artisan man, woman, and child on the other side? I won't help you if it's just blood you're after."

"So you *do* have sympathies, then. I suspected you might."

154

I frowned. "Artisans and Craftsmen die just the same," I said. "Their blood doesn't spray any different. I can hardly tell it apart anymore." And I had seen far too much of it already. I ripped a knot of grass from the earth, then closed the crater it left behind with nothing but a thought.

Patrick watched. He swallowed before he spoke. "No one will die that needn't. I'm not mad with revenge."

"Aren't you?" I asked, incredulous. "Sinking a bullet into Lord Tanner sounds an awful lot like revenge."

"My plans for revenge are scratched into the walls of my throat, Nina. I've never spoken them aloud, but I assure you, they are there. And they don't involve the innocent residents of Belavere City."

"Your union had no such reservations when you blew up the school," I reminded him and swallowed thickly.

"It's different now."

"How?"

"Because I'm in charge." He said it with such finality, as though the topic brooked no further argument.

"And what of Domelius Becker?" I asked next. "What will you do with the Alchemist?"

His posture changed. Up until that moment, it seemed he had been leaning in closer and closer. Now, he blinked, turned back to Kenton. "That ain't your concern."

"It is currently *everyone's* concern," I countered.

Patrick smiled carefully, in a way that was meant to cover the anger in his throat, and I was immediately reminded of him as a boy spitting in the dirt. "If it's idium you're worried about, I'll ensure you have what you need, when you need it. Past that, I won't be discussing alchemy." He turned to stake me again with his stare. "And *you* won't be askin'."

I looked away instinctively, but I wasn't done. "What I want to know is, if you have the Alchemist, then why haven't you made yourself an entire army of Artisans?"

He stroked Isaiah's head as he answered. "Do you know how much terranium is needed to make one dose of idium?" he asked.

I realized I didn't. I hated that I didn't.

"Three pounds," he said in the wake of my silence. "The Lords' Army is currently fifty-thousand strong, and a fifth of them are swanks." He looked over at me. "We'd need—"

"Fifteen tons of terranium," I said quietly.

Patrick's eyebrows rose, impressed. "And that'd only match them in magic. Not in number."

I sighed. "The mines wouldn't yield even half that."

"And what *could* be mined is already heavily guarded by the House."

The thought brought me comfort, though I'd never tell him that outright. I quailed to think of what so much unregulated idium could do in the midst of a war. I let out a breath. "So, *you* have the Alchemist, and the House has the terranium. A stalemate."

"For now," Patrick said rigidly, as though a bolt were tightening his jaw.

And therein lay those future plans, after he'd delivered Tanner a bullet.

"If you have no stores of terranium," I said carefully, sensing a looming end to the conversation, "then where did the idium come from? The dose you gave me when you thought me too dumbstruck to refuse?"

Patrick's eyebrows rose. "Would you have refused?"

I pressed my lips together. Shook my head reluctantly.

He grinned wryly. "I didn't mean any coercion by it. I only meant it to quell the aches and pains. I hear idium has wonderful healing properties—"

"How did you get that terranium, Patrick?" I asked once more, and for a moment, it seemed as though he wouldn't answer.

But he clicked his tongue. "By doing terrible things," he said. "But you already knew that, I'm sure."

I rolled my eyes and turned away from him, imagining him stealing into mines and smuggling lumps of ore out in his pockets. It was better than the truth he alluded to, which probably involved blades and guns.

For a moment, we sat in tense silence, a bevy of questions still sloshing around my mouth. When I next looked over, Isaiah had settled his great head on Patrick's knee. Patrick looked near asleep, head tipped back once more, the sun turning his skin golden. He was ruinously handsome. I'd be a fool to deny it.

I said what had perched on the tip of my tongue since the conversation began. "We'd all be better off without it."

Patrick's eyes opened slowly, though he did not look at me.

I continued. "If it were up to me, I'd take all the terranium on the continent and I'd blow it to pieces."

A short laugh escaped him, then another. In the intervals between, he seemed to expect me to take it back. When I didn't, he said, "You can't possibly think so."

I shrugged. "Terranium—idium—it divides us. It's a guillotine. Those in power will always use it to exploit the rest."

"And what of those sick or injured?" he asked. "You'd deny them bluff as well?"

"It's a plight on thousands of households across the Trench," I countered. "There are other, less toxic medicines. Besides"—here, I gave him a pointed look—"are Craftsmen not the strongest among us? The hardiest?"

He smiled ruefully. "That's what they taught us, didn't they? When we were kids. Artisans were the thinkers, but the Craftsmen?" He gave a low whistle. "They were the people of action. No one more capable of toilin' than a Crafter: the only one with the bones and muscle to withstand the hardship."

It was the creed of the House of Lords. The mantra of my Scurry schoolroom teachers.

The Artisans honor Idia's mind, but us? We honor the rest of her.

Who will shift the Earth on its axis, once the idea has been conceived?

I'd rather be weak-minded than weak-boned, my father had sniffed. *Ain't gonna think me way out of the grave, am I?*

"You surprise me," he said eventually. "I thought *you* of all people would see the good in idium. You likely saw the very best of it in that school, in that city. I remember how big your eyes were when we were kids in that courtyard." He was careful not to look my way. "You drank it all in."

"There was much to be amazed by," I said. "Before it all blew up in smoke."

He appeared remorseful for a moment, and I sensed he had more to say on the subject, about the good of idium and how he'd change the world one vial at a time, but instead he said, "You must have been lonely, travelin' around all those years by yourself. I imagine it's why you hate the silence."

I felt suddenly exposed and crossed my arms tightly. "I kept myself occupied."

"Not so easy for a lady like you to stay hidden. To avoid pickin' a side. It's a wonder you kept it up for so long."

"A wonder, indeed." I couldn't stop that needling, burrowing into my flesh.

"Makes me wonder why you bothered at all." His eyes tracked a convoy of sluggish clouds. "Why would you turn your back on the House of Lords, on Tanner, on all Artisans, to go on the run? I can only imagine what they must have asked of you, for you to take off like that."

You would do what is necessary to protect this city, would you not?

I shuddered for only a second, but he saw it. I sank my nails into the palms of my hands until they screamed. "I never gave them the chance to ask it of me, Patrick. I was gone before the dust settled."

He looked at me as though I'd disappointed him, turning his eyes away and making a noise in the back of his throat.

"Play a game with me," he said then. The coin was back in his hand, dancing over his knuckles.

"A game?"

"Yes, Nina, a game. Now, you might look and talk like a rich girl, but we don't have bridge or croquet here in Kenton, so you'll have to settle for a poor man's game."

"Are you claiming poverty?" I scoffed. I flattened the lapel of his well-tailored coat as I said it and thought I saw his neck tense at my touch. "Strutting around with your pocket watch? Never seen a miner's son with such polished shoes."

He sighed. "Do you want to play my game or not, princess?"

Sweet victory. "Fine."

"Heads, you answer a question. Any question." His eyes bore into mine.

"And tails?" I asked.

"Tails, I'll answer one of yours."

I nodded, perhaps too eagerly.

He flipped the coin in the air, and it landed heavily on the ground between us.

"Heads," he said, and the profile of Lord Tanner glistened up at me.

I braced myself.

"What was it like in that school?"

Not the question I'd expected. "Shiny. Flip it again."

Patrick tossed the coin into the air. "Heads. What did they teach you?"

"Life drawing, painting, clay modeling, performing arts, earth Charming," I listed. "Those were my favorites."

He threw the coin in the air. "Heads." I stared at the coin, exasperated. Patrick looked indifferent. "Did you ever think of home while you were there? Did you ever regret your choice to be an Artisan?"

"That's two questions."

"Pick one."

I shifted uncomfortably. "I tried not to think of home. Not much back there to think of."

"Not your family?"

I gave a tight-lipped smile. "Flip the coin."

He did so without looking at it. "Heads. Did it bother you to be surrounded by frauds?"

I stared at the traitorous coin and bristled. I supposed there was little point in lying. "Sometimes."

"Heads. Did *you* ever feel like a fraud?"

"Does this coin have another side?"

He flipped Lord Tanner's face over. A canary glinted back at me.

"Answer the question," Patrick said softly.

Anger burgeoned between my ribs. "Every day there. And all the ones since."

He nodded. Another test, it seemed. One I seemed to have passed this time. He tossed the coin. Lord Tanner's profile sat face up in the grass.

"God, have mercy—"

"Did you ever think of leaving?" he asked.

I sighed. "No."

"And did you ever think of me?"

The coin lay forgotten.

Catastrophe waited between us, something that ought not be touched or turned over. The grass whispered, my chest ached, and Patrick's eyes were more all-encompassing than the redolent sky.

I bit my bottom lip, and his eyes traced the movement. Then I took the coin from the grass and tossed it into the air. "Tails," I said. The spell broke, though he moved no farther away. "Do you truly believe your father is alive?"

He spoke without blinking, lips barely moving. "He's alive," he said. "I only need to know where he's being held."

"And you'll tunnel beneath?"

"And *we'll* tunnel beneath." He gestured to the coin before me. I tossed it once more into the air and watched it land. Heads.

"What did he ask you to do, Nina?"

A jolt of panic rattled through me. It wasn't necessary to ask who *he* was. The venom coating the word was clarity enough. It seemed Patrick wasn't expecting an answer, or at least not an honest one. Already he turned away, the question futile.

I wished he looked as off-balance as I felt. I hated feeling so unsteady while he remained completely self-possessed. Did he not feel the ground shifting beneath us?

With effort, he tore his eyes from the horizon, extracting a cigarette from his pocket and lighting it. The smell reminded me of Scurry, of the single-room town house I'd been born to—bricks and plaster impregnated in ash.

He turned with an open case, offering me one, but I shook my head in distaste.

"You don't smoke?" He raised his eyebrows, surprised.

I shrugged. "Can't stand the smell."

"Have mercy," he muttered, throwing the cigarette into the grass and stamping it out with his foot. He stood then, Isaiah following suit. The dog lapped at his fingers, expecting adventure. "Come on, Scurry girl," Patrick said, offering his hand. Confidently. Expectantly.

We were twelve in a courtyard again, only this time, the name was a caress, the rumble of his voice cradling the words.

"Is this the part where you drag me back?"

For a moment, he seemed to consider it. "Temptin', but I get the impression you'd only pick the locks. You said you wanted to see Kenton Hill, didn't you?"

I stared at his hand like it bore teeth. "And you're planning on escorting me?"

It seemed he'd grown bored of my hesitancy, because he bent to take my hand from my lap and pulled me upright.

His hand remained around mine for longer than necessary, thumb pressed to knuckles, fingers curling over mine.

Every inch of his skin burned hot.

"If you plan to skulk about town, I'd better come with you."

"And what if someone recognizes the infamous earth Charmer?"

"Who, Nina Clarke?" he said, finally dropping my hand. "Never met her."

CHAPTER 22

NINA

We walked slowly back alongside the canal, keeping a careful distance between us. The men fishing at its edge barely paid us any mind as we passed them.

"Is there no river for them to fish in?" I asked Patrick. Ahead, the tall brick walls came closer, riddled in lichen and soot, slowly blacking out the sky.

Patrick shook his head. "No water outside the canals," he said. "We're too far from the mountains, and too high. If I was a godly man, I'd say Idia chose this place to build her canals because we needed them most."

I peered at him. "You don't believe there's a God?"

Patrick chuckled, low and bitter. "Oh, I believe there's a God," he said. "But I'd spit in his hand before I shook it."

I got the sense that I should ask no more questions about that, though I desperately wanted to. I thought of what I'd seen in all those towns and wanted to tell him that I felt the same.

"I've never seen a canal so clean," I said instead. "How did you manage it?"

"We have experts."

"Experts in drawing pollution from the water?"

"Something like that."

"And if there's no other water, then why choke it off?" I wondered. "Your farms must be suffering."

"We don't have farms, Nina. The land here's no good for farming. No good for much but coal."

I looked at him incredulously. "But how are you feeding all these people, if you've blocked all method of import?"

"Now, I never said there were no imports, did I?"

Oh, of course, I thought. *The tunnels.*

He grinned. "Always hungerin' for all the things you don't know." He shook his head. "Have you forgotten all those union members outside this town? We ain't the only ones fighting the fight. There are plenty who are willing to trade."

We reached a skinny path between the canal and the brick facade, and he gestured for me to go ahead of him. His breath whispered against my neck from behind, and I shivered. "So you make your deals with them, and they pass along their goods?"

"In exchange for coal," he said, "and safe passage." The words crept over my shoulder, slipped beneath my collar.

"Safe passage to where?" I asked, stopping halfway down the alley. I turned and looked at him.

He was staring ahead at the busy street where people hurried on foot and horse and newer modes of transport back and forth in an endless parade. One seemed to be operating a one-wheeled apparatus with his feet alone. Patrick turned wary, forehead creased. "To wherever the tunnels can take them," he said. "Any town in the northwest, really, so long as it's this side of the Gyser River."

"That's how you manage it?" I asked. "All of it? The weapons, the communications. It's all underground."

He tsked, and his jaw flexed distractingly. It drew my eyes downward. "I thought you'd have figured that much out by now."

I thought of the miles upon miles of tunnels that would need to exist between towns, the impossibility of such a complex network, all buried beneath Lord Tanner's feet.

"The tunnels have saved people," he said, taking a small step back, reestablishing the distance. "Entire villages. When the Lords' Army comes in, the rebel towns have a way out. They can escape or hide until the gunfire stops. Have you ever seen a town razed, Nina? Have you seen what their police do to them?"

I had. I'd watched it unfold around me, just barely avoiding the raining missiles and exploding cement. Girls carried away by their ankles, boys shouting over the punctured chests of fathers. Lines of rebels with their knees sinking in mud, gun barrels to their heads. Screams bursting the walls of your middle ear.

Patrick nodded. "So you've seen," he said. "And it's why you couldn't take their side."

I didn't like the way he said it; like he knew me. Like he'd already unraveled all my secrets, there for the taking. "You haven't mentioned why I can't take *your* side," I told him, stepping intentionally across the boundary he'd created. I wanted his insides to flinch in my presence as mine did in his, and I got my wish. His nostrils flared; a fire lit behind his eyes. He suddenly looked starved.

"You speak like your union hasn't done anything as terrible," I said cuttingly. It was true that I'd seen towns wiped from the Trench by the Lords' infantrymen. I'd seen all the blood and the bullets spraying. But there was a time before all this, when the cords of my soul hadn't yet been severed, when I didn't know what death looked like, and the first to show me was the Miners Union on the day of the first attack. "If you have any misconceptions that I sympathize with you, I should dispel them. I've seen both sides of this fight. You both bleed the same. Both scream the same. Both leave women without husbands and children without parents. You're two sides to the same coin."

Patrick looked at my finger now prodding his chest, pushing the first button of his waistcoat against the bone of his sternum. When he looked back up at me, his eyes had softened somewhat, the fire tempered. "I don't believe you," he said.

I wanted to punch him. He held up his hands to placate me, clearly reading the violence in my expression.

"I only meant that I don't believe you're without sympathy. You likely have too much of it. I can see it in your fists," he looked down to where I'd bunched them. "In your throat," he said, and I couldn't help but swallow as his eyes touched it. I was burning, burning. "You're a miner's daughter," he reminded me. "Ain't never met one not filled with all the soot their daddies brought home with them."

Suddenly I was a child again, and my father sat staring at the stove with a slack jaw and wet eyelashes.

Patrick nodded knowingly. "I bet you remember what it was like when he came home—filthy, the soles of his shoes separating from the damp. And you'd listen to him cough and wonder if he'd drown in it this time. And then he'd start swallowing anything wet. He'd sink himself in booze and bad bluff, and you'd be happy for him to do it, because it quieted the rattling in his chest, didn't it? It made it so he'd sleep, eh?"

Twelve years of evenings just like it. Each night the same as the last. My father growing steadily thinner and less present. I pressed my lips together to stop their shaking.

"You know exactly why we started this fight," Patrick said now. "You're just too scared to join it."

I swung at him, throwing my fist around in a wide, wild arc. Instead of hearing it connect with his jaw, I found myself wrapped up, my back to his front, his hands clamping over my wrists, his lips by my ear.

And every muscle of his chest and stomach pressed against me. We were both burning, our skin flaming beneath the fabric.

"Get off me!" I heaved. "Crafter scum."

"Crafter scum, eh?" He snickered, though there was anger there, too. It broiled between us, mixed with a hundred other things too tangled to examine. I struggled to escape his hold.

"Easy," he said, as though I were a skittish horse. "God, woman. Did your daddy never teach you to punch a man?"

I wanted to tear his eyes out. "Let go of me, Patrick. *Now.*"

"I intend to, Scurry girl," he said. "And we'll speak of other things if your sensibilities can take no more, but know this—" And here he pulled me closer, so that I could feel all the hot points of his thighs and hips and the solid wall of his chest. "I'm making it my mission to change your mind about us Crafter scum, and about the union as well. Because I know you, Nina Harrow," he said. "Better than you think I do. And I know you'll pick the side worth fightin' for."

Slowly, my muscles slackened.

He let me go then, gently loosening the cuffs of his fingers and letting me slide my wrists free.

But his hands lingered near my waist a moment longer, and I felt the current of his pounding blood through my clothes. And for a fleeting moment, I imagined his hands sliding beneath them, running up my sides, around to my stomach. My breath sounded like a gasp. "I thought I'd already picked a side," I said. My voice was someone else's.

There was a moment of hesitance, and then his hands abruptly fell away. A careful distance resumed. "Perhaps out of necessity." It sounded strained. Guttural. "But soon, you'll be enlisting for the cause. I'll make sure of it."

· · · · · ·

As soon as our feet found the cobbles, I felt Patrick's hand at my forearm. Without breaking stride he fitted my arm into the crook of his. "Don't get ideas," he said quietly, watching the people that passed, people who looked at him and tipped their caps. "If you walk these streets, you walk them on my arm." Isaiah trotted along beside Patrick, one eye on his owner. Everyone watched him, it seemed.

"Why?" I asked. I didn't like the way my skin pricked at his touch. I imagined sinking into the folds of his coat. Being swallowed by his shadow. It was both unnerving and . . . tantalizing.

No, not tantalizing. Just unnerving.

"Because you're quite recognizable, Nina. And there are a few around here that don't take too kindly to Artisans."

An image of those wanted posters floated to mind, and I shuddered. "You receive the bulletins here?"

"Of course," Patrick said. "Our Scribbler gets the same bulletins as any other province."

My head turned sharply. "Aren't you worried they'll alert the House of—?"

"There's only one," Patrick interjected. "And she's loyal to us."

A noise of exasperation escaped me. My eyes began darting to the streetlamps and shopwindows, expecting to find my own face staring back at me.

"I don't allow Artisan propaganda to make its way onto the street," he reassured, watching my face closely. "You needn't worry."

"But if—"

"Just stay on my arm," he said, looking ahead, "and you'll be fine."

A woman holding a basket of folded clothes passed them; she nodded once to Patrick, then looked resolutely at her feet. "They won't come with their pitchforks and fire?"

Patrick patted his pockets for cigarettes, then seemed to remember that I didn't like them. "If they think you're with me, then they won't even look at you."

We passed a scrapyard and took a right turn, where the streets were lined with horse carts, coal bins, men in soiled shirts bellowing in accents even thicker than Patrick's. They shoveled coal and pressed iron rods into open stoves. They softened metal and hammered it with oversize mallets. The cobbles disappeared under thick layers of grime, and the sound was immense—a symphony of metalworkers.

It was clearly a part of town a lady did not venture to. Yet, I walked through its middle on Patrick's arm and no man came to leer at me. There were no shouts in my direction, no whistles or gestures or threats. Instead, the Crafters only continued in their work. It seemed Patrick was a stern parting water wherever he went. No one stepped into his path.

One factory loomed larger than the rest, its large doors open to the many workers within. Chimneys sprouted from its extensive roof, chugging smoke into the sky. The entire building seemed out of place, too big for a small town, parts and scraps patched together to make a giant.

Patrick saw me staring. "The Coal Works," he said easily. "The pride and joy of Kenton Hill, actually."

I frowned at all the smoke. Inside, giant copper drums towered over the workers and lined the walls. Their plumes fed into those chimneys above. Even from here, I could feel the heat of them, could smell the sweat of the Crafters.

Like all the buildings in Kenton, the gut of the factory was networked in those same copper and steel pipes, but this time they fed into the ground. They were great tentacles that snaked from the belly of the coal drums and sunk into the floor, presumably feeding gas underground.

"This is how you light the town," I marveled, more to myself than to Patrick.

He nodded. "And how we heat the boilers, and the stoves."

I laughed. "It's brilliant."

"It's a work in progress," Patrick said. "Coal gases are toxic. We've been trying to learn the best ways to keep this factory stable. You ever seen a gas explosion?"

I shook my head.

"It ain't pretty."

"You're inventors," I murmured.

"I can't take credit for the Coal Works," he said, though my incredulity seemed to satisfy him. "This is the genius of the oldest Colson brother."

They were a family of innovators, then. Of enterprise. It was little wonder they had taken hold of Kenton Hill and rallied an army. People in brink towns wouldn't turn away the promise of more warmth in the winter.

"Come on," he said, glancing at his pocket watch. "Day's waning."

We walked for quite a time, crossing canals on latticework bridges and weaving down busy lanes.

I looked about all I could. I breathed deeply, even if some of it was ash. We passed residences and entered a street of merchants, shopwindows of every shape jutting out onto the pathways with their bold lettering. A milliner displayed an aviary of hats. An apothecary and chemist competed side by side, their windows starkly contrasting. One held a cage of live mice, glass jars of minced plants, and a nude picture of Idia. The other held warning posters for symptoms of diphtheria, cures for dry mouth and lunacy, and a rather punishing breathing machine, if the metal braces were any indication.

I slowed our walk to a crawl to look closer at everything, to peer in and see the people lining the counters. The trolley rattled past. Passengers jumped from its carriage in hard-soled boots. A slack-eyed preacher leaned on a dustbin and hollered half-hearted predictions of doomsday.

War didn't exist here. Of all Kenton's oddities, this was the most notable. The patrons went about their business as though the nation's conflict were just a column of newsprint.

"It seems unfair that you can live this way," I said outside a cobbler's shop, watching as women met in the street, kissing cheeks. "Your union started this war, and yet its hometown is the only place granted amnesty?"

I turned to find Patrick staring. I hadn't realized he'd been looking at me so closely. It made my face heat, but I didn't want to give him the satisfaction of looking away.

"You still look at everythin' the same," he said offhandedly. "See through it all."

I wondered if I was meant to respond. "Is that going to be a problem?"

To my surprise, he nodded, leading me across the street, where a warehouse waited with open doors. "To be sure."

The warehouse was more a barn somehow dropped into the middle of a shopping district. Its doors were bolted back to allow crowds of people to funnel to its middle, where table upon table waited, laden with produce, meat, thread, steel tools, china, chickens. People queued in short lines before each, talking briefly with vendors before making their trade.

There seemed to be no particular theme, no rhyme or reason to the order of items.

"What is this place?" I asked, barely aware of Patrick guiding me to the side near the paint-stripped walls.

"A market."

I watched patrons accept their wares and leave without payment, stuffing goods into their baskets. They hopped from queue to queue, collecting corn, then sprouts, then leeks, and potatoes. "They don't pay? Is it charity?"

He chuckled humorlessly, and it fell over my shoulder, curled into my ear. "Not charity. Just fair share. None of us here are wanting anymore."

I watched as mothers came and left with full baskets, none taking more than the others. "You're communists," I accused.

Patrick tilted his head. "Yes and no. We don't share everythin'."

"But you share food," I guessed. "And coal, water, gas. No one pays."

"They pay for the whiskey," he said, "and the hats."

"And no one goes hungry," I finished for him.

"No one goes hungry." He nodded. "And no one goes cold." I found myself watching him as he spoke, his tone fading into something more resonant. "Everyone does their share, takes their share. The businesses are still independent, and they trade how they want to. But everyone is fed and given a chance." He looked out at the array of vendors. Or volunteers, I supposed. "What they do with it is up to them."

I observed the tables, the emptying crates beneath. "It doesn't seem like enough food for an entire town."

"It ain't," he said, and I detected something heavier in his voice. "Scottie and Otto will be back this evenin' with more from Dunnitch."

"All of it needs to be brought in?"

"Yes. Though finding good harvest is half the trouble. The Lords' Army has been aiming their Charmers at them—flooding the pastures and crops or setting fires if the towns announce a strike. We only get pieces left over after the Artisans have taken what they like."

"But you said no one goes hungry." And certainly, it did not seem like the people of Kenton Hill went hungry.

"We make a lot of deals, Nina, in a lot of different places." He lit a cigarette then, unable to bear the temptation any longer. "We find it, however far we need to go."

"And I imagine it's rather difficult to say no to the leader of the Miners Union."

"Son of the chairman," he reminded me, exhaling a gust. "You hungry?"

I was rarely not.

"Come," he said, taking my arm once more. "There's a teahouse next door."

CHAPTER 23

PATRICK

The teahouse was, unfortunately, filled to the brim with wives and their mothers and the widows who'd ventured out for the day, and Patrick was loathe to step into their henhouse.

There was no quicker way to stir gossip than to step into a teahouse.

But Nina looked weary. She limped slightly as she walked, no doubt suffering in shoes that did not quite fit. There was a purpling in the corners of her eyes that Patrick suspected came from the clobbering Scottie had given her. He ground his teeth.

"Stay," he said to Isaiah, and the dog sat heavily by a lamppost.

Patrick thought it unlikely Nina would allow him to take her to a doctor. She'd evidently missed the one he'd sent to her room that morning. But he supposed he could offer her a chair, a warm drink, some fucking tea cake.

He sighed internally and stepped inside.

The moment he crossed the threshold, he was accosted. A widow named Mrs. Hedley stood from her wicker-backed chair, ignoring her tea, the pleas of her companion, and took two tight steps toward him.

Her hot hand collided with Patrick's cheek, and he bore it with good grace, blinking back the reverberations. "Hello, Mrs. Hedley," he greeted her.

Patrick was aware the shop had fallen quiet, all conversations halted.

172

The entire place seemed to hold its breath in wait for Mrs. Hedley's repercussions.

Colson & Sons were famous for their repercussions. But they weren't in the habit of dragging widows down Main Street by their housecoats.

"You cut my son lose, you hear me?" Mrs. Hedley spluttered, nostrils flaring. She was raised up on her toes to better raze him down. "Turn him out. I won't have him workin' for you!" A hairpin sprung free, making her look altogether unhinged.

Nina moved closer to Patrick's side, clearly mystified. He wondered how insulted she'd be if he pushed her back out the door and out of harm's way.

Deciding against it, Patrick sighed. "Sam is his own man. If he no longer wishes to work for me, all he has to do is say so."

Spit collected on the woman's lips. "He's a *child*!"

"He's eighteen now, Donna," Patrick said, quieter now. He nodded his head politely and stepped around her. "He ain't a kid."

Mrs. Hedley reared up, her hand raising of its own accord. "You'll have him go into the ground alongside his father!" she screamed, but before she could land a second slap, her friend had wrapped her arms around Mrs. Hedley's middle. In a tangle of handbags and hats, they wrestled out of the teahouse and into the street. Mrs. Hedley kept bellowing, one swollen finger jabbing the air in Patrick's direction, *"Fuckin' Colsons took my husband! You're not havin' my boy. You hear me, Pat?"*

He heard her. Every bloody word.

And so did Nina.

She stared through the windows, confusion on her face. "What does she mean?" Nina asked. "What happened to her husband?"

Patrick bit down a curse. This foray into Kenton was meant to charm her.

"We should sit," he said, leading her through tiny spaces between patrons, to a table crowded by a pink-papered wall and a mounted cabinet filled to the brim with figurines and decades of dust.

Nina took her seat without protest. She even waited for Patrick to take his before demanding answers. "Where is her husband?" she repeated tersely.

"Dead," he sighed. The rest of the teahouse had resumed conversation at half-volume; he felt their eyes on the back of his neck.

Nina paid them no mind. She seemed to be trying to thread a bolt into his forehead, with the aim to crack it open and see inside. A pause, and then, "Did you *kill* him? Is that what the Colsons do?"

"This is hardly the place to discuss murder. I brought you here for tea."

"I'd rather know the man I'm agreeing to work for," she said. "You can keep the tea."

It was hot in the enclosed space. Her ringlets curled tighter in the humidity, falling from the clasp at her neck into her face. They made her look more herself.

Patrick flexed his fingers. "All right," he said slowly. "Did I kill Mrs. Hedley's husband? Sam's father? The answer is yes, and no."

She sat back, seeming to take Patrick in anew. Perhaps she was reshaping that image of a twelve-year-old kid in her mind, carving out space for more. "What happened to him?"

Patrick shrugged. "Went into the tunnels," he said. "Didn't come out."

"Tunnels *you* ordered him into," she guessed.

"Yes. Tunnels I ordered him into."

She scowled. "And they collapsed? She blames you for that?"

"People have to blame someone."

She went quiet and bit her lip, deep in thought. He could almost see the tangle beneath her brow being teased out piece by piece.

"Patty," said a voice. Mrs. McCallister, the tea shop owner, was suddenly hovering over his shoulder. "Haven't seen you here in a while."

"With good reason," he sighed.

"You certainly stir things up, eh?" she glanced at Nina, then did a double take. "Is that—"

"A good friend of mine," he said curtly. Mrs. McCallister's mouth closed, and she nodded once. "What can I get you?"

"Tea," Patrick said. "And cake."

Mrs. McCallister rolled her eyes. "What *kind*?"

Nina smiled at her. "I saw some lavender bread in the display," she said. "It looks beautiful."

Mrs. McCallister brightened immediately. "Oh, it ought to, love. Was me Ma's recipe."

Nina's head tilted to the side. "How do you make it rise so perfectly? Mine always fall dead flat."

"It's in the yeast. Lager is better than stout."

Nina's eyebrows rose in fascination. "Really?"

The women chatted a minute longer, discussing the intricacies of lavender cake, and all the while, Patrick watched Nina. He watched her smile stretch and her cheeks rise. He saw the way she held her spine straight, her neck long, shoulders back. She had an elegance about her, one that didn't match Kenton Hill. Too regal for pubs and tunnels. Artisan-hewn, so much so that the Scurry in her was barely recognizable.

But it was there. Patrick could see it.

Then again, he was looking for it. Probably closer than he ought to.

There were specks of pigment across her nose, beneath her eyes—faded but discernible. Every so often her Eastern tongue got the better of her, elongating her vowels. She looked people in the eye when she spoke, her chin level and not floating somewhere up with God. All of it reminded Patrick of that courtyard girl—the one whose hand he'd held in Belavere City. The one whose cheek he'd kissed.

The one he'd thought of every day since.

"Pat?" Mrs. McCallister was saying. She was waiting for the answer to a question he hadn't heard. Nina stared back at him, amused. "I'll have what the lady is having," Patrick said.

Mrs. McCallister walked away with a knowing twinkle in her eyes.

Lord, Patrick admonished himself. *She's just a woman, Patty. Like any other.* But he shouldn't look at her so closely, or she might recognize the wanting.

"So," Nina said now. "You've started a revolution. You're feeding the hungry. Protecting allied towns with your tunnels and bolstering ingenuity within your own walls."

Patrick's eyebrow rose. "Makes me sound like a bloody hero."

"You'd have me believe you were, wouldn't you?"

God help him, but Patrick enjoyed it. The challenge. The prickling aggression.

He leaned closer until she was the only one who could hear his reply. "I told you I would try to get you on our side," he said. "But I won't trick you. I'm no hero."

"Then what are you? Why are these people so afraid of you?"

"Because I kill their husbands and drag their children out of their rooms in the night."

"The truth," she demanded. Her voice was sharp as a guillotine, slicing the air in two.

Patrick almost smiled. "All right," he began. "The truth is, my family is in the business of justice."

She frowned at him. "What does that mean?"

"Sometimes it means feedin' people, helpin' them find safety," he said. "Other times, it means dynamite and bad deals and men with bullets between their eyes."

He paused, waiting for it to sink in. He saw the fear when she swallowed, when the gooseflesh rose along the column of her neck.

"Oftentimes," he continued, "the business requires me to do both, and the people here know it. They've seen it. That inspires fear in a lot of 'em. But it inspires trust, too. The village needs somethin' big and bad to stalk about in the night. They feel safer havin' it, even if they're scared of it." Patrick looked around at the guests of the teahouse. "As you said, the war hasn't touched this town, and they know they have Colson and Sons to thank."

"The big bad thing in the night," Nina echoed.

Patrick nodded. "That's the whole of it. I do sorry things for the greater good of this town, and that's all you need to know."

"And what about the rest of the world?"

"That's someone else's village."

The tea arrived in chipped cups and mismatched saucers, but steam rose pleasingly from the bread, and Nina's attention was absorbed. She placed her hands carefully in her lap, as if to keep them from clawing at the food.

Patrick scowled. "Waiting for somethin'?"

Her eyes did not leave the plate. She must be starving. "Would you like—"

"Just eat, Nina."

And she did. Artisan etiquette be damned, she nearly devoured the slice whole.

She grinned, satisfied, when the food was gone. "Lord, that's good."

"They don't have lavender cake in your big city?"

"I haven't been to the city in seven years," she said, dusting crumbs from her fingers. "We can stop pretending I've been living a life of luxury, if you please."

The clatter of the door ricocheting off plasterboard interrupted further conversation. A gust of dry, cold wind swept through the tables, danced among legs, and Patrick turned to find Otto in the entrance, chest heaving, cap in hand. "Patty," he huffed, looking over the heads of other patrons. He paid no mind to the groups of people, who stared aghast and backed their chairs away, expecting trouble.

And who could blame them? Otto was made for trouble.

That was what he'd told Patrick the day he'd caught Otto thieving cigarettes from the market. He'd been barely seventeen then, thin as a post, teeth bared. *You're asking for a whole lotta trouble, thieving from John Colson*, Patrick had told him.

Was made for trouble, he'd spat. He'd scrapped like a prizefighter all the way back to the hotel, had stopped only when the barrel of a pistol was pointed at him. Patrick's father had taken one long look at the boy and said, *Trouble is just what we need.*

Patrick stood.

"There're hawkers in the market," Otto said simply, and every eye in the teahouse turned to Patrick.

Problems and fixes.

"Stay here," he told Nina, swallowing his tea in one gulp.

She was already on her feet. Already rounding the table. "No," she said firmly.

"God, help me."

Patrick threw a handful of coins onto the table, wove back through the diners, and followed Otto out onto the street.

"*Hawkers*, Patty."

"I heard you," he said, seething, striding back toward the market. "Keep the lady away."

Patrick could hear the staccato of Nina's boots following close behind. Otto dropped back to intercept her.

"Touch me, and I'll rip a hole in the earth beneath your feet," Nina told him, her voice deceptively sweet.

Patrick groaned, then held a hand up for Otto. "Let her be," he growled.

If she wanted to see who Colson & Sons were, then let her.

Hawkers were a growing thorn in the side of Kenton Hill. Lately they seemed to lurk in every dark corner, every dripping alley, but never were they so bold as to trade in the open market.

They were getting brave. An example would need to be made.

Hawkers traded bluff, or at least, they claimed to. It was once intentionally rationed out to miners before they entered the tunnels, which suited the wives. Where there was less liquor, there was less gambling, less holes in their walls, less piss in the bed. It seemed a welcome compensation until the men stopped waking up. The wives would find their husbands wide-eyed and staring in the morning, lips still stained the color of ink.

The Artisans had long ago stemmed the influx of bluff to the mining towns, but it leaked through the gaps between their fingers. It found its way down the canals and into the veins of those who still craved a quiet head. Those like Gunner, who still saw walls collapsing all around them.

With terranium stores now as scarce as idium, the hawkers' bluff was even more diluted, more toxic, cut with a cocktail of opium and arsenic and whatever else could be found.

Patrick stalked back through the barn doors into the market and spied them immediately.

Two hawkers, both men. They stood in long coats by oil barrels with chalk on their boots. A single chalk line across one's boot signaled to those who knew—it was a silent message between dealer and buyer. One of them was Ferris Manley. The last time he'd been caught dealing, he'd lost one of his remaining teeth for his efforts. Evidently, it had not been warning enough, since he now stood in broad daylight, chalking his boots.

The other hawker saw Patrick coming and had the good sense to bolt. He had slipped out of reach before Otto could give chase.

"Leave him," Patrick barked to Otto. "We'll catch up with him later." He needed Otto to stand by Nina.

Ferris looked like he'd swallowed a hornet. His mouth fell open, revealing the few teeth that remained.

"Good God, man," Patrick said, stopping a foot away. "You smell like a pig."

Ferris had the decency to quail. His fists clenched at his sides. He looked around for help that wouldn't arrive. "Pat," he said, nodding warily. "I've just come from the stables."

"Aye," Patrick said. "Shovelin' shit today, were you? You haven't thanked me yet, for getting you that job."

Ferris swallowed. "Thank you." There was anger in those watery eyes, far more than there should be for a man in his current position. Fear and dumb rage wrestled within him.

"Now, Ferris," Patrick warned, heat rising in him by the second. Soon, the world would go red. "The last time I caught you sellin', I was very generous. I swapped your bad bluff for the horse shit and gave you another means to make a living, didn't I?"

Ferris turned puce. "He took me fuckin' tooth," he seethed, pointing a shaking finger at Otto. "With a pair o' pliers."

"Only one," Patrick agreed. "A fair trade, I'd say, for all the shit you'd strewn through Main Street. Now I come and find you spreadin' it round the market as well?"

Fear won. Ferris held up his hands. "Please, Pat," he uttered. "I owe some money to . . ."

"To who?" Patrick asked, though he knew the answer. The fake bluff came from the coppers, and the police weren't dumb enough to sell it themselves.

Ferris's lips pressed tightly together. "That job you got me pays next to nothin'."

"And yet it's the only one you're worthy of in this town."

Anger took the stage. It rose up Ferris's neck and spilled out his mouth. "Fucking *Colsons*," he spat, though the words quivered. "You think you're better than any of—"

He didn't finish the sentence. Patrick's fist landed squarely in Ferris's mouth and sent him reeling, falling backward over barrels and onto the ground.

Vaguely, Patrick heard the collective gasps of the people nearby, the crack of his knuckles against Ferris's nose, cheeks, jaw, but he only saw red. He only felt heat and aching adrenaline in his shoulders, in his fists. He felt the wet pulp of flesh beneath his knuckles, and nothing else.

Not until a hand began pulling intently at his back.

"*Patrick!*" someone called, frightened. "Patrick. Stop!"

Then the ground quaked.

A collective shout rent the air as the ground swelled and settled, a monstrous groan emitting from its depths. The tables toppled. Wares spilled across the ground. Dust was shaken free from the rafters above and rained down on their heads. But it was only a moment. A second of noise and movement. There and then gone, as though they were all the contents of a bottle that had been picked up and shaken.

"Patrick!" Nina said again, though this time, she stood over him. Her hand gripped Patrick's collar. "Enough."

She looked scared.

I tried to tell you, he thought.

Ferris was crawling backward. But it was not Patrick he stared at, horror-stricken. Instead, he stared through swelling flesh at Nina, blood bubbling on his lips. "That's—" he stammered, his elbow collapsing beneath him. "She—"

Patrick stood and blocked Nina from view. "You stick to shovelin' the shit in the stables, Ferris." He bent to take the man's collar in his hand. "Next time, it's a bullet, not a fist." A river of blood spilled over the man's chin.

Patrick pulled open Ferris's coat and took the bluff from his pockets. The man shook beneath him, barely clinging to consciousness. He tried to speak, though his tongue was uncooperative. "Thasss . . . Thas Nina—"

"No," Patrick said. "Don't say her name." Then his fist came down one last time, and Ferris went slack.

The market had emptied of patrons. Only a few vendors remained to collect strewn produce, but they averted their eyes.

"Boss?" said Otto, a toothpick between his lips. "Want me to take him somewhere?"

Patrick shook his head, then took a handkerchief from his pocket to wipe his hands clean. "Leave him," he said. He'd let the others see the chalk on Ferris's boots. "Take all this to the canal and throw it in." Patrick passed over the bluff in its small brown paper parcels.

Otto nodded and left quickly, whistling as he went.

Patrick let out a sigh, tension gathering in his shoulders. Then, finally, he turned to face her, wondering what expression she might wear.

He found disgust. Fear.

Fuck.

Before he could stop her, she stalked past him out into the street.

Better that she understands, he thought, though acid trickled down his throat, eating holes through his insides.

CHAPTER 24

NINA

Dim afternoon light leaked through Kenton Hill's streets as we made our way back to Colson & Sons. Isaiah led Patrick and me, and I kept my eyes straight ahead, determined not to see the swell of his knuckles.

He's a dangerous man. It should have come as no surprise.

He was a revolutionary, a mob leader, and a miner. Most miners had more muscle than they could be trusted with.

He isn't a boy anymore. I reminded myself. *He tried to tell you.*

So, he was the judge and the executioner. I wondered how often he broke eye sockets like it was a transaction.

Kenton Hill was a town run by one man. I wondered if he knew how unbalanced it was, to have collected so much control, to be the sole puppeteer. Had he considered how easy it would be for someone to snip all the strings when only one hand held them?

I folded my arms over my chest rather than take his arm. I was wire-taut.

Would he have pummeled that man to death? He certainly seemed intent on doing so. And over what? A bit of bad bluff?

I thought of the man in the pub, quailing beneath Patrick's gaze, Sam's puce-faced mother, the hawker's head as it hit the dirt. Was this the Colsons' idea of peace?

Kenton Hill suddenly didn't seem so miraculous as the light faded. The copper and steel works lost their gleam.

Even with the waning daylight, the townsfolk had not slowed. The laneways kept their frenetic pace, and I was shocked to remember there was no curfew here, not like the ones imposed elsewhere. Even so, a particular buzz wove its way from conversation to conversation as we passed.

"Jack, are you headed to the meetin'?"

"Meetin's at eight, you dunce, not seven!"

"Another meetin'? Not that I'm complainin'."

I frowned. "What meeting?" I said without looking at Patrick.

"Town meeting," he offered. There was a cigarette between his lips that he lit with a flourish. "At the hotel."

"Run by you?"

His eyelids seemed heavy. Smoke billowed from his lips. "In lieu of the chairman."

"And what's the meeting about?"

He shook his head minutely. I got the impression that I exhausted him. "The usual," he said. "The coming winter, food rationing. Mostly people come to complain, and then we fix whatever's broken." He talked about it like it was a millstone he was tied to.

I squared my shoulders. "I'd like to go."

"I bet you would." He said no more, just puffed on his cigarette.

I gritted my teeth. "I've got my own complaints to air."

"Oh, I don't doubt it." He looked skyward as he walked. The floating lights were beginning to spark to life of their own accord. For a moment I was distracted by the improbability that they should exist. "It's beautiful," I admitted, trying not to sound too complimentary.

Patrick watched me as though I were mystifying. I wished he'd stop. I was trying to keep my blood cool, my pulse slow. I wanted my wits about me, and they were quick to scramble in his presence.

Was it just that he was dangerous? Had I become one of those desperate women clamoring to feel alive? Wasting in idleness so severe that anything thrilled me?

How pitiful. And yet.

Perhaps it was merely his looks—not clean-cut, but intense. It struck me anew with each glance. A sharp, vicious beauty. The destructive kind. By day's end, I'd be peppered through with shot.

Maybe it was just the tether I'd kept with the Patrick of my youth. The softer Patrick, the skinny kid with dirty hair. Glimpses of the boy made me more sympathetic toward the man.

"Whatever your grievances, you can write 'em in a letter and send them to me," Patrick said now.

I stopped on the path. Patrick took two strides, then turned to me with apparent irritation.

"Why can't I come?" I was fully aware of how petulant I sounded.

"Because you ain't a resident," he said, stamping the cigarette beneath his boot. "And your face will distract the entire pub from the agenda."

"I'll sit in a dark corner, then."

"You'll sit in your room," he said. "And I'll have a doctor come see you."

"I don't need a doctor."

"Nevertheless, you'll see one." Already he was walking again. "You've had your time on the town, exactly as you asked."

I scoffed. "Did you truly think I'd be placated by *one* small outing?"

"And what a fine outin' it was," he said grandly. "I bought you tea and cake."

"And clobbered a man blind."

He turned and found me one pace behind. His chest was an inch from my nose. "You'll wait in your room for the doctor."

A different woman might have given in then, their stomach shriveling as mine did. "You planning to carry me up there?" I asked. "Throw me over your shoulder?"

His eyes flashed. "You say that like it isn't *exactly* what I'd like to do."

I swallowed. "It's a lot of stairs, Patrick. You wouldn't manage."

"Careful." He crouched until his nose was level with mine, his lips a hairsbreadth away. "That sounded an awful lot like a challenge."

Heat washed over me, a thousand small flares sputtering beneath the skin. I narrowed my eyes. Tried to pretend like I wasn't on fire. "You wouldn't dare."

"But I *would* dare, Nina," he breathed. "I'm just bidin' my time. Don't give me an excuse."

There was an instinct to close what little distance remained. I ignored it. "You're so confident you could get me in bed just like that?"

For a moment, he only watched my lips, and I was a heartbeat away from letting him have them, bravado be damned. My thighs pressed together, my stomach jolted with fresh thrill. He was going to kiss me, right there in the street.

But Patrick's eyes suddenly sharpened, and he leaned back, amusement dancing across his face. "Didn't say anythin' about a bed, now did I?"

He left me standing there alone, my face ruddy red, the tightly spooled cord in my chest unraveling.

CHAPTER 25

NINA

Colson & Sons was overflowing with patrons.

They trickled out the door and onto the street, littering the walkways. Isaiah wove between their legs, then disappeared inside, and Patrick sighed, cursing quietly at the crowd.

"You'd better pick me up now, Patrick," I murmured as we approached. "You'll lose me in these crowds."

He gave me a withering glare. "What are my chances of bribing you to stay upstairs?"

"I have no need for money."

"Or sense, apparently."

Some of the patrons looked up as we approached. Patrick grabbed my wrist, his long, roughened fingers enveloping it and winding my arm around his. "Stay near to me," he said low in my ear. "There're a lot of people here who hate me, Nina. Do you understand?"

"No," I said bluntly. "In fact, the more I see of Kenton Hill, the less I understand."

He scrubbed at his face. "Just do this one fuckin' thing, all right? Stay by me."

The people stuck out in the cold parted for Patrick; a few nodded to him genially. One man called out "All right, Patty?"

They now stared at me openly, and I chose to allocate their quizzical expressions to the oddity of an unfamiliar face in town, rather than the possibility that they knew exactly who I was.

The racket within the pub was such that I'd rarely heard before. The walls were too close, the ceiling too low to bracket all these people standing shoulder to shoulder.

The same woman as before stood behind the bar, shouting, "Beer only! Beer only at meetings, you bunch of louts! I'm not pourin' any fuckin' whiskey with this many in a room! Mind your manners!" And so the pints were meted out by the staff at terrific speed. Everywhere I looked, glasses sailed overheard, finding tabletops and greedy hands.

Patrick cut through the crowd easily. Some patted him on the shoulder, but Patrick stopped for no one. He pulled me along at his side, and his hand gripped so tightly I almost complained.

The men watched with interest. The women looked on with disdain.

"He's got a bird on his arm," someone muttered, none too discreetly. "She looks right familiar, don't she?"

"That's the Charmer," another said. "Caused a bloody earthquake in the market today. Didn't you hear?"

"Shit. Is that really her?"

An old and familiar dread climbed my throat. "They know who I am," I whispered to Patrick, my voice wavering.

He turned and glared down at me. "*Now* you're scared?" he asked. "Where's that clever mouth gone?"

My face heated. "I suppose I needn't worry. You'll just flay them within an inch of their lives if they come too close."

"Ah," Patrick said, dropping my hand. "So you *do* understand." He turned and nodded to the door that would lead to the stairwell. "If you don't want me defendin' your honor, you can head on up to that bed you mentioned us sharing."

My collar felt suddenly too tight. "I suspect my *honor* has never entered your mind."

"Oh, it has," he said darkly. He leaned so close that his mouth hovered over my ear. "Say the word, darlin', and I'll carry you up those stairs."

I could see the pulse in his throat. His scent corralled me.

"You're an arrogant fuckin' bastard, you know that?" I muttered contemptuously, vowels trailing.

"I am," he admitted, backing away an inch, but only so much as to look me in the eye when he spoke. "Or perhaps I just like invokin' that Scurry tongue of yours. It comes out when you're mad."

I aimed a quick jab at his stomach, which he caught easily. "Lord," he muttered, fingers slipping around my hand again. "We need to teach you to fight properly, darlin'. Surely, they breed quicker hands in Scurry." He gave another of those barely suppressed smiles, the ones that he'd failed to fight back. "Come on," he said, turning to the table before us.

He slapped a hand on the shoulder of none other than Scottie, who stood the moment he turned and spied Patrick, offering him his seat.

"A full house, Pat," he said, adjusting the vast waistline of his trousers. "We expectin' trouble?"

Patrick gestured for me to take the seat instead. "Always expect trouble, Scottie."

The round table hosted three other men. Two younger than me, I thought, and one older. The older one peered at me as I sat. He was large. Imposing. He sat with his legs crossed, a pipe between his cracked lips. A prominent brass-colored tooth glinted at me.

That he was a Colson was obvious. It wasn't the eyes—they were a warm brown rather than Patrick's blue. It was his expression. Careful, dauntless, overladen. I got the sensation I was an insect beneath glass.

"Nina Harrow, this is my older brother, Gunner," Patrick said.

Gunner shared a look with Patrick that stretched for a long moment. "Shouldn't she be behind a locked door somewhere?" His voice was a hoarse rendition of Patrick's. He seemed exhausted. Irritable. Moments from rage.

Patrick merely nodded, taking a glass of nondescript liquor from the table and downing it all at once. "She certainly should be, brother. And yet, I've brought her here." Whatever message passed between them seemed to change hands silently. Gunner sighed, smoothed his beard with one hand and toasted me half-heartedly. "Nice to fuckin' meet you," he said, then stood to leave. "I'll be at the bar."

I swallowed, my neck prickling uncomfortably. Perhaps it would have been wiser to go upstairs.

Next was a man with badly mussed hair and a boyish chin. His eyes quivered, unfocused, and mimicked Patrick's in color—surely another Colson.

"Me baby brother, Donny," Patrick gestured, taking Gunner's abandoned seat beside him.

Donny stared past me as he spoke. "Milady," he said, and he reached into the air, presumably for my hand. I suddenly recalled young Patrick referring to a brother who couldn't see well. I gave the man my hand, and he kissed my knuckles.

"Glad to meet you, Donny," I told him.

"Fuck me," Donny said, dropping my hand abruptly. "Is she a *proper* lady then, brother? Sounds like an Artisan or some such."

"She's as proper as they come, Don," Patrick muttered. "And she sounds like an Artisan 'cause she is one."

Donny turned his head in my direction. "Scottie brought you down the tunnel then, did he?"

I frowned at the man in question. "Something like that."

Scottie took a large swill of beer and grimaced as he swallowed. "Sorry about the knock to your noggin, hen," he said, then looked sideways to Patrick for approval.

Patrick's jaw ticked, and the big man put his drink on the table and looked down into his lap.

"I'm Briggs," said the only other occupant of the table. He was a tall man with a mop of shockingly red hair and a friendly disposition. He stood to shake my hand and offered a genuine smile. I nodded to him.

"So, then," I said to the group at large. "You're Patrick's browbeaters, are you?"

They each stilled completely in the act of lounging or drinking and stared at me, speechless. Then Donny broke, snorting into his glass. Scottie followed, then Briggs, and finally Patrick.

"What tales have you been tellin' her?" Donny asked Patrick. "Ain't you s'posed to be convertin' her to *our* side?"

Patrick's eyes met mine. I hoped he couldn't see me swallow reflexively. "She'll come round," he said simply, assuredly.

"So, what are you then, Nina Harrow?" Donny continued. He had Patrick's devilish charm, his confidence, but he was boyishly limp-limbed and languid, unburdened by the same duty his brother was.

I looked furtively to those patrons closest, lowered my voice, and said, "A Charmer." I did not elaborate as to the medium.

"Blimey. Another one, Pat?"

Patrick merely took a deep drag, but my attention darted between them, perplexed. "Another one?"

"Pardon," Donny continued, ignoring me. "But I don't give a figgy for your station. I meant what *are* you? Are you beautiful? Married? Someone tell me if I should be romancin' her—"

"Not unless you want to spend the night in a canal, Donny," Patrick said evenly.

"Ha!" Scottie barked. "He couldn't charm a fish if he were a worm."

Donny scowled. "Just so you know," he said to me, finding my hand on the table, "I've got much more than a worm. It's more the size of a—"

"Shut the fuck up, Donny," Patrick groaned, stubbing out his cigarette. "You said you were goin' after the lads from now on."

"That's not true. I'm happy to tip my cap at anythin'—"

"God almighty. Let's get this debacle over with," Patrick said, standing abruptly.

"But it's not half seven, Patty," Briggs said, leaning back to view an old grandfather clock by the wall, its glass cracked.

Patrick looked out over the packed pub. I followed his sights, to where a woman was beginning to climb to a tabletop and two men were tussling, though the lack of space made them unable to do more than grab each other's ears. The piano playing had ceased so that it could be pushed to the wall and allow more room.

"Close enough," he said. Then he walked to the bar. I watched him talk briefly with the woman pouring pints from a tapped keg. I saw her shoulders rise and fall on a sigh, and then she dragged a large brass bell from beneath the counter.

As soon as the bell began to clang, the noise died.

The fighting men froze mid-headlock. The woman on the table awkwardly crouched down, unsure what to do next.

Patrick took a swig of liquor straight from a bottle, closed his eyes briefly, where few could see him galvanize himself, and then climbed atop the bar.

No one clapped. No one called to him. There was only the quiet clinking of glasses and taut anticipation.

"Couple of messages," Patrick said, apparently with no other prelude on offer. "First—a shipment of goods and produce arrived this afternoon. Our market tables will be full tomorrow." A cheer. Fists pounded the air. "But"—Patrick called, and the crowd silenced like a school of admonished children—"if we see the same chaos that ensued last month, some will go without. Do you hear me, Randerson?" Patrick looked over at a man sliding halfway down his stool in an attempt to melt into the floor. "If you start breakin' the queue, Scottie will haul you out. Wait your fuckin' turn!"

The man nodded into his drink. "Aye. Sorry, Pat," he muttered.

"There was a hawker intercepted at the market earlier today. His wares were thrown into the canals. Anyone with information about the origins of the . . . *bluff* he was carrying will be handsomely thanked. And if need be . . ." And here Patrick paused. "We will conduct another search, home to home, to find all those in possession and the people responsible for producing it."

A collective titter rippled across the crowd. A few women raised their eyebrows at one another.

Patrick ignored the rousing.

"These are desperate times," he said, walking across the bar top. "Our miners—many of your loved ones—are still belowground each day in places we can't reach, doing what is necessary for the Union. But despite the pressure, we won't fold to the strain on our backs!" He held up his pint, matched by every other patron in the pub.

"They haven't figured us out yet, have they?" Patrick shouted, the cords of his neck straining.

"NO!" the crowd roared, and I jumped in my chair as it was jostled from behind.

"It's a time war we're fightin', but we are resilient. We've held our breath beneath ground for centuries—can we can hold it just a little longer, for our freedom?"

"YES!" Hollering ensued. The woman on the tabletop stood tall in her apparent elation and knocked her head against a brass pendant light.

When the last hurrah died, Patrick wiped the sweat from his brow, sniffed once, then said, with no small amount of resignation: "Right. Complaints?"

The herd surged forward, all of them at once. I watched Patrick's jaw tighten.

It went on for longer than I could stand.

"The drains round Blinder Street need clearin' again! An' not by old Frank—his knees don't take the strain and the job don't get finished."

"The Eastern mine is bogging, Pat—soon the whole fuckin' hill will slide right into town!"

"Those Wembley kids are runnin' free in the street, day and night. Left cat shit on my damn doormat again! If they can't be controlled, I'll—"

"I want fair compensation from that lousy dust collector. He broke a wheel and spilled soot all over my hydrangeas!"

Such trivial grievances. None seemed worthy of mention in wartime, and I grew quickly irritated. But Patrick listened, nodding to each complaint as the woman I presumed to be his mother scribed them. The sheets of parchment before her piled at an alarming rate.

How entitled these people were? How utterly oblivious to the fires outside their fortress?

From the looks on their faces, Donny, Scottie, and Briggs shared my opinion. Their expressions soured with each passing minute.

I watched Patrick carefully, saw how he took the brunt without remark or reaction. I wondered how many pieces made up the whole of him, beyond his bloodied fists and the flask inside his vest. Beyond the dog waiting for him by the window bay and the tin lighter he'd kept since his childhood . . . Had the boy I'd met been snuffed out somewhere between twelve and twenty-five? I desperately wanted to ask.

I also wanted to feel nothing for him at all. *You don't know this man*, I shouted in the chambers of my mind, banging the walls to ensure I paid attention. It did nothing to drown the sudden defensiveness clawing inside me as these people made their demands.

But you do know him, another voice hummed. *It all began with him.*

Eventually the grievances diluted to things like soil quality and a "peculiar smell" behind the scrapyard, and I sensed the meeting was finally concluding. Patrick's mother banged her pencil on the countertop and put her fingers between her lips, whistling at an aching decibel.

"We're done," she shouted, glaring at the crowd. They fell deathly silent. "No whiskey. You can have another dark mild before you trot off home, but if you fight, Gunner and Scottie will be escortin' you."

A low rumble of conversation arose, but no dissent.

I thought most would leave—the pub had grown oppressively hot. Instead, someone began clanging the keys on the piano, the volume rose to an earsplitting revelry, and the men and women continued on with a sense of ease, apparently lighter after having aired the soft inconveniences in their lives.

"Bunch of whinging pricks," muttered Briggs as he lit a cigar with a match. "It'll be a busy day tomorrow, boys."

Donny nodded. "I'll take care of the coal collector. He's on the bluff again, droppin' dust all over the place."

"You and your brother need to find where on God's green earth it's comin' from, Donny," Scottie said. "Ain't no point takin' their bluff where they can make more."

Donny scrubbed his face, looking tired. "It'll mean another raid."

"Fuck me," Briggs mumbled, pulling deeply on the cigar. "I'd prefer the fuckin' tunnels—"

"Shut up, Briggs. We're in *company*," Donny said sharply. Briggs eyed me with suspicion and fell silent.

I bristled. "Patrick told me about the tunnels."

"Did he, now?" Donny seemed unperturbed. "Did he threaten to leave you down one of them?"

My jaw ticked. "No," I said. "Though leaving me in a tunnel wouldn't render much use."

Scottie was smiling at me, entertained.

"No?" Donny said, leaning his forearms on the table and looking smug in his gold-buttoned waistcoat. "Taken a fancy to you, has he? Well, bully for you—whatever keeps you aboveground."

I wanted to shake the foundation beneath us, just enough to topple him from that high horse.

"I take it you're here to help us clear out the water rats, too," Donny continued, sipping his liquor.

"She ain't here for the rats, brother" came Patrick's voice from behind my shoulder. I turned slightly to find him standing with his hands in his pockets.

"Ah, Patty," Donny shook his head, sniggering. "Tell me you didn't bring her all the way out to the brink just so you could bend her over?"

My hands itched to slap him.

Scottie buried his fist in his mouth to quell laughter.

I looked up to find Patrick grinning, as amused as Scottie, it seemed. He placed his hands to the sticky table and leaned toward Donny. "I brought her all the way out here to bend *earth*, Donny," he said. His brother's face went immediately slack. "No need to dig your own grave. I promise Nina here can do it quicker."

Scottie broke then, laughing so uproariously his head tipped back to the ceiling. Briggs stared at me wide-eyed.

"No shit!" Donny said simply. "You fuckin' found one?"

"The *only* one, Don," Patrick corrected. "And here you are, insulting her where she sits," Patrick resumed his seat. "You ought to apologize." He said it casually, though there was that hint of malice in his words, making it clear that it wasn't a mere suggestion.

"Aye. Sorry, milady," Donny said, holding his hand out to take mine again. For the second time, he kissed my knuckles. "That was right fuckin' rude of me."

"Your foot's so far down your throat, Don, it's a wonder you don't choke and die." Briggs muttered.

"If only," I said, and they all snorted, Donny included.

"Bloody hell. She's a beauty, ain't she? I can tell. Guess I've already blown me chances."

Patrick nodded, upending yet another glass of amber liquor to his lips. "Aye," he rasped, not looking my way. "I'm afraid she is."

A scuffle ensued then. People crowded near the entrance called out in reproach as they were pushed aside. I caught sight of three black pointed hard hats adorned with Belavere's emblem before a firm, slender hand grasped my upper arm, hoisting me off my chair. "Move it, girl," came a feminine voice, Northern accented and scorched.

"Go," Patrick said to me once, short and sharp. He and the other three men had already rounded the table, heading straight for the hard hats.

The woman who I presumed to be Patrick's mother pulled me to the stairwell door, pushed me through, and followed after me. The door clicked shut behind us.

Tess Colson pressed her ear to the door. "Shut up," she hissed, and I realized that I was panting.

The police had come.

"Why are they here?" I breathed, blood pounding against the drums of my ears.

Tess did not look back at me. "They live here, darlin'," she said. "And as far as Belavere City knows, they do a stellar job of policin' the entire province, while we pay them handsomely to do the opposite."

"I meant, what are they doing *here*?"

"If I could hear a fuckin' thing, I might tell you," Tess said, then opened the door until a slither of light split her in two. I crept hesitantly closer at her back and peered over her head.

The patrons had fallen into silence again. It was the ringing kind. The violent kind. The mere creak of a floorboard might incite a brawl.

Fingers squeezed around the handles of heavy pints. Bodies turned to the black steepled hats in their faded black uniforms. The police stood with long batons in their hands, glaring at a room of curled knuckles and bared teeth.

"Hello, boys," Patrick said to them. "Got the uniforms out of your trunks for a night, eh? What's the occasion?"

"Colson," said the officer in front. He had sagging undereyes and a bent nose. His front teeth pleated and gave him the overall impression of a dunce. "Is your mother in?"

"She's indisposed," Patrick replied, even-tempered, eerily calm. "What can I do for you, Kirkby?"

"Had a man come to me door tonight, Patty. Looked like he'd been kicked in the face by a horse. The name he gave was Ferris Manly."

"Ah, Ferris," Donny shook his head. "He tends to let those mares get away from him in the stables. Slippery hands don't hold the reins right."

Kirkby grunted. "Gave me a little tip though, did Ferris. Told me that he had a very peculiar encounter with a woman he believed to be an earth Charmer, of all things. Said it was Nina Clarke!"

Utter silence, except for the lighter Patrick struck to light his smoke. The room held precariously by the tips of his fingers. "Did he?" Patrick said eventually, seemingly indifferent. I, on the other hand, felt my blood freeze. "Ferris says a lot of things, Kirkby. He's a bluff hawker, after all. I wouldn't pay him any mind."

"Said I might find this Nina Clarke here, in *your* company," Kirkby continued, stepping surreptitiously closer. "There's a mighty big reward on that swank's head, Patty. Far more than me and my colleagues get paid for our . . . discretion."

Men rose in their place. The sounds of their chair legs scraping across the floor filled the room. The balance teetered.

Kirkby seemed undaunted. "You brought a woman into market today," he said. "Took her around town, too. Loads of people've been whisperin' about it." He waved an arm around the room, and indeed, several people averted their eyes. "Rumor is, it's someone new. Funny accent. What's the newcomer's name, Pat?"

Patrick answered without delay. "Harrow," he said. "Of Scurry."

"Vaguely reminiscent of your last wife, Kirkby," Gunner said loudly, stepping forward to stand beside Patrick. "Only this one never ran off with the night soil man."

Kirkby slammed his baton down on the nearest table. A glass bounced and shattered. Those nearest backed away several paces.

Patrick gave no reaction at all.

Before me, Tess Colson ground her teeth.

"You can check with your masters for the records, if you like," Patrick said. "You'll find the name. Miner's daughter."

"Bloody Ferris," Gunner chuckled. His brass tooth flashed. "That horse must've kicked the wits out of him."

"Nevertheless," Kirkby replied. "Ferris said there was a strange quake in the ground at the market this afternoon. Reckons there were plenty of witnesses there who can attest to it."

Patrick looked around with a raised eyebrow. "Does he now? Well, if anyone here wishes to speak to the esteemed officers of our great Belavere . . ." He stepped forward and turned in a circle, arms out. "Do so now."

There was hardly a mutter. Just a creak in the floorboards, the whisper of bodies shifting. Gunner took a pistol from his coat, checked the barrel casually, then replaced it. He sniffed, rested his elbows on the bar. "You'll find no witnesses here, Kirkby." His voice was hewn from some deep, dark place in the earth, and it gave me the strange sensation of being buried. "Why don't you go back home to that empty bed now."

Kirkby turned puce with rage. "Fuckin' Colson boys," he muttered, spittle collecting on his lip. His hand tightened around the baton.

Through the crack in the door, I could see nothing but men with flared nostrils and women with taut fists. The entire tavern somehow smelled of hot flowing blood.

"Not your brightest idea, comin' in here tonight," Patrick said quietly, darkly. "We agreed you'd bring any concerns to me privately. Save all the . . ." He gestured to the angry crowd around them. "Ill will."

Kirkby seemed to become slowly aware, through the haze of his own fury, that he was vastly outnumbered. That his two uniformed comrades were gape-mouthed and backing furtively away. His eyes shifted to the glass shattered over the floor, then to Patrick, Gunner, Donny, and the others—none of whom had bothered to draw a weapon.

Kirkby teetered. "We'll speak about my new payment," he said, pointing a finger at Patrick. "House of Lords is offerin' a hundred, so I want a hundred—for my tolerance."

Gunner took two heavy, menacing strides before Patrick caught him around the chest, preventing his advance. "Enough," Patrick said, unflinching. "I'll be comin' to find you tomorrow, Officer," he said, waving Kirkby off. "Off you go now. Bar's closed."

"You're a crook, Colson," Kirkby grunted, spitting on the floor. "You and your mongrels."

Donny barked. Briggs crowed with laughter. Gunner bared his teeth, not arguing the accusation. The coppers turned their backs.

Tess let the door swing shut, muffling the returning conversation outside. "Lord almighty," she said slowly. She appraised me from crown to toe. "You've caused quite a stir."

I swallowed. What I'd done in the market had been foolish.

"My son went on and on for *months* about how useful you'd be," Tess said now, peering closely at me. I could see with total clarity the prisms in her eyes. "I told him it wasn't worth the risk."

Despite her shorter stature, her slightness, I felt smaller in her presence. I shrunk in my place. "Yet," I rasped. "Here I am."

"There you are," Tess agreed. "Do you understand the gravity of your position here, miss?"

I nodded, though I feared I only knew the half of it.

"Good," she said. "We've got an entire town to protect, to provide for. We do what must be done, however unseemly it is. If we must rid the world of one prissy Artisan to remain hidden, then I myself will pull the trigger."

I blanched. My chest rose and fell seismically. "I don't mean any harm to your people," I said unevenly. "Whatever you do, I'm sure it is only to ensure their safety."

For the first time since arriving in Kenton Hill, I was peacekeeping. Twisting words to please. Shame clawed at my throat.

Tess Colson only snorted. "Safety?" she echoed. "You think safety is all we want? No," she said, picking a loose thread from my sleeve. "If that was it, we'd not have started a revolution, now, would we? What we want is a fair fuckin' chance."

I did not have the gall to break eye contact.

"Do you really think you can help us with that, Miss Harrow?"

I pressed my lips into a thin line, tried to regulate my breaths. *Run*, my blood beckoned. *Run.* "I can carve the tunnels Patrick tells me to," I managed. "Whether it's a help to your cause is no concern of mine."

"Ah, yes," Tess nodded sagely. "A war-shy neutral." She said it the way one would describe an infection. "So, your plan is to dig some holes, then catch a fare to far-off lands, eh?"

"Yes," I said, my voice regaining strength. "Patrick made me a deal, and I accepted."

"Is that a promise?"

"It is."

"And are you a woman of your word?"

"In this instance, I'd be shot for breaking it," I reminded her.

She grinned, surprise momentarily brightening her features. "Just don't break any hearts along the way, miss. Keep your pretty eyes where they ought to be—on those far-off lands."

My mouth dried, but I nodded once, ceding to the warning.

The clamor in the pub seemed to have died down. The door pushed open, and Patrick appeared. He eyed the two of us, standing none too far apart, with immediate wariness. "They're clearing out," he said to his mother. "They've had enough booze for the night."

Tess nodded. "And Kirkby?" She was still staring at me, inspecting the curls falling free from their pins and the collar that closed at the hollow of my throat. "We pay that dullard enough."

"Well, Ma, unless you want me to kill him, we'll be payin' him some more."

Tess turned her head to Patrick, skewering him with her expression. Either he had the skin of a marble statue, or he was far more used to her mettle than I. Even without her glare on me, I withered.

"Bribin' coppers only shuts 'em up for so long," she snapped. "Your father taught you that."

"The coppers haven't worked a day in seven years, Ma," he said tiredly. "They send their special scribbles to their lords in the city saying all is well in old Kenton, and it lets us live another day. We need them here, alive, and willin' to turn their heads."

Tess watched him with reproach. "Put her back behind a locked door, son." No guesses as to who *she* was. "We've had enough trouble for one day."

She strode past Patrick, through the swinging door without a backward glance.

My jaw unclenched.

"In case it isn't already clear," Patrick said, eyes closing. I wondered if he'd fall asleep right there against the wall. "That's why you should've stayed in your room."

It didn't seem right to argue while he looked so . . . tired. I said nothing at all.

"There're a lot of people in this town who'd like to stick it to me, Nina. If they were clever, they'd use *you* to ruin my plans."

I thought of all the people in the pub tonight, placing their woes at his feet, but then standing with him in the face of police. I wanted to tell Patrick that there were also people who relied on him. Admired him.

"Can't trust a single one of 'em," he muttered to himself, then pushed away from the wall. "Off you go," he said, gesturing to the stairs. "I'll have someone bring you something to eat."

I raised my eyebrows. "I can't eat in the dining room?"

"There ain't one."

"Then perhaps I could eat in the pub?"

He raised his eyebrows. "Are you asking for more of my mother's company?"

I shivered delicately. "I think she threatened to shoot me."

He grinned. "Not to worry. She'd like to shoot just about everyone."

This didn't seem any less worrisome. "I'll say goodnight then." I turned toward the stairs.

"Sam will be up soon to keep watch," he said, and I tried not to hear it as a punishment. "Do me the honor of not threatenin' to bury him?"

My lips twitched.

"You'll be meeting Margarite tomorrow," he continued. "Seven sharp. I'll have Sam wake you and escort you downstairs."

I turned, my foot already on the first step. "Who is Margarite?" I asked.

He didn't answer right away. Rather, our eyes caught on each other's, and there was a long pause. Prismatic blue shifted, melted. A jump along his jaw. I wondered if there was something in his middle that cracked and spilled out, as it did in mine. "You'll see," he said.

Keep your pretty eyes where they ought to be—on those far-off lands.

"Good night, Patrick," I said again.

"Night, Scurry girl."

Twelve flights of stairs to the top, where Sam's wooden stool sat empty and waiting. I thought of his mother, red-faced and furious in the teahouse. I thought of his father, buried in an abandoned tunnel.

Guilt filled me, and I silently vowed to be kinder to Sam when I next broke free of my room.

But for tonight, I only wanted sleep. I wanted cherry blossom wall-paper and a swollen ceiling. A long stretch of heavy quiet. One day in public among the kind of noise I'd craved, and already I was spent.

I walked past door thirteen, with door fifteen looming invitingly, just out of reach.

But door fourteen opened on the right as I passed it, creaking on its neglected hinges. The room's occupant stepped out, tall and wide-eyed. He froze at the sight of me.

"*Nina?*" he said.

"Theo," I whispered.

Only I wasn't sure the name ever truly left my lips.

CHAPTER 26

PATRICK

Donny and Gunner awaited him in the pub, and the brothers left without another lick of whiskey.

"Come on, boys," Patrick muttered, heading straight for the door. "It's been a long day."

They walked along brightly lit Main Street until they reached the first canal, then followed it downstream, not stopping until the rooftops shrunk and the pasture peeked over the tiles.

Ferris Manly was asleep, face down in his straw cot, beside horses of a pedigree far above his own.

He reeked of liquor and horse shit. A half-empty bottle had fallen from his hand and spilled out onto the hay. His face resembled pulp.

"Look at this sorry lump, eh?" Gunner said, dragging on his cigarette. "Took me a case of single malt to get him this fuckin' job."

Patrick shared his indignation. On occasions like this, he wondered if it wouldn't be more efficient to just rid the world of men with Ferris's character than entertain fantasies of righting the ship.

"Well," Donny muttered, stubbing out his own smoke against a wooden post. "God rest his soul and all that."

The horses were quiet in their stables. Even they seemed accepting of Ferris's fate.

"Oy," Patrick called loudly and kicked the sole of Ferris's foot. "Up you get."

The man came to slowly, eyes rolling. His pupils dilated at the sight of Gunner leaning over him. "Hello, Ferris," Gunner said.

Even as a boy, Gunner had been possessed of the ability to shrivel a man where he sat. Patrick wagered there were none in Kenton Hill who did not fear him. He'd seen the turn of their pallor in his presence.

Ferris now resembled a trapped rodent, trying to curl in on himself. Already, he blustered. "I—I didn't—"

"Didn't what, Ferris?" Patrick asked.

His breaths snagged in his chest. His syllables came ever more disjointed. The Colsons hadn't yet touched him.

Donny took a pistol from his pocket and pointed it in the vague direction of the cot.

Ferris quaked. The unmistakable smell of piss scented the air.

Gunner didn't move. He looked to Patrick, now confused. "Mercy killin'?" he asked. "I thought we was here for sport."

"We are," Patrick assured him. "Put the fuckin' gun down, Donny."

Donny reluctantly lowered his gun, nose wrinkling.

"Scottie and Briggs are just rounding up some of your colleagues, Ferris," Patrick told the man on the ground. "They'll be joining us in a moment."

As though summoned, feet could be heard slapping off the compacted dirt outside. Briggs stuck his burly head into the stables. "Got 'em, Patty," he said.

Patrick nodded. "Get him on his feet, Gunner. Let's see how fast this pig can run."

Gunner grabbed Ferris's arms, ignoring his whining protests. "Gunner," Ferris coughed. "Please, Gunner . . . We were friends."

Gunner merely scoffed, taking Ferris's scruff in one hand and forcing him out into the night.

Standing like strays between Scottie and Briggs were five others, all known former hawkers. All now in more morally gainful positions. The Colsons gave second chances, just not to traitors.

"Hello again, boys," Patrick said to them, making his voice louder than the growing wails of Ferris. "Pardon the interruption to your evenin'. We've brought you here to help us decide your associate's fate." They shifted uneasily, not wanting to look at Ferris, nor any Colson. They all stared at their boots instead. Except one, who glared at Patrick with obvious defiance.

"All of you," Patrick continued. "Have been given new jobs. A fresh start, if you like."

"Shovelin' shit," said the bold one, Leon. "Or chasin' rats round the canals."

"But employment nonetheless," Patrick countered, undeterred. "And yet, Ferris here has decided to throw away the opportunities handed to him. You look like a betting man, Leon." Patrick held aloft a coin, flipping it to show both sides. "If it's heads, then I shoot Ferris as he runs."

Leon's eyes went wide. Ferris whimpered behind Patrick.

"Tails, and I'll let you decide who gets to shoot him."

Leon looked once to Ferris, pupils widening, and then he nodded. "I want to flip the coin meself."

After a brief contemplation, Patrick threw the coin to him, "Be sure to give it back, won't you? Times are hard."

Briggs and Scottie chuckled.

Leon's fingers shook around the coin. He squared his feet and shoulders as though preparing to throw a grenade. He gave Ferris a nod in solidarity, then flipped the coin on his thumbnail.

It spun and spun, then fell and fell, right into the waiting cradle of Leon's palm.

He smiled, loosened a breath, looked to me exultantly. "Tails," he said, grin stretching.

"Very good. And who's your pick?"

He took no time at all to answer. "Donny," Leon said. "My pick is Donny."

Patrick nodded.

Donny clicked his tongue and winked an unseeing eye. "Why do they always pick me?"

Patrick smirked. "When you're ready, Gunner, cut Ferris loose. To make things fair, we'll give young Donny only one shot. What say you, Leon?"

Leon gave a curt nod, an air of smugness lifting his chin.

Ferris had stopped wailing.

Donny had yet to draw a gun.

"Let's see how fast you scamper, Ferris," said Gunner. "He'll be headed downwind, Donny."

Patrick felt their spectators lean forward, the sport getting the better of them.

"Ready, Ferris?" Gunner called. "Take your mark . . . steady . . . and he's off!"

Ferris was surprisingly agile on his feet, despite a small stumble upon release. He was twenty feet away before Donny had even brushed his coat aside. Ferris's legs pounded the dirt back toward the cobbles.

His colleagues whooped and cheered; Leon was the loudest, barking a laugh skyward.

Donny cocked the hammer of his pistol and raised it in the general direction of Ferris, though the gun barrel erred to the right. "Am I straight on, Patty?"

Patrick lit a cigarette. "Straight enough."

The end of the lane was near enough for Ferris to smell the victory. He closed in on the corner, fading into the late evening mist.

An almighty bang rented the air.

The bullet made whorls of the mist.

In the distance, Ferris fell.

The brick walls carried the sound upward with the smoke, and Kenton grew silent once more.

"How'd I do?" Donny asked.

"Square in the back of his head," Gunner answered.

Donny cursed. "Was aimin' for his arse."

Leon's expression had fallen, arrogance as shot as poor Ferris. Fear always filled the hollow.

The rest of the men stared back and forth between the felled man and the blind man, disbelief rebounding.

"Thanks for joinin' us, boys. And just so there's no confusion, know that your pastimes are not welcome commerce in the marketplace. As for your new positions of employment," Patrick stepped toward Leon, eclipsing his view of Kenton Hill. "You could do worse than horse shit and rats." Patrick's head filled with flickering lantern light and groaning timber and walls made of mud. "Show some fuckin' gratitude that I don't throw you down a mine shaft instead."

Leon shrunk, his brow spotting with perspiration, thoughts of the tunnels turning him quiet.

It was late. Patrick was tired. He wondered if perhaps tonight would render any sleep.

"Be sure to turn up to work in the morning, boys," he said, giving them his back. "As demonstrated here tonight, your life depends on it."

CHAPTER 27

NINA
EIGHT YEARS PREVIOUS

In the sleeping quarters of the National Artisan School, students were not permitted to enter one another's dorms beyond the stroke of nine. So, naturally, the corridors were full of quick-moving shadows by a quarter past the hour.

At almost midnight, long after I'd fallen asleep at my desk, the door to my room inched open.

I startled at the sound, disoriented. My cheek ripped away from the porous page of a book.

"Did you doze off again?" Theo murmured, closing the door quietly behind him. He entered with an air of casualness. This meeting had long since become a habit of ours, though we'd made no plans to meet tonight.

I scrubbed a hand over my face, sleep clinging. The wax from the candle had dripped over its holder and into the saucer beneath, flame barely sputtering.

Theo seemed amused. "Should I go?"

"No," I mumbled. "No. It's all right."

He walked to my chair and turned my face to one side. "You've got *Pholinger's Interpretation of Modern Aesthetics* on your cheek."

"It wasn't very enlightening."

"I'd gathered," Theo said, smirking. Whenever his lips quirked like that, charged particles raced through my core and ruptured like tiny supernovas.

Infatuation, Aunt Francis had called it. *Not to be confused with love.*

Theo took my hand, led me to my bed. Without a word exchanged we lay on our backs, my head cradled in the crook of his arm. We stared at the ceiling. I felt his lips descend into my hair.

I'd read poetry that had described romance as being a descent into madness. A kind of precursor to pain. That wasn't how being with Theo felt. Being with Theo was levitation. I was weightless here, when usually I felt encumbered. It sometimes took great effort to drag myself from place to place.

Sometimes I thought of him as the water he charmed. I was buoyant with him. Helpless to the current. I went where he took me and rather liked the lack of responsibility.

Theo drew a box from his pocket and held it in the air above us. It was emerald green, made of leather. No bigger than the canyon of his palm.

"Had one of the fourth year Smiths make it," he said, removing the box's lid. "And a Cutter as well." He pulled a green jewel from its depths. Swinging from it was a gleaming silver chain, thin as spun sugar. He lowered it gently onto the bridge of my nose, then left a kiss beneath my ear.

I grinned, pinched the necklace between my forefinger and thumb and inspected it closely. It was small and precisely cut and the color of poison. Pricks of some inscrutable emotion lanced my throat. I'd never owned something quite so beautiful. "What's this for?"

"For you," he said simply. "It's been a year since we stepped out."

A year and two days, actually. "I—I don't have anything to give back to you," I said feebly. So often, it seemed, I sounded less than I was.

Theo turned my chin to see the expression I tried to hide. Damn that grin. "Don't fret, Clarke. I've got no need for presents."

I relented, a wavering smile stretching across my face. "Thank you," I told him. "I've never owned jewelry."

"Never?" he frowned. "Did your parents never gift you any? An heirloom, even?"

My stomach tightened painfully. Close—so dangerously close to the lie. To the truth. "Everything was left behind when they passed," I invented. I was rather proficient in storytelling, so said the scribbling teachers. "I was quite young. Not old enough for necklaces."

I could see him taking those tidbits and adding them to some invisible inventory. I wondered what the collection would look like if it was laid out on the bed: dead Artisan mother and Crafter father, born in Sommerland—the source of my strangely blended accent. What killed them? Influenza, so common near the brink. Who raised me? Aunt Francis, a spinster. Now I was here. End of story.

At some point in our acquaintance, the scant offerings of my history had failed to satiate Theo. These days, he asked questions frequently. I suspected it was why Aunt Francis had not endorsed our relationship from the beginning.

"Do you miss them?" Theo asked me, tracing my bottom lip with his thumb. There I went again, floating up to the ceiling.

"Sometimes," I said, though it was my own mother and father I thought of.

I closed my eyes, momentarily drugged by his soft caresses. Sometimes my body reacted to touch as though it'd been starved of it. I supposed it had been.

"What were they like?"

"My father was worn," I said. "My mother was sad."

His voice lowered to a whisper. The candle on the desk finally sputtered out. "Were they kind to you?" he asked tentatively, and the tenderness with which he said it did not make it feel like so big an invasion.

"Sometimes," I murmured. "Sometimes they were too wrapped up in their troubles to remember me at all."

He became so quiet that I opened my eyes, missing the sound of his voice. I couldn't see him well in the dark, just the familiar outline of him.

The movement of his eyelids. "But you were young," he reminded me. "Very young when they died."

I tried not to tense. "Yes. I was young."

"And it must have been a difficult life for them. There aren't many who would endorse a marriage between an Artisan and a Crafter."

I said nothing. I didn't need to widen the divide between him and me. Between myself and everyone.

"Sommerland just declared intentions for their first strike, actually," Theo continued. His hand had stopped its hypnotic ministrations. "The sheep farmers and wool millers are all walking out at the blow of the whistle in two days. Bloody Miners Union." I saw his head shake in the dark.

My lips pressed tightly together. "You think them fools." It wasn't a question.

"My father says you can't strong-arm a governing house to increase wages by simply walking out. After all, we have Tailors! We have Smiths and Masons. If the Crafters won't pick up their tools, the Artisans will use their mediums. The millers and farmers of Sommerland will soon see how irrelevant they are."

"Irrelevant," I repeated. It rolled off my tongue like a tidal wave. "Do you believe Crafters irrelevant?"

"Of course not," he laughed. "Nor does my father, or the House of Lords, by the way. I only mean to point out how easily the Crafters will be persuaded, by merely giving them the illusion that they can be easily replaced."

"There's only one Artisan for every ten Craftsmen," I reminded him. "Surely, they won't be so easily duped."

"I think Tanner knows how persuasive hunger will be when the wages stop altogether. Sommerland has a lot of children who will go without food for as long as the strike holds."

"And the House of Lords will be in their stately homes, with their cooks bringing five courses each evening."

Tension coalesced in the air, as it tended to where Theo's father was concerned. Lord Shop was determined for Theo to follow in his political footsteps, and yet Theo often seemed to me as though he wanted to resist. He would never say so aloud. It was only ever evident in the tightening of his lips, or the way his eyes hardened at his father's mention. And his father was mentioned quite a bit. It was a large part of Theo's popularity among our peers.

"Speaking of dinner, father asked if you would join us this weekend?"

I grimaced. I'd already declined the last two invitations. Recently, the lord had taken a keen interest in me. I wondered, and not for the first time, what Theo's father would do if he knew where I truly came from.

"For what it's worth, I *would* like to have you there this weekend at dinner. It'll be much less insufferable with you in the room."

I peered up at him, but it was too dark to see if he meant it. He pulled me tighter to his chest, and I was floating again, lighter than oxygen. His hands grazed the curve of my spine.

"Come with me," he said, then pressed his mouth to mine.

We stayed that way for a while, his lips taking hostage of my cheeks and throat. Eventually my nightdress was swarmed above my hips and the ribbon at my bust had come undone, and I was pieces of airborne dust, not really of any substance at all.

CHAPTER 28

NINA

In the first year of unrest, I'd hocked Theo's emerald necklace to a boatman in Baymouth. It had bought me canal passage on a tightly packed long rig. Sometimes I wondered where that emerald necklace had ended up.

On the highest floor of Colson & Sons, Theo followed me inside room fifteen and closed the door behind him.

The two of us stood a foot apart, a pipe moaned at the wall, the cherry blossoms distended, and weak orange light filtered through the window.

"Clarke," he said. The name clicked off the roof of his mouth, as it always had.

He was a little taller, his jaw a little darker—shadowed in week-old growth. His edges weren't as sharp, the perfectly tailored robes with their severe lapels now gone. I realized that I'd hardly ever seen him without them.

I noticed his hair did not wave so deliberately. It seemed a little overgrown. He wore suspenders and an undershirt tucked into faded trousers. There was a small cut beneath his left eye, a bandage around his wrist. If he weren't otherwise wholly familiar, I might mistake him for a Crafter.

"Theo," I said again, my hands tightly gripped behind my back. What else to say to the man you once loved? "You're here."

I didn't float. I felt as if I weighed a thousand unmovable tons.

"As are you." His hand rose and fell, drowning in hesitancy. "Are you—are you all right?"

I grimaced. Nothing either of us said would feel adequate. "As all right as one can be. Are you . . . ?" My eyes stuck to the bandage.

He followed my line of sight. "It's just a sprain. The tunnels are hazardous."

"The tunnels?" I parroted, baffled. "Are you mining?" I couldn't imagine a person less suited. He was toned and straight-backed, but not muscular, not fortified the way Crafters were, like a bullet might bounce off their skin. Theo looked breakable. Had he always been?

He chuckled darkly. "Difficult to imagine, I know. Yet here we are, Clarke. Two Charmers, turned miners. Patty told me he was looking for the earth Charmer. I hardly allowed myself to believe that he might succeed." He took stock of me as he spoke. "You look shockingly good for someone seven years on the run."

I blanched. There was accusation in his voice. "As it happens," I said slowly. "I've become rather proficient at it."

"And it never occurred to you that I might wish to know if you were all right?"

There it was: the canyon between us. "Would it have made a difference?"

"*Yes*," he said immediately, unequivocally. His stare was stony.

"I couldn't risk that." Surely he understood why.

"Everyone was after you, Clarke. And your aunt . . . I searched in the rubble all night."

Shame seized me. I saw again the dust that fell like rain, tiles that moved like rippling water.

Heat practically misted from Theo's nose as he exhaled. "You disappeared in the smoke. I thought you'd *died* or been taken hostage." He'd never spoken to me with so much venom, or indeed, any venom at all.

I'd earned every bit of it. "I had to leave," I said weakly, "so that neither side could take me." Those words struck where I'd intended. His eyes—the same warm brown they'd always been—hardened.

Everyone was harder now. War, I'd learned, sapped gentleness from the core.

"I looked for you," he said. "For a long time, Clarke."

And what would you have done with me, if I were found? "I'm sorry," I said instead. And I meant it, all the way to the bone. How many times had I been tempted to write to him in those months? In the end, I hadn't dared risk it. "You were loyal to the House," I reminded him. "Ready to fight. And I . . . I didn't want any part in it."

"You picked your side the second you left Belavere City, Clarke."

"It's Harrow," I said, a surge of mettle returning. "And I don't have a side."

Theo raised an eyebrow, looked pointedly to the cherry blossoms, then back to me. "Yes, you do, Nina. It's the same side as mine. Mining tunnels."

If only Professor Dumley could see his protégés now. "How long have you been here, Theo? What about your lordship?"

"You didn't hear?" he asked, skeptical. "I was ousted from the House."

I gasped lightly in disbelief.

"I'm surprised you didn't read about it," he said. "It was quite the scandal."

"What could Lord Shop's son possibly have done to offend the House?"

"He sent secret missives to brink towns, warning them of imminent raids."

Again, I was caught short. "You sent *warnings*? Under Tanner's nose?"

"I admit it was foolish to trust a Scribbler of the House," he said, clearing his throat awkwardly. "But she and I had formed a . . . close bond."

I took that to mean he'd been fucking her, though he didn't say it. He glanced away uncomfortably.

"That was two years ago now. The headlines feasted on it—*Water Charmer Accused of Treason*—and I found my way out into the brink. It took the Miners Union all of a few days to catch up with me."

"Two *years* ago?"

He nodded. "I've been holed up here ever since."

I shook my head in disbelief. "I knew those canals were too clean."

"They were in a shocking state when I arrived," he said. There was the Theo I remembered, jovial and vain. "Tunnels full of seeping water, too."

I worried at my lip with my teeth. "So, you joined the cause, just like that?"

He lifted his arms half-heartedly. "I'm a volunteer."

"And the town just welcomed you in?" I asked.

"Hardly," he rolled his eyes. "A man took a shot at me once, early on."

I believed it.

"But the Colsons tend to make examples of those who go against them. We struck a deal: they offer me their protection, and I get idium twice yearly and the joys of clearing the water from their tunnels."

"So Patrick doesn't keep you confined to your room?"

Something in my voice must have been too familiar when I spoke the name. Theo cocked his head to the side. "You've met Pat, then?"

I nodded but didn't say more, and I didn't know why that should be. If there was anyone in the town I could spill myself to, shouldn't it be Theodore Shop? "I'm glad to see you," I said instead, relief escaping me by way of a smile.

He smiled back at me; his hand rose to cup my cheek. "You're exactly as I remember you."

A match had been struck. It sizzled on its end, slowly expending itself. Waiting. Waiting.

I stepped into him.

His arms wrapped around me, encasing me in his familiar frame. He smelled different but held me just the same. My arms overlapped around his waist, and my head fell to his collar. I was surprised to find that I'd grown taller.

I was desperate for comfort but unsure where to find it.

"Do you want me to stay with you?" he asked.

I shook my head.

"My door isn't locked, Clarke." The words wove into my hair. "I'm just down the hall. Number fourteen. Do you understand?"

I understood, but I unwound my arms and stepped out of the circle of his. I wouldn't be in this town for long. I intended to leave it without bringing anyone with me. I would do only what was necessary, only what I must. And then I'd be gone.

Both Nina Clarke and Nina Harrow would cease to exist.

"There's a meeting with Margarite in the morning," he said. "I'll see you then."

I nodded, not asking how he knew I'd be in attendance. My chest filled with air I could not expel.

"I've missed you," he said, looking at me before he closed the door.

And then it was just me, the bowled ceiling, the groaning pipes, two large holes pierced through my heart.

CHAPTER 29

NINA

The meeting was not in the pub, as I'd expected, but in the town's square.

Sam knocked on my door before dawn broke, and I followed him out onto the landing. Waiting there was Theo and, by some perplexing design, Polly Prescott.

My school friend had hardly changed. She had the same tightly ringed black hair that floated just above her shoulders, dark skin, and warm eyes. Now there was a horizontal scar across the bridge of her nose, and her hands were incised with a thousand old abrasions—a Scribbler's hands.

She smiled somewhat shyly when she saw me. "They'll let anyone into the club nowadays, I suppose?"

A noise of exasperation left me. I looked to Theo for explanation, but he only shrugged.

"*You're* Kenton's Scribbler?"

"I'm afraid so."

"And you—you're—"

"A member of the cause?" she offered. "I am."

"We could start a musical group," Theo added grimly. "Polly was always a fair alto."

I only remembered Polly to have been a kind friend. Quiet. "Squid," they'd called her. Each winter and summer break she'd remained behind in her dorm, rather than travel home to any waiting family. "How on earth did you find yourself *here?*" I wondered aloud.

"I came to Kenton Hill three years ago," she shrugged. "When I arrived, Patrick offered me a choice—work for him or work against him. Not much of a choice at all, really." She said it without resentment. "Kenton Hill is about as safe as it gets."

Sam was tapping his foot impatiently on the first step. "We'll be late," he said.

We walked down Main Street together, the sun just beginning to touch the backs of our necks. The first residents were stirring, the whole of Kenton rubbing sleep from their eyes. The streets were eerily quiet.

"What exactly will this meeting entail?" I asked no one in particular. Theo and Polly walked casually, not needing Sam to guide them down each alley.

"I imagine Pat will be putting you to work," Theo answered, taking my arm and intertwining it with his as though the past seven years hadn't elapsed and we were out for a walk together. I pretended to fix a pin in my hair and extricated myself. "Work?" I asked.

"I suspect he's about to finally reveal his next big plan," Polly mused, burying her hands into her coat pockets. "He's had us in the dark for months."

"His plans to get to the capital, you mean?" I said without thinking.

Polly, Theo, and Sam all slowed in their walk, their eyes pinned to me from three different directions.

"That's the plan?" Theo asked. "He told you that?"

I went quiet. Swallowed. "Well, I don't know the finer details, but—"

"I suppose we'll all be in on it shortly," Polly interjected. She gave a surreptitious glance in Sam's direction; he was listening with grave interest, mouth agape. "Best not to say anything more out in the open."

Sam walked us toward the middle of the town, following the curve of facades until we reached a brick arch opening.

On the other side was a large square, each side cordoned in blackened warehouses and shops. Street vendors and buskers were already beginning to set up their tables in each corner. The buildings themselves had a hint of abandonment to them.

The signage indicated a treasury, though half the lettering was missing. The police house waited beside it, but the windows were boarded. Its roof was in ruins and burned black with some previous fire. A large bulletin board bolted beside the archway sat empty, no decrees from the House of Belavere adorning the cork.

"What happened here?" I asked, turning in a slow circle.

Sam only shrugged. "No need for Belavere officials anymore, except for Polly. That over there was the food dispensary, and the trading post was in the corner. The police station was smoked out years ago."

This left only one side to the square, which held an array of dilapidated storefronts, one of which hosted a bold, flaking sign: MARGARITE'S MODERN LADIES, SEAMSTRESS EXTRAORDINAIRE. Its windows were so clustered in misshapen mannequins that for a moment, I was outright alarmed.

I was further baffled when Sam led us directly to its skinny maroon door, the paint here woefully blistered and peeling.

Sam knocked once, and a cascade of red flakes flurried off the wood.

I looked sideways at Theo and Polly, who seemed oddly at ease. "Who is this woman we're meeting?" Clearly, the shop was no longer open for business. If the windows were anything to go by, it was now a mausoleum of wooden corpses.

The door opened before they could respond, creaking desperately on its hinges.

Scottie stood on the other side in the same miner's clothing he only ever seemed to wear.

"Mornin', Sam, Polly," Scottie greeted, moving his tremendous body aside. "Teddy."

Theo rolled his eyes. I noticed that his demeanor had turned sullen. He kept close to me as we stepped inside.

But Polly smiled easily as she crossed the threshold. "I believe you owe me a debt, Mr. Brooks," she said, patting Scottie on the shoulder as she entered.

"Aye," Scottie grunted. "Though a merciful woman would let a man win his money back?"

"I've won five out of five games, Scottie."

"The cards are on my side today, Pol. I can feel it."

She shook her head, apparently comfortable in his presence.

"Miss Nina," Scottie said, nodding to me. Then he shut the door behind us all, locking three separate bolts.

The air in the shop was thick. It moved, stuck to us. Sunlight fought valiantly through the dust. It smelled of damp plaster.

Those strange mannequins were arranged all over the shop floor, headless and stripped of any fabric, their limbs bent grotesquely. A wall lined with shelves and ladders stood bare save rusty shears, the odd needle. An old sewing machine and crank collected cobwebs on its bowed desk, and I pictured ghosts threading cotton through the wheels.

Leaning against that desk, Otto and Briggs passed a cigarette back and forth. The oldest and youngest Colson brothers had convened by a basket of yellowing fabric, both alike and drastically unalike. Gunner was already swigging from a flask drawn from his coat. In Donny's hand was a wrought-iron cage encasing, strangely, a singular canary.

Tess Colson leaned her back against the empty shelving and did not spare Theo, Polly, or me a glance.

And then there was Patrick, Isaiah at his feet. He looked, once again, as though he had not slept. My eyes stuck to the circles beneath his.

"Thanks, Sam," Gunner said abruptly. His loud voice seemed offensive in such a small space. "Now, fuck off."

Unperturbed, Sam whistled as he left, kicking a thimble gaily, and no one spoke in the interim.

But there were looks exchanged. Tess stared at Gunner until he put his flask away. Polly and Otto exchanged nervous glances, the latter clearing his throat awkwardly. Patrick pinned his eyes on Theo's hand, which had briefly touched the middle of my back as I'd stepped into this strange circle of associates.

It was exceedingly uncomfortable. Quiet. Close.

"Right," said Donny after a while, blessedly breaking the tension. "Is the kid gone?"

"Get it over with, son," Tess said to Patrick. "I've got a hotel to manage."

Patrick lifted his chin. I could practically feel the exhaustion wafting off him. "First, some formal introductions—"

"Idia, save us," Gunner moaned. "We *know* who's who, Pat."

Patrick continued, closing his eyes briefly at the interruption but otherwise pretending Gunner hadn't spoken. "You've all been brought into the circle because you're valuable—a necessary function in the Miners Union. You're also here because, for whatever reason, we've deemed you trustworthy." Here, Patrick's eyes touched on Polly, Theo, and finally me. "Whether by nature or because a deal was struck."

I wondered what deal he'd struck with my two former classmates, for surely he wouldn't trust an Artisan by nature.

"Some of us have known each other all our lives. We've bled together enough that trust comes easy. Others have joined our party . . . more recently. For them, trust is conditional."

I frowned. "What does that mean?"

"It means we'll put you on that ship in *parts* if you double-cross us," Tess said. The look in her eye left little doubt that she would do the cutting herself.

I looked quickly away and closed my mouth.

"There's a plan coming together, with far more complexities than any other we've endeavored, and every one of us will need to offer their expertise. For most of us, that means the usual mining. Scottie and Otto know the tunnel pathways better than anyone. They're the navigators."

Otto nodded. "Spend more time in the dark than out of it," he said cheerfully.

Patrick continued. "Briggs here is a clay kicker, though his particular area of expertise will no longer be needed." Patrick's eyes flickered to mine. "He'll handle the struts. Gunner and I are grunt labor—we'll move the dirt topside. Donny is our listening post. Mrs. Colson looks after things up top while we're in the hole. And then there's Nina Harrow," he said as though he couldn't quite believe he was saying it. "Our very own earth Charmer. There doesn't exist a better team of diggers." Patrick took a breath, exchanged a quick glance with his mother. "We're tunneling all the way to Belavere City, ladies and gents, as quickly as we can."

A hush ensued, save the static crackle of Patrick's decree.

"It's two hundred miles or more, Pat," Otto breathed, permeating wariness. "Under the Gyser River. Right into enemy territory. You know the Artisans are listenin' for vibrations in the ground. Burying land mines in wells for us to stumble onto."

Patrick nodded. "The mines tick. We'll hear 'em before we hit 'em."

"We ain't ever dug farther than Fenway," Briggs said. "And that tunnel's buried now."

Tess sighed. "And why do you think we brought in a fuckin' earth Charmer?"

Briggs gave me a furtive raised eyebrow. I felt a prickle of discomfit.

"As for the river," Patrick interjected, "Theodore here will accompany, of course. He's already improved the existing tunnels running south and west. He'll divert the water, should it become a problem."

"Oh, it'll be a fuckin' problem all right, Pat. It's the fuckin' *Gyser* River."

The Gyser River was the continent's longest and widest. It barreled through the Trench at impossible speed, splitting the brink in the east from Artisan-populated towns in the west, including Belavere City. "You can strut that tunnel in as much timber as you want and pack it full of Charmers. They'll still drown the same. It's impossible."

"Then by all means, brother, back out." Patrick said. The dare sounded like a bullet sliding into its chamber.

Gunner glared, his upper lip curling slightly to reveal that strange tooth. But he said nothing. In the space of his inaction, Patrick continued.

"That goes for anyone else who wants no part in this. It'll be dangerous. I won't claim that the path will be smooth—and even if we get there, there's no promise of return."

"I don't suppose you'll tell us what you intend to do in Belavere City, assuming we make it through?" Theo asked. He did not shy away from the volume of his own voice. He looked Patrick square in the eye.

But Patrick remained impenetrable. "Two years ago, a mission into the city took a turn, and several men were taken prisoner at the National Artisan House. I intend to retrieve those men."

Tess turned her back at the mention of prisoners, muttering something I could not hear.

Theo seemed unsatisfied. "Surely that's not all you plan to do. I've proven my loyalty to you enough times, Pat," he said, standing his ground. "I deserve to know the full scope of things."

Patrick raised his eyebrows at Theo's tenacity. "Your job is to get us through those tunnels without them flooding. What more should you know, Charmer?"

"I should know if the people I'm leading into the capital intend to gun down every Artisan within reach."

Gunner scoffed. "Fuckin' swanks," he muttered, making it clear that he didn't think gunning down every Artisan was necessarily a *bad* thing.

Polly cleared her throat. "I should like to know the same." Her voice was more diplomatic than Theo's but just as sure. "I'm on your side," she said, her gaze shifting from Patrick to Otto, "but innocent people needn't die."

"Agreed." Patrick nodded. "No innocents should die."

Theo frowned, unconvinced. "And you intend to pop up in the middle of the city without needing to raise a weapon?"

"Ah, but we intend no such thing," Patrick said, and Donny chuckled quietly. "That'd be suicidal."

Theo frowned. "Then—"

"Thirteen years ago, Nina and I stumbled upon a cellar in the National Artisan House." His eyes darted to mine for only a moment. "If we can tunnel into that cellar, we'll have gained entrance to the House."

I thought of ghostly linens and dry cake. Of Patrick's hand squeezing around mine, begging me to be quiet. One look at his expression told me he was remembering the same.

Theo's jaw ticked, and I could guess why. His father, Lord Shop, still presided in the House. "Do you plan on blowing the House to pieces?" he asked. "Like you did the school?"

Patrick tilted his head. I wondered if Theo had meant the barb to strike. If anything, Patrick seemed to be genuinely considering the option. "It'd be a sure way to win the war, eh?" he asked. "Blowin' up all those lords."

My heart pounded suddenly. I looked around at all the wooden mannequins, and my head replaced them with pieces of people. I squeezed my eyes shut. When I opened them again, they would be gone.

Patrick checked his pocket watch, "Don't fret, Teddy. If I blew up *your* daddy, I'd almost certainly be blowin' up my own in the process. I intend no such thing."

"Seems like a wasted opportunity, Pat," Scottie said. "Do you know for certain that the prisoners are bein' held in the House?"

"No." Tess interceded now. "He doesn't." There was so much strain in her voice, it was a wonder she hadn't screamed it. "He isn't even sure the prisoners are still *alive*."

Patrick looked at his mother with barely suppressed irritation.

I couldn't tell how Tess Colson felt about the prospect of her husband's death. There was no hint at acceptance or despair. There was only festering anger. I could practically see it sprinting across her skin.

"The House of Lords has always worked against us at a disadvantage. They don't know where we are, or who we are. We could attack at any time. They might have the superior weapons in their Charmers and Masons and

Smiths, but we have the element of surprise. We demonstrated how we could crumble their buildings around 'em once." Patrick's eyes darkened. "What would stop us from taking their National House, then?"

"Hostages," Otto said, nodding at his feet. "Takin' bloody hostages."

Patrick nodded. "A few months ago, Polly received a scribble from Belavere City. It was a notice sent to every province in the Trench. Polly?"

All eyes turned to the Scribbler, mine included. She blushed slightly, but nodded and recited in a neutral tone. *"Union fugitives remain in custody. The House implores rebels to lay down arms and release its hostages. Surrender brings salvation. Long live Belavere."*

"That's how I know they're still alive," Patrick said sharply. "Tanner won't kill 'em. He's using 'em as shields."

"Gutless bastard," Gunner muttered, a violent edge reaching his voice.

"Our aim is to find our men and bring 'em back safely," Patrick said. "By whatever means. If a few lords should die"—and here he looked directly at Theodore—"it will only be to save ourselves. We'll be outnumbered. Easily overrun. Our own weapons will be nothing compared to their mediums. This isn't a mission for glory," he said, ensuring they each understood what he asked of them. "We remove the shield first. We'll go back for the heart when the time is right."

"What do they mean, hostages?" I said suddenly. I looked directly at Patrick, watched closely for any flicker of reaction.

"What?" Gunner grunted. "He told you—"

"The notice called for the *Union* to release its hostages," I continued, ignoring Gunner's clear lust for revenge. "What hostages?"

The rest went still and quiet.

Patrick smiled disingenuously. "Perhaps they're talkin' about you three."

But it was so obvious a diversion that I could only assume Patrick hadn't been prepared for the question. I knew he could lie better than that. "I think they're talking about Domelius Becker. The last Alchemist."

Theo tensed beside me, but I barreled on. "If you gave them Becker, they might exchange their hostages."

Patrick's eyes were closed off. "That," he said, "is not up for discussion."

Polly gripped my hand at my side imploringly. "Nina—"

But I brushed her aside. "You wouldn't make the sacrifice? Not even to save your own men?" I asked. "Your own *father*—"

"*Enough*," Patrick said with so much ice that the room seemed to shrivel, everyone retreating slightly. When Patrick next spoke, the words were hard as granite, low and deathly final. His eyes pierced mine. "All you need to know, Nina, is that I've got reasons for the choices I make. And someone must surely make them. I won't fault anyone here for bowin' out if you've weighed the danger and my own intentions and found it not worth your while." He drew a deep breath. "But you will decide in this room. Now."

There was a restless silence, quickly punctured by Scottie, Otto, and Briggs stepping forward next to Patrick, tipping caps and adjusting their waistlines.

The Colsons were a unit, if a dysfunctional one. They waited together for the rest of us to accept or rescind.

Polly stepped forward next. She stood tall and held her hands in front of her elegantly.

Theo followed suit, looking once to me to convey some sort of message. "I'm for the cause," he said. "So long as you keep your word."

"I always do," Patrick said in return.

This left me standing alone on the outside of the circle, my jaw straining under the pressure. "You're a liar," I said quietly. The words were only for Patrick, yet everyone but him seemed to react to them. Theo looked outright alarmed.

"You say you won't fault us for walking away, yet you couldn't possibly allow us to walk away now, knowing what we know." I knew he heard the question I didn't ask, of what would happen to me if I were to turn my back at this moment. What he would do with such a liability.

Patrick didn't waver. "You'll need to weigh the risks carefully then, won't you?"

The dust motes in the air collided and sparked. My heart raced.

Everything was a test. I knew, just as he did, that the fate of his plan rested with me.

I filled my chest with air, gritted my teeth, and stepped forward.

The collective seemed to sigh in relief. Theo more so than any other.

"We begin today," Patrick said, divesting himself of his coat.

"Today?" I gaped, then noticed all the men, even Theo, seemed to be readying themselves for something. "I thought we were to meet Margarite."

There was a smattering of laughter.

"You'll be introduced in a moment," Patrick said, extracting several pieces of parchment from his breast pocket. "Polly, could you have these sent off for me?"

Polly took the letters from him. "I'll leave you all to it, then," she said. Then she turned on her heel and made her way to the door.

"Where is she going?" I asked Theo in a quiet aside.

"The old post house," he said. "That's where the Scribbler's cranny is."

I frowned. "It looked abandoned."

"It is," Patrick said. "Save for Pol."

Otto and Briggs were, at that moment, taking the ends of the large circular rug and rolling it up. "'Scuse," Briggs said to me, and I moved my toes from the rug's edge.

As they rolled, they uncovered roughened timber flooring and a large wooden trapdoor. Scottie took the latch and lifted it away. A black abyss appeared beneath.

Patrick walked to its edge and peered within. "Nina," he said. "Meet Margarite."

I frowned, then moved forward to peer inside. I was immediately swarmed by the smell of fresh earth. The drop seemed interminable. "You must be kidding me."

And one after the other, each man clambered down the ladder in their miner's wear. Briggs rummaged in a cupboard first, then reappeared carrying a medley of shovels, picks, and hammers. He balanced them on his shoulder as he descended belowground.

I looked up at Patrick questioningly.

"Best to keep certain things out of sight," was all he said, donning worker's gloves. "This ain't a tunnel I want anyone stumbling upon."

Theo sighed heavily and disappeared down the ladder, leaving only myself, jaw agape, and Patrick and Tess, who headed for the door of the shop rather than the hole in its floor.

"Keep a close eye on the girl, son," Tess remarked, then proceeded out into the square. Patrick went to bolt the door behind her.

"I think she likes me," I murmured.

Despite all that had just transpired, Patrick laughed. As he came closer, I could see the tiny rivers of blood in his eyes. "Did you not sleep?"

He seemed bemused. "What?"

"You look tired. Did you not sleep last night?"

He stared at me for a moment, then shook his head. "You'd think she'd ask about the great hole in the ground," he said to Isaiah, who had laid down by the trapdoor's opening. "Or the presence of her fellow Artisan peers. But no, she asks if I got any bloody sleep."

I said nothing. I simply waited. If I had to guess, I'd say he didn't get a wink.

"No, Nina. Not much sleep to be found in the night."

"You look terrible." A lie.

He ignored it. "The hole isn't deep. Only twenty feet or so, but it will feel a whole lot deeper. There are lanterns, so you'll see well enough. Just breathe. If you feel faint, just say so and we'll take you back up."

I raised an eyebrow. Only days ago, he'd had me dragged through the tunnels. "Why the concern?"

He raised one single finger and tapped the back of my hand. "Because you're scared," he said. "You ball your hands up when you're scared."

I abruptly loosened them. "No, I don't."

"You do," he said simply. "But my guess is that you ain't afraid of being underground."

I bit my tongue and shook my head, rather like a petulant child.

"So you're afraid of *us*, then." He nodded, confirming something I'd never admitted to.

"I'm not afraid. I simply don't feel comfortable being stuck underground with men I hardly know."

"Well," Patrick said. "I'm afraid those are the terms of our agreement, Nina." He held an arm out. "Ladies first."

I put my weight on one hip, crossed my arms. "*You* first."

He sighed. His tone gentled. "No one will touch you, Nina. They wouldn't dare. You have my word."

"And what does your word count for, exactly?"

He gave me a piercing look. "That's the question, isn't it, Scurry girl? Exactly how much can we trust each other?"

CHAPTER 30

NINA

Wet rot, peppery root, kerosene fumes, and ten bodies stuffed in a small pocket. It climbed into my nostrils and clung. The canary tittered, stressed and desperate.

I wondered if the miners shivered the same as me when they burrowed inside the earth's crust. I wondered if they heard it hum the same dirge, cautioning the prey that clambered into its mouth. Or was it just the idium in my blood that made me hear the creaks and groans and warnings in the walls?

How did they come below each time, knowing they'd be unable to dig their way out?

My body wanted to crouch, though there was room enough to stand straight. Even Scottie, who was surely one of the tallest men I'd ever seen, stood easily. The timber rafters did not graze his head.

We stood in a narrow antechamber before the shaft. A shaft that would sink a person far deeper than they ought to go. Three dim lanterns flickered gaily, unfazed by the finite air.

They all looked to Patrick as he entered as though it were routine. He wore stained Crafter clothes, just like the rest: a cotton shirt rolled up to the elbows, suspenders, trousers, thick-soled boots.

A picture of my father in identical wear blazed to mind, limping toward me.

The shaft held three people, and it was one person too many. I found myself between Patrick and Gunner, my shoulders pressed so closely to their chests that they could feel every quake of my body. The shaft clanked down interminably in almost complete darkness, save for one insubstantial lantern. The air turned gaseous and torrid.

It wasn't fear of the tunnels that made me shake. It was pressure. To be encased by so much to which my mind connected sparked fire all over my body, down my spine. Professor Dumley had once told me that when Artisans restrained their magic in the presence of their medium, it was a kind of starvation. That was how I felt now. Starved.

How long had it been since I'd feasted?

Gunner operated the pulley. With each grunt of exertion, sweet remnants of whiskey filtered through his pores and filled the shaft. We descended at a pace that was surely unsafe. I stumbled slightly.

Patrick caught my elbow as I fell into him. I felt the wall of his muscles suddenly heating me. "Just breathe," came his voice, coiling into my ear. He spoke more softly than I knew him to speak. His hand slipped away from my elbow, down to my waist, and he leveraged me upright again. "Gunner won't drop us."

"I might," the man rasped. "If this Charmer of yours turns traitor on us."

Bile rose in my throat. My hand reached toward Patrick, unbidden.

"No threats, brother," Patrick warned. "The lady and I have an agreement."

Gunner didn't question further. He merely cursed as the rope in his hand bit into the skin, and then finally, finally, the shaft clattered gracelessly atop solid ground, and cool air rushed in.

Theo, Briggs, and Donny awaited us, lanterns already lit, the canary cage set down before a vast wormhole channeling through the earth beyond.

Here, the ceiling was much lower. I ducked my head to exit the shaft, and Theo came to me immediately.

"Are you all right?" he asked. I'd forgotten how much he used to ask it, a habit returning. He reached for my hand and gripped it in his, pulling me through.

Patrick stared at where Theo and I connected. There was a tick along his jaw.

"You know each other," he said to Theo rather than me. It wasn't a question.

Theo simply nodded once. His hand tightened around mine. A signal.

Patrick's eyes swept to me, crystalline blue, and I felt the distinct urge to pull my hand free, make it my own again.

As it was, Theo gripped it too tightly.

"Get started, boys," Gunner intoned. He pulled buckets and timber from the shaft and into the tunnel. "Ladies first. And Teddy, do somethin' with all these puddles, would you? I want dry boots when I walk out of here."

"For the last time," he said through gritted teeth, "it's Theo."

"Don't sulk, Teddy. Come on, get rid of these puddles before we all catch our death."

"You're with me, Nina," Patrick said. He walked past me, disappearing down the wormhole where the light couldn't chase him.

I gave Theo a resigned look, and he returned it. It reminded me of how we'd once parted ways to attend separate classes. "Good luck," he said, offering a quick grin.

I followed the walls slowly, my hands to either side, my heart galloping, watching as more gas bulbs ignited ahead, illuminating the path. My skirt dragged heavily through bog.

I collided with Patrick, his form suddenly there where before there'd been nothing, and I grunted, almost slipped.

"You're clumsier than I remember," he said, his face just visible. A deep frown lined his forehead. He knelt, upturning a square barrow with four wheels. He tied a rope to one end.

"You could have given me some warning that I'd be belowground," I grumbled. "I would have dressed more appropriately." Already, the skirt felt weighted. My back ached from it. The white blouse was likely ruined.

"Well, you dropped your skirt in front of me once, Nina Harrow. By all means, do it again."

I whacked him, my hand glancing the back of his head.

"You disappoint me," he said happily. "That deserved a closed fist, at the very least. One of these days, I'll teach you to hit me properly."

"Keep talkin' and it'll surely come to me."

"Ah, there's that Scurry mouth." He tied off the rope with a flourish. "Like cornering a feral cat."

I tasted blood when I swallowed, breathed deeply to collect myself. "You might just be the most infuriating man I've ever met."

He stood, as well as a man his height could stand in close conditions. "I'm honored. And what of Teddy, son of a lord. What is *he* to you?"

The bloodlust lingered. "Your exact opposite."

"Figured that much out for myself. First time he came down here, he fainted, started mumbling hymns in his sleep."

"He's kind. Intelligent. Well-spoken."

"That's not what I asked," Patrick interjected. "I want to know why he looks at you like he's the judge at a country fair and you're the prize pig?"

"A *pig*?"

"A steak then, if you like. Or a sponge cake."

"I'd *like* not to be described as something to eat."

"And yet," Patrick said, looking back down the tunnel to the shapes that disentangled from the dark. "I bet that boy would take a bite."

I shook my head. He was jumping to conclusions. "We knew each other well when we were apprentices, but we haven't known each other since."

Patrick waited for more.

I sighed and relented. "He broke it off with me before we graduated."

Patrick's eyes dipped to my mouth. Suddenly, he felt too close. "And did you love him?"

"Yes." I shivered.

"And he you?"

"I believed he did."

"And do you love him still?" He asked it so quietly I strained to hear. His face took on the visage of a ghost, lantern light only settling on the sharpest bones.

Breath weighted my lungs, and my feet sunk another inch. Why did all things become heavier in the dark?

"It isn't your business to know who I love." But I said it to the ground, where there was no brilliant blue. Beneath my skin, blood raced.

Silence. Sounds suffocated on the hot air. Patrick waited an interminable moment, until it was impossible not to look at him again. "If it's all the same to you," he said, low and exact, "I'm inclined to make it my business."

I was twelve years old in a courtyard, and a furtive hand slipped vials into my pocket. *You've got a mind of your own*, the boy said. *Don't let those fuckers take it.* And then he faded from view.

· · · · · ·

The work was simple enough. I was to break sideways through ground, Patrick and Otto would collect the loose dirt in the barrow and careen it down the line to Gunner, then Briggs, who would take it up the shaft. There was a secondary tunnel that ran under Kenton and out to pasture, where the earth would be discarded via a pulley mechanism, according to Briggs. Theo would control the water, which seeped through hidden veins, ravenous for empty space. The walls bled with it incessantly, the ceiling a leaking faucet. I was drenched before I could even begin.

Donny began with me at the prow. He had what looked like a doctor's stethoscope, slightly rusted, its lead mangled. Its earpieces clung to his neck as he crouched beside me, humming some worker's tune he'd dredged from the recesses of a memory I'd long ago shut away.

"How will I know which way to bend the tunnel?" I asked, my fingers itching to start.

Donny stopped humming. He turned his face in an approximation of where I stood and polished the head of the stethoscope on his shirt. "I'm captain of the ship, darlin'," he said. I wondered how his squatted knees did not protest. "Just dig where I point, all right?"

I was skeptical. "And, erm . . . *how* will you know which way to go?"

Donny tapped his temple with a boyish grin. "Got a built-in compass," he said. "I was gifted second sight, when the first was taken from me—"

"He listens for the flow of water and keeps us away from it," Patrick interjected. "I've got the compass." He held one up. It was edged in rust and clouded. "Stop windin' her up, Donny, or we'll tiptoe out and leave you here."

Donny nodded, unapologetic. "Righto. Onward, milady."

I felt each one of the men fall still behind me. Someone lifted a lantern to better see. Before me, my own shadow was cast onto the wall.

I lifted my hands. I welcomed the expansion of my mind, as Professor Dumley had once directed me. I felt my awareness of the earth unfurl, tenfold in size, commands rushing from the channels of my nervous system at light speed.

Then I felt the earth as though my fingers were touching it.

And I tore it to pieces.

The dirt took the shape my mind bid it to, large chunks crumbling away, the walls of the tunnel elongating before me, the ceiling climbing to allow room to stand. The wall moved back, back, an invisible pressure pulverizing it, roaring in my ears, a trillion mites burrowing through.

And I was caught in the ecstasy of it.

"Stop!" called a voice. "Fuckin' hell, STOP HER!"

A hand on my arm. Not the hand I was expecting: Theo's, precise and warm and sure.

"Hold up," he told me. "You're scaring our friends."

I'd already dropped my hands, and the dirt stilled. In its absence, a monstrous groan resonated all around, like the hull of a ship straining against the waves.

I turned to find the men some distance behind me, perhaps twenty yards. The path between us strewn with matter. It piled in mounds, some of it threatening to reach the ceiling.

Through a gap in the wreckage, Patrick held up a lantern and looked around. Then he stared at me like I was an earthquake, a specter of disaster.

CHAPTER 31

PATRICK

He got down on his belly on the incline of a black mound and counted the seconds passing as the walls settled.

They wailed for longer than they should without folding inward. *Five . . . six . . . seven . . . eight.*

Accompanying the groan was the blare of a hand-wrenched siren that only existed in his mind. A miner's siren. *Run, hurry, there's men below the surface.* He had to shake his head to dispel it.

But the walls held. The ceiling settled. A ways ahead, Nina looked back toward him, her face streaked in mud. If he'd had a talent for art, he'd have wished to freeze time to paint her, just the way she was.

Theodore had his hand on her wrist again.

"*Fuck* me." Gunner was panting. "Fuck, fuck, fuck." His voice trembled. He hammered a fist into the ground where he knelt.

"It's all right," Patrick said, his hand slapping Gunner's back, feeling the sweat and panic that had accumulated there. "She's held. Walls are up."

Gunner shook regardless, Briggs beside him and Patrick in front. Three trembling fish in a barrel. The canary screeched.

"Briggs?" Patrick called, his stare still plastered to the woman with hands fit for a malevolent god. "Reckon we're gonna need some more men."

"You fuckin' think so, Pat? *Bloody hell.*"

"Go topside. Tell Mrs. Colson to find some men with empty pockets and deaf ears to move all this dirt. We need strutters, too."

"Three, Pat?"

Patrick thought for a moment. "Better make it four."

"All right. Give me a minute, me fuckin' balls got lodged somewhere near my lungs."

"And while you're up there," Patrick added. "Tell my mother . . . that the timeline has been accelerated."

A beat passed, and then, "By how much, Pat?"

He thought through it. Twenty yards in twenty seconds. *Twenty fucking seconds.*

"Tell her we'll be there in four weeks." Beneath the pounding adrenaline, there was hope burgeoning. Patrick grinned.

Four weeks.

"Come on, Gun," he said now. "We need to get some timber on these walls."

His brother was still breathing too heavily, his hands on his knees. But Gunner nodded, wiped his nose.

On his belly, Patrick slid through the spaces left between ceiling and floor, the lantern he carried now the only one that hadn't flickered out. Water seeped through the ceiling. "Teddy," Patrick called. "Might be a good time to use some of your Artisan shit on all this water, eh?"

Theodore looked down at him, seemingly in no hurry, and Patrick got the inkling that the Charmer rather liked seeing him crawl through mud.

In any case, Nina withdrew herself from his hold. Patrick's jaw loosened.

Theodore raised both hands with his palms down. The water seeped back into the ground, absorbed once more. In the ceiling, the leaks receded, diverted for now.

Patrick finally stood straight in the pocket Nina had left in her wake, leaving the lantern at his feet.

"All right, Donny?" Patrick called.

"Think I'm fuckin' deaf now, too," Donny answered. "Are my ears bleedin'?"

"Just the one."

Nina watched Patrick with an unfathomable expression, and he her. The crater bitten out of the wall loomed threateningly. "Should I keep going?" she asked.

"No," Patrick said, a smile in his tone. "You most certainly shouldn't."

A crease appeared between her brows. She looked at Donny's bloodied ear, and then at the wreckage beyond Patrick's shoulder as though only now truly seeing it. "You said 'as quickly as we can,'" she reminded him.

Patrick swallowed. "Aye, I did. But we can only go as fast as it takes for us to make the hole safe. And that groaning you heard?" Nina's eyes went to the ceiling, as though she heard it still. "Disruptions in the earth. We want to avoid the weak spots. Donny here"—Patrick jutted a thumb toward him—"he has the best ears on the continent. He'll hear any danger a ways off. You listen for him to tell you when to stop."

Nina wiped her hands on her muddied skirt. "Oh," she said meekly. "I'm sorry. I—I got carried away."

Immediately, Theodore wrapped an arm around her shoulders. "You don't need to apologize," he told her, and Nina's lips pressed together. She fell quiet.

Patrick saw it then, the tight coil stuffed inside Theodore's middle. It sprung at every opportunity to steer Nina. To keep her within reach.

Patrick wondered how long it would take for her to spring back at him. "We'll clear the dirt from the tunnel," Patrick said now. "We'll need a few hours—"

"I can help," Nina offered, almost eagerly. "I could move it topside?"

But Patrick was already shaking his head. "The shaft can only hold small loads at a time, and it only has a hand pulley. If it snaps, we're stuck."

She seemed put out.

"Things move slowly down here," Patrick said, the smile creeping back into his voice—he couldn't help it. "There's a sleeping monster in these walls. Best we don't wake it."

It seemed she wanted to argue. Her hands wrung together.

"You can't do *all* the work, Nina," said Theodore, rubbing his hand along her arm.

Her lips pressed once more into a thin line. She nodded, then stepped out of Theodore's reach and raised a hand. Clods of dirt rose in midair and landed gracelessly in the wagon between them. "I'll do that much, at least. Save your shovels," she said.

Patrick only nodded once, though inside, he marveled. Never before had he seen so much power. The ease with which she wielded it. "Donny, keep an ear to the wall."

"Don't you worry. I'll keep an eye on things, Pat," his brother responded, winking in no particular direction.

"Shut up, Donny."

CHAPTER 32

NINA

The sun was still high when we breached topside again and spilled out of Margarite's Modern Ladies.

The air was cool and clean, and I filled my lungs with it.

After six hours, Patrick had called a halt to the work. By then, I'd carved five miles out of the earth, bending slowly around to the south.

My hands no longer itched. My mind was pleasantly languid, the tangles of thought now elongated and buoyant, without much resistance to them. I was afloat.

The other men, Donny gripping Gunner's shirtsleeve, began their weary stagger over the square and through the brick arch, no words exchanged other than the mention of a pint. It was a repeat of a memory—men mired in filth from the mines, lighting cigarettes and spilling into the nearest drinking hole. In my levity, it did not rankle. It felt different, an alternate world.

"Come on," Theodore bid me, holding his hand out. There was a silent expectation that I would take it. "I'll take you to your room. Get you something to eat."

Eat? I wasn't hungry. I was filled to the brim.

Still his hand hung between us. It seemed second nature to just reach for it, let it cover mine, allow him to decide where I would go.

But the sky. The air. Miles of cobbles and all my rushing blood. The last thing I wanted was to return to my room.

"I think I'll walk for a while," I told him.

The hand fell. "Then I'll join you."

"No," I answered, perhaps too quickly. "It's all right. I won't stray far."

His brow furrowed in concern. "I thought you might want to redress. You're covered in mud." His eyes flickered down to my blouse.

I quickly crossed my arms over my chest, suddenly worried that if I looked down, I might find it had turned translucent.

"The Colsons won't like you walking about alone," he persisted.

"Like I said, I won't stray far."

He seemed confused. Off-balance. "There's a rally this evening," he said, brow still creased. "They have them every month in the marketplace. I can collect you from your room and take you there." He didn't await an answer. "In fact, if there's ever anywhere you wish to go, I should come with you."

I wanted to remind him that I'd spent the last seven years alone and survived well enough, but I knew he was trying to be kind. I nodded in acceptance. It seemed he would not take his leave without it.

A twinge of guilt bled its way into my heart that I should want him to leave at all.

"It begins around dusk," he said, glancing to the horizon. "I'll be at your door just before." He placed a hand in his pocket, nodded reluctantly, and meandered away, looking over his shoulder once, then a second time.

"Ah, you broke the poor bastard's heart," came a deeper voice. Isaiah was suddenly sniffing my ankles, panting excitedly, and I turned to find Patrick standing on the stoop to Margarite's. He bent to ruffle Isaiah's ears. "Good dog," he told him.

I grimaced. "I suppose *you* won't let me walk awhile?"

"We've been workin' underground all day, and you want to walk?"

"Yes," I said unequivocally. I was pulsing with energy.

"Good god, woman," he said. "Fine, let's take a walk."

"You could always leave me to it."

"Not a fuckin' chance."

Patrick turned to bolt the door before we left, hiding the locks from view for a moment.

I tilted my head, a thought occurring to me. "How many tunnel entrances are there?"

Patrick wiped his hands on a kerchief he pulled from his trouser pocket. "A few."

I frowned. As many tunnels as secrets, then. "Will I get to see the others?"

"And why would you need to see them?"

Together, we stepped out into the square.

I rolled my eyes. "You're a paranoid man, Patrick. I don't intend to run away."

He nodded his head. "Good," he said. "Might hurt young Teddy's feelings if you took off."

"Hardly. And he's not a boy."

"Ah, Nina," he drawled. "We all turn back into boys when it comes to girls." He patted his pockets with fumbling hands. "Will you be offended if I smoke?"

"Yes."

"Goddamn," he muttered. "You might be the death of me."

Isaiah bounded ahead of us, apparently keen to be home.

I noticed how quickly we fell in step beside each other. He offered his arm, and I took it, trying not to fixate on the flex of the muscle beneath his sleeve, the warmth emanating all the way through. The sunlight painted him gold.

"Four weeks, Isaiah," he said quietly. "Four fuckin' weeks."

Isaiah, too taken with the smells of the town, didn't answer.

I didn't need to ask what was in four weeks. I swept away a clod of dirt from my blouse.

"It was . . . remarkable, what you did." He squinted down at me against the cascading light. "I've never seen anythin' quite like it. How do you feel?"

It was hard to answer his question. I inhaled a certain amount of pride. "Like a thousand wires inside me have all been snipped free."

I smiled. For the first time, the thought of using my medium wasn't tainted by quiet shame, not with him. Patrick knew it all. He knew exactly where I'd come from.

"It's been a long time since I leveraged so much magic at once. I'm out of practice."

Patrick whistled low, then shook his head. "God help us all, then," he said, averting his eyes.

I was a lit match.

"What of the rally?" he asked now. "Will you give me another chance to persuade you to the right side?"

I rose my eyebrows at him. "I assumed I'd be made to stay behind."

"Look me in the eye and tell me you wouldn't pick the locks the second my back were turned."

I only grinned.

He grinned in return, clicked his tongue. "S'pose it wouldn't be wise, leaving you alone at Colson's while every man, woman, and horse looked the other way. You'd be a sitting target."

I rolled my eyes. "Is there truly anyone in this town who would go against you?"

"Can't be too careful," he muttered. "But you should come to the rally. Let Teddy take you."

"Theo."

"Whatever."

Suspicion crept in. "Why are you being so gracious?"

He shrugged.

"And why are you letting me come to the rally? Do you think it might turn me?"

"I get the feeling it'd take a lot more than one party to convince you."

"Party?" I repeated, confused. The only rallies I'd witnessed included a lot of slogan-shouting from an increasingly bloodthirsty crowd. "No politician's speech?"

He sighed. "It'll be quick," he allowed. "After that, it's just drinking and dancing. If there's one thing this town can agree on, it's how to do both at the same time."

I tilted my head. "Do you dance?" I thought of all those stuffy Artisan School dance lessons to a string quartet in a marble-hewn ballroom. Men with ramrod spines and upturned noses.

"No," he said flatly. "I only drink."

We reached Colson's much quicker than seemed possible, given our slow amble. At the door he disentangled my arm from his, but he did not immediately drop my fingers. His were hot. Burning. For a moment, the pad of his thumb skated across my knuckles.

Once more, I counted the stolen seconds before he let me go. *Three, four, five, six.*

He blinked rapidly, relinquished my hand.

"Are you not heading inside?" I asked.

He shook his head and put his hands in his pockets. "I'll see you at the rally."

"I have nothing appropriate to wear," I told him, my fingers itching once again, though not for their medium this time.

"I'll have somethin' sent up," he said. "Mrs. Colson will bring you supper."

"Please thank her for me."

"Nah," he said, smirking at some joke I'd missed. "Better if I don't." Then he nodded once, eyes flickering to mine in a way that made my heart stutter, then stepped back into the lane, dusty coat billowing out behind him.

I stood there a whole minute, waiting for my blood to cool before turning to go inside.

CHAPTER 33

NINA
SEVEN YEARS AGO

The Artisan Fellowship Ball was an annual event inviting future graduates to dine and dance in the splendor of the National Artisan House,
where a stowed-away ballroom was dusted off and dipped in gold.

On the outskirts of the dancefloor, I felt Theo's fingers slip out of mine.
He held his hand out to a girl with an exuberant headdress, then left me
in the corner alone.

I watched as he spun her among the sea of other couples, an inexplica-
ble hollowness carved from my middle.

"Is that Theodore I see with Jane Winter?" said a voice from my side.
Polly was resplendent in white silk, her dark hair coiffed high on her head.

"You don't wish to dance?" she asked.

I shook my head.

"Me neither. I've never felt more out of place."

I bumped my shoulder against hers. "We've worked as hard as any of
them, haven't we?"

Polly grimaced. "Harder, probably."

But I felt what she felt, the undeniable sense that we were imposters.
The worm and the squid.

For a while, we simply watched the party pass us by. To me, it looked like theater: costumes and gleaming teeth and false smiles. Around the government ministers, all manner of near-graduates swarmed—Cutters and Scribblers and Masons and Smiths all vying to have their name remembered, collecting insurance they wouldn't be sent somewhere unseemly beyond graduation.

As for me, I imagined a foothill hidden in the colossal shadow of a snowcapped mountain, an easel with fresh canvas, a board wet with paint, someone who loved me. It was, really, all I wanted.

Theo offered his hand to yet another of our classmates.

"What plans do you have after graduation?" I asked Polly.

She grimaced. "I've been posted in Hesson."

A brink town. It seemed all the new Scribblers were sent to the ends of the Trench. Polly took a sip of champagne and said, "It seems foolish, doesn't it? To send Artisans so far from the capital on the precipice of a war?"

It was uttered with such bluntness that my lungs stuttered. The party continued to ebb and surge before us in great mocking contrast. We weren't to talk of such things—to spread panic. "The union members are being disbanded," I argued quietly. "It was in the papers."

"The papers lie all the time. Just last week, a train cart was blown to pieces on its way to the city."

I swallowed, trying not to look too surprised, lest someone around us notice.

After a considerable silence, Polly said, "Do you ever imagine that perhaps the idium got it all wrong?"

A few nearby wallflowers were staring now, their ears pricked. Several paces away, Theodore's father, Lord Shop, caught my eye.

He turned his cane in our direction.

"Shh," I warned, snatching Polly's hand. I ushered her sideways. "Outside. Come on."

We wove through the throng and escaped through the open doors, our heads ducked and faces turned away. Gardens stretched out before us, neatly hedged and haloed in golden light from hundreds of torches speared into the flower beds. The music of the party settled into gentle waves, and Polly and I were alone, save the few couples stealing private moments behind peony bushes.

I pulled Polly into a dark corner, not too close to the exit. "They're lying to us," she continued, as though a wall inside her had been knocked down and she couldn't stem the river. "I don't think they have control over *any* of it."

"I'm sure it's—"

"War is *coming*, Nina. They know it, and they won't tell anyone." Polly was trembling. Her fingernails bit into my palms. "My father says that half the policemen have abandoned their posts already. *Half!* They're all Craftsmen. How are we to win a war if our own army is made of the enemy?"

The word *enemy* struck me. Her parents were Crafters. She'd once belonged to the brink.

"They'll think nothing of killing people like us, Nina. *Nothing.* They're stronger than us. Crueler."

I went quiet. There had been a boy in my Scurry schoolroom who'd routinely held me against a brick wall in the yard and forced black beetles past my lips. I still remembered the way they'd tasted. I wanted to argue with Polly but found I couldn't.

Instead, I embraced her. "Even if what you believe comes to pass," I said, "we'll still have the greatest minds working to keep all of us safe." And as I said it, I realized it was true. What would bullets and dynamite matter next to an army of thousands who could turn the land against them, crack the earth beneath their feet, and bury them whole?

"They're lying to us, Nina," she said into the tender flesh of my neck.

"Nina?" came a voice. "Polly?"

I felt her disentangle from me immediately. She wiped her eyes and smiled at the newcomer. "Theo."

"Pardon the interruption," he said, eyes darting between us.

I was quick to take his arm and guide him away from Polly before she could say something she regretted.

"Is she unwell?" he asked me, looking back at her.

"Just feeling sentimental," I said. "Too much champagne." I leaned my head against his shoulder to hide my face.

"What did the two of you talk about?" he asked, his suspicion plain. I wondered if Polly's voice had traveled too far in the ballroom.

I considered lying, but panic climbed my throat, and there was no one I trusted more than him. So instead, I asked him the question on the tip of my tongue. The question we had, each one of us, wordlessly agreed not to utter. "Theo, what will you do if this war comes to pass?"

He rolled his eyes. It seemed so often recently that his eyes rolled when I spoke. "Don't be dramatic. There's nothing to fear."

"You and I have *everything* to fear. Do you truly believe that we won't be put on the front lines?"

He pinched the bridge of his nose. "Nina, stop. Enough with this."

My voice was small. "Enough with what?"

"With this . . . *naivete*! We aren't children anymore."

I breathed, once. Twice. "What is that supposed to mean?"

"Good God, Nina. It means we have responsibilities to uphold. Did you really think we could just hold hands forever and ignore what we *are*?"

A knife incised my chest, twisting inward toward my heart. "Are you prepared to follow any order then?" I asked. "Whatever it might be?"

Theo shook his head at me, exasperated. "Nina," he pleaded. "What other choice is there?"

There *was* another, looming there in the dark. "We could refuse," I said. "You and I. We could refuse to be their weapons."

I watched a shutter fall over his eyes. The knife sunk deeper. "What?"

"We could do it, Theo," I said, taking him by the wrists. "We have minds of our own. Why should we let them take that from us?"

"Shh," he hissed, looking over his shoulder, disentangling his wrists from me and raising his hands as though to fend off an animal. "Lower your voice. We're surrounded by every lord of the nation."

"Theo." And now, it was me who pleaded. "Please. Think about it." Beneath my collar was the emerald he'd gifted me a year previous, when the future had seemed very, very distant. I reached to grip it through the fabric, a habit I'd developed. "The only thing that I want . . . is you." I was painfully aware of how pitiful I was.

His head dropped on a sigh. He shook it, and when it rose again, he looked tired. Sad. "Nina," he said. "Once we've graduated, I'm leaving for Thornton. I—I'll take my ordainment there."

In plunged the knife, to the depths of my pulsing heart.

I tried to identify Theo in the person who stood before me and failed. He seemed a stranger. "What?" A gasp escaped, I was afraid my lungs were caving in. Theo looked away.

"When?" I managed.

"The day after the ceremony."

"And you've already decided?"

"I have," he said. His chin shook, but his eyes—they were steel. "I have to, Nina. I have to go."

"For . . . for how long?"

"Two years."

It seemed an uncrossable amount of time. "Does—did your father—?"

"My father suggested it, yes," he answered. "If a revolution breaks, he thinks they would need a force there to man the docks. This is my duty, Nina."

I reeled. "And what of us? Of me?"

Theo met my eyes, and for a second his facade broke. "Tanner wants you here."

"That isn't what I meant."

His chest rose, swelling with that final missile. I wondered how long he'd kept it loaded and aimed. "Nina, we're only eighteen. I think it best we part ways."

There was more. More about the nature of change, and how it creeps up on a person. He apologized and apologized until I was riddled with his reasons. I stared at the earth beneath his feet as he spoke and wondered why I could so easily move it, but I couldn't move *him*.

CHAPTER 34

NINA

When Theo collected me at dusk, as he promised he would, he did not hold out his hand.

His eyes widened at the dress I wore. A dress that, I feared, had been purloined from some sorry wife's wardrobe. It hugged my waist in romantic red and lined my spine in buttons. At first glance in the wardrobe mirror, I thought I looked striking. On second glance, I was scandalized by the way my breasts threatened the sanctity of the bustline. I had to wrap a shawl around my shoulders to look properly decent.

Theodore cleared his throat, keeping his eyes dutifully ahead.

We walked by Sam down the treacherous stairs, out through the pub, out to a blanket of stars close enough to touch. In dim light, the town's lanterns looked like magic.

The trolley rattled past, brimming with passengers—a train's carcass trundling down Main Street, following a gentle curve out of sight. Steam rose from the pavement, starlings swarmed above, and a chorus of pounding feet passed us by, everyone headed in the same direction.

Theodore drew a cigarette from his pocket and lit it, and I raised an eyebrow.

He shrugged in response. "At first, I couldn't stand them. Now I can't stop."

I caught a laugh between my teeth before it could escape. "What would your mother say?"

"Wouldn't say much of anything I'd imagine. She's dead."

My stomach lurched. I stopped in the street. "Theo, I'm . . . I didn't know. I'm sorry."

"It's all right, Clarke," he said, flicking ash to the pavement. "Everyone's lost someone, haven't they?"

Yes, everyone had lost someone. "How did she—?"

"Influenza," he said, and his hand surreptitiously slipped around mine, pulling me onward. "Right after the laboratories in the South were raided. The reports said the Craftsmen had taken all the terranium meant for bluff. We couldn't find any in a twenty-mile radius. The fever took her a week later."

My conversation with Patrick came to mind immediately.

How did you get that terranium?

By doing bad things.

"I'm sorry, Theo," I said. And I didn't pull my hand away, not until we reached the marketplace. People thronged near the doors, and children, abandoning their parents for the evening, chased one another in circles.

"If you find yourself wanting to leave," said Theo, "just say the word, and we'll go back."

"Why should I want to leave?"

He grimaced. "It can become . . . rowdy."

I must have looked to him like I was still eighteen years old, a debutante. Not a girl from Scurry, or a woman seven years in the shadows.

"Do you remember the night of the Fellowship Ball?" I asked him, letting him guide me into the giant barn, cleared of its vendors' tables and wares. The crowd was gathering before a low wooden stage in the back corner, and we followed suit.

Theo nodded, his neck now mottled red. "What of it?" he asked warily.

"You danced half the night with every girl we knew." On the stage,

Scottie set down a podium, and I kept my eyes on him instead of Theo. "As many as you could. And I stayed by the wall."

Theo sighed, his eyes closing briefly. "Yes. I thought it might be better to try and . . . slowly separate myself, I suppose. I think I was trying to ease the blow. It was idiotic of me." His regret sounded genuine.

I nodded. "It bothered me for a long time."

Theodore shifted nervously, and I envisioned him again, walking past me in the halls and pretending the two of us had never been. Pretending he couldn't see me breaking. Crumbling.

"You left me as well," he muttered. Patrick climbed onto the stage. "Left me in the dust."

"You left me behind well before," I answered, and a millstone inside me disintegrated.

Patrick was doused in shadow, but I saw that he'd changed his clothes, bathed, perhaps even shaved. His hair remained as wavy as it had been when he was a boy. He was hundreds of heads and shoulders away, but I still saw those small pieces of him.

What seemed like the entire town chanted the Miners Union creed: *From each what they can give, to each what they need. By dusk our work is done—at dawn we fight!*

Scottie brought a small gramophone onto the stage, a long coil of wire, and what was possibly a reconstituted trumpet. Castoffs that did not belong together, but when Patrick raised the horn to his lips, the gramophone crackled, and his voice was magnified louder than ought to be possible.

I laughed in surprise.

"Good people of Kenton Hill," he said, and the crowd cheered. Every one of them settled, their faces turned to the stage and the man presiding it. "Yesterday, our brothers in combat successfully raided the docks of Dorser and took two shipping containers of artillery out of the hands of the Lords' Army."

An uproarious response. Women clapped, men raised their hats in the air.

"With control of the Dorser docks, and the ones in Morland and Baymouth, we will take over imports and exports, and that which has been withheld from us by our own government will be sought offshore instead!"

More cheers, louder now. It struck me that Patrick had an aptitude for this—a politician's vigor, whether he would admit it or not. He was utterly compelling.

"Every success, every inch gained, has been gained with nothing more than the grit of laboring Craftsmen!"

"And what are we?" Theodore said quietly, beneath the applause. "Showpieces?"

"We will take back the land we have worked for generations. And God help those so unfortunate as to stand against us!"

Around me, people exploded in a frenzy, cheering, whistling, shouting slurs and curses and devotions simultaneously. Patrick returned his strange microphone to Scottie, pushed his sleeves up to his elbows and left the stage. He descended into a sea of back claps and vanished.

Music started, a man with a fiddle on a far wall played a quickening melody. He was joined by another, a man with a harmonica, another with a cello. A small grand piano with two wooden legs and two steel substitutes was unveiled beneath a dustsheet, and a woman took the stool before it. The song shook the starlings from the rafters, and soon, pairs stumbled and laughed along to a country dance I'd not seen since childhood.

A small smile crept across my lips. I clapped along with the other spectators.

Theo left my side momentarily and returned seconds later with a tin cup of wine. "It's bitter," he said. "But not so bad once you get used to it."

I downed the entire cup before the first song ended, the piano notes still warbling among applause.

Overhead, those endless twinkling manufactured lights hung. Kenton Hill's very own galaxy. A young woman was asked to dance by a timid young man. Little girls twirled amid a group of cheering adults. A harried contingent served spit pork and potatoes at the door, and the fiddler played notes at such dizzying speed I could hardly make sense of his fingers. I had the sudden image of my old music composition class, where dozens of students hovered over the shoulder of a professor, trying to untangle the majesty of his quick play. I felt, and not for the first time since arriving, that I was in someone else's misshapen dream.

Without preamble, Theo turned to me. He hesitated before speaking. "I was an idiot back then," he said, clearing his throat. "I should have danced with you all night."

He likely didn't remember that I had begged him for reprieve. I had never wanted to dance in that room, before all those watchful eyes.

"Let me make amends." He held out his hand. "Please, Clarke."

It seemed too joyous a moment to say no, and I thought it might be nice to dance with him again, the man I'd loved as an adolescent. He led me out into the fray.

The next dance was a folk number, and Theo turned me until my back met his chest and held my hands out wide in the starting position. Had it really been years since we'd practiced these steps in the Artisan dance hall, laughing and falling over each other's feet?

We followed the flow of dancers in a circle. Theo led me with expertise. Feet pounded the plywood and reverberated in my bones. My borrowed red dress arced when I spun, and I didn't try to stem the gaiety, the freedom of it. My shawl slipped from my shoulders and puddled around my elbows. As always, the tendrils around the frame of my face sprung free, and when I finally looked back at Theo, he was smiling at me—not, it seemed, at the simple happiness of barn dancing.

And it made me sad that I no longer saw him in the same way I used to.

The song ended abruptly, with both of Theo's hands around my waist in a way our old instructor would have deemed improper. The crowd clapped politely. Theo's chest pounded beneath my hand. His dark eyes hooded. He bore down on me.

"No—"

"Pardon, Teddy," came a merciful voice, and I disengaged from Theo's embrace while I still could.

Patrick stood close by with a strange expression; his jaw fastened, eyes flashing.

Theo's smile fell. He looked between me and Patrick, and something fraught brewed in the space between the two men.

But Patrick spoke genially enough. "I'll need to steal her for this one." And he held his hand out to me.

If we'd still stood in the Artisan School, where Theo's status had counted for something, he might have laughed in Patrick's face and spun me away. Then again, he wouldn't have been challenged in the first place.

But this was Kenton Hill. Theo's expression darkened. "If Nina wishes."

I swallowed.

Patrick's gaze softened considerably when he looked at me, but his hand waited.

I thought I saw him grin when I placed my fingers in his palm. He nodded to Theo. "Enjoy your evenin'," he said, and turned his back.

Patrick pulled me deeper into the flock of dancers, his fingers interlocking with mine. I had a mind to look back at Theo and say something, but a new song had begun, and Patrick turned and gathered me to him automatically, as though it were second nature.

I was immediately coalesced in warmth and the heady mixture of subtle cologne, fresh linen, washed skin.

I couldn't tell if his pulse sprinted as violently as mine. Was he a drug for all the women he touched?

The music was light and fast, the couples whirled by around us, and yet Patrick seemed in no hurry to lead me into the current. We swayed very slowly against the tide.

Looking at him became difficult. "I thought you didn't dance?"

"I don't," he said. "But evidently, *you* do."

I tried to put on a frown, but I was a slave to my thundering blood. "Am I not permitted to dance with anyone else?"

He looked over my head, eyes surveying the crowd. "If you want to, you can dance with all of them. Lord knows every man in here is imaginin' it."

I scoffed. "You can't know the thoughts of every—"

"Their eyes've been following you since you walked in. You're gonna get them in trouble with their wives."

I blushed fiercely. "They have not."

"They have."

I looked at the wall of his chest. My stomach knotted. "I can't tell if you're complimenting me," I admitted. "Are you?"

"Just sayin' how it is," he said, as though he were describing the weather. "Are you a woman who needs to be complimented?" He ceased his surveillance to look down at me. I wished his eyes were any other color.

"*Every* woman should be complimented. Especially by the men who cut in to dance with them."

"Then, you have very pretty freckles."

"You're jealous," I said boldly, though I could hardly believe it. "Why should you be jealous?"

"I can't say, Nina. But there it is."

"You can't say?"

"No," he said flatly. "I can't. Can *you* say why your heart's beating out of your chest?"

Mortification flooded me. Deep in my belly, there was a quickening as good as an admission.

Patrick nodded, and there was no arrogance to it, just a deep, inscrutable knowing. "So then, we both have things we can't speak on."

We swayed back and forth, his hand diligently pressed to the middle of my back, not daring to move a single inch lower, oblivious to the crowd around us.

"We all turn back into boys when it comes to girls," he said again, though I wasn't sure if he was speaking to me or to himself. "Perhaps we can let it just be that."

We should let it just be that, I thought. *And nothing more.* "Do you intend to intercede every time another man looks my way?"

He grinned. He couldn't seem to help it. "I intend to put the rest of these boys to shame and spoil you for anyone else."

My breath stopped. *Why should my breath stop?* "Says the man who can't dance."

His grin turned devilish. "I said that I don't dance, not that I *can't.*" His chest swelled beneath my hand. "Hold on, Scurry girl."

His hand flexed at my back and pulled me against him, so that my chest pressed into his. I felt my nipples harden beneath the chiffon. The muscle of his stomach flattened against my own, and he whirled us suddenly sideways. We broke into the circle of couples, me laughing in shock, and the music, the cacophony, came swarming back in.

I hardly knew the steps to the dances, and it didn't seem to matter. Patrick was, by contrast, proficient in all. He smiled wickedly, laughed as he caught and released me, spun me back into his arms, linked my elbow with his. His neck was hot where my hand touched it. When I mock curtsied at the end of a particularly quick song, his eyes sparked and he ran a hand over his face, as though it physically pained him.

The music slowed, became fluid and gentle, and I thought that might be the moment where he returned to his many duties, and me to my corner. But instead, he gingerly caught my waist in one hand and clasped the other around my palm, turning us both in an endless circle.

Silence ensued, and we stared at each other until I could hardly stand it.

I was the one to break first. I lowered my gaze. "You *can* dance," I accused. "Where does a miner learn how to dance like that?"

He made a show of being offended. "You've got an awful memory. Didn't I demonstrate my abilities in that courtyard for you?"

I remembered it then—Patrick whirling about in the dust, children giggling behind their hands. "You looked insane."

"As I recall, you were claiming that Crafters didn't like music or dancing." He looked about us pointedly. "You can eat those words now, if you like."

I rolled my eyes. Smiled.

For a while we simply turned in our own small, warm space until my head grew heavy and the music grew indistinct. After a time, I found my head had come to rest against his shoulder, though I didn't remember putting it there. I felt restful, pleasingly drunk—on what, I could not say.

"You're too beautiful to be real," he said suddenly, softly. With my ear pressed to his chest, I could feel the words, too. "There's your compliment." His fingers traced a very careful line then, slowly up my spine and back down, and in their wake, they left a trail of fire.

And I thought, in that moment, of the same picture drawn over and over until every single line was precise, and yet I still hadn't rendered a perfect replica of him. "I drew pictures of you," I told him, giving him this one small piece of myself. "In school."

He didn't speak. Just pulled me round and round in a small orbit.

I swallowed. "I was scared to forget you."

The sound of his heart beating made me think of caves under leagues of sea. "I never had a hope in the world of forgetting you, Scurry girl."

And I wondered what had made me so unforgettable. Was it the secret we'd unraveled together, or was it the inner workings of fate?

How to stop a rising tide, the rapidly expanding cell of a storm?

If I'd known it then, in that barn, I might have reduced that night to the whims of wine and music.

I might not have tilted my face to his and seen firsthand the sureness burgeoning in all that blue.

He shook his head. "I'd hoped you were hideous."

I smiled. "And I'd hoped you weren't an arse."

"Well," he muttered, eyes lowering to my mouth. "We don't always get what we want." And then he kissed me.

Or perhaps I pressed my lips to his first. I was balanced on my toes after all, reaching, reaching, and then his mouth and mine touched, and it was whisper-soft and intoxicating. Unstoppable.

I blazed to life.

The song changed, became rapid and throbbing again, and the moment evaporated. Spell broken.

I descended back onto the soles of my feet, releasing his neck, but his arm remained wrapped around my back.

You're a fool, I thought.

"I . . ." he stumbled, swearing beneath his breath. It was odd to see him falter. "I'm sorry," he managed. I gathered he had little practice with apologies.

I tried not to sound breathless. "Are you?"

"Not even a bit," he said. "Nevertheless, it was . . . impolite."

"And everything you've done so far has been beyond reproach?"

"I hope not." He grimaced. "Sounds dull."

I tried not to smile. Truly, I did.

"Walk with me," he said then, eyes still glinting. "You've tortured me enough."

But he didn't look like a tortured man. He looked and laughed exactly like the boy of twelve I remembered. He took my hand and pulled me through the rivulets of people. By the tapped barrels along the wall, I spied Tess Colson watching her son with a curious expression. She marked his course with a smile far gentler than I thought her capable.

There were others who watched us leave—many in fact, but I paid them no mind.

· · · · · ·

The open lane brought fresh air. Children ran screaming, as was mandated by childhood. I'd spent many nights just the same, bolting down the street in some game while the grown-ups drank in the warmth of the pub. There were differences though, between my youth and the one tearing through Kenton Hill. These boys and girls weren't without shoes.

They wore knitted jumpers. Some squeezed bits of cooked pork in their hands, the juices slipping over their knuckles.

I'd stopped walking, and Patrick with me. He followed my line of sight to the children, then looked at me quizzically. "Thinking of stealin' one?"

"I don't think I was ever that free," I said. It seemed to come from a vault I'd left unlocked. Even I was surprised to hear it aloud.

Patrick frowned. "You never played coppers and thieves?"

"I did. But I don't think I looked like them." I could explain it no further. I just knew that my cheeks had never shone that brightly. I'd never bellowed with such abandon. Always, always, I knew that the game's end would come long before Fletcher Harrow emerged from whatever hole he was drinking in. And when he did, it was a fickle bet he'd be able to make the walk home.

"No," Patrick said. "Reckon I didn't, either."

There was a saying in Scurry, that the anger of the parent leaves traces in the blood. Babies got their eyes from their mother and their bloodlust from their father. Their mum's bitterness, their grandfather's right hook. All of us born with hereditary rot in our bellies. It seemed these children had been spared it.

But Patrick and I, we were sure carriers.

"They've never heard the whistles, Nina. That's what it is."

I thought he might be right. Sometimes I heard them in my nightmares. Whistles, canaries, and earth caving in.

We continued up the lane at a languid pace. In the nimbus of lanterns, pairs sipped bottles and laughed. Polly Prescott sat on the steps to the tea shop and pressed her shoulder to Otto's. I wondered if she felt freedom in sitting without her legs crossed at the ankles, without a kerchief beneath her arse or wires in her undergarments. She tipped her head back and laughed at something Otto said. I wondered if she thought of Belavere City at all.

"What about you?" I slipped my hand in the crook of Patrick's arm, the fever of the night making me brave. "Did you ever play coppers and thieves?"

"Darlin', I'm playing it every day."

I sniffed a laugh. "I suppose you are."

"Haven't lost yet," he said, kicking a stone from his course.

But along the way that game had become life, it seemed. He'd some-how grown into a man responsible for the running of an entire town, a political revolution. I wondered when the game had lost its fantasy. "Would you explain it all to me, if I asked you?"

"I can't yet read your mind, Nina, much as I'd like to. Explain what?"

"How the Union formed," I said. "How it all started."

He hesitated, but only for a moment. There and then gone. "It started with me."

This I knew already. He'd blown the whistle. "You told your father about the idium we found."

"I did," he said. "But even before that, my father was already having meetings in the pub every week, talkin' about change. Talkin' about the police. We've only got three left now, but there used to be an entire outfit of coppers. Bigger brutes I've never seen. They killed a miner in the street when I was a kid for spitting on an officer's shoes. Beat him with their ba-tons until his skull caved in, right outside the pub. People were angry after that, of course, but none more so than my father. He wanted every one of them dead." Patrick stared up at those plucked, strung-up stars. His usual tiredness returned. "It was like he'd already determined what would hap-pen. Had everything mapped out, just needed a reason. Something big enough to make even the most mild-natured man pick up a gun."

I stared, wide-eyed. "And then you got off the train."

He nodded slowly. "And then I got off the fuckin' train. My father had Kenton's miners corralled around the jailhouse by the end of the week, and they set it ablaze. My mother hardly spoke to my dad again after that, because he made me and Gunner come along, and we saw it all."

I could almost smell the burning ash on the air, hear the pounding fists on the inside of the glass as two boys in the street watched monsters take the shape of men.

Patrick looked over his shoulder. "Whatever is alive and well in those kids back there, I reckon it was snuffed out in Gunner and me that very night."

We had walked beyond the streetlights and claimed the middle of the lane. There was absolutely no one to stop us. I had the strange urge to spread my arms and try to balance on the cobbles. Instead, I asked, "What happened next?"

"The coppers that remained were kept scared enough that they didn't report what happened, and in return, they got to keep the pay the government continued to send to the dead ones. My dad and the others built a tunnel to the nearest port, and they began making their deals, hoarding weapons. He started traveling, using false names and talking in more pubs about the idium. He said it was like a contagion spreading. Hundreds quickly pledged to the Miners Union, which meant more tunnels, more guns. They communicated through coded telegrams back then, sending messages underground—we couldn't trust the Scribbler we had at the time. The strikes were effective, and Dad said it wouldn't be long till the whole government buckled. Eventually, he started talking about blowing up the school." Here, Patrick paused, and his voice resembled fraying thread. "And I begged him to target anything else."

I swallowed shakily, the smell of sulfur and smoke collecting in my nose. "Why did he do it?" I managed.

He'd walked ahead of me, letting my arm fall. I suspected it was to offer me distance. But he had the decency to look me in the eye when he said, "Because that school was the epicenter of the Artisans' universe, and we had a message to send."

That was war, wasn't it? *Look at the buildings we can crumble. Look at how many we can kill.*

I nodded weakly, a tear escaping over the curve of my cheekbone. "He was right," I murmured. "It was the center of everything."

He stepped toward me, then thought better of it. He buried his hands in his pockets. "My father was—*is* a good man. I might not be painting a pretty picture, but he's not evil. He sent warnings. We thought the city would be evacuated."

"The House of Lords didn't take the idea of a rebellion so seriously back then," I said, wiping my fingers beneath my eyes.

Patrick's voice turned wry. "Or perhaps they knew we would attack, and they *wanted* the Nation to see what barbarians we are."

And didn't that sound right? All those caricatures in the newspapers of blood-smeared Crafters—men willing to bury an entire generation of Artisans under rubble.

I wished I could stem the tears. "How did he do it?" I asked. "How did he get into the school?"

But Patrick shook his head, and for a moment, I thought he swayed where he stood, or perhaps it was me.

"No, Nina," he said. "Not him. Me."

Of course.

"We dug a tunnel from the outskirts of the city to the center, all of us. Scottie, Briggs, Gunner, Donny, Otto. Two miles long, right underneath the building. But it was me who set the explosives and the wires. It was me who detonated it. My father was miles and miles away, celebrating in Colson's."

I remembered the sensation of the floor rising and sinking, the walls and ceiling splitting, lights exploding. All those beautiful things, covered in plaster dust. I thought of Patrick, belowground, wiring the boxes that would pitch it all into a crater.

"I swear to you, Nina," he said now, eyes hard. "We didn't know you were all waiting above it. If I had . . ."

I exhaled, then eventually, finished the sentence for him. "If you had known, you would have pushed on the plunger anyway, because you believed it was right."

His jaw rolled. "I like to believe I wouldn't have. I need to believe that."

I didn't much care to pick apart whether he was lying. I was running through cracking halls, Aunt Francis pulling on my hand.

Then, back in Kenton Hill, Patrick's arms went around me, and I was swallowed in warm darkness. I buried my face in it and waited for the shaking to stop.

"Just breathe," he told me. "It'll pass."

Slowly, achingly so, it did. And he pressed his cheek to mine, as though he was trying to steal the tears slicking my skin. "I'm sorry, Scurry girl," he said, and it felt years old, heavy with burden. His face came away as wet as mine, full of ghosts.

We walked the remaining journey without exchanging a word. Just my hand in his, all the way down Main Street and through the pub and up the stairwell. All the way to number fifteen.

And he bid me goodnight before I thought he would, and turned to retreat, and it was me who stopped him. I clasped his hand when he tried to reclaim it, and without saying a word I asked him if he would kiss me again.

He shook his head, slowly, painfully. "The night's grown too sad for it, Nina."

But there had been joy, too, hadn't there? There'd been laughter and flushed cheeks and racing hearts. And he wanted to. It was written all over him.

"Men turn into boys when it comes to girls," I reminded him, though I had no right. "Perhaps we can let it just be about that."

He looked at me, tormented, a card house quickly folding. And I couldn't say why I pushed him, or why I felt suddenly starved. In truth, I wasn't thinking at all. I only felt, and whatever it was, I was sure he felt it, too.

So when he crowded me against the door I was already expecting it, and I hardly moved, hardly breathed. His hands slipped over my waist and around my back, and his voice ghosted over my lips. "I'll wake up tomorrow, and you'll have been somethin' I imagined, I'm sure of it." And then his lips pressed to mine. Briefly, softly, and so heart-wrenchingly gentle.

And then they lifted, and I felt deserted.

"Sleep well," he told me, hands disappearing from my body. "I'll send Sam up." He was descending the steps long before I could muster any sensical response.

I touched my fingers to my lips. Vaguely noticed that they trembled. Then, I smiled so widely that I thought they might crack.

It was a while before I moved, before my heart slowed and my muscles uncoiled. I turned to number fifteen and went inside, listening for the snick of the doorjamb as it shut, and still, all I could see was his face. I leaned my forehead against the wood.

"Enjoy your evening?" said a voice, and I jumped.

There was movement in the shadows. A figure sitting on the end of my bed. It lifted something to its mouth, and I heard the glug of liquid, the subsequent exhale.

"Theo?" I asked, stomach turning. "What are you doing in my room?"

"Waiting," he said. Then he stood, and the light slinking in from the street threw him into relief. He saluted me with an amber bottle. "Having a drink."

The words were elongated and slurred. A warning bolted across my skin. "I'm tired," I told him carefully. "Perhaps we can talk in the morning."

"What are you doing, Clarke?" he asked. "Pardon, that's not your name, is it? Not anymore."

I eyed the door handle. "Theo, you shouldn't—"

"He's a dangerous man." He stalked forward, and in the dark, he seemed taller, more daunting. "You haven't been here long enough to see that, but I have."

"Theo. I don't know what you're talk—"

"I watched you," he said, stepping closer, into another prism of light thrown through the window. "I watched you dance with him." His face had changed. Liquor had dragged out the circles beneath his eyes and twisted his lips, turning him cruel. "I watched you *kiss* him."

Fear slid down my throat and into my belly, dousing the fire and leaving only ice. I swallowed. "It isn't what you think."

"What do I think?"

"I knew Patrick *before*, Theo. Before all of this. When we were young."

He nodded at the ceiling. "Ah. A romance rekindled, then."

"No—"

"And what will happen to this . . . *romance* when he finds out why you're really here, Nina?" he asked. "When Patrick finds out who sent you?"

My fingers clenched. "Theo, please . . . someone might hear—"

"Or worse," Theo continued, "what will happen to *you*, when Tanner learns you've been seduced by the man you were sent to bury?"

CHAPTER 35

NINA
ONE MONTH PRIOR

It took them seven years to catch me.

In the watery lanes of Delfield, an entire contingent of infantrymen in their navy blue uniforms chased me all the way to the ramparts. At the spearhead was a man who struck me so hard with his baton, I did not wake for an entire day.

When next I opened my eyes, I was in the National Artisan House, albeit not a part I recognized.

A nurse hovered near the door, and the second I roused, she disappeared through it like a startled cat.

There was an open cupboard of medical supplies, a spongy cot mattress beneath me, a tall, stained window, a persistent pounding against my skull. My head felt two sizes too big, a burden on my neck. When I rolled it to the side, I caught my reflection in a tin cup waiting on a side table. It showed a girl with a pair of blackened eyes, her head swathed in white bandage.

Get up, I thought. *Go. Get out of here.*

I only managed the titanic effort of swinging my legs over the side of the cot, of sitting upright, before the door was thrashed open.

Tanner walked in, and only then did nausea find me, cresting and breaking in great rolling waves. I leaned over the side of the bed and vomited.

"I'll have the nurse return shortly to clean that up," the lord said, pins gleaming on his lapels, buttons polished. I thought he looked thinner, older. "Hello, Nina Clarke."

I said nothing. It had always been best to say nothing.

He tilted his head, perused me from head to toe. "Good God. You are revolting, aren't you? Those who lie with dogs come away with fleas, I suppose. You've been sorely missed, my dear."

I spat the remnants of bile before him onto the checkered floor.

"Come now. Surely your foray into our world left you with better manners than that. I remember you to be quite the young lady. I must admit, the first time I laid eyes on you, I was surprised."

"Surprised I didn't walk in on four legs?" I rasped.

"Ha! Quite," he laughed. "I had no idea they still taught children in Scurry to speak in more than monosyllables. But you defied my expectations, Nina. And again in your schooling, when you continued to impress your professors! It bothered me quite a bit at first. I'd expected you would fail, and I don't usually like to be wrong." He paused, and in the silence I closed my eyes, shuddering inwardly.

"But in your case, I was pleasantly dumbfounded. A girl from the brink, excelling as a Charmer? And the very first earth medium we've been blessed with in more than a hundred years!" He sat on the nurse's chair by the cot, brushing loose hair away from my eyes. I wanted to bite his fingers clean off, spit the bones out. "We had a nice time together, didn't we? We shared tea and biscuits, and you were such an enthusiastic little thing."

"I was a *child*," I croaked. Small orbs of light were forming in my periphery, closing in.

"You were. And what followed was an extended period of adolescent rebellion." His hand closed around my jaw, angling it up toward him. "And now you are home, and ready to live up to all that idium you stole."

My eyes were shut again, weren't they? Better this way, to speak to the dark. "I won't—I won't bury people."

He sighed. "I know you sympathize with them, Nina. It is difficult to ignore your roots. But you, of all people, should find some opportunity in all this. A chance to put right what was wrong. A chance to take revenge, for all the wrongs done unto *you*."

I shivered. "Shut up."

"Your father, may his soul rot—he does not deserve your sympathy."

"Shut up."

"He was too far gone to notice you. Wasn't he? Always too dosed or drunk to protect you the way a father should."

That swelling tide rose within me again. A river of vomit, though not a speck of it seemed to find the lord's shoes.

"And your mother, she was already in the wind," Tanner shook his head sadly. "God says vengeance is righteously sought by the aggrieved, Nina. And I believe vengeance is yours."

I shook my head, brain matter sloshing to either side. If I'd been capable, I would have carved a hole in the earth right then and pitched us both into the crumbling black. I slumped toward the window. "I'm not fighting your damned war," I mumbled. "Best put me in an iron cell and hope I don't find a way out."

He chuckled. "And what good would you be to me there? No. I won't be your jailer, Miss Clarke. But I might be your executioner."

Pain lanced in every direction. I realized his thumb was digging into my temple, where the flesh seemed most tender. He worked a groove into the skin, and I cried out.

"I will drop a ten-ton stone on your head, and the world will have lost a very accomplished Charmer. Let me make this perfectly clear. If you are of no use to *me*, then I will make you useless to *them*."

Fear closed in. It eclipsed my mother and father and Scurry and cells made of iron.

Tanner's mouth was at my ear. "So, you will join our side. The side you so brazenly stole onto, and you will be of use. Yes?"

I swallowed. Nodded.

And what did it say of me, that I gave in so quickly?

"Good." He released me again. "That's good."

He let me sit there and pant and shake, a scolded dog bent to sub-servience. He patted my leg. "Don't worry. I won't be sending you off to crumble mountains onto every poor mining town in the brink. We'll still need them, after all, once this war is won."

Was I crying, or was blood running down my face?

"This nation does not run without those mines, I'm afraid. A fact the Craftsman haven't been able to accept. There is only one particular town I wish to bury, Nina. And it won't be easily squashed. The Miners Union wants you badly enough that I believe if I dangled you out in the open, they'd bring you right into the fold."

Which town? Surely any town was a price too high. "And once I'm there?" I asked. "What then?"

"Well, we'll need to ensure you won't scamper off, won't we?" He turned his body to the door. "Nurse?" he called. "Would you bring in our guest?"

From the hall came a soft whimper, a shuffling of feet across tiles. The nurse appeared in the door again, and with her she dragged the arm of someone unwilling. Someone who, though frail, resisted.

She had the air of a person whose mind had departed their body. She stared off vacantly, at the walls and ceiling but never at me. Her light hair had been cropped short, and still the curls matted. Sharp lines cut across her forehead and webbed the corners of her mouth. Her feet were bare and her toes curled in nervously as though they wished to burrow beneath the floor.

It took a long moment for me to recognize her. After all, she'd been a younger woman at last glance, and me, a girl of just eight.

"Ma?" I whispered. And the pounding in my head doubled.

She seemed unable to unstick her eyes from the wall, but her bottom lip trembled.

"Ma," I said again, as forcefully as I could. "Ma? It's *me*. It's Nina."

There was an air of death about her, as though it might reach out and snatch her away at any moment. Tears shook on the pink rims of her eyes.

Still, she didn't look at me.

I made to move toward her, and she flinched.

"Alive and well," Tanner said. "I do enjoy a reunion."

But she was far from well. Far from the woman meant for bigger places. Now it seemed those bigger places had devoured her whole and spat her back out.

She was both a stranger and my first love.

I turned to Tanner and spat in his face. The way a miner's daughter should. "What have you done to her?"

He wiped a handkerchief over his nose and mouth, barely managing to hide his fury. "I've opened my doors to her. She's been with us for some time now, haven't you Ms. Harrow?"

And still, Rose Harrow said nothing, did nothing. Beneath her breath, it seemed she hummed something; a child singing to soothe herself, a song I vaguely recalled.

"Ma—"

"Quiet little thing. Sneaky, even. I looked long and hard for your parents when you were a child, Nina. The moment your name came across my desk, in fact, and I saw through that half-cocked plan Francis Leisel devised. Your father was simple enough. A Scurry terranium miner. But your mother? She was nearly impossible to locate. You'll never believe where I found her."

Another shiver, a whimper. Rose Harrow hummed louder.

"She was working as a servant, right here in the National Artisan House!" Tanner clapped his hands as though it were all a gag. "There was an understanding, you see, between the Crafters that served us and kept sensitive information from public knowledge. Hold your tongue, do your duty to the House, and we may reward your family members with opportunities Crafter-born children rarely receive."

"Idium," I whispered.

"Correct," Tanner nodded. "It seemed your mother had been under our remit for some time, for *your* sake, obviously. A selfless mother, indeed." He looked over Rose Harrow with none of the fondness his fair words suggested. "Though her service to us did not necessarily mean we had plans for you, it appears you made those for yourself, Miss Clarke. When I found her, she was relieved of her position immediately, of course. With you in the Artisan school, I couldn't help but think the proximity would prove too tempting for her. She was much louder on that occasion, if I remember. The histrionics of women have always confounded me. You'd think she'd be pleased to hear what her daughter had become, but alas, she fought the policemen who escorted her to the train station and all the way out of the city.

"I found her right where I left her, in the squalor of Trent, but not quite as loud anymore, and only half a wit remaining. It seems the brink has not been kind to her."

Nausea swelled once more. I saw my mother sewing buttons on a knitted sweater, kicking rocks into the riverbed. *We're made for bigger places, you hear me?*

"We've become well acquainted, your mother and I," Tanner continued. "And I plan to keep myself acquainted with her while you fulfill your duties to the House."

Fresh tears slipped over my cheeks as I stared as this shadow of my mother. I felt the weight of every wall cave in on me. "What do you want me to do?"

"Well, that's where the complication lies, Nina. You see, we need you to find their headquarters, of course, in order for you to bury it. But you're not to do so straightaway! You'll need to bide your time. Earn their trust."

"For what?" I asked. "Why earn it only to break it?"

Tanner curled his fingers into his trouser legs. "They have something that belongs to us."

CHAPTER 36

PATRICK

Behind the empty bar, there was a bottle of rum no one had touched in years.

It was distilled by John Colson, drunk sparingly and only on dire nights. On its label were the words: *For the recess of head and heart.*

Lord, but Patrick longed for a recess.

The bottle was drawn from its shadows and placed on the bar top, where Patrick stared at it for long moments, head awash.

But he didn't drink from it. He wouldn't until his father was the one to pour it. If John Colson were here, he'd set two glasses down, fill them to the brim and tell Patrick that there is little more dire than a woman.

Patrick sat himself on a stool—one that faced the door to the stairwell—and drew a coin from the inside of his sleeve. "You're a fuckin' fool, Pat," he said to no one. He flipped the coin in the air and let it fall as it may. Tails.

So he'd stay here, then. He would not go back up to her.

A strange combination of relief and anguish followed.

He returned the bottle of rum to its dark corner and wiped his mouth on his shirtsleeve, trying not to imagine it all again. At this moment she was likely hanging her shawl, unpinning her hair, unbuttoning that torturous dress. She was closing her eyes and trying to rid herself of the night's events, enough to fall asleep. She would fail. He would fail. They would wake with burning impressions all over their bodies from where the other had pressed.

"Fuck," he growled, and stalked toward a door behind the bar.

Through the kitchen and out to the courtyard, past the chickens and a sleeping Isaiah, who awoke and greeted him immediately. Patrick stopped to stroke his downy head, then whistled for the dog to follow him to the cottage door.

The windows glowed orange—a bad sign. He'd hoped Tess and his brothers had remained at the marketplace.

The kitchen was already warmed when he stepped into it, the round table occupied by Gunner and Donny. Isaiah went to Donny's feet and puddled gracelessly. He panted up at them all, oblivious to the tension arriving the moment Patrick closed the door behind him.

He waited for either of his brothers to speak, and when they didn't, he took off his coat, hung it, and said reluctantly, "Let's have it, then."

Gunner was tight-jawed. He looked at Patrick squarely when he said, "We had an agreement. No fuckin' the swanks."

Donny offered nothing. He seemed to sink into his chair, readying for a long argument.

Patrick merely tilted his head to the side, scrutinized his brother through his furrow. "A rule we came up with for Donny and the other boys."

"So, it's different rules for Patty, then?" Gunner grasped a mug on the tabletop like he might break it. "Very convenient, eh?" From the corner of his mouth, a speck of inky black slipped free.

Patrick stared at it, laughed darkly, then stepped forward until he was close enough to bend his face to Gunner's. Patrick lifted a thumb and smeared the bluff from his brother's lip, then held it up for closer inspection.

Gunner shrunk. His eyes averted.

"Yeah, brother," Patrick muttered, inches from Gunner's face. "It's different rules for me." He was close enough for Gunner to throw his head, to take a swing. When he did neither, Patrick shook his head and paced in a circle, scrubbing his face.

"Pat?" Donny asked, not without apprehension. "What's it like to fuck a Charmer?"

"Watch your mouth." Patrick felt the last tethers of his patience snapping. "And no one's fuckin' anyone."

"I just wondered if there was anythin' special about it, is all."

"Shut up, Don," said their mother, appearing in the doorframe behind the table. "Go to bed."

"No," Patrick said. "Donny, take Gunner home. Make sure he doesn't fall into a fuckin' canal along the way. His wife's waiting for him."

Gunner raised his head. "Pat—"

"I'd wring your neck, Gun. But it seems you do a fine enough job of that all on your own. Get the fuck out of here."

For a moment, his brother seethed, fists balled, and Patrick almost wished he would throw a punch.

But he didn't. Gunner only sniffed pitifully. "Yeah, I'll go," he muttered, overbalancing as he stood. He was a head taller than Patrick, broader in the shoulders, yet somehow half his size. "But you just remember what we said, eh, brother? Them Artisans you're collectin', we can't trust 'em. You told us to keep our distance."

"And so long as I'm running the tunnels, the trades, the meetings, the rallies, and the *fuckin'* coppers, I'll keep telling you whatever I like, Gunner. Unless you want the job?"

Silence fell. Each one of them knew it couldn't come to pass. The bluff had hold of Gunner, and so Gunner had hold of nothing.

"What about you, Don," Patrick said then. "You got eyes on a promotion?"

"Was that a dig?" Donny frowned. He turned to their mother. "That one was surely a dig—"

"Go," Tess answered, her lips thinly pressed. "Now. Take your brother."

"Am I s'posed to lead him, or he me?"

"Just keep to the left, and if you hear the trolley, jump out of the fuckin' way."

Donny muttered under his breath as he collected his coat and Gunner's.

"I don't need a bloody keeper. I'm fine," Gunner said, but when he met Patrick's expression, it brooked no further argument. The two of them disappeared through the door, and Patrick tipped his head back and closed his eyes.

Tess waited, her hip against the frame, arms crossed over her chest. "Well?" she said eventually, when it seemed her son would say nothing at all.

Patrick breathed once, twice, cooling his temper. "The foray into Dorser failed," he said, sitting at the kitchen table with a metastatic groan. "The shipping containers were already empty. A decoy, probably. They knew we were comin'."

Tess nodded. "Scottie told me. That's three of the last four missions thwarted." She peered at Patrick, gritted her teeth to keep back what she so wished to say. "You can't tell 'em, Pat." She said, and she meant anyone, everyone. "They can't know."

Patrick didn't argue the point. Panic spread quickly in Kenton Hill. They were all tinder in a waiting box, at any moment set alight. There could be no friction. "The crew've been told to keep it quiet."

"Otto has a big mouth when it comes to that Scribbler. I think he's in love with her."

"He'll keep it quiet."

"Ten to one, son. Ten to one says it's one of the swanks gettin' word out."

Silence again. Above them, a boiler sourced the air temperature and clanged to life. Gas funneled through copper pipes. A fire would light beneath the cistern. Winter was approaching.

Patrick shook his head. "They're watched, day and night," he said. "They only know what we tell 'em. It ain't the swanks."

"Then find whoever it is," Tess said simply. "And throw 'em down a shaft."

Patrick nodded. He lit a cigarette, watched the first euphoric exhales spin eddies into the ceiling. "Out with it, Ma," he said eventually, closing his eyes, bracing.

But a moment ticked by, then another. Enough moments to warrant the opening of his eyes. He found his mother looking away, oddly distant. "Been a long time since I saw you like that, Pat. A long, long time."

His mother and he were well practiced in speaking this way, in half sentences. No mincing. She meant the dancing at the rally. The foolishness of it.

But he'd been a kid once, hadn't he? A kid in the lane, playing coppers and thieves.

"You used to do that a lot."

He frowned. "Dance?"

"Laugh," she said. "Have fun. You were sunshine once."

But no longer, because someone had to step up. Someone had to gather the storms.

Tess tsked. "She'll leave this place, son. You know that she'll leave."

"Or she'll stay," he said, but it was feeble. "If she can be convinced to our side."

Tess sighed, and it was world-weary. Formed by years of trial. "You should prepare for the eventuality that she won't, son. Pick another. There're plenty of other girls for you in Kenton Hill."

Were there? To him, their faces were indistinguishable, their outlines hazy. He felt they might pass straight through him. He had begun to think that he'd been waiting all these years to see *her* again. Even more worrisome, that he'd brought her here because of it. "I just need some time," he said. "She's one of *us*, Ma. I know she is."

Patrick didn't look to see the pity in his mother's eyes, the sink of her shoulders. But he heard it when she said, carefully, quietly, "You shouldn't waste time hopin' people will change, son. They never do."

Patrick stood. He didn't want to reenact the many rows that had split the seams of this kitchen when his father had been here and Tess still believed he could be persuaded from his course. Patrick and his brothers had heard them from that one bedroom upstairs, one ear pressed to the mattress and the other blocked by a pillow as the roar downstairs seemed to grow and grow.

"Four weeks," Tess murmured. "It ain't enough time to change a person's mind. Lord knows a decade weren't enough to change your father's, and now he's—"

"Captured," Patrick cut in.

"Dead," Tess said forcefully, white knuckles clutching the back of a chair. "There ain't a hope you'll find him still alive, Pat. You need to stop pretendin'—"

"You're able to abandon him so easily." Patrick's fists shook with the urge to be buried in a wall. But he spoke evenly. "Not me."

No, not Patrick. He felt his father knocking at the insides of his skull. Other people had a tendency to forget what Patrick couldn't when it came to John Colson: the cast-off parts turned into toy trains, the easy jokes, and a hand wide enough to span two of his. In the mornings, his father would submerge his head in a bucket of water to rinse dust from his eyes, and they'd come away bloodshot. He'd sit at the table, draw a sketch of some strange imagining: a lantern, a filter, a kettle, a trolley. Tess would shake her head in wonder and ask him how he came to such ideas, and John would pull Donny onto his knee and tell her that he was going to fix up the whole world. A place crafted by hand, out of spit and steam, all before the whistle for second shift blew. *No son of mine*, he'd said. *No son of mine in a pit.*

And he'd found a way. It would only take a war.

He was too stubborn to die, Patrick knew.

Tess shook her head again, and from one breath to the next, Patrick thought she grew older. "This idea you have in your head of victory? It's a delusion. We already have all the victory we're gonna get. A safe home, fair gain, less men belowground." Her eyes welled. "Everyone gets what they need, Pat. God bites the hand of those who try 'n' take more." Suddenly, she coughed into her hand, bending almost double, and Patrick rounded the table to her side, held her shoulders until the spluttering slowed.

He sighed. "Your God turned his head from this place a long time ago, Ma. We're the only gods here."

She sat at the table with Patrick's guidance, leaning her head on her steepled hands, eyes closing. "You sound so much like him, Pat. That's what's hardest." She said it so softly he could barely hear it. "You're some of him and some of me, and we don't get to pick which parts we give to our children. You're a mess of the two of us—his head and my heart. Both'll get you killed."

"I have to finish it, Ma. I promised him."

"Aye," she said. "And there's not a day I don't hate him for it."

Patrick left. No time to sleep, no time to lament. Just a knocking in his brain, a tingling on his mouth, a looming clock in the periphery winding down the seconds.

"Don't wait on her, Patrick," his mother called after him as he walked out into the night.

CHAPTER 37

NINA

W hat will happen to you, when Tanner learns you've been seduced by the man you were sent to bury?"

Theo came closer.

He reeked of whiskey. Whiskey made good men angry and angry men violent. I hid my shaking hands, lifted my eyes. "You assume it's me who's been seduced?"

It was enough to give him pause.

"Do you give me no credit at all, Theo?"

He rose onto his toes and back onto his heels, the neck of the bottle dangling precariously in his grip. "You planned it?" He sounded mollified, at least in part.

I shrugged in a way I hoped seemed offhand. "Is seduction not the quickest way to ruin a man?"

He blinked twice. Then he slowly raised the bottle to his lips and swigged, contemplating. "You looked at him a long, long time, Clarke. Same way you used to look at me."

Perhaps jealousy was the quickest path to ruin. I barely recognized him in those shadows, menacing and brash. The drink propelled his voice, made me flinch inwardly, but I hid it. "We were sent here to find the Alchemist, Theo, and in two years, you've been unable to. Patrick's careful. It'll take more than trust before he reveals where they're keeping him. It'll take—"

"Love," Theo finished. "Is that your plan, Clarke? Are you to make him fall in love with you?"

I wanted to tear my own heart from my chest. "Yes."

"A tall order to achieve in a few short weeks," he muttered, his expression no less severe. It seemed at any moment he might slip over the knife's edge. "That's when they're planning to raze the National House, you realize? Four short weeks."

"I need more time," I muttered, and this, at least, was true.

"Then you'd better dig slower." It ricocheted across my skin. "You know as well as I do, if they reach the city, the game is up."

I wanted so badly to sit. To think.

"We should be frank with each other," he said then, now close enough that I could smell sour breath. "Why don't you tell me what orders Tanner gave you?"

You're on this side, I reminded myself. *This is your side.* "Find Domelius Becker, then bury everything."

He watched me for too long, until I felt undressed by his eyes. "And you're willing to carry it out?" he asked, voice steeped in doubt.

I'd made a promise to myself to not think of it, to not imagine sinking Kenton Hill into a pit. "I don't have a *choice.*"

But Theo seemed to be weighing things in his mind, trying to find the side to bet on. "What threats did Tanner use to persuade you?" he asked, and hidden beneath all the whiskey and jealousy was a muted concern. He softened.

"Execution," I said shakily. "For myself—and for my mother."

Theo's eyes went wide. He turned away, ran his free hand through his already mussed hair. "I—I didn't know," he said.

"How could you?" I frowned. "You've been here."

He nodded to the shadows.

"And what were you threatened with?" I dared to ask.

"Threatened?" he asked. "After Crafters robbed the laboratories, stole the last Alchemist, and left my mother to die?" He shook his head. "There were no threats, Nina. I was an ordained lord for the House, and when our Right Honorable head gave me my orders, I simply followed them, as I'd pledged to do."

"So the scandal of your exile was—"

"A lie," he nodded. "A very thorough one. How else could the Miners Union trust me? They needed to think I was already a traitor to the House."

I had no right to reproach him, but still, I did. I was here under duress, while he was here of his own volition, though I supposed the result would be no different. My hands would be as dirty as his.

"I volunteered myself, Nina, if you can believe me so stupid." He looked around the room with distaste. "And in return, Tanner made me a promise."

I quailed. "What promise?"

"You."

I froze.

Theo turned his back to me, gazing toward the window and the town beyond. "He promised me that he'd find you. Finally, after years of my pleading and petitioning. Of doing every fucking thing asked of me, he finally agreed." When he turned back, his grin was contemptuous. "They looked for you at first, did you know? I badgered my father, badgered anyone who would listen, to try harder. But eventually, they gave up. Assumed you dead. They stopped looking. Except *me*. *I* kept looking. I found your supposed first address in Sommerland and learned that there had never been a girl born to the name Nina Clarke. I looked at the registry from the year of our siphoning, and you weren't there, either. There *was* a Nina Harrow, though. A girl from the brink. Her name was blackened out with so much ink, it was nearly impossible to read the indentations." He exhaled deeply, his shoulders falling. "I learned that you'd lied to me. All that time."

I said nothing as he swayed. Guilt wrapped a hand around my innards and squeezed.

"I began to wonder how a girl from a pit like Scurry could become an earth Charmer, of all things. It's so incredibly unlikely. An act of God, surely." He scoffed, stumbled. "The more I dug, the deeper it went. The idium isn't a prophecy. In fact, there is no such thing as prophecy, only alchemy." He shook his head. "I wondered if you'd tell me, Nina. I've wondered for years . . . was it an accident? Or did you figure it out when you were still Nina Harrow and decide to make yourself into something big?"

I was only twelve, I wanted to tell him. *I was twelve, and I couldn't go home.*

"I found the vials in a cellar," I told him. "And overheard someone talking about them. I stole an Artisan vial and swallowed it."

He huffed an acknowledgment. "Clever. Though, you always were. Smart, but quiet about it. That's what I loved about you." For a moment then, he seemed lost. A muscle along his jaw throbbed.

"I couldn't tell anyone," I said softly. Even to me, it sounded like a weak excuse. "What was done was done."

"And you couldn't trust me, because I was the son of a lord." The words dripped with bitterness.

"I considered confronting Tanner. I almost burst into his office and threw all my findings onto his desk, but that day, a group of miners were caught outside the National House with boxes of dynamite, and I watched them shoot down four police officers before they were subdued. One of them took a knife out of his pocket and dug a copper's eyes from the sockets, held them up like damned trophies." Even now, the memory seemed to nauseate Theo. "For all his faults, what Tanner says is true. The Miners Union are barbarians. Animals." He took another swig. When he blinked now, his lids stayed closed for long moments. "I made a decision then about which side I'd rather have in charge."

I wondered if it were John Colson who'd lifted the knife and taken a dead man's eyes. He'd been among the group arrested that night. "You chose to avenge your mother?"

"I chose the Artisans" came the answer. "I chose Belavere Trench the way it was *before* war ruined it. Tanner had the idea to bait the Miners Union out of hiding, to allow them to take one of us into the fold. And in return, he agreed to find you. He promised to keep you safe." Theo approached, though his legs wobbled. His hands slipped awkwardly around my neck, and he held my face, blinking at me as though I'd just now materialized. "Two years I've been here, working for the Colsons. Trying to find the damn Alchemist. But always hoping for *you*."

I kept very still. Very quiet. When drunk men looked at you, they saw not one but three. A one in three chance they'd miss.

"And my prize is watching you dance with someone else?" His eyes narrowed. "Ha! It's almost funny. Is it a fair punishment, do you think? For breaking up with you?" His fingers loosened, rather than tightened. The whiskey, thankfully, choosing the course of melancholia. Theo backed away, hands dangling limply at his sides.

"I'm not punishing you, Theo," I said gently. "I'm doing what I must."

He wiped his nose. "They're bad men, Nina. Patrick Colson will kill you if he finds out."

"I'll need your help," I said, a net constricting around me. "*Please*, Theo. I'm begging you to say nothing. Don't interfere."

"You think so little of me, that I'd give you away?" He seemed more hurt than offended. "No. You go ahead and play your game with Patrick Colson." He stalked in the direction of the door.

"Theo?" I beckoned, suddenly panicked. "Theo, what are you going to do?"

"I'll watch, Nina," he grunted. "I'll just stand back and watch."

"I'm only doing what I must," I repeated. I hated how desperate I sounded.

"As will I," he muttered. "I'll have a scribble sent to Tanner."

"A scribble? But . . . how?"

"Polly."

I faltered, confused. "Tanner sent her as well?"

"Of course," he said. "We're Artisans, Nina. She's on the right side of this." With one last hollow look, he left, the door bouncing off the jamb, and I rushed to lock it. I smothered my mouth with my hands and swallowed a sob.

Fuck. Fuck.

Somehow, I made it back to the bed. I crawled under the sheets and curled onto my side without bothering to undress, to take my shoes off or pull the pins out of my hair. I shook violently.

There had been other nights like this, praying the mattress would swallow me, chest so tight it felt like it was constricted in rope. Too many nights to count, though never quite as piteous.

In a continuous matinee, I thought of Tanner and Theo and my father. Of my mother and how delicate she had become. I thought of miles and miles of tunnel. And I thought of Patrick.

I sank my face into the faded quilt and screamed myself hoarse, begging God to explain to me, just this once, why it had to be *him*, and why it had to be me.

And the price of it all seemed insurmountable. All those men and women and children.

All of it, for idium.

I lay there and wrestled with it until the shaking subsided, and then, exhausted, I told myself that I would do what I must.

CHAPTER 38

PATRICK

Thirty feet below Margarite's, the tunneling party stood in water that reached their shins.

"What fuckin' use are you, Teddy?" Gunner spat. He seemed tortured by the aftereffects of the bluff. "It's turned into a lake overnight."

"Aye," added Briggs. "The struts are already shiftin', Pat. The dirt beneath is erodin'."

Theodore looked down the belly of the tunnel. Not at Patrick, not at Nina, not at the other men. "I need a day to get rid of it," he said in an empty voice. "Maybe two."

Gunner scrubbed viciously at his face. Donny sighed.

Briggs clapped his hands together. "I'll stay down here with Teddy. See if I can't start fixin' the timber along the way."

Patrick handed Briggs the canary cage without looking at him. His stare was saved for the back of Theodore's head. "Is it one day that you need, or is it two?"

"Two," Theo said. "To dry it up properly. And to find where it's getting in."

"Fuck me, Pat," said Gunner. "Here we fuckin' go."

But that was mining. Two setbacks for every victory. An inch gained and another lost. Patrick thought they ought to be pleased they wouldn't be bucketing it out by hand.

"Be thankful, brother," he said, patting Gunner on the back. "The day is yours. You can sleep off that pounding in your head."

Gunner turned for the shaft, grumbling under his breath about not being suicidal enough to return home.

Patrick turned to take Donny's sleeve, but Nina was already there. She had threaded her arm with Donny's. "If you topple me," she told him, "I'll trip you up on purpose."

Donny grinned widely. "Shit. She sounds like *you*," he said to Patrick, who scowled.

"If you topple her, *I'll* trip you every day for the rest of your sorry life."

"Ma would clobber you," Donny said assuredly, his chin high. "I wouldn't mind hearin' the sweet sounds of wood on your arse, just like when we were kids—"

"Does he always have so much to say?" Nina asked, leading Donny onward.

"'Fraid so." Donny said before Patrick could answer. "Have you any interest in hearin' a story? I've got one about young Patrick hangin' by his underpants out a girl's window."

Nina's eyes lit up.

"Shut up, Donny," Patrick said. "Remember, you won't see my fist before it hits your face."

They clambered into the shaft, and Gunner pulled them topside, but before the lantern light disappeared from view, Patrick saw Theodore standing in all that water, watching them all with a strange, bottomless expression.

· · · · · ·

Patrick concealed the pit with the trapdoor and brushed his hands clean. Donny and Gunner were already exiting Margarite's, taking advantage of their rare free day to do whatever they wished. Patrick ought to tend to the many outstanding concerns of Kenton, starting with the eastern mine and the reports of unstable ground.

But Nina stirred in his periphery, feigning interest in the mannequins. Not moving off immediately, but not speaking, either. She had said nothing to him since she'd arrived at the shop that morning, nor had she met his eye. In fact, she seemed gray with exhaustion.

"You didn't sleep?" he asked, his breath swarming dust in the air.

Her cheek ticked, and still, she didn't look his way. "Not well."

He sighed, dread in his lungs. Best not to delay sorry news. "Do you want to pretend last night never happened, Nina? Is that it?"

He'd give her that, if it was what she wanted.

She took far longer to respond than any man could stand. He felt her grappling with it, lips parting and shutting. Finally, she said, "No. I don't think I can."

Lord, how he wished for a look inside her head, to watch the cogwheels turn. "Do you regret me already, then? It usually takes a little longer, I'll admit."

She grinned at the floorboards, and it morphed her entire face, disarming him. "Long enough to hang you out a window?"

He ran his hand over his face. "Fuckin' Donny."

Her grin widened. "Must've been quite the night."

Patrick felt his blood rush south. The light was glancing off the ends of her curls, the tip of her nose, the side of her neck. She bit her lip to keep from laughing, and though he hadn't found the fun in repartee of late, she seemed to enjoy teasing him, and he had begun to crave the sound of her voice.

He suddenly pictured himself trapping her against a wall again. He wanted to feel her soft body pressed once more to his. To run his hands over every agonizing curve of her.

Perhaps it showed on his face, because Nina's cheeks flushed pink. He was beginning to crave that, too.

Patrick's lips quirked, just slightly. "If it's to be a night of regrets, I make sure to be very thorough."

She cleared her throat. "And exactly how long is this line of women who regret you?"

"Are you asking for a list, Scurry girl?"

"God, *no*," she held up a hand to fend him off. "Please forget I asked."

"You sure? I could introduce—"

"I'll make you a deal," she interrupted, stepping closer. "I'll hear your list if you hear mine."

Patrick's smirk vanished. Something vicious lashed his insides. He thought of faceless men he'd never met and heard a trigger pull. To stop from giving himself away, he pressed his lips together.

And she glowed, victorious.

Goddamn. He could stand to lose more fights, if this was the reward.

"Come on," he said. "There's somewhere I want to take you."

It was a good excuse to take her hand, and wind it into the crook of his elbow. She didn't question him as he led her out into the square, through the arch and along the canals, crossing the industrial district and then out, out, out into the hills.

He thought her color was returning. She walked on the tips of her toes, turned her face up to the sun. She panted and complained as they climbed a hill full of chestnut trees, but her grin never quite disappeared.

When at last they reached the top, Patrick extended his arms and said, "Welcome to the Colson brothers' stronghold."

That stronghold now only comprised five sandbags, waterlogged pickets, and a couple of upturned crates. Most of the timber had rotted now, or lay broken.

But Nina brightened all the same. "Quite the fort."

"It's seen a few battles," Patrick said. "Duncan McCallum tried to bust in with a broom once."

"And did he manage it?"

"Course not," Patrick said. "Donny has dangerous aim. Threw a volley of chestnuts at him."

She chuckled, then smiled at the view and breathed in deeply.

Patrick followed her gaze to Kenton Hill below them. Eventually, he said, "Does it remind you of home?"

She responded, "Not even a little."

"Never been to Scurry," he said conversationally. Then saw the way her shoulders tensed.

"May it stay that way."

And he wanted desperately to know what it meant—if it was as bad as he guessed, or worse.

Instead, he said, "I'll walk you back. You can take the day to rest."

"What will *you* do?" she asked, not moving an inch. "What do you do with your days if you're not digging?"

Nothing good. "Today, I'll visit a friend," he said. "One I've been meanin' to speak with."

She narrowed her eyes. "A *friend*."

"Yes. A friend."

"I wasn't aware you had any."

"You know," he said as he took her hand, "you make a lot of assumptions." They began downhill, and when she didn't pull her hand away, his chest loosened. He wondered how scandalized she'd be if he kissed her again.

"Can I meet this friend?" she asked. "If only for proof of existence."

"Another time," he grimaced. "This friend is a while away."

"Not in Kenton?"

"No," he answered. "Dorser."

She halted, lace grass swilling around her. Her forehead creased. "Dorser? But that's—"

"A three-hour journey underground," he finished. "Four if you're slow."

She narrowed her eyes, crossed her arms over her chest. Patrick wondered if she intended to look fierce instead of just beautiful. "I'd like to come."

"No." Patrick chuckled and continued walking on without her. "Not a chance."

She followed. "Is it a woman you're meeting?"

Patrick did not show her his smile. "Careful. You sound jealous."

"Then why can't I come? Are you still afraid I'll run away?"

He considered the question carefully. "No," he said. "And you don't seem very fast, in any case. I'd catch you."

A flicker of annoyance. "I'll remind you that it took six months for you to catch me."

"It took six months to *find* you. Catching you was simple."

She stopped on the hill, braced her hands on her hips, which only drew his attention to them, which led to imaginings of how he'd span his hands around them, grip the flesh, lift her—

"Then I'll make you a deal, Patrick Colson. Catch me, and I'll let you be on your way to Dorser. But if I make it to the fence at the bottom of the hill, you'll bring me along."

Some keen sense of thrill was rising in him. On the air was the same scent of pollen and smoke he'd inhaled as a boy, and Nina looked spun from gold light. At any moment, the illusion would vanish. "Then *run*, Scurry girl," he said. "I'll give you three counts of a head start."

Her eyes widened, as though she'd never expected him to take the bet. "One . . ."

She took off, bolting downhill in waterlogged boots, arms windmilling, glee in her wake. He bit back a laugh. "Two . . ." he shouted.

Down, down, down she ran, and Patrick took his cap in his hand. "Three."

There was a knack to running on grass-knotted terrain, and Nina didn't have it. She was already nearing the bottom of the hill and the gate beyond, but Patrick gained on her quickly, throwing himself into the sprint. His feet traversed the ground with ease. She was almost within arm's reach.

He heard her laughter, and he thought its sound could end a war.

The gate was a stone's throw away, and he reached for her easily, finally, like it was the most natural command his body could obey.

But the ground beneath him suddenly trembled, and it lifted and cracked in the exact spot he was about to place his foot. He was forced to overcorrect and tripped. *"Fuck!"*

And Nina reached the gate, her whole body saved by the palms of her hands as she went hurtling into it. She turned with flushed cheeks, sparkling eyes, a smile the size of a continent.

Patrick looked up at her from hands and knees, one trouser leg stained green, his hands grazed. "You dirty little cheat."

She spun in a circle, basking in victory. "Craftsmen have the natural physical advantage. I only evened the field."

"You *tore up* the field, little coward."

She laughed as he rose from the ground, brushing dirt from his hands. "A deal is a deal," she said, exceedingly pleased with herself. "I'll accompany you to Dorser."

He shook his head, exasperated. "This friend I'm meeting—it might get dangerous."

"I'd gathered that already," she said, straightening her blouse. "But as I've just demonstrated, I can take care of myself. I might even have to protect *you*."

He cursed beneath his breath. "Change your shoes," he said. "You'll meet Donny, Otto, and Polly in the pub. I'll be there within the hour."

"Polly?" Nina asked. "Why Polly?"

Patrick moved toward her, felt her intake of breath when it seemed he'd reach out and touch her, and it took everything to keep his hands to himself, to ignore the way she looked at him. Instead, he pushed at the gate by her back. "You'll see," he said.

CHAPTER 39

NINA

When I was a child, and scared, I could imagine peace where there was none.

I could redraw my own cot into a feathered bed, the kitchen into a dining hall, my father at the head of the table and my mother still there. All of Scurry made new.

I did it again now, putting fraught things away in drawers. It was shockingly easy to do in the presence of Patrick, where the heat of him clouded every other thought. I could imagine I wasn't balancing on the precipice of a cliff.

The five of us—Patrick, Donny, Otto, Polly, and I—had entered a new pit, one Otto referred to as the southeast line, its entry point not disguised like Margarite's tunnel. This one was simply dug into the bottom of a hill in Kenton's outskirts.

The ceiling was at least tall enough to allow a person to stand, the walls wide enough that my shoulders didn't brush the sides. It seemed a well-traveled path. There were even points where two people could walk side by side. We carried nothing among us, not even a birdcage, and so I assumed we weren't making the journey to trade.

The men stayed ahead, walking at a quick clip without uttering a word. I walked just behind Polly, who hummed to herself, apparently familiar with the affair.

It remained baffling to see her amid the dirt.

"Who is it that we're meeting?" I asked her quietly.

She shrugged as though it hardly mattered. "A dockyard master probably, or another union member."

I searched for another safe question. "And why have *you* been brought along?"

"They never really tell me," she said easily.

Ahead, Patrick, Donny, and Otto were nearly out of sight. Polly and I had fallen behind. It seemed as good a place as any to speak frankly.

My voice became a whisper. "Theo said you were sent here," I said carefully, "by the same person who sent me."

She slowed very slightly, her eyes on the men ahead, pupils widening. "Lower your voice," she warned, though I couldn't have been quieter, and the others were only echoes along the walls. "Yes," she said.

"For the same purpose as Theo?"

She nodded, her discomfort obvious.

"And you've found nothing?"

It took her a moment to answer. "I've found a lot I didn't expect to find." It sounded cracked and broken. I thought of Otto and how closely they'd been seated on that step. "As for Domelius Becker, very little."

And I sensed, though I couldn't be sure, that she was as trapped in the same corner as me. "What were you threatened with?" I asked. "Or are you here out of honor?"

She huffed a dark, bitter laugh. "No honor, just the promise of a bullet from either side."

"Polly, we—"

"We can't speak here," she murmured, so lowly I barely heard it. "Come to the pub tonight. Better to talk where there's too much noise for anyone to hear a thing."

We said no more.

For three hours we walked until my feet and stomach and back protested, until the ground seemed to slope upward and the walls narrowed. And then, a shaft lift.

"Up you go," Otto said, proffering a hand to Polly to lead her inside. He held on a second longer than necessary, and I watched Polly smile at her feet.

When I entered, Patrick took my arm in his hand and maneuvered me to the back, so that he stood in front of me. "Don't say a word," he said. "And please, Nina, no Artisan shit, all right?"

"I'm not an imbecile."

"Promise me."

Did anyone ever deny him? "I promise."

I thought I heard him mutter something about fools.

Patrick and Otto operated the pulley, then blocked the lift in when it reached its peak, and we filed out.

Light spilled in, not from above, but ahead. The tunnel opened, and the ground turned to cement underfoot. The walls were spotted with snails. Through the blinding yellow light, I could make out a rocky shore, timber piers, a hundred docked sailboats. It seemed we were concealed in a culvert tapering to the sea.

We hadn't taken five paces when Patrick said "Wait here," and we stopped. Donny and Otto positioned themselves in front of Polly and me. Donny said "Smells like rottin' fish in here," and Otto shushed him.

Within moments, sunshine and sea were interrupted by three figures. All men. All armed.

"Hello, boys," Patrick said, as though we weren't convening secretly in the mouth of a giant drain. "What've you got for me?" From his mouth coiled small spirals of smoke. There was a lit cigarette in his hand, his body positioned in a way that blocked me out entirely. I strained to see.

One of the shadow men was taller than the others and stood at the spearhead of their formation. He hefted something over his shoulder and let it clatter to the ground—a sack. He said absolutely nothing. The other silhouettes lifted their pistols very slightly. Nervously so.

Danger seeped in from every corner, collected in my throat.

"That's it?" Patrick asked coldly. If he had a weapon of his own, he did not raise it. I wished he would. I shuffled unwittingly toward him.

"Two rifles, three boxes of grenades, a pistol, two boxes of powder." The voice was hoarse, dispassionate. A wracking cough followed. A sniff. "It's all we could save, Patty. Take it or leave it."

Patrick exhaled again, toed the sack on the ground, then turned to look over his shoulder at us. "Take it or leave it, the man says. What say you, Donny?"

"I say they can kiss my arse."

"All right," Patrick said, throwing down his cigarette. "Lionel, kiss Donny's arse and we'll call it even."

The pistols inched upward. "We were fuckin' *made*, Pat. The coppers searched every dock. Every boat."

"Then you didn't hide my guns well enough," Patrick said in a tone that was contrastingly conversational. They could have been discussing the weather. "There were forty *cartons* of rifles. Two hundred boxes of grenades—"

"In *shippin' containers*, Patrick! Where the fuck am I gonna hide shippin' containers?"

"In these very convenient tunnels we dug for you, Lionel. The same tunnels you've used on more than one occasion to run from all the razing and arrests." Patrick waited, but the man named Lionel didn't respond. Patrick checked his pocket watch. Clicked his tongue. "Did you sell me out, Lionel?"

The figure bulked. "I'm not a fuckin' *traitor*." He spat onto the ground.

Patrick ignored him. "I paid very good money to have those containers sit in your particular yard, Lionel, on a very particular day, and my men arrived to find them already empty. And now, you give me some guns and a few bangers and tell me that's all you saved?"

"It's all I could get away, Patty. The coppers came early. We were caught by surprise."

"And yet, you had time to open a container, fill a sack, then hide it away somewhere."

The tunnel chorused the words. The sea rushed the pylons. Inside my chest, my heart thrashed against the walls.

"So, did you tip 'em off, Lionel? Or did you skim a few weapons away for yourself, long before the police showed up?"

Lionel, even in the dark, appeared cornered.

Patrick sighed. "Come on, man, which is it? Are you a traitor, or a thief?"

The guns twitched on either side of Lionel. My feet inched farther forward, but Otto's arm barred further progress.

"I'll tell you what," Patrick said then. "I've got a better idea. Pol?"

Polly stepped forward, body tensed.

"Scribble this will you, Polly? Make it anonymous. Write to Belavere City and tell 'em there's a man named Lionel Billings sacking containers in the Dorser Shipyards. Tell 'em he's got a few crates of contraband bluff in his warehouse."

The longer Patrick spoke, the whiter Lionel became. "Wait. WAIT!" he yelled when he saw Polly shut her eyes. "All right!" he said. "I skimmed some guns off the top. There! I admit it. That's what's in the sack." He looked furtively between Patrick and Polly.

Languidly, Patrick held a hand up. "Never mind, Pol. Scratch that last."

Polly opened her eyes, then stepped back behind Otto.

Lionel wiped his forehead. "I'm sorry, Pat. All right? It were only three guns. Three out of a few hundred."

"Three of the *Union's* guns," Patrick said. "Of which I paid you handsomely to keep for me."

"Yeah, in fuckin' bluff," Lionel said, anger rising. "Do you know how hard it is to move it round here? There's coppers on every corner."

"Say no more, Lionel. I'll have Scottie and Otto come through in the morning. They can take it all off your hands."

"They can't take my fuckin' bluff—"

"Then they'll take your hands."

Lionel seethed. "I ain't listenin' to threats—"

"It ain't a threat, Lionel. It's a promise." Even from a distance, his voice skittered over my skin. The temperature seemed to dip. "You should know this: I don't make a habit of handin' bluff over to men of bad character. Even less so to fuckin' shipyard guard dogs selling it to poor folk for more than it's worth. I made a concession when it came to *you*. I made a promise to myself that I would only do so while the relationship served the Union. Have you stopped serving the Union, Lionel?"

Lionel twitched. "Imma proud fuckin' member. Have been since the first attack."

"Good," Patrick said. "Then I won't be needing to take your bluff . . . or your hands," Patrick turned and locked eyes with Otto. "Grab the guns. It's time we were on our way."

Lionel stepped forward, a hand out. "What about payment?"

Patrick turned back slowly. I thought I heard whips strike the air as he responded. "What payment?"

"We agreed on a vial of proper Artisan ink."

Patrick laughed coldly. "Yeah, well, we agreed you'd keep my bloody guns out of the hands of the House, didn't we, Lionel? You get to keep the bluff we've already gifted you, and count yourself fortunate I don't take everythin' you've ever touched."

The man blustered. The guns glinted. "I stole those fuckin' containers and stowed them in me yard, like you asked! Those coppers could've had me arrested!"

"And the Miners Union thanks you," Patrick said without a hint of feeling. "We'll be in touch the next time we need a plan completely cocked up."

Otto retrieved the sack, paying no mind to the twitching pistols at the men's sides.

"You think I'm scared o' you, Patty?" Lionel spat, voice quaking with ire. "You've brought naught but a boy, a blindman, and a couple of whores with you—"

Patrick stopped in his tracks.

Donny stepped forward. "Ah, I wouldn't do that, Lionel," he said, all levity in his voice now gone. It was the first time Donny had ever made me nervous. He suddenly seemed every bit the Colson brother Patrick and Gunner were. Cold, unforgiving. Dangerous.

Patrick didn't speak right away. Instead, he turned slowly, until he was facing Lionel again. I felt Polly edge onto the tips of her toes, as I did.

Neither Patrick, Otto, nor Donny drew a weapon.

"Say that again for me," Patrick said in a voice made of smoke and violence. It curled down my chest and between the hairs on my head, making them stand on end. I was possessed with the sudden urge to throw myself in his direction. "*Patrick*," I said in warning.

He didn't turn.

"You want to skive a poor man of his dues, Pat?" Lionel continued, blinded by anger or ego. "Why don't you send one of those pretty girls over here, and we'll part with no bad blood. All debts paid."

Foolish man. Did he not smell the blood on the air?

"Lord almighty, Lionel," Otto uttered, scratching the back of his head. "Don't say we didn't warn you."

"Ah, Lionel, now you've gone and spoiled a whole lot of blood between us," Patrick said, and finally, his hand reached into his waistcoat.

The waiting hammers cocked.

Gun barrels rose and leveled with Patrick.

And it was odd, wasn't it? That I should suddenly fear for the well-being of Lionel, and not Patrick, who was faced with three men and two guns?

Patrick said "Donny?" and it seemed an order. "Otto?"

Otto moved quickly, grabbing Polly and me by our shoulders and pulling us against the tunnel wall.

But I saw it all. I watched all the moving parts.

The men and their shadows pulled their triggers. The bullets exploded from their chambers. Nine or ten, the reverberations deafening. And somehow, the bullets clattered in far-off places; it was unclear if any hit their target. And when it was over, Patrick finally pulled a gun from his holster and shot a single bullet, and Lionel toppled backward, skull slamming upon the culvert floor.

Then there was only the ringing in my ears, Polly's breath on my cheek. My throat throbbed as though I'd shouted, and I wondered if I had. I might have screamed his name. Sound lagged.

But he did not seem harmed. No blooms of red sprouted along his back. He did not descend to his knees and then to his chest. He stood tall and straight and pointed the gun at the remaining two men, their own weapons now lowered, smoking, spent. They held their hands up and backed away. I sensed their fear, their confusion.

"Take Lionel's body home with you," Patrick told them. "And when I call on you next, don't walk into this fuckin' tunnel with guns."

The men hesitated, then as one, nodded. One of them said "Yessir" in a voice that bordered on a boy's. I blinked the light back, trying to see them clearly.

They retreated, dragging Lionel between them, and Patrick didn't turn his back until they were swallowed by that circle of yellow and out of view.

Patrick turned. He closed his eyes briefly, then picked up the sack of weapons and threw it over his shoulder.

Otto hustled Polly to the shaft, with Donny at his other elbow. "Come on," he told her gently, disappearing with her into the dark.

And I was aware that my chest rose and fell too quickly, and that my body was coiled tight enough to break the bones within. Patrick saw that, too, and when the wall behind me began to crumble, giving way to my trembling hands, he held up both of his. "Shhh," he whispered, suddenly inches away. He stroked my face once, twice. "Easy." The walls cracked. "Nina, calm down. You're all right."

But my head shook of its own accord, and a sound escaped my lips.

And it seemed, though I didn't know how, that he understood.

"I'm all right, too," he said instead. "Look at me, Nina. Nothing hit. I'm all right."

A squall of breath left me, and my head fell to the crook of his neck and shoulder. And I didn't give a thought to anything but just that. Just warm skin and the arm around me.

"We're safe," he said, and it was so soft.

Soft enough to end a war. Soft enough to break me.

CHAPTER 40

NINA

The trip to Dorser had, at minimum, confirmed two things.

The first was that Patrick had the Alchemist alive. There was no doubt of that.

The second would require an interrogation.

Oddly, they hid the bag of guns we had retrieved from Dorser inside a grate on Main Street, of all places. Otto lifted the heavy iron cover in broad daylight, taking no notice of the passersby, and Patrick jumped through into what appeared to be not a drain, but a fully equipped bunker.

I gave them all a look of bewilderment.

"They've dug them out all over town," Polly told me.

"I thought you said no one could get into Kenton?"

"Can't be too careful," Donny uttered, pulling on his suspenders.

Colson & Sons was roaring before nightfall, its walls straining to hold everyone inside.

It was growing colder out, so the windows stayed closed. No patrons lingered on the street. It seemed all of Kenton was tucked inside the base of this lopsided, narrow building.

After I'd bathed and changed, I found Polly downstairs in a corner, sipping a dark and mild alone. She was hidden between a man with a patched bowler and the cloudy grandfather clock. Somehow, she'd managed to commandeer a stool and a small bar table. It was cluttered with abandoned pints.

Polly was surveying the crowd in a perfunctory way. When our eyes met, she sighed, took a large swig, then nodded reluctantly.

I wound my way to her, knocking shoulders and elbows as I passed. I had not seen Patrick or anyone else I recognized since I'd descended from my room, but I knew they would arrive soon. Patrick had told me as much when he walked me to my door. He'd insisted Sam go home for the evening, that he wouldn't be needed.

I'd raised my eyebrows at Patrick. "Am I to take it you trust me now?"

And he'd considered the question carefully, pushed a stray strand of hair behind my ear, left the skin searing. "Ask me somethin' easier."

I braced myself. "Do you *want* to trust me?"

"More than I want most things."

He left a kiss on my cheek, then turned to leave.

My body had leaned toward his retreating back. "Will I see you downstairs later?"

"I'll find you" was his only reply. "If you don't want to be found, you should stay up here." A promise. A warning.

Now, Polly watched me approach. She had to raise her voice for me to hear her. "No drink?" she asked.

I shook my head. Lately I was balanced on a tightrope, and liquor would send me over the edge. I stood as close to Polly as I could, leaning my arms on the sticky table. Then I waited.

Polly sighed, her eyes on her lap, muttering something I couldn't hear. Finally, she lifted her face with something like resolve. "After the attack on the school, my parents wanted me to return home in the South until the fighting resolved. Remember when they all assumed as much? That the fighting would be short-lived?"

I didn't answer. Her eyes had taken on a distant sheen, and I was concentrating on her lips to better make out the words over the din.

"But I couldn't go. I had a contract already, you see? All the Scribblers did. We'd received them before we'd even graduated, and mine was Hesson. Do you know it?"

"Oil mining." I nodded. I'd lived there for a few months, working as a launderer. It was a festering sore of a town.

"Before we left, all ninety of us were called to the National Artisan House, and Lord Tanner came down to the atrium himself. He handed us each our contracts in person. I remember thinking it was quite an honor," she smiled sardonically. "And then he gave his speech. *Each of you is headed for a different point on the compass. And there's no telling the dangers you'll face in our current state of conflict, the hardship you may endure. By fulfilling your contract, you become men and women on the front line, and we at the House understand the gravity of this task. Which is why any scribble you send that might* help *our efforts will be greatly rewarded. Any whispers you pass along will not be forgotten.*" Polly's eyes snapped to mine. "It's customary for first-year fellows to be sent out into the brink towns. It takes years to work your way back in. But Tanner promised quick promotions to those who proved themselves . . . informative." Polly gritted her teeth.

"And you didn't want to go to Hesson."

"I was loathe to be sent anywhere east of the Gyser River, actually. Does that make me sound snobbish?" Her chuckle was weak. "I was a lot more timid back then. Suddenly I was being thrown into the most sullied divot of the Trench. I was terrified. I would have done anything to be brought back home."

I felt an inkling of pity for her. Perhaps it was conceited to think one-self above a place, but I'd seen most towns this side of the continent, and very few had turned my stomach the way Hesson did.

I spoke gently. "So what did you do?"

"I listened," she said, eyes glazing again. "I strained my ears for any information I might be able to pass on to the House. There was nothing at first. Long months of nothing, and I was miserable." She swallowed, moisture welling in her eyes. "The men and women there detested Artisans. They knew me as one right away, even though I hid my mark. When they saw me in the street, they shouted slurs at me, even threw things. I learned which routes to take home to avoid people. I covered my head to make myself less recognizable. But eventually, when the fighting worsened, a brick came in through my window. I started sleeping every night with my mattress against the door, so I would know if anyone tried to come in."

I took her hand in mine, pity swelling. "But you found a way out?"

She nodded. "I fell sick. Influenza was spreading and I found myself completely debilitated. Horrible fever, a cough so severe I thought my ribs would crack. I figured I would die, and I was relieved." A single tear slipped free of her lashes, but she wiped it away before it could run. "I dragged myself to the hospice, but they were overrun. I slept for days on a pile of blankets on the floor with a hundred others and simply waited to die. I couldn't even conjure enough strength to scribble my parents a farewell note.

"But then, bluff came. Crates of it."

I rose my eyebrows. "The Miners Union?"

She nodded. "They'd raided the bluff stores and stolen mountains of supplies. It had been all over the newspapers the previous weeks. And then suddenly, it was in Hesson. The whole town was awash in whispers. The common belief was that the bluff had come from a warehouse in Baymouth."

"So, you gave the information to the House."

"The moment I had regained strength enough to form a legible sentence," she said. "A week later I received a new posting—in Baymouth."

I frowned. Baymouth was certainly a more favorable province then Hesson, but it was no closer to Belavere City. "Not much of a promotion."

"Neither was the next posting, after I'd given the House information about a group holding Union meetings. They sent me to Trent after that, and when I learned that Trent was receiving weapons from the Eastern ports, they sent me to Dorser," she shook her head. "Some places were better than others. But mostly, it was more of the same. People who knew what I was loathed me. Nowhere was safe. The House sent scribbles promising promotions, and I became their loyal spy, following rumors around the continent like a rat."

"And then you wound up here," I said. "How?"

"Quite by accident," she answered. "The Colsons frequent Dorser, as you've seen today. That's where they do the bulk of their trading. They have supplies smuggled in at the ports, and there was a name that kept floating between conversations. No last name. Just *Pat.* I was passing along inventories to the House about the boats coming and going, and some of them I couldn't account for. Always it was tied to the name Pat.

"And I couldn't help but think that whoever this Pat was—if he really existed—was a critical player, and if I could find him, I could go home. So I spent a lot of time at the docks. It was quite naïve of me really, as though I could simply confront him, or follow him. It was idiotic, and it almost killed me."

I frowned. "Who almost killed you?" I asked. "Patrick?"

She laughed. "No. He saved my life."

I took her drink from her hands and helped myself to a mouthful. "I think I might need something stronger."

"I thought you weren't drinking?"

"How did Patrick save you?"

She gave a faint smile. "A dockside is a poor place for a woman to linger at night. I was confronted by two men fresh off their ship. God knows how long they'd been aboard. If the way they tried to tear off my clothes was any indication, I'd say it had been a while."

My stomach turned.

"Patrick says he heard me screaming. He shot them both in the head, right there in the open. Then he helped me upright, gave me his coat, and asked for my name," she grinned wryly then. "I remember the way his eyes sparked when he heard my accent. *And what breed of swank are you, Polly Prescott?* he asked me. I told him I was a Scribbler."

It was a sad story, certainly not one that should warrant a smile. But it was there in my jaw. I bit it back.

"I passed out after that," she said. "When I woke up, I was in Kenton Hill."

"Patrick brought you back himself?"

"Through the tunnels, I presume, though I don't remember it. I simply woke up to John Colson at my bedside, telling me outright that I was in the center of the Miners Union, and that if I helped them, they'd make sure no man or woman ever touched me without my permission again."

"And you didn't believe them."

"Of course I didn't," Polly said sadly. "What I believed was that I'd found my ticket out of the brink, at long last. I wrote a scribble to the House. I told them the place they'd been looking for all these years was Kenton Hill. I thought I'd be brought home the very next day." She shook her head again, heavy with remorse. "That was nearly three years ago."

My chest hollowed. I supposed I was more aware than anyone that Lord Tanner knew exactly how best to utilize us, his greatest tools against the enemy.

"You know," she laughed, "I came here expecting . . . well, I'm not sure what I was expecting. But it wasn't this place," she said. "It wasn't these people."

"Gangsters?" I asked wryly. "Hawkers? Prostitutes?"

"Community," she said seriously. "Kids. Neighbors . . . friends."

I watched her closely, and whatever she thought of made her smile. "You haven't been here long, Nina. But you'll see it, too. Try *not* to." Her eyes had stuck to something—or someone. When I looked, I saw Otto shucking his coat by the door, his forehead iridescent with sweat. A group nearby cheered at the sight of him.

I watched conflict pull at the corners of Polly's eyes and lips. She swallowed. "Despite the pretty lights and the jokes, remember that they'll kill us the moment they figure us out. They'll do anything to keep this place hidden, Nina. *Anything.* Do you understand?"

I nodded, and something unfurled within me. Was it terror or defiance?

"We're stuck between two guns now," she said. "That's all there is to it."

But of course there was more. There was Otto, whom she could hardly look away from, and all of Kenton Hill. All of it pearled in my vision.

And wasn't that the true evil of war? That it didn't have the decency to strip the humanity of those we killed?

"I can guess why you're here, Nina," she said to me now. "You don't need to tell me. But promise me, before you do it, you'll give me enough warning to turn my head. I—I don't want to see it happen." She closed her eyes, as though the scene were unfolding here and now. All these men and women buried beneath mountains of dirt. "Either that, or bury me with them. God knows there'll be no peace for me after this." She swallowed the rest of her drink and wrapped her arms tightly around her middle.

I felt suddenly sick, but before she walked off, I asked, "Would you do it if you were me?" It came out rushed, desperate. After all, I'd run from these very thoughts for seven years. I'd refused to confront them. "Could you do it?"

She gave me a look that said, very plainly, that the question was pointless. A drain to circle. "Can *you*?"

I pressed my lips together. There were two guns, as she'd said, and the answer to that question could fire either of them. It was safest to say nothing. It wasn't that I didn't believe Polly—she seemed as reluctant as me, someone with no real loyalty to Tanner. Someone who, like me, had no interest in tearing this town apart. But Patrick's voice had arisen from some hidden depth. *Trust no one*, it said.

She watched me for a moment, then stood and waved to Otto. The piano belted a new melody at that exact moment, and the drinkers and dancers brayed.

I thought of Polly traipsing from town to town, leaving fire and ashes in her wake.

· · · · · ●

Patrick reentered the pub when it was at its most raucous.

I didn't see him so much as sense him. I felt the crowd disperse, the air stricken, the music slow for half a second. Or perhaps it was all in my mind, the pressure mounting atop me showing its first effects.

He grinned when he saw me. It was small and fleeting; he tore his eyes away to hide it. Took off his coat, addressed a few patrons who slapped his shoulder or raised their glasses and hollered.

He made his way slowly through the swarm, quickly nodding and untangling himself from the people who sought to speak to him, until finally, finally, he was close enough to touch. He lowered his mouth to my ear. "Come on," he said, his voice drowning all the others. "It's about time I bought you a drink."

I narrowed my eyes at him, trying to appear unaffected by how close his face was to mine. "You own all the liquor," I reminded him.

"Then I'll buy it twice."

He pulled me to the bar, then disappeared behind it, pouring two glasses of whiskey. He left bills beneath the till drawer.

Tessa Colson was noticeably absent. The bar was tended instead by a burly man with a low-slung apron and a spotty teenage boy.

"Where's your mother?" I asked. "Is she well?"

Patrick passed me a glass. "Everyone deserves a day off sometimes," he said. He held his drink up. "To topside." An old miner's toast. He clinked his glass against mine and swallowed the liquor in one gulp.

I watched it disappear with wide eyes. "God. You'll be dancing on the counter by the top of the hour."

"Have some faith, Nina." He reached back to retrieve the bottle. "I can hold off for at least another two."

I laughed. He appraised me furtively. "I should ask you if you're all right," he said then. "After the events of the day."

I thought of those flashes of light and the smell of gunpowder, Lionel dropping in a heap with a single hole in his forehead. I repressed a shudder. "I shouldn't have expected much else from a gangster."

"Revolutionary," he corrected. "In any case, it was the opposite of what I wanted you to see." The regret rung clearly.

My answering grin was weak. "Don't mind me, Patrick. I insisted on coming, and I've seen men shot before."

"But I do mind you," he said simply, and the heat of his gaze was too intense to hold. I looked away, warmth creeping up my neck.

"Come on," he said. "Sit with me."

We returned to a table occupied by Donny and Gunner, engaged in an arm wrestle. The surrounding onlookers were placing bets, shouting at either brother with increasing frenzy. As Patrick and I sat, Gunner smashed Donny's hand down onto the tabletop, cracking it down its middle, and half the spectators exalted while the other half groaned. Money was snatched, the winners quickly dispersed with their take.

"I let you win," Donny said, swiveling in the direction of Patrick and me. "Who's this?" he asked.

Patrick rolled his eyes. "Who d'you think?"

"Not *you*, you pouty bastard."

I suppressed a laugh. "It's Nina."

Donny grinned rather suspiciously and pulled a chair out with too much grandeur. Gunner stared at me in a way that told me I was not welcome at his table.

This wasn't a revelation. I hadn't been oblivious to Gunner's quiet contempt.

I sat in Donny's offered chair and stared straight at the oldest Colson brother. When the silence stretched, I gathered myself and said, "Is there something you wish to say to me?"

In my periphery, I saw Patrick lean back in his chair with a smirk. "Good luck, brother," he said.

Gunner waved me away, a vein pulsing in his neck. "Why don't you go on up to your room. I ain't in the mood for any swank bullshit tonight."

I sniffed. "That's a shame. I'd written a poem just for you."

Donny smirked and shifted to the edge of his seat.

"Yeah?" Gunner chuckled darkly. "Then you can recite it to your pillow, darlin'."

"I want to hear it," Donny said immediately, and Gunner kicked him. "*Fuck.* Ouch!"

I cleared my throat exuberantly.

"In old town Kenton, come quick,
While Gunner boy swings his dick.
And the ladies will sigh,
For his balls have gone dry,
And his cock is the size of a prick."

What followed was a ripple of shocked silence, first broken by Patrick, who laughed around the rim of his glass and watched Gunner closely. Then Donny slapped the table and hooted, startling the patrons nearby. Gunner, for all he was worth, did his best to remain stoic. But seconds passed, and I refused to look away. Donny almost slid off his chair in hysterics, and eventually, Gunner's lips twitched upward despite himself. His eyes brightened. "She's got some bullocks on her, Pat, I'll give you that," he said, finally lifting his stare from me. He shook his head and lit a cigarette.

I turned to see Patrick quietly chuckling, watching me.

"Bet they didn't teach you that at your fancy school," Gunner continued. He had turned his body just slightly, now including me in the fold. This was how brink men often were—hard and calloused, but simply won over if you showed them your mettle.

"Not quite," I allowed.

"Then you learned it from some dirty Craftsman," he tsked. "What would your ma and pa say?"

"My father was a miner," I said, and watched Gunner's eyes pop. "He taught me that poem when I was four."

"Nina's from Scurry," Patrick offered.

"Scurry?" Gunner replied, his interest seemingly piqued. "What do they dig for over there?"

"Terranium."

"Ach," Gunner grumbled. "Nasty fuckin' work. All that rock and dynamite."

I shrugged. "Soot isn't much better."

"Aye, but I'd take it any day over bloody terranium." He saluted me with his pint. "To your dad," he said, and took a swill.

I kept my features measured and brought my own drink to my lips, taking the barest of sips.

Otto and Polly joined the table then, falling into chairs with flushed faces and wide smiles. The shadows darkening Polly's eyes had disappeared. Otto spoke to her conspiratorially, and she laughed.

"What're you laughin' about?" Donny said. "I heard you say my name, Otto."

"I was tellin' Polly about the time we stole horses from Old Parker's barn, and you accidentally saddled a donkey." Otto chuckled. "This was back when we were kids and Donny could still see a lick. Not enough to tell the difference between a horse and an arse, obviously." The table fell into a fit of laughter.

"But you're forgettin' the rest of the story, Otto," Donny grumbled. "The part where you fell clear of your horse with your trousers caught in the stirrups. He had to walk back into town in his underwear."

Otto sobered, and the rest roared harder, even Patrick, who mussed Otto's hair.

"How you two weren't thrown into the fuckin' clink astounds me," Gunner guffawed.

"Ah, Patty took two bottles of whiskey from the bar and walked it over to Old Parker. Made me take the donkey back, too," Donny said. "He promised not to go to the coppers."

My lips felt as though they might crack from overuse. I realized I hadn't smiled often over the past seven years. And something else was thawing away, releasing me. I watched them all taunt and pick at one another, listened to the stories of their younger selves. Every so often, Polly and I locked eyes, and I remembered what she'd said about trying not to see it—this patchwork affection among them all. I found I was jealous.

During an interval of conversation, Patrick reached over and took the bottom of my chair. In one smooth movement he scooted it closer to his own, so that parts of our arms glanced each other's, though to look at it would be to see nothing of consequence—the pub was brimming and there was hardly much room for anyone to stand without touching another—but a current flared to life beneath my skin.

I couldn't help but steal glances up at him, and each time I was struck with how engrossingly handsome he was. Had I ever suffered an attraction so devastating?

I hadn't.

And the realization hit me like a freight train. I knew then that I couldn't do it.

I looked at the longstanding friendships before me, in this pub alone. In the market and hills beyond, there were whole families, neighbors greeting neighbors. Freedom and dancing. All this good among the bad. And then there was Patrick.

I couldn't do it.

I wouldn't.

But then what?

Two guns, Polly had said.

Amid the chorus to "Sleep, Whistle, Sleep," Theo arrived.

The pub was a din of off-key singing. Patrons had their eyes closed and their arms over one another's shoulders, swaying back and forth in time with the piano. Polly was sitting on Otto's lap, and I with my arm pressed tightly to Patrick's.

Theo was covered head to toe in mud.

It caked on his face and cracked where he frowned. His eyes were rimmed red and he looked bone tired; he measured Polly and me and the drinks in our hands in a deadened way.

Warily, I put an inch between Patrick's arm and mine.

And Patrick noticed. I felt his eyes land heavily on me, then bounce to Theo.

The din receded.

"Theodore," Patrick said casually, though surely, he'd noticed the fissure down Theo's face. "Get a drink. Join us."

But Theo's eyes only skittered as far as Patrick's hand, which had reached around the back of my chair and rested just short of my shoulder, not touching, but sending a message as clear as if it were.

Theo reserved his response for me. "Enjoying your evening?" he asked, voice empty of emotion. Next, he addressed Polly. "And you?"

Polly swallowed. She stood from Otto's lap and smoothed out her dress. "I should be off to bed."

"*Sit down,*" Theo said, more aggressively than anyone ought to among so many miners. All three Colson brothers stood from their seats, as did Otto. A more menacing sight I'd rarely seen.

The pub quieted.

"You've had a long day, Teddy," Patrick said, in that low, rumbling voice. "Perhaps you'd better turn in, eh?"

But Theo's anger seemed to evaporate, right there on the spot. Perhaps it was the hulking figures that stood taller than him, shoulders wider than his, that cooled his blood. He smiled genially. "I've only just arrived," he said, ignoring Gunner at his shoulder with great effort. Theo sat. "Stay awhile longer, Polly," he said with faux politeness. "Let's have a drink."

Slowly, the Colsons and Otto sat, though Patrick and Gunner traded wary looks. "Why don't you get everyone a beer, Otto," Patrick said. "You owe us about a hundred of 'em."

"I'll get them," I said, immediately standing. In truth, I needed a moment of reprieve.

I left before anyone could stop me.

At the bar, the keep didn't ask for payment. He placed a tray of pints on the counter with a meek "Here you go, miss," and hurried on to the next customer.

I downed an entire drink before stepping away, wiping my mouth on my sleeve. When I turned, it was only to nearly upturn the entire tray on Theo's chest.

I froze.

That same tightness remained around his mouth, his eyes. He stood not half a foot away from me. "Had a productive day, did you?" he asked.

My gaze shifted to the patrons nearest, then over his shoulder.

"Yes, he's watching you," Theo said icily. "So smile. Offer me a drink."

He was right. I smiled at Theo, lifted the tray for him to take a pint.

"Make any progress?" Theo said now. "Or did you and Polly simply sit on their laps all day?"

"*Don't*," I said, my smile wavering slightly. "You don't get to say that to me."

"Forgive me. I've been in a hole all day. My patience is a little spent." He waited expectantly, and for a moment I was torn. Telling him everything and telling him nothing both felt like a betrayal.

"They met a man in Dorser who gave them guns," I said quietly. "That's all."

"That's all?" Theo queried. "And what of the person we were sent to find?"

"It's not as though I can simply ask him where he's hiding an Alchemist, Theo." I laughed as though we were exchanging jokes. I hoped from this distance that Patrick couldn't see the strain beneath the surface.

"And I can't keep creating leaks and pretending I don't know how to fix them," Theo gritted out. "I've bought you these extra days, Nina. *Use* them. The sooner we can leave this hellhole, the better."

"The sooner I demolish it, you mean." I said it beneath my breath, but he heard it still. How was it that voices could crest and fall all around us, but be of no consequence to him? Had he already buried them in his mind?

"I'm aware of the enormity of the task, Nina." His voice had grown softer. He sighed, and his shoulders fell. "Perhaps I can—"

But Patrick had risen from his seat, and his intention was clear. "This isn't the time to discuss it," I interjected.

"When *is* the time?"

Patrick drew nearer. "I don't know, tomorrow night?"

"I can't keep this up forever, Nina."

I just had to find a way out of this mess. Lure the two guns away. "I need more time."

Theo leaned down nearer to my ear. "Then use it wisely, Clarke. And be careful."

I nodded, and before Patrick could arrive, and Theo could melt into the crowd, I finished another pint.

Patrick watched the ale disappear with suspicion. His eyes stuck to Theo's retreating back. I wiped my chin furtively and tried to plaster on a smile.

"Are you all right?" he asked without looking my way.

"Fine," I said. "Theo was just apologizing. He becomes ill-tempered when he's tired."

"Does he?" Patrick said, looking down at me. "In two years, he's not so much as raised his voice."

I gave a little shrug. "Using your medium is exhausting. I suppose it got the better of him today."

But Patrick's attention was on the swinging door Theo had disappeared behind. His head tilted to the side. "When we caught up to him in Dunnitch, he told us he was searchin' for a girl," he said. "He meant *you*." It brooked no argument, no room for denial.

I shifted uncomfortably. "Perhaps."

"He's still in love with you," Patrick continued, sounding oddly contemplative. "I've gathered that much, but I'm having trouble with the probability of it." And this time there was black suspicion.

My stomach roiled. "The probability?"

"Of the two of you ending up here, of all places," he said. "In a town the rest of the country has forgotten about. How unlikely it is, that he found you after all?"

The tray in my hands slipped an inch, and his eyes tracked the movement. I tried to look indignant. "*You* brought me here," I reminded him.

He nodded, taking the tray from my hands and placing it back on the bar. "Like I said, it's the probability of it. Perhaps you were destined to find each other."

I laughed, the first swells of giddiness bubbling up my throat. "God, I hope destiny has something more in store for me than the boy I loved when I was eighteen."

Patrick simply watched me, eyes on my lips, following the next drink I tipped into my mouth. I was sweating. The room seemed hot as a furnace. Noise clambered the walls in my ear, and the fabric of my blouse suddenly itched unbearably. Patrick would see my flushed skin and think me drunk. He didn't suspect, didn't know, would never hold a gun to my temple with his finger on the trigger. *Bang.*

I took another drink.

"Go easy," Patrick warned, brows pinching. "You'll drown yourself."

And indeed, I had begun to feel as though I was underwater, where all sound was transmuted and dull. It was very inviting.

"If *he* is who you want," Patrick said next, nothing but blue eyes expanding and retracting in my vision. "I'll step out of your way. But you'd better tell me now, Nina."

I shook my head. "No" I might have said. It was difficult to tell. I took his hand without making the conscious decision to do so, and perhaps I overbalanced, because his other came to my shoulder, and he said, "Whoa, there."

In my periphery I saw Polly and Otto dancing again, and her arms were wrapped around his neck. The pianist made room on his bench for Scottie, who thrashed on the keys. I found a half-glass of abandoned whiskey on the table. Patrick said, "You'll regret that," and made to take it away, but I held on. I found his face in the soup of faces and drank the lot while he watched warily. "You're very handsome," I told him. "Even when you scowl."

Perhaps I told him again about those drawings of him in the rubble of the Artisan school. Perhaps I told him other things, too, like how scared

I had always been in those halls, how scared I was still. Utterly terrified every second of the day. I had no idea if any sensible thought colluded with speech. It was so difficult to tell while underwater.

At some point in the night, however long it lasted, his arms came around me—were we dancing again? Faces spun on a carousel. The ground had fallen away. I shut my eyes and leaned my head against his chest and was struck by the steadiness of his heartbeat.

How did we get here? I thought.

"God knows, Scurry girl, but here we are," he said. And I wondered if he'd somehow found the lock to my chest and was bleeding it of every good and terrible thing I'd ever done.

CHAPTER 41

NINA

I had strange dreams.

Gun barrels coughing smoke in the air, shaped into portraits by Theo and his precise hands—a rendition of my own face with two different sides to it. There were trolleys and tunnels and Isaiah, who brushed against my legs and frolicked away. Patrick and Polly and Theo and me, all seated on a train tumbling onward, onward, beyond our control. One by one they jumped from the moving carriage at uncertain intervals, beckoning for me to follow, while I plucked the spokes of a dandelion clock and hoped it would tell me when to go.

I awoke to lurid light filtering through the curtains, cutting my face in two. Dust motes squalled in the beam, the air felt heavy, the bedding too oppressive, and I shucked it off with sudden, violent desperation.

I groaned quietly and pressed the heels of my hands to my eyes. Slowly, my mind churned, presenting me with snatches of the evening prior in frightening distortion. It had been a long time since liquor had gotten the better of me.

My leaden arms fell to my sides and my hand met with coarse, stringy fur. It moved up and down beneath my touch.

My eyes snapped open.

Isaiah waited several inches from my face, his body as tall as the bed-frame, his head on the mattress, stretching to reach me.

"Hello," I rasped uncertainly, and his tongue unfurled from his head.

Beyond Isaiah, another sound found me—soft breath, in and out.

I bolted upright.

In an armchair before the hearth, Patrick slept with his chin on his chest.

My slamming pulse slowed at the sight of him—purple eyelids, crossed arms, legs slack and too long for comfort. He seemed softer like this, the sharp edges of him muted in sleep.

I suddenly recalled a whisper in my ear telling me to lay down, to sleep.

He must have carried me to my bed, up all those flights of stairs.

I was dressed in the same clothes I'd worn the night before, less my shoes. There was a jug of water and a waiting glass at my bedside. A pocket watch with his initials etched into the back. The time was nearly noon.

"Lord," I mumbled. I'd slept half the day through.

Patrick sighed in his sleep. Shifted slightly. Isaiah went to him and pooled at his feet. The fire behind him sputtered weakly.

In the Artisan School, there'd been many male and female models cycled through the classrooms for us to draw or carve or sculpt, to learn the human form. But mostly, the bodies had just been bodies. I'd often struggled to see the splendor.

But I thought this man before me ought to be carved into stone. My fingers itched to recreate him. I wondered if it was because he was truly special, or if it was that tether between us. Perhaps it colored my view.

I looked at the hands wringing in my lap. How intolerable it was to think of cutting him away while he was so close.

"You speak to yourself when you frown" came his voice.

I startled. Gripped my chest in fright.

Patrick watched me beneath heavy eyelids. "Always mouthing things under your breath. Like you're having an argument with yourself."

I exhaled in a gust, sparks of floating light igniting. "Sometimes I am."

"Hmm. Don't imagine anyone wins." The timber of his voice did damning things to my insides. My blood raced. His eyes swept the length of me and everywhere his gaze touched, warmth followed. "How do you feel?"

Like I'd been trampled. Like I wanted to feel his mouth on mine. "Fine."

"Drink the water," he said, gesturing to the bedside table. "It'll stave the headache."

There was, indeed, a pick grinding a fine hole into my skull. "Thank you." I swallowed it gratefully. Then, self-consciously, I said, "You slept here all night?"

"Sam had the evenin' off," he explained.

I frowned. "And you think I'll disappear if I'm not guarded?"

"It's not a matter of keepin' you locked in," he sighed. "It's keepin' . . . *others* locked out. But in this case, you insisted I stay."

"I—I did?"

He nodded, his eyes traveling down to my waist. "Many times."

Mortification flooded me. He gave a weak smile. "I'll leave if you want me to."

"No," I said, too quickly. Already I'd wasted half the day. Theo couldn't flood the tunnels forever. "Unless," I stumbled, "you have somewhere to be?"

"Usually," he admitted, "but not today. Gunner is taking a shift in the east mines. I've left Donny in charge of the market. I heard from Briggs at dawn—there's a new leak in the tunnel. The Charmer will need another day to patch it."

"Theo."

"Yes, him."

Guilt and gratitude mixed together, quelling the warmth in my middle, though not completely. I shook them away. *Use these days wisely.*

"You speak in your sleep, too," Patrick said then. "I'm starting to think you might never shut up."

I rolled my eyes. "What did I say?"

"Somethin' about guns," he said, repositioning. "Two guns."

Dread pooled in my mouth.

"After that, I couldn't say. I fell asleep. Didn't wake up until Briggs came to the door."

I tried not to show my relief, tried to breathe normally. Patrick didn't seem suspicious in the least. In fact, he seemed satisfied. "You sound surprised at the thought of sleeping," I noted.

"I don't sleep well," he reminded me, and I wondered if what he meant was that he didn't sleep at all. That there was never enough peace for him to sleep.

He exhaled in a gust and looked my way, and I returned my gaze to my lap. I couldn't quite explain the fear that lingered, only that it wasn't a fear for my life. It was the anxiousness of being alone with someone who makes your blood sprint.

"I fear I made a fool of myself last night," I uttered.

But he shook his head. "It was a trying day. You were only letting off steam."

Perhaps, but hadn't I forbidden myself from drinking long ago? Wasn't there enough danger without liquor loosening my tongue?

I should count myself lucky I hadn't said something incriminating and awoken—or not—at the bottom of a canal.

"I want to ask you somethin'," Patrick said, and it brought my gaze back to his. I wondered if it was always his intention to swallow me whole.

"I have questions, too," I said. And here it was, that irreversible moment.

He pulled that damned coin from his pocket. "Shall we flip to see who gets the first one?"

"That depends," I said without humor. "Will it be a fair toss? Or will you use your medium to manipulate the outcome again?"

Silence. I thought I felt the tick of his heart. He rolled his jaw slowly before speaking. I counted one breath. Two. "What gave me away?"

"Besides the blatant cheating?" I asked. "And the bullets that didn't hit?"

He tilted his head.

I sighed. "You went home with a bottle of magic in your pocket, Patrick. What twelve-year-old boy could resist the temptation?"

He nodded, even smiled at the accusation.

"I used to imagine you on that train back here," I said. "I wondered if you'd thrown the ink out the window or given it to someone else. Stupid, isn't it?" I asked him.

"No," he said. "It's likely the only sensible choice there was."

"But you were only twelve."

"I was," he agreed. "And angry as a bull."

I nodded. "You're a Smith?"

"An untrained one," he said with a shrug.

"Of lead, I presume. Or perhaps steel. Why keep that from me?"

He looked into the fire, perhaps to give himself a moment to cultivate an answer. "You asked me last night if I trusted you," he said. "I confess, I don't come by trust so easily."

"Do your men know?"

"They do."

"Theo and Polly?"

"They suspect, but I don't tell them everythin'."

I fell quiet. I let the knowledge settle around me and took him in anew. "So, then, we're both kids from the brink turned Artisan imposters."

His mouth twitched. "You're smiling," he said. "Why?"

"It's nice not being the only one." I paused. "Can I ask one last question?"

He nodded warily.

"The last Alchemist is alive."

He didn't answer, only turned that coin over in his fingers a few times. "Sounds like you're tellin' me, not askin'."

"Is that a yes?"

"You'll need to give me an answer to get an answer."

I braced myself. For one fleeting moment, I thought he might ask me something with a catastrophic answer. And I wasn't sure I could lie.

He weighed his words carefully. "I promised you a ticket out of here, to somewhere safe. Away from the Trench."

I waited, his question banking up in the silence.

"I wondered . . . if I could prove to you that I could protect you . . . if you'd ever consider this place, here with me, as somewhere safe."

He didn't rise from the chair. Didn't adjust his position. And yet it felt as though he had just grabbed me by the rib cage and squeezed.

"You want me to stay in Kenton Hill?"

He nodded slowly, and in the following seconds I felt completely translucent, as though a mere bob of my throat or the flicker of an eyelid would be too telling.

But he had cast his own veneer aside. Behind those simple words was a deep wanting, and I saw it plainly. It mimicked my own.

"How did we get here?" I asked aloud, the question genuine. I could no longer see the paths behind us.

He smirked, though his eyes remained tight. "You're making a habit of askin' me that." His tone implied he didn't much care how we'd arrived. He waited patiently for my answer.

I knew I should tell him yes, that I'd consider it, consider him. It was the obvious answer. Theo and Polly would want it.

Get closer to him, make him trust you. Find the Alchemist.

I could see how quickly he would fall in love with me. It seemed almost as though he were predisposed to it. That his mind was already made.

What I could not fathom was how *I* was not to fall in love with him.

I was failing already. Tumbling into it.

Somewhere in Belavere City, Lord Tanner stalked some government parlor and my mother sat waiting in a cold cell, and I was here, unable to do what I must.

So, I did nothing. I remained here plucking at dandelion petals and hoping the correct course would present itself. I had pulled Patrick willfully into a trap without ever deciding to do so.

I was sinking, and soon, there wouldn't be a way back.

But there had to be, somehow. Surely there was a way through?

Patrick waited, just feet away, and he remained a force to be reckoned with, taking my hand and pulling me through the throng. Whispering reassurances and sinking a vial of promises into my pocket.

If there was a way out, surely it was with him.

CHAPTER 42

PATRICK

He felt every second passing like a stone added to a pail. It grew steadily heavier in his grip, harder to hold.

But there was no rebuff yet, just a maelstrom behind her eyes. Flushed cheeks. Wild blond hair strewn around her face. Full lips, parted in indecision. It was the longest he had seen her survive a silence.

She was, to him, a walking contradiction. Crafter and Artisan. Soft and strong. Vulnerable, yet difficult to read. Wickedly smart and painfully beautiful. A headache to any man trying to divulge all the secrets she was made of.

He was a selfish creature, he knew. Was it not enough to try and persuade her to his side of the fight? Did he truly need to keep her, when what she wanted was escape?

No, not escape. Freedom. It was a long time she'd spent in hiding. In Kenton Hill she was finally unfurling, he could see it. She had come alive here. If it was freedom she sought, he could offer her that. Maybe it would be enough for her to stay.

He hadn't meant to ask it of her yet. There'd been a plan in mind. A more extended period in which to draw her in. Perhaps he'd fumbled things now.

But he didn't think so. Difficult as she might be to understand, he wasn't misreading her when she admired the hills and laughed at his brothers and marveled at Kenton's machinations. She no longer resembled a tightly wound spring. She went quiet when she looked at him, and that was how he knew.

In truth, he had never considered a wife. No one had ever enticed the idea for him. His devotion was spent on his family, his town, his people. He'd imagined his life would dwindle on that way, him expending himself on their behalf. On and on the fighting would go. Deals and tunnels and problems, and he would die eventually, somewhere amid all the noise with no great love to leave behind. Just the pub, the stacks, the mills, the mines. Kenton and the rest of the world churning on without him.

There was no room for a wife in all that.

But if he could find his father and end this war, perhaps room could be made. No more blood or interminable problems to solve. No need to worry that someone he loved might be tangled up in the mess. Lately, he really thought it might be possible. He held on to more hope than he'd admit to Nina, who still hadn't answered the fucking question.

He imagined her in his bed each night, lying with her head on his chest, all those curls splayed over his skin.

Then he imagined her in someone else's bed, and felt every muscle in his body seize. Blood pooled in his mouth.

Yes. He'd have to make room for a wife. He'd find a way.

Suddenly, Nina's eyes glazed, tears threatening the rims, and Patrick stood.

"Wait," she said, holding a hand toward him, staving him off. "I— there's something I need to tell you first."

She moved her legs to the edge of the bed and stood, beginning to pace. She pulled her blouse at the throat and said "It's too hot in here" despite the frost on the window, the dying fire in the hearth. Her cheeks had turned ruddy and splotched.

Patrick closed the gate on the fire to snuff it, went to open the window.

She didn't speak, only breathed heavily. Isaiah watched her from the rug with a tilted head.

"Just tell me," Patrick said. He was nearing insanity. Lord, but being near her was a descent into madness.

"My mother fled Scurry when I was a girl," she began, wiping her palms over her hips nervously.

Patrick's chest tightened. "I'm sorry."

"But she was a good mother," she said, eyes flashing defensively. "Before . . . before she left." Nina seemed to hover on the edge of something.

Patrick waited, uncertain what to do.

"She was a beautiful artist, and she taught me to draw and paint. She would steal coins out of my father's pockets while he slept to buy supplies. She used to insist that I was made for bigger places and I knew she meant the Artisan school. She filled my head with dreams of going there when I came of age. And then she left, and I never understood why."

She didn't go on. Didn't seem able to. She swallowed and shut her eyes. "She's been taken prisoner by the House," she said then. "As a way to punish me, I suppose."

Patrick exhaled, his chest a cage his heart sought to break out of. He felt awash in that old hatred again—for the House and Tanner and every peer who'd come before him. "Tanner is a monster," he said, his loathing plain and hot to the touch.

He wondered why she'd never mentioned her mother before, or if she'd just decided, this day, that she trusted him enough.

Nina picked at her fingernails; her eyes flitted to the ceiling as though searching for something—resolve, perhaps. "I'm telling you, because you have something that can free her, as well as your own father."

Patrick frowned. "Of course I'll—"

"I'm not talking about tunnels," she said, impatient now. "Patrick, I'm talking about the Alchemist. Domelius Becker."

Patrick stilled. He saw the direction of her thoughts without her needing to speak them. "Nina—"

"He can be traded, Patrick. There is nothing more important to the

House of Lords than idium. Give them their Alchemist, and Tanner will give you every last prisoner, our parents included."

But already, Patrick shook his head. She didn't understand war games. How to transact with politicians. "I can't do that, Scurry girl."

She visibly deflated at the words. "Please," she said, desperate. "You *can*. You're just choosing not to."

"There's another way to get them out."

She let loose a sound of frustration. "Is idium more important to you than their *lives*, Patrick?"

"Nina—"

"Answer the question," she insisted. She didn't yell or scream, but her voice shook, quaked. "Is idium more important than your father? Than my mother?"

He wished he could tell her something different. "Idium . . . is everything," he told her. "It's the key to this war, Nina. To progress. I wish it weren't so, believe me."

Her eyes welled, and she nodded, turned her body away from him.

Surely she understood. She wanted the same thing as him, after all: true freedom. She knew what he knew, didn't she? There was no other way to win than to utilize the Artisans' very weapons against them.

Patrick stepped toward her, eyes on the sweeping curve of her neck and shoulders. "I'll get them both out, Nina. I swear it." And he wasn't one to make promises he couldn't keep.

"You're confident you can do it?" she whispered, and when she turned her face to him there were tears spilling onto her lashes. "And come back?"

He had to come back. There was no other choice. For Colson & Sons and the Miners Union and Nina. There would be life after the fighting stopped. There was room for more. "If your mother is alive and willing," he said, "then I'll bring her back."

Her hands shook. She brushed the tears away from under her eyes. Then she nodded and squared her shoulders, shaking off the maelstrom. "Then I'll stay here."

"With me," Patrick added, stepping closer. "To be clear."

She peered up at him, and he was moments away from abandoning honor. "Say it."

"I'll stay with you."

"Because I won't be able to leave you alone if you're close by," he said, reaching her at last, tracing the underside of her jaw.

She shivered. Heat crept up her neck from beneath her shirt.

"When it's all finished, Nina, I'll come knockin' on your door. Do you understand?"

She swallowed. Nodded. He wondered if she was aware that she was rocking onto her toes, stretching upward.

"I'll keep everyone safe. And when it's done, you'll be with me." He kept his lips a hairsbreadth from hers, watching her eyes close and her breaths shorten. He needed to be sure it was the same for her, this need. This incessant fucking desire. He thought he might come undone, right there, to see her so wanting. "Is this what you want?"

"Yes," she said on an exhale, her hands slithering into his collar.

It was all the assurance he needed. He closed that last inch, and his mouth finally, blissfully, descended upon hers again.

It wasn't like their other kisses, hesitant and whisper soft. This was unrestrained, crushing. He pressed his tongue to the seam of her lips, and they parted on a gasp. Gold bloomed behind his eyelids. She tasted like victory. The sum of all he'd ever craved.

How many moments had he imagined her in his hands? A hundred? A thousand? Could she feel the core of him rearing, clawing her into its recess?

What will I do, he thought, *if she claws her way out?*

CHAPTER 43

NINA

He left me in the room to wash, to change my clothes.

"Meet me downstairs," he said. "I want to take you somewhere." He took his fingers slowly away from my face, like it hurt to do so, and shook his head to himself as he led Isaiah out the door.

Afterward, I stood there alone with my thrumming heart. I traced my lips to check if they were real. Perhaps they would dissolve and I'd come awake from a dream so cruelly vivid it left marks.

I smiled. I buried my face in my palms and relished in the lingering adrenaline until it ebbed away. *You'll stay*, I told myself. *You've picked your side. You will stick to it.*

I'd open a tunnel all the way to Belavere City and free my mother. I'd remove Tanner's leverage, then be free to do as I pleased.

I didn't know if there was a true end to this conflict. But even if it continued, I'd be safe here in Kenton Hill, where the people knew me as Nina Harrow, and the threat of killing the last Alchemist kept the House from crushing it flat.

There was a way to save this place.

And what of Theo? invaded sense. *Polly?*

Polly didn't necessarily want to betray the Colsons any more than I did. Theodore, however, was another case entirely. He came from a life of

Artisan privilege, and it was clear that Kenton's charms had made little impression on him. Not to mention Patrick, whom he sometimes looked at as though he'd like nothing more than to bury him himself.

So I couldn't tell Theo. He might care about me enough not to throw me at Lord Tanner's feet, but he would certainly never see Patrick's plan executed without trying to stop it.

Polly was the key, then. She was the sole channel of communication between us and the House. If Tanner could be misled, then Patrick and his men had a chance. I'd watched him deflect those bullets, hadn't I? He was a Smith, and I a Charmer. We had the Alchemist. We had a way in. I just had to show Polly there was a way to remove one of those two guns pointed at her.

But the Colson brothers could never learn why we had come here. If they ever believed themselves betrayed, our safety was forfeit. Patrick's affections for me, however strong they might be, were not strong enough for that.

I would seek out Polly and speak with her. A new plan would be made. *And Theo?*

I saw no hope that he would abandon his loyalties to the House. He was angry, eager to leave. I reasoned that he had to be kept in the dark, and that when the moment came, he would have to accept that we were on different sides of a war, that he would take the opportunity to leave safely, at a time that would not completely hobble Patrick's plans. He only needed to be kept ignorant for a while longer.

I hoped enough of the old Theo lingered that he would allow me this choice.

Hope erupted.

I bathed hurriedly with warm water that chugged out of the brass pipes. I emptied the basin with the pump and lever—genius. I wore a dress too thin for the cold air, but in a pleasant pale blue. I defined the curls of my hair and pinned them up as I always did. When I was done, my reflection in the armoire mirror didn't seem all that terrible for someone whose liver had pickled overnight.

Sam was waiting in his chair outside the door. "Hello, miss," he yawned, tossing a polished ball from hand to hand.

"Hello," I said, hesitating. The ball rose and fell, rose and fell. "You must be tired of sitting there."

He shrugged. "Better than minin'."

I grimaced. "Is Patrick really so worried someone might come to attack us?"

"Nah," Sam said. "Ain't no one stupid enough."

"He doesn't trust us," I said aloud.

"Of course not. You're Artisans. But I don't think it's exactly that."

"Then what is it?" I asked. "If it's not to keep us in, or to keep others out?"

"I think it's to keep me off the street, miss," he said. "Me dad got buried in the tunnels. Sometimes Patty invents jobs just to keep people paid."

I considered the burden of it, of ensuring everyone had what they needed. "Sometimes I can't tell if he's as good as he is bad." I wasn't sure why I admitted as much to a boy.

But the boy in question seemed to take care in his answer. For a moment his face tightened in thought. "He's bad to those who're bad. No idea if that makes him good, though."

Perhaps Sam and I weren't of the authority to decide who was good or not. But I thought Sam's father might be thankful that Patrick had kept his son out of the tunnels and off the streets. "Goodbye, Sam."

He nodded, lit a cigarette.

I descended the flights of stairs with a genuine grin, and my limbs felt lighter. I got the strange urge to jump down to the landings, slide down the rails. I was eager to be near him again. Too eager. I could still feel the sensation of his lips traveling over my mouth, my throat. In my mind, I crashed out of the stairwell and Patrick was waiting, already taking my weight in his hands and kissing me again.

I pushed the swinging door open to the pub and there he was, his hands in his pockets and his back to the bar top. He turned at the sound of my footsteps.

For a brief moment, a spell was cast wherein only Patrick and I existed—the rest of the universe reduced to a slither. He grinned and offered his hand. I blushed as I reached to take it.

And then the illusion was blown to pieces.

From some distant rooftop, a familiar siren whirred.

The sound grew, stampeding down the lanes, permeating walls and rib cages. It droned outward, upward, pitching.

I was transported back to childhood, sitting beneath a kitchen table, my back mashed against a brick wall.

Patrick's face drained of color.

On the street, voices shouted, "*Collapse!*"

"Collapse," Patrick whispered.

And sprinted for the door.

CHAPTER 44

PATRICK

When Patrick was a boy and the siren sounded, he thought of monsters rising from the depths of vast seas and swallowing ships, fire raining from the sky, titanic gods slinging bolts of lightning to the anthill towns beneath.

His thoughts weren't so different as a man. That sound, it rendered muscle from bone. Squeezed your heart of every last drop of blood.

The door's window popped on its recoil, his boots hitting the cobblestones in the next moment. Someone shouted to him, "East mine, Pat! *East!*" As though he couldn't see the frantic crowd funneling in that direction, disappearing down alleyways, shovels already in hand, screaming to the windows above. "East!" they shouted. *"Hurry! Hurry!"*

How many would be lost this time? Ten? Twenty? Would Gunner be among them? *No*, Patrick thought, over and over.

He cleared one alley, ran full out down Citadel Street, then Penance. The siren droned, doors crashed open, and people erupted from the depths of buildings with pails and spades and anything that could break earth. All of it was carried to the edge of town, to the foot of a yellow hill. Already there were people racing up its side to the pit above. Patrick ran to do the same. The people trapped below had minutes, seconds left in the hourglass. No air to breathe. Just the thin hope that someone would dig deep enough.

Even from this distance, Patrick could see the frame of the pit entrance had caved inward, the ground beneath it bowled.

And suddenly the yellow hill came alive. It shifted, awakening from a long, deadened sleep, shelves of grass sliding away. The entire fabric of the hill distorting before Patrick's eyes. A wave of black hurtled toward them, flowing from the summit, slipping down, down.

"LANDSLIDE!" Patrick bellowed at the same time as twenty others, fifty.

Patrick grabbed the jacket of a man running by to pull him back. There were already too many on the hill, too many falling as the earth beneath them fluxed. Soon, they'd be trapped, too, devoured by the mud swarming their ankles.

"RUN!" Patrick shouted. For the wall of mud wouldn't stop there. It would barrage over the fence and through the alleys, through windows and doors. It would buckle walls and bury those, too.

He saw Scottie struck dumb, mouth horribly agape. "Holy fuckin' God," he intoned as Patrick grabbed his arm.

"GO!" Patrick begged, pushing, herding as many as his arm span would allow. He shoved them backward until their minds caught up with their feet. Screams rent the drums in his ears. *Back over the fence. Fall. Stand up. Run.* The roar of a terrible beast intoned behind them, harrying its prey.

And then Nina appeared, sweat slickened and breathing at a tremendous pace. She ran with her skirt scrunched in her hand, toward the landslide rather than away from it.

"Nina!" Patrick shouted. Scrambling for her, through the river of scattering bodies. "NINA! STOP!"

But Nina was now clear of the crush. She clambered over the fence, her dress ripping. She grounded her feet in the grass and lifted her chin, as though the wave of mud about to eclipse her was an old friend and she was there to greet it.

The earth shook.

CHAPTER 45

NINA

The wall of dirt came crashing downward, ripping tree roots in its path, ever closer.

Strong enough, I knew, to demolish buildings. Behind me, at the town's border, was the fenced yard of a school, the children within shoving through the door, hiding beneath their desks. Nothing to save them now but brick and mortar.

I climbed over a low fence, ripped my skirt free when it caught, and wove through the torrid sea of bodies rushing in the other direction, abandoning their shovels and picks. I heard Patrick shout my name, again and again.

But the crush of dirt was nearly upon us, close enough to swallow us all. Specks of it hit my face, sharp as knives. Seconds left.

Adrenaline flooded my chest, coated my tongue. Idium bloomed in my blood.

If someone had asked me in that moment, I could have told them the precise texture of all that earth, the way it would taste—copper, grit, sharp and mired. Its smell and the color and exact weight. All of it burst into my mind. I felt its ridges and planes and the exact points of momentum. I raised my hands, felt the expanse of all that earth in the widths of my fingers.

Then I bent it all.

I crushed it in on itself, brought billions of tumbling particles to a grinding halt. They were impossibly heavy. Heavier than anything I'd commanded before. I gasped beneath the weight of it. It rose up before me like a wave, and I shuddered beneath it, holding it steady.

But then slowly, ground shaking, I forced it back, back, then held it steady. I held it until the rumbling stopped, until I felt my mind might burst, stray pebbles and clumps tumbling to my feet. It settled in enormous mounds a foot from the fence line, splaying up the hill. But it did not breach the town.

And all went silent, the ground no longer shuddering, no longer roaring. Only the scream of the siren from Kenton's belly.

"Nina!" called Patrick. And quite badly I wanted to heed that call, but instead, I climbed. I climbed and climbed, my shoes sinking into the mud, up and over the mounds. And behind me I heard others follow, climbing through the formicaries and shouting to one another again. *Get to the pit. Dig. Idia, please, grant them a few minutes more.*

Halfway up and a man's fingers wriggled their way out of the soil, grasping at air. I forced the dirt to reveal him until he was uncovered to his waist. He slumped forward and I didn't stop to slap the dust from his lungs or offer my hand. There were so many others.

I heard shouts of "Here! Here!" and the thwack of shovels slicing the dirt. All those people swallowed up in the landslide somehow reaching for the surface.

But I tracked on, my legs screaming, up, up. Until the summit was reached, the ground a concave. Sunken atop whatever maze existed below.

I sunk to the ground, my hands to the earth. Closed my eyes.

"Get the horses! The barrows!" a voice shouted—Patrick's. He was running for the pit entrance, half destroyed as it was. He wound rope around his waist and secured it tightly. Scottie followed, donning a strange hat with a burning filament in its front. He passed one to Patrick.

"Wait," I said. Was I shouting? "WAIT!"

Patrick turned, his expression firm. "Stay here."

"I can help," I said, nearly tripping on my skirt. "I'm going with you."

"*No*," he heaved, adjusting the lamp on his head. The look he gave me was stricken. "You will stay right fuckin' here. You hear me?"

"Are you mad, Pat? She's an *earth Charmer!*" Scottie blustered, his voice rising over the din of the rest.

"Your brother's down there," I said forcefully. "I can get him out."

"We've got minutes, Pat!" Scottie shouted, his face ruddy, spittle flying. *"Minutes!"*

Patrick only eyed me a second longer. Then he squared his chin. A veil came over him. "You stay behind me," he said, the words bitten out through the cage of his teeth. "If I tell you to go back, you go back."

"Let's go," I gritted out. "We're wasting time."

"COME ON!" Scottie begged, pulling on Patrick's shoulder. "Now, boss! The horses'll pull you back."

Patrick closed his eyes and shook his head. He spoke while winding the same length of rope around my middle and tying it tightly. "There's two shafts; sometimes they can withstand a collapse. If we're lucky, some of the boys will've made it back inside the one nearest. We need to crawl to the pulleys, find the cables and bring 'em out. The horses will pull 'em up."

"How many?"

"Twenty-five, give or take," he said, and it sounded like a knife was twisting inside his chest. He gave me one last strained look. "Protect yourself. *Please.*"

I nodded.

Scottie fed in the rope we were tethered to as we ducked beneath the splintered rafters. Patrick hurried ahead of me with his head bowed. The earth slanted violently downward.

The ceiling had crumbled, leaving little room to move in. Within a few feet, Patrick was on his haunches. I felt the groans in the walls, smelt the freshly aerated earth. "I smell gas."

"If you feel yourself getting dizzy, tell me," Patrick panted. "I'll get you out." His hands felt along the ceiling, the sides, the ground. His headlamp blinked off and on. "We crawl from here."

"I can widen it," I said.

"There's a seam beneath us. It might not be safe."

"You just watched me stop a hundred thousand tons of earth from flattening your parish, Patrick. I know what I'm doing."

"One small disturbance, and it all comes down on top of us!" he rasped. "You won't be able to charm us out if you can't breathe."

"We don't have time to crawl, Patrick!" My breathing felt labored, the gas finding me already. "Move out of the way."

"If we get this wrong, they die. *You* die."

"*Trust me*, Patrick," I begged, exasperated.

He gave me a look of wild desperation and cursed. "All right," he panted. He flattened himself against the wall and grabbed my wrist. "All right." He helped me forward until my shoulder was pressed to his chest, as close to the hole as I could get.

I realized that he was shaking badly, that he was terrified. Beneath his breath, it seemed he was praying. There was no time for reassurances. Somewhere beneath us, ninety fathoms below, men waited in the earth.

I carved away at the walls, pushed the ceiling up, gently, carefully. I listened for the moans of the earth, for any telltale splits. But it all melded away at the bid of my mind, until it was wide enough to walk through at a crouch. Patrick let me lead him down, down, holding the loop of rope at the small of my back. We hurried through, two mice in a maze. Slipping, panting, growing more and more woozy with each small descent.

Finally, Patrick's headlamp caught the glint of steel—the shaft, mostly barricaded in clay. My mind pulled at it with waning strength, the earth slower to move now. Patrick took to it with his hands, clawing clods of it away with manic determination until the void could be seen, still there, its frame holding. Echoing up from the depths, I thought I heard a soft plea. *Help*, it said, and evaporated quickly.

Patrick fished the cables hanging from the pulleys. He unwound them from their anchor point, fingers fumbling. "Carry these out to Scottie," he huffed, his chest heaving. "Be as quick as you can."

"What of you?"

"The gate jams in a collapse," he said. "I need to be here to let them out."

"It should be me who stays," I panted. It seemed there wasn't enough oxygen. "If the ceiling falls, I can charm it."

He shook his head, sweat trickling over his jaw. "If you think I can leave you here—"

"Patrick," I spat, grabbing his shirt in one fist. "I can do this. I promise I'll come back." And perhaps he saw the blaze in my eyes, felt the idium pulsing through me. "There's no time. *Go.*"

And though it seemed to tear at every fiber of his being, he swallowed, nodded. He grabbed the cables in his hand. Gripped my neck in the other. And his lips met mine for one fervent moment. And then they were gone. He ripped the strange lighted hat from his head and put it on my own. "I think I've fallen in love with you," he said gruffly. "So you'd better fuckin' come out, Nina. Promise me. *Now.*"

I blustered. "I . . . I promise."

And then he disappeared into the gloom.

And I crouched in the dark and waited, my heart thrown from one wall to the next.

There was little time to recover. It didn't take long for the cables to become taut, stretched to capacity. I flattened myself against the outer wall and waited the interminable wait for them to move.

What seemed like a millennia later, the pulleys screeched, the cable within forced over its wheels. It moved in painful increments, the void filling with an awful grating sound, the clanks of steel and the groan of timber reaching me. But the lift was rising. The wheels spun in their mechanisms. The cable sped by, the clanking grew closer and closer.

And then I could feel it beneath my feet, something heavy rising from the belly of the world, forced from its middle. The lift ground to a halt when it hit the ceiling and the cable couldn't pull it any further.

Dizzy, I scrambled to the lift's doors. I pulled on the steel lever that clamped the gate shut. Moans within, shouts. I threw all the weight I had onto the lever, and inch by inch, it moved. A crack appeared, widened. Twenty, thirty fingers fed through the gap, prying the gates apart.

And then Gunner spilled out, landing on his knees, coughing violently. Blood seeped from his eyebrow, into his beard, already black with soot.

Behind him, twenty or so men appeared in the weak glow of my lamplight. Some held up by others, some slumped to the floor with their back against the walls. All of them gasping for breath, blackened by the earth, visible only by the stark reflections of their eyes.

"He sent the *Charmer* in?" Gunner panted, his voice nothing more than a scratch. But he smiled up at me, spitting a gob of soot to the ground. "Figures."

I swayed, seeing two of him. "This Charmer is going to get you out," I told him. "Unless you'd rather stay?"

He exhaled and it might have been a laugh. He accepted the hand I offered to stand on shaking legs.

I glanced over his shoulder, to the men behind him. "Can they walk?"

"They'll fuckin' crawl if they must," he rasped. "Lead the way."

I kept my hands to the walls as I ascended again, looking over my shoulder constantly to the train of miners following. The unconscious men were carried on backs, the conscious dragged their feet and sucked breath through hollowed cheeks.

I thought of things my father said when I was a child, about air temperature and gas in the head and lead feet that wouldn't move when commanded. *That's what the tunnels do*, he'd told me. *They make it so you can't run, can't see right. When you realize it, it's already too late.* I hastened, feeling my brain slosh to one side. I couldn't get enough oxygen.

"Easy, there," Gunner said at my back. "One foot in front of the other, girl. It's just a bit of gas."

I nodded, though it distorted my vision, sent fragments of picture into a moving kaleidoscope. I fell down and felt no pain, just hands pulling me upright again.

Men moaned. The walls sung a dirge. The tunnel extended on and on, its length somehow doubling, then tripling.

"Almost there," I said aloud.

And then, in a cage swinging from the hand of a miner, a canary gave its last warbling titter and became silent.

"Stop," Gunner said, his hand grasping my shoulder. My lamplight fell onto his stricken face, his slackening mouth. It made a ghost of him.

Then, from deep in the earth there was a catastrophic shudder. It rippled first from somewhere deep below, then through my fingertips, the soles of my feet. In my mind, a billion separate and connected sparks sputtered.

"Gas!" one man yelled.

"A blast!" another heaved.

"GO!" Gunner growled, shoving me forward with all the strength his arms allowed, and I was pitched headfirst into the gloom ahead, the walls around us trembling.

Rafts of dirt fell from the ceiling, clodding the path, filling it with rock. I blasted each blockade backward, again, again. The walls held so long as my hands glanced them, then collapsed soon after. Twice I heard the bellow of a man struck. The shouts of the others to keep moving. Keep moving.

Too heavy. It was too heavy. If it all fell at once, I wouldn't be able to lift it away.

And then, ahead, there was a light. It permeated the dust and the falling rock.

And Gunner pushed at my back, screamed "RUN!" into my ear, and the walls descended and crumbled all around.

But I pressed my back to the wall, my palms to the ceiling, and I let him pass me by. I counted the men who barreled through, and held the hill atop us, refusing to let it cave in. *Just a few more men*, I told myself. *Nine. Ten. Eleven men. Stay standing, Nina.*

But the mind can only hold so much, and I lost count of the bodies that collided with mine as they passed, lost sight as the grit poured into my eyes, and inch by inch, my mind slackened. There was simply too much.

So I let it go, and I bolted for that shrinking light ahead. I felt rock slamming into my back, my calves, piercing my skin, and I let it all crumble in my wake. I forced my muddied eyes to stay open and begged my legs to carry me out into the air.

CHAPTER 46

NINA

I remember this: broken clouds scudding overhead, a strange, muted ring spiraling in my ears. Dirt beneath my nails. A hand on my heart, then my neck.

Patrick's face. Gunner's.

Time lagged. I heard speech disconnected from lips, felt touch long after fingers were gone. I blinked, but darkness lingered.

"Nina!"

"She took too much gas to the head. Give her a minute."

"She held up the whole hill, Gun. The whole fuckin' thing."

"I know, Pat."

"Nina, can you hear me? No, don't get up. Just lie there a minute. Breathe."

I thought I might lie there for an eternity. Let those clouds sail by while I slept and slept and slept. My limbs had never felt heavier, less familiar.

But slowly, the rest trickled in. I smelled the gas on the air. I frowned at Patrick's tormented face. "How many?" I tried to ask, and it seemed he heard it.

He sighed. Relief slackened his face. Gunner slapped him on the shoulder and smiled. "See? She's all right."

"How many?" I asked again.

Patrick was close enough that I could count flecks in his irises, spaces between lashes. "All of them, Nina," he told me. "You got them all out."

Then he pressed his lips to mine, with no mind paid to his brother beside him, and I felt the warmth flow from him into me.

When he drew back, I saw something new in his expression. A sunbeam in all that darkness.

I wondered if it was a picture I'd ever be adept enough to paint. Clouds, skies, muddied skin, and a man who might be, at that very instant, declining into love.

"Take her home for me, Gunner. Please."

Gunner nodded without argument. His arm slipped beneath my knees.

"I can walk," I said, though when I sat upright everything tilted, the world slipping sideways off a plate.

"It's the gas," Patrick said unnecessarily. "Gunner will carry you."

"No, he won't," I protested.

"He will. And you'll let him."

I groaned. "You aren't coming?"

"I need to stay," he said. "There were others caught under the mud in the slide. Some unaccounted for."

"They'll be dead by now."

"Aye," Gunner answered. "But it would've been half the parish without you, Harrow, myself included. Know that."

My throat constricted, the trembling earth and screams and pounding feet returning to me. Those poor people. Tears pricked at my eyes.

Patrick took my chin in his hand, the grit on the pads of his thumbs pressing into my skin. "Breathe," he said. A command. "I'll come find you after."

After he dug up those bodies. Delivered them to their families. A sob escaped.

He was nothing but blue eyes, a strong grip. "No fallin' apart until I get back. You hear me?"

"Y-yes," I answered, mind still awash, the ache in my throat dulling.

"You go and rest. Wait for me."

Yes, I thought as he faded into shadow. *Of course I'll wait.*

· · · · · ·

I awoke in Colson's to the clamor of many voices, the uneven gait of Gunner, the scratch of his shirt buttons against my cheek.

"Gunner! You're alive!"

"How many came up, Gun? We heard from Donny they all got out. But it can't be true, can it?"

"Who's that? Is that the *Charmer*?"

"Nina?" This last voice was the only familiar one. Theo. "Good god. *Nina!*"

I was suddenly jostled. Gunner grunted. "Watch it, Teddy! You want me to fuckin' drop her?"

"What happened to her?"

"Nothin'. Just got a bit of gas rattlin' round her head. She'll be good as new in a couple hours. Leave her be."

I groaned. Tried to force my eyelids to open.

"Give her to me," Theo persisted, incensed. "I'll take her."

"Get out of the fuckin' way, Ted."

"Stop," I tried to say, but it was barely a whisper. I blinked at the underside of Gunner's beard, then at Theo. "Put me down. I'll walk."

Theo's face flushed. His pupils dilated. "What happened to her?" he repeated.

"She saved a whole lot of people, that's what," Gunner grunted.

Theo's eyes pierced mine. "You went into a collapsing *mine*?" he asked, as though I were a reckless child.

"She held up the whole fuckin' hill, you little shit," Gunner spat. "Get out o' the way."

"I said I'd take her." Theo made to pull me from Gunner's arms.

"Put me *down.*"

"You wanna keep all your teeth, Teddy?"

351

"For God's *sake*!" came another recognizable voice. This one harsher. Tess Colson came into view, the cords of her throat tight and pulsing. "Put the girl *down*. She's not a grenade."

Gunner sighed deeply, grumbled something beneath his breath. Theo released his hold on me and allowed Gunner to settle my feet on the ground.

I stood on loose limbs. "Thank you."

"Get out o' my sight, boys," Tess said, though her eyes were pinned on me. "And Gunner, leave the Charmer boy alone. Pat's orders, as you well know."

"She's unsteady on her feet, Ma—"

"I've got her." And her stare cut so severely, that no further argument could possibly be broached. Gunner rolled his eyes, sneered at Theodore, and dropped my wrist from his grasp. "I ought to thank you, Nina," he told me, inclining his head. "I was thinkin' I'd die down there."

And though he said it to me, I was sure I saw Tess's chin wobble, her eyes gloss over. By the time Gunner turned to face his mother, it had gone. She patted him on the shoulder as he passed by, averting her eyes, and Gunner paused to lay a swift kiss in her hair. "I'm all right, Ma. You ain't gotta cry."

"Go home," she warned him. *"Now."*

"Nina," Theo said, "let me get you upst—"

"Off you go, Charmer," Tess said cuttingly, knocking her shoulder into his arm as she passed. "Surely there's some other way you can make yourself useful."

Tess took my elbow, and before I could glance at Theo again, she ushered me through the swinging door. Her arm went around my waist as we ascended the stairs, and I at least had the wherewithal to hide my surprise. "Come on, darlin'," she motioned, allowing me to lean my full weight against her side.

On the third flight, she cleared her throat, adjusting my arm across her shoulders. "Is it true?" she asked. "You stopped that landslide?"

I tried not to think of the weight of the hill on top of me. "Of course," I said. "I had to."

"Hmm," she said, and nothing more.

In room number fifteen, Tess deposited me gingerly onto the bed, then turned the mismatched knobs over the bath, filling it first with steaming water, then cool. She helped me out of my dirt-encrusted dress. She held my hands as I lowered myself into the water. The scowl it seemed she'd been born with never left her face.

"Tip your head back," she instructed, then doused my hair with a pitcher. I suppressed a moan at the mercy of it. To feel the grime slipping free of my skin. To luxuriate.

Somewhere in the trenches of my memory, my mother had done as Tess Colson did. She combed fingers through the snarls of my hair. She added scented oil to the water. I closed my eyes, half there in Scurry, half here in Kenton.

"The gas don't linger too long," Tess said, perhaps as softly as she was capable of. "The room will stop spinnin' soon."

"It's not the gas," I replied. "I've just overextended myself."

When Tess didn't reply, I almost slipped away into sleep. The water lapped at my throat. She washed the mud from my hair. My ears filled with nothing but a gentle rhythmic pulsing.

"I've always envied Artisans," she said suddenly.

It was a curious enough comment for me to lift my eyelids. "*You* envy Artisans?"

"You sound surprised," Tess smirked. "Don't all Artisans assume we Crafters envy them?"

I delayed my reply. It seemed important to get it right. "Artisans are arrogant by nature," I said. "They believe even the sky envies them."

"You don't count yourself among 'em?"

"No," I said simply, chewing over my next words. "I . . . I know your son has the Alchemist holed up somewhere. And that the Union managed to steal a certain amount of terranium in the South."

Tess's eyebrow quirked. "Is there a question in there?"

"Have you never been tempted to take some idium for yourself? Surely Patrick would—"

"I'd never allow him to waste ink on an old woman like me," she said easily. "There's not much in reserve. Very little, in fact, and Pat doesn't trust many people."

I considered what her words could mean.

Tess tipped warm water over the crown of my head again. "My son said you were there with him at his siphonin'—that you found the idium together."

I couldn't quite interpret the intensity in her gaze. "Yes."

"Only you picked the Artisan ink, eh? And you stayed in the city."

I frowned. Nodded. I wondered if an insult were to follow. How dare a Crafter girl betray her very blood?

But Tess sighed. "I would've done the same, in your shoes. There was a time I would've swallowed anything to get me out of this place." She grimaced, replaced the pitcher to the floor. "You look around Old Kenton now, and you wouldn't recognize it. But once, it was just soot and misery. I was jealous of the Artisans in their sparklin' buildings. Jealous of their other finery, too. The dresses and coaches and balls and feasts. Their magic. It all seemed like such a dream, didn't it? You must've imagined the same."

I nodded but didn't speak.

"I've never been to Belavere City," she said then. "Never left Kenton, in fact. Girls weren't allowed to siphon when I was young, only boys, so I cut my hair with shears and tried to muscle my way onto a carriage in my brother's clothes. Didn't work, of course. I was thrown out on my arse before I could make it to a seat."

I laughed at the story despite myself, and Tess grinned. "Was worth a try." She shrugged. "My best hope after that was to find a good husband. One that wasn't quick to anger. One that wouldn't waste away on bad bluff. And even if I was lucky enough to find a good man, it was still likely the mines would take him, like they'd taken my father."

"And then you met John Colson?" I guessed.

"The innkeeper's son." She nodded, passing me a washcloth, a nail-brush, a bar of soap. "He promised me a lot of things, let me tell you. He were a Crafter, through and through. But I always thought he might've had an Artisan's imagination. He was always makin' somethin' out of nothin'. He promised me an easier life. A life free of the mines. He'd take over his family's wasted business, sell his inventions and oddities on the side. Our children would never step foot beneath ground, he promised." Tess shook her head. "I was a fool, and I believed him. I had always prayed for daughters, but when Gunner came, then Patrick and Donny, all I wanted was to keep them out of the mines."

I braced myself. I knew the ending to this story already.

"But you can't rise above the mines out here in the brink," Tess stared out the window, eyes glazed. "It's not designed that way for us Crafters. The money is always too tight. By the time Gunner came of age, we weren't a penny better off than the day we'd married. Colson & Sons was barely holdin' on, and there wasn't any other choice but for Gunner to go into that damned pit with his father." Here Tess's lip trembled, just as it had downstairs when her eldest son turned his back. "There was a collapse on his very first day. Did Patrick tell you that?" she asked.

I shook my head, my heart pounding hard enough to disrupt the bath-water.

"That's why he is the way he is," Tess closed her eyes. "Got stuck in an air pocket and almost died. His father kicked his way through a wall and dragged him out. And you know the cruelest thing in all of it, Nina? The worst part is—"

"They have to go back down the next day," I answered. "And cheat death again."

She nodded, jaw tense. "Most of the men here, they'd never admit it, but they spend most of their lives afraid. Afraid of the dark, of small spaces. Their lot in life is to live and work in fear. For Crafter women, we live our lives listenin' for the whistles, the sirens. We make plans for what will happen to us after our fathers and husbands die." Tess shook her head as the corners of her eyes grew wet. She blinked away the tears. "I don't envy the Artisans their dresses and parties any longer. But I envy them their sons and daughters, who'll never step foot in a pit. I envy them their clearheaded men. I envy them the ease of sleep." She sighed. "I owe you my sleep tonight, Nina. You saved my son." She didn't look at me as she said it.

"You don't need to thank me," I told her. Something oily and foul slithered into my stomach as I said it, reminding me of what I'd once intended to do to Kenton Hill.

Tess wiped her eyes, dried her hands in her apron and stood. "Patty . . . I think he might be in love with you. Has he said as much to you yet?"

I pressed my lips together and said nothing, staring at the reflection of the light on the water.

"He will," Tess told me. "You ought to start preparin' your response now. Once that boy sets his sights on somethin', mountains won't move him."

"He asked me to stay," I admitted, sinking a few inches deeper into the bath.

"Hmm," Tess mumbled. I wasn't brave enough to observe her expression. "Then I'd ask you to break his heart sooner rather than later, if indeed, you intend to break it."

My eyes snapped to hers. "I don't intend to."

"Good," she said, grinning slightly. "I doubt he'll let you leave now, in any case. I've never seen him so infatuated."

"I think I mostly infuriate him."

"Trust me, darlin', he's always lookin' at you, even when you think he's not."

I looked down at the water again, holding back a smile. It still seemed unbelievable that I should be the one to enthrall a man as enthralling as Patrick.

Tess sighed. "You should know he's intent on seein' this war through to its end, come what may. A smart woman would factor that into their decision-makin'. He won't be convinced to sit it out, especially after comin' this far."

I nodded. "He is determined to rescue your husband."

"My husband is gone," she said. And it was not cutting, or bitter, or devastating. It simply was. The ghosts in her eyes swirled on. "He was dead the moment he founded the Miners Union, Nina. There ain't a damn thing waiting for my son in that city but more blood. And he won't stop until he's won or he's dead."

It was a story with a sad ending no matter the outcome. She read from it as though it were imprinted on the walls of her chest, a future she couldn't avoid. "It ain't our lot in life to live easy, Nina," she said. "Men like Patrick die young, and the people who love 'em live on without 'em."

She retrieved clothes from the wardrobe and laid them on the bed. She looked back at me one last time. "Don't fall asleep in that water. Best you get out soon." Then she left, taking her ghosts with her.

She's wrong about men like Patrick, I thought.

She's wrong about women like me.

The bathwater became still as a lake, monsters hiding beneath the surface.

CHAPTER 47

PATRICK

All the people who'd gone under the mud came back up. Four came up dead.

Their bodies were with their families, in their kitchens or laid out on their beds, the grievers sobbing, whispering prayers on their knees on the sides of corpses.

But only four this night. Only four, when it ought to have been a hundred, perhaps two. A crew of trapped miners, a school, and a row of housing before that raging landslide.

It was midnight before Patrick persuaded his tired body up those stairs. He'd had the good sense to wash, redress before he went to find her. He felt he could never again stand the stench of wet earth. He'd scrubbed and scrubbed until every particle was lifted from his skin, nails, hair, and still, he felt gritty with it.

Sam was asleep in his chair, and Patrick passed him by like a phantom, his feet dragging, his heart pounding. The door was unlocked. He pushed it inward.

Nina was curled up in sleep. Moonbeams found her through the window and left squares of light on the blankets. She breathed softly, her parted lips so achingly perfect it made his stomach tighten.

He closed the door silently, and she didn't stir.

Patrick laid himself beside her, the shape of his body mimicking hers. He thought he could waste away hours looking at her. This close, he could trace the ridge of her cheekbone, touch the small scar on her jaw, be awed by all the finer pieces of the picture.

She blinked away dreams, and he was grateful to have her hazel eyes now, too. It was quite a relief to drown in them. "Ask me again if I trust you," he whispered, burying the fingers of one hand into the light curls behind her ear.

He could hear her swallow. "Do you trust me?"

"There's no one I trust more," he said.

And when she finally settled against his chest, he held her, and it was the easiest thing in the world to do. Even as she shook with the day's dealings. Even when she finally broke apart under the tremendous enormity of all those lives and all that darkness.

"Thank you," Patrick told her, again and again, until his eyes closed and her shuddering slowed. "Shhh. I'll keep you safe."

And then he slept. He slept like a man who'd never seen the winding snake of a tunnel, who had never felt the darkness as a vise, pressing in from all sides, pulverizing bones to dust.

CHAPTER 48

NINA

I awoke wrapped in Patrick.

His breath on my neck, my back to his chest, his hand on my stomach, my nightdress bunched indecently high. I felt all the hard planes of him against me and had never felt as restful. How little it would take to shut my eyes and sleep another day.

My stomach, however, would not be ignored. It growled insistently.

I rose with the intention of finding food for the both of us. Surely Patrick would be hungry when he woke. God knew when he'd last eaten.

His discarded pocket watch on the bedside table read just before six. Dawn broke beyond the rooftops; I would likely meet no one but Sam in the stairwell, nor in the pub or the kitchen. I slipped a coat over my clothes without bothering to dress properly.

Sam was snoring with his head lolling on his chest. The stairs creaked as I descended but the rooms on each landing were quiet. Barely any sounds from the street permeated.

I was almost to the bottom when I heard a thundering from above. Feet pounded the steps as they descended, intensifying as they neared. I frowned at the way I had come, watching a window shudder in its frame.

Patrick appeared, barreling around the banister. His hair stuck up at every angle. He remained shirtless, as he had been in sleep, trousers unbelted and hanging loose on his hips. The way he panted made the muscles of his chest and stomach expand in distracting ways. Truly, I had never seen a man more magnificent.

I swallowed, blinked rapidly. Then said, "Is someone chasing you?"

He braced his arms against the wall and hung his head, cursing. "God *almighty*, Nina. It's barely daybreak. I thought . . . I thought—"

"What?" I asked. "That I'd left?"

His cheeks hollowed and filled. "No, I—"

"I'm only finding breakfast," I told him, trying not to stare at his body. Trying to ignore the warmth pooling low in my stomach at the sight of him. "I'll return soon."

But Patrick shook his head, descending the last of the stairs. "I'll have it brought up," he said. "That's what I pay the cooks for."

"I'm capable of procuring some toast," I argued. "And I'm hungry."

"You aren't even properly dressed," he countered. "And your feet are turnin' purple with the cold."

"So are *yours*."

"Come back upstairs with me." He drew closer, and I stopped breathing.

Like all his commands, this one was difficult to ignore. He was close enough that I could feel the heat emanating off his body. His fingers reached and threaded slowly with mine, tempting me back to him.

But I was, in fact, very hungry. "I'll only be a moment."

"I can think of better ways to fill the moments," he said in a voice like smoke. His other hand wound gently around my lower back.

I inhaled sharply, my thighs squeezing together as he closed the space between us, and his scent overwhelmed me. It felt like coercion—a very effective coercion. "I realize that everyone else around here does whatever you ask of them, Patrick, but if you think I've agreed to stay here just to fall in line and obey orders, then—"

He sighed at the ceiling, cursed beneath his breath.

"Then you'll be disappointed to learn that I'm not that kind of woman. And—"

He kissed me. Took my waist in both hands and pressed me back against the wall. His lips covered mine, stunning me, and then unraveled me entirely.

The seam of my lips parted on a gasp, and he took advantage. His tongue stole my breath in long, luscious sweeps, forced a gasp from my chest. Then his hips pinned me there, and hot, liquid wanting filled my core, disintegrated every other thought.

Somehow, my legs found his waist and wound around him. My hands delved into his hair. The coat I'd thrown on puddled around my elbows, and when his lips disentangled from mine, a sound of longing escaped me.

"It's early," he murmured. And his voice was thick with need, heavy with it. The hard ridge of his arousal pressed into me. "Come back upstairs with me."

I nodded, not caring much if he took me here in the stairwell.

On the top floor landing, Patrick barked at Sam to go home, and the boy went wide-eyed and fled, possibly mistaking the urgency on Patrick's face for something else.

Patrick pulled me back into the room I'd just escaped, and it seemed we were both taken by something uncontrollable. A spring tension pushed to the limits of its constructs before it broke, gave way. He pulled me off the ground and onto his chest so that my mouth was aligned with his, so that our lips could connect again. We were drunk. Desperate. I let my coat fall to the floor, then wrapped my arms around his neck, urgently pressing my body against his. He cursed against my lips.

I found my back pressed onto the bed, the wide span of his chest hovering above my own. He braced his arms on either side of my head, and my fingers found the valleys between the panes of his chest, then his stomach. I felt him shiver.

"Last chance to change your mind, Nina," he said, drowning me in perfect blue. As he spoke, a finger glanced the column of my throat, drew a line down my chest to the ribbons of my nightgown, pulled them free.

I watched those eyes turn wild, ravenous. "You've got this one last second to tell me to leave."

In answer, I kissed him. Amid all the noise, the endless machinations of this world, there was little else I knew better than that I wanted Patrick Colson. That I was willing to do whatever it took to stay here, like this. I'd traveled to every village and parish on the continent, but that any other man might have captured my attention seemed unfathomable to me now. None came close. There was only Patrick and his secrets and these walls.

How had that happened? How had he eclipsed everything so swiftly?

He pulled the ribbons down until the bust followed, the cotton sleeves slipping free of my shoulders, the lace hem creeping slowly over the swell of my chest until it caught on the peaks of my nipples. Patrick's eyes ignited.

A thousand brilliant bursts of light ruptured in me when he looked at me this way, like I was crafted precisely for him. Like I was the only woman who had ever existed.

I whispered, "What have you done to me?"

He shook his head once, jaw flexing. "No," he groaned. "What have *you* done to me?"

He lowered his head to my chest and gently pressed his lips to the curves, making a reverent path to my throat, and something inside me surged, clawed for the surface. "Undress me," I begged him. "Please."

A sound of deep relief escaped his lips, and he sat upright on the bed, pulling me with him. With deliberate slowness, he drew the hem of my nightgown back over my thighs, his hands bunching the fabric at my hips, skating over my sides as he lifted it higher, and all the while, his eyes followed the trail. Lust flooded across his features as each new part of me was exposed, his hands tensing, jaw tightening. I wondered if he could feel how heavy my breasts became under his eyes, how the blood quickened beneath my skin. Soon the nightgown fell away, and Patrick curled his hand around my jaw. "I've never seen anythin' so perfect," he told me. And perhaps a million men had said just the same to a million lovers, but never quite like Patrick, whispering it into my skin, lifting my wrist and sealing his lips over the mottled scar where a brand had once been, making every nerve ending writhe beneath it.

He left me alone in the middle of the bed and stood at its side, fingers making quick work of the buttons at his trousers, and they fell away.

It seemed every inch of him had been carefully drawn, precisely carved, and I could hardly stand to look away from him, but there was something more I needed. I met his stare. "Touch me," I said. There was no waver in my voice.

I saw his eyes flash with hunger.

And I was sure he could see the same in me, how I breathed too fast, squirmed as he stood there, too far away, too devastatingly masculine. He bore down over my body slowly, holding himself just slightly out of reach, as though inspecting which part of me he would take first.

"Where, Scurry girl?" he murmured, and it thundered through my own chest. His fingers skimmed over the hollow of my stomach, and even this simple touch made me tremble. "Here?" he asked, and he watched me closely as his roughened hand traveled lower, lower, down to my sex, fingers teasing. He watched my back arch, my mouth fall open, and it seemed to unleash something wild in him. His mouth sank to my collarbone, then to my breasts, lips closing on one peak. I moaned his name.

I gripped his head in my hands and held him there, his fingers still massaging expertly, learning me instantly. "*Please*," I said, and I undulated against the pressure of his palm, seeking more, more, desperate for him.

"Ah, how I'd hoped you'd beg, just like this," he said against my skin, and his palm pressed down hard.

"*Patrick!*"

"Hoped you'd whine like that, too."

I was shivering, legs trembling, my hips moving instinctually, needing more. His smoky voice was a drug to me.

"Do you know how many times I've imagined fucking you?"

I forgot how to breathe, how to think. There was only this, only him.

He guided the head of his erection inside me, and my head fell back, my mouth opened in shock.

"Holy god," he uttered. Only he was looking at me, like I was some divine entity.

For an eternity I was lost in all those devastating sensations. The shudder of his chest, the urgent pulsating of my hips, begging him, pleading with him to satiate this burning. Each time I thought the ends of the earth had been found, the intensity increased. Each thrust pushed me further into insanity, made my nails dig into his shoulders. My body moved in discordant ways, hungry, ravenous.

"This is how I want you every single time," he told me, his tongue playing with the skin behind my ear. "Just like this. Undone. Wild."

My inner walls were tightening, and I watched his face transform into one of agony, acute pleasure. He captured my mouth and growled my name.

And I turned to shafts of light, rivulets of music, the shiver of stars misaligning.

CHAPTER 49

PATRICK

Patrick had never understood the possessive tendencies of men in love. Possession was for gold, land, idium. But something primitive and marrow deep lashed against his rib cage when Nina looked at him, and he thought, though he knew it was brutish, that he wished to claim her.

He took every measure to delay the moment they would have to leave that room. He had food brought to them, fruit and toast and pastries, and he watched every crumb disappear into her mouth. As soon as it seemed she was done, he pushed the tray aside and lifted her into his lap while she laughed at his impatience. He claimed all of her that he could, while he could, in this six-by-nine-foot realm of theirs. Eventually, the world beyond would come flooding in. The moment wouldn't keep. He had a town to tend to. It seemed an unbearable task.

How quickly he had become addicted to hearing her breathe his name, the sounds of her climax, the pinch of her nails digging into his back. He took her again, then again, marveling at the many curves and valleys of her. He wondered if he'd ever feel fully satiated, or if he would always walk around with this yearning now, this knowledge of her entire body and the way it felt. And if so, whether it was possible to accomplish anything ever again, or if she had ruined him.

The rest of the day's intentions had been laid to waste. Twice, Donny had come knocking at the door asking for Patrick, and twice Patrick and Nina had ignored him. "Brother, if you need me to break down this door and save you, just use the safe word. Has the Charmer bested you?"

"Fuck off, Donny," Patrick had called, and Donny had snickered on the other side of the doorframe.

Nina lay naked against him, one leg entangled with his, her stomach pressed to his hip. She had her eyes closed but didn't sleep. She smiled as Donny's footsteps receded.

One of Nina's fingers drew patterns on Patrick's chest. Swirls. Mazes, perhaps. He'd never felt quite so peaceful.

"I wish I could draw you," she murmured sleepily. "I'd be able to get it right this time."

He frowned. "You must miss it," he said. "Art, I mean."

A pause. "A little."

"I'll find you some supplies," he said immediately. "You can paint and draw until your fingers fall off."

"Awfully generous of you."

"I have a mind to keep you here by any means," he murmured, following the underside of her breast with his fingers. She shuddered. "Bribery included."

He felt her body surge slightly beneath his touch. He was quickly learning all the ways to make it respond to him. It was the most enthralling puzzle he'd ever encountered. A kiss beneath her jaw tipped her head back, her hips were ticklish, her inner thighs especially sensitive—she gasped every time.

He suspected she was marking him just as quickly. It seemed every place her fingers traveled set him on fire.

With nothing to stop him, he lowered his mouth to one pert nipple, delectably pink. His groin tightened painfully at the sound of the moan she emitted. Truly, if he had his way, he might hold her hostage in this bed forever, so he could elicit these songs from her at any moment.

Her chest flushed, her stomach dipped and rose with need. She tried to pull his face to hers but instead, he resisted. He traveled lower, skating down the length of her body until her legs rose on either side of his head, and his tongue parted her.

"Patrick," she whimpered, again and again, eyelids fluttering. It was his favorite picture of her, he'd decided. Lips wet and glistening, throat exposed with her head back, cheeks pinkened. Those fall-colored eyes becoming uncontrolled.

He brought her to the very cusp, where it seemed the fall into blissful oblivion were inevitable, then watched her lunge for him, pushing him upright. She wrapped her legs around his waist and lowered herself onto the hard length of him, immediately picking up a rhythm that had already become intuitive to them both. He relished the way her body slid up and down his, how her stuttered whimpers collected in his mouth. He braced his arm around the small of her back and angled up into her, pulling her down as tightly as he could, as close as he could, and watched her rapture cascade.

He followed soon after, groaning her name into the hollow of her throat, tangling his fist into her hair. If there were pleasures greater than this, he'd never heard them told. He descended back into himself with languid reluctance and found her still here, wrapped around him.

They fell in a tangle onto their sides.

It was peaceful enough here that he thought he might be able to sleep. He closed his eyes. "Tell me a story," he whispered into her ear.

She stirred lazily, half-dazed. "What kind of story?"

"A story about you. Before we met. In Scurry."

Her eyes opened, a line appearing between her brows. "Wouldn't you prefer a happier story?"

He shook his head slowly, dropped a soft kiss to her throat. "I want a real one."

"If you insist on touching me like that, I shouldn't be expected to speak."

He noted her hesitancy and was unsurprised. In the brink, childhood was a balled-up wad of troublesome things. Watery dinners and long winters and red-raw palms. Policemen with swinging batons. Mothers who cried. Fathers who shouted and split their knuckles against the wall. From the little Patrick had gathered, Nina's upbringing had been no different.

She stalled at first, and Patrick wondered if he'd accidentally broken the spell they'd cast. But she didn't withdraw, didn't turn her face. She closed her eyes, and through their touching flesh, he felt her heart race.

"There was a river behind our house," she said. "My mother used to take me swimming in it. Taught me to pick the mint leaves along its edge and make tea with them. We watched the narrow boats and she tried to teach me to sketch or paint them. She told me the boats were headed for Belavere City. She promised we'd go there together one day."

Patrick stayed very quiet. He sensed pain laced into the words. A pain that wrenched at her even now.

"One day, I woke up at dawn and she wasn't in her bed. She wasn't in the kitchen, either. And somehow, I knew. I knew she was on one of those boats headed for the city. I ran to the river just as she was passing. I chased it for a mile at least, screaming for her, all the other passengers staring at me. All except for her. She didn't even have the courage to look at me one last time. She hid her face beneath her hat and turned her head away."

Patrick's fingers had become clamps. He swallowed the knot caught in his throat.

"I still wonder sometimes how she could do that. How could someone leave their child without a word? Without a single glance? I know now that she wanted to give me a chance. Another kind of life. But she didn't look back.

"I stood on that bank until sunset. Then I went back out the next morning, and the next. For the longest time, I was sure she would come back. That's the cruelest part of childhood, I think. You don't know how to stop hoping."

There was no tension in Nina's body as she spoke, no severity in her tone. Only acceptance. She spoke as though the story belonged to someone else.

Patrick thought of that small girl on the Scurry riverbank, waiting for her mother to return, and was incensed. The troubles he'd traversed as a child paled compared to this.

Patrick looked at Nina, at her blond curls and rose-stained lips, and imagined her as a girl, the breaking of her heart a gradual progression. He wondered whether, if it were possible to go back in time and hold her hand, it would have made any difference.

Patrick drew Nina closer until she was curved perfectly around him. He kissed her shoulder, her jaw, the space between her eyes. He muttered, "She was a fool," and, "I'm sorry," and, "Thank you."

"For what?" she asked, her lips a hairsbreadth from his.

"For giving me that piece of yourself," he said. "I swear to you, I'll look after it."

And then he kissed her endlessly. Until it seemed she'd forgotten the river and its bank. Until she'd forgotten anything but this small world. Patrick Colson and Nina Harrow, succumbing to that which had simmered and seethed between them like a growing tidal wave.

CHAPTER 50

NINA

At dusk, Donny came again to pound on the door. He threatened to break it in and drag Patrick out.

"In case you forgot, Pat, an entire fuckin' pit caved in day afore. The whole town's waiting downstairs for you!"

The bath Patrick and I shared had become tepid, yet neither of us made any move to rise.

"I'll be down in a moment," Patrick called, sighing with tremendous reluctance. "Hold 'em off for a bit, will you?"

"They've come to hear *you* speak, Patty. What am I s'posed to do?"

"Play 'em a song," Patrick suggested, playing with a tendril of my hair. "Pass out a round of drinks."

"They're four deep already, Pat. Hurry up!" He hit his fist against the door one last time, then stomped away, cursing us both loudly.

"And so, it ends," Patrick muttered beneath his breath. He held my fingers in his beneath the water, but now rose them to press his lips to their pads. Then he lifted himself from the water, the streams running down all those fine muscles. He stepped out of the tub and collected a towel with which to dry himself.

"If I asked you to wait here until I get back, would you do it?" he asked me.

I grinned at him, resting my chin on the lip of the basin. "Not a chance."

He groaned. "Every man, woman, and child out there will be wantin' to buy you a drink," he said, donning his clothes in distractingly practiced ways. "It'll be midnight before I can tear you away."

I laughed. "So you *are* the jealous type." I rose from the bath and stepped out.

Patrick was suddenly before me, hands sliding around my wet waist, "It's not jealousy. It's greed."

The way his tone graveled, pulled at the cords of my resolve. Heat descended into my belly. "Haven't you ever heard of the risks of having too much of a good thing?"

"Not in this case," he said, then drugged me with his fingers skating down my neck.

I exhaled shakily. "You won't distract me. I'm coming with you."

He sighed, then released me. "Don't say I didn't warn you."

The thrum of the pub rang up the stairwell, pulsing the windows in their frames on each landing. Even at this early hour, someone belted the piano keys, voices walloped, the unmistakable thunder of dancing shook the floorboards when we alighted the stairs.

I raised my eyebrows at Patrick. I noticed he had already stowed away that light in his eyes. The peace that had been on his face was gone. Back was the careful veneer, that knife-sharp glare. But his hand remained on the small of my back, gentle and sure.

"Are they . . . celebrating?" I asked incredulously. It seemed in poor taste.

"Don't judge them too harshly," Patrick said. "They've come to expect catastrophic loss when a mine collapses. Yesterday feels like a miracle by comparison. It *is* a miracle," he said, his gaze boring into mine. His fingers touched my cheek. "I'll apologize now for what's on the other side of this door." Then he pushed it open.

Uproar descended upon us.

A voice screeched, "The Charmer! There she is!" and it seemed the entire sea of faces turned simultaneously.

A discordant cheer rent the air. Glasses clinked above heads. Men waved their caps and women covered their mouths with their hands. Some of them wept. Several children, none of them taller than my hip, swarmed my legs and gripped hold of my dress. They hugged me, shoved limp dandelions into my palms, pulled me forward into the crowd. I looked over my shoulder, silently pleading for help, and found Patrick leaning against the wall beside the door, hands in his pockets, a small grin on his face.

I was swallowed by the horde a moment later, and Patrick disappeared from view.

I felt as though my hand was gripped and shaken by a hundred different people, all their faces floating into view and then abruptly disappearing, replaced by more.

"Thank you, Miss Harrow. Bless you."

"You're a gift from God, surely."

"Me brother were in that shaft. We owe you his life."

"I've always trusted Patty Colson. Always! And now he's brought you to us."

"You consider yourself a Kenton girl now. If there's anythin' you need . . ."

It went on and on. Somewhere in the mix, I caught a glimpse of Theo and Polly. They sat together in a bay window. I looked long enough to make out Polly's pinched expression, Theo's balled fists, before they were eclipsed once more by another wave of drunken gratitude.

Eventually, Gunner clawed me out of the scrummage. His large frame appeared at my side, and his presence alone was enough to make those clustered nearest take a step back.

"All right, you dolts. That's enough for one night. Let the girl breathe, for fuck's sake. She ain't had a single drink yet." He offered me a wink, a sly grin beneath his wild beard, then gripped my upper arm and pulled me away.

Gunner brought me to the bar, found a stool for me to sit on, and glared at anyone who tried to approach. They quickly diverted, and though the floor space was entirely occupied, a foot of space was left around me.

Tess appeared before me with a pint. She said nothing, but her hand patted mine before she departed.

"Well, fuck me," Gunner grunted, staring wide-eyed after his mother. "Don't tell me you cracked Tess Colson?"

I shrugged. "Turns out she rather prefers you alive."

Gunner let out a laugh the likes of which I hardly thought him capable. He appeared a different man. "Only sometimes, I assure you."

All around us, it was more of the same. A tumble of dancers slammed their feet on the boards as they skipped around their partners. When the most inebriated spilled their drinks on another, it was met with not ire, but laughter. The bay windows were steamed and sweating and Tess pulled a large brass bell over her head and rang it. Its peals were met with more cheers.

"A round on the Colsons!" she shouted, and the piano rejoiced.

I watched it all with a growing warmth. The thrill in the room—I'd never seen a thing like it, not in the pubs of Scurry or in the ballrooms of Belavere City. Nothing existed in those places that could replicate this. They were, each one of them, a single piece of a larger joy.

Happiness swept through me. I let it.

I turned to Gunner. "Thank you for the rescue," I said.

But he shook his head. "You're stealin' all my lines," and he clinked his pint to mine.

Just then, Tess Colson climbed onto a chair behind the bar, and her voice rang out at a decibel that seemed supernatural. "QUIET!" she shouted, and it served to silence at least half the crowd. "Scottie! I'll mash your head in if you don't quit."

Scottie, who'd once again commandeered the piano, saluted her with a wayward grin, then promptly fell off the bench.

"Right. The Union meetin' is about to commence, and at least half o' you aren't an official member," Tess said. The comment was met with resounding dissent. "But I've got no earthly hope in hell of movin' you out o' me pub. So, if you insist on stayin', commit to shuttin' your trap!"

There were a few brave or stupid souls among the wash who cheered or whistled in response. But upon the glare Tess issued, they soon fell quiet.

Patrick appeared behind the bar and helped his mother from the chair. It seemed she wobbled on her descent, though Patrick shielded it from view.

"Go on, Patty!" Gunner cheered drunkenly, and the crowd laughed. They looked to Patrick expectantly as he stood on the chair, then on the bar top.

And so did I. I marveled at the boy in that courtyard who had become this man—arresting and steadfast. I saw precisely what Kenton Hill must have seen in him. Someone unswerving.

I felt as though I understood it then—the toll paid to keep a place like Kenton Hill safe. To keep it aboveground and functioning. What wouldn't one do, to preserve something so invaluable?

"I call to order this extraordinary meeting of the Miners Union of Kenton Hill. Tonight, we'll be skippin' formalities."

His spectators bellowed.

Patrick's eyes swept to me, held.

And I knew what he would do in the next moment. I shook my head and thought of Theo sitting somewhere in a corner, watching.

Patrick knelt down and held a hand out for me. "Do me the honor, Scurry girl."

My hand shook. Whatever commendation I'd receive next would be undeserved. And would they see it on my face, when I stood before them all? Would they know that my intentions here hadn't always been pure?

But Patrick's fingers took mine, and Gunner's hands hoisted me from behind. And suddenly I was standing beside Patrick, and the people of Kenton Hill were calling my name as a chant. My real name.

"Yesterday, Kenton Hill suffered a loss of four men. But we were also gifted the safe return of many more, the likes of which we Crafters have never seen. They went home yesterday evening to their families, slept in their beds, awoke this morning to a new day. And for that, we have exactly one person to whom we ought to give thanks."

He spoke to them, but he looked at me. He lifted a glass of whiskey into the air. "First, we toast those fallen, Idia claim their souls."

Glasses were hoisted into the air. They remained poised, waiting.

"Next, we toast our old Kenton, whose hills we have sworn to defend," Patrick's voice rang out as though he stood on a summit. It was reverent. Commanding. "And last, we toast Nina Harrow, who lifted an entire hill off our backs."

I was deafened by cheers, all of it coalescing to a shrill ring. Patrick drank his whiskey, and his stare robbed me of breath.

He smiled. I smiled, too, more widely than I ever had. And he took me up in a kiss in front of everyone, giving in to whatever enslaved us right there on the countertop.

Sound came punching back, full of joy. The barriers between me and Patrick, between me and Kenton Hill, seemed in that moment entirely surmountable. We would break into Belavere City and free our loved ones. We would take down Lord Tanner, and I would never need to live in fear again. All problems could be rectified.

That evening was colored gold. It glinted from every corner, every eye. Patrick led me to a table with his brothers, Scottie, Briggs, and Otto, and I blushed as Donny made countless inquisitions about what Patrick and I had been doing upstairs all day.

"Playing checkers, were you?" he asked while the others jittered. "Cards? You can tell me if my brother don't know how to keep a woman entertained, Nina. I'll keep it in confidence."

Finally, Patrick kicked the leg of Donny's stool sideways. His brother went sprawling onto the floor, and the others broke into hysterics. "Fuck me, Pat! I was only askin'."

"Ask her again," he said. "I dare you."

Donny sensibly kept his mouth shut.

The crowd eventually thinned, patrons tipping their caps or waving to me as they left. The night grew late when I saw Theo and Polly across the room again, still seated against that bay window, drinks untouched, expressions unchanged.

Theo stared a hole right through me, though his eyes flickered more than once to Patrick's hand on my knee.

"I need to help my mother in the kitchens for a while," Patrick said into my ear, and I resisted the urge to try to drag him upstairs.

"I can come," I replied, turning toward him. Donny and Gunner were already standing, bidding the others goodnight.

Patrick shook his head. "No need," he said. "But I'll be at your door later." He pressed a kiss to my cheek. It could have been a gentlemanly gesture, except for the way he lingered, except for the words skating across my skin. "And you'd better let me in. I might break my neck crawlin' in through that window."

I laughed and let him leave without argument. I watched him rebutton his waistcoat and follow his brothers behind the bar, all while two pairs of eyes lanced me from afar.

It seemed there was a conversation that wouldn't keep till morning.

CHAPTER 51

NINA

I excused myself, muttering about fresh air, though the excuse wasn't necessary—Scottie and Otto had taken their leave, and Briggs was, by that hour, sagging over the table.

The moment I stood, so did Polly and Theo. I warned them away with a glare. How would it look for all three of us to exit at the same time, with no chaperone?

They let me slip through the doors first. A few smokers and liquor-numbed gawkers said my name as I passed over the stoop, and I smiled politely. They paid me no mind as I crossed my arms over my chest, started down Main Street, then took a sharp turn down the alleyway that bordered Colson's.

There were no floating lights here. Nothing but rats and a vicious chill. I hadn't thought to bring a coat.

I heard their footfalls before they came into view. Polly and Theo stuck close to the walls, tucking their hands away from the cold as I did.

Polly's face seemed stricken. Theo's roiled with something I tried not to notice.

"We should make this short," I suggested, my voice low and careful.

Theo rolled his eyes. "We've been here longer than you, Nina. Trust me, at this hour, there isn't a single one of them that will manage standing on two legs, much less notice our absence." His voice was clipped.

I sighed. "Whatever it is you wish to say, Theo, say it."

Theo's eyes flashed, and I immediately regretted my tone.

"Congratulations," he said, and it might as well have been a slap to the face. "You made quick work of it."

I frowned. "Quick work of what?"

"Of making Colson fall in love with you. Even if it took a landslide to get the job done."

I blinked once, twice. "You think *I* caused that landslide?"

Polly fretted at Theo's side. "Stop it, Theodore."

"I was in Dumley's lessons with you, Clarke. I know better than anyone what you're capable of. It was effective, I'll admit, having him watch you save his people like that. But it was also stupid. If you lost control, you could have buried the Alchemist, for all you knew."

"It's *Harrow*," I said. "Not Clarke. And I didn't charm that landslide."

"Then stopping it was an utter waste of your talent—in fact, you've sabotaged half your mission from happening at nature's own hand." The way he said it made me think he didn't believe me, that he easily thought me capable of such a thing.

"*Enough*," Polly pleaded, her voice a whisper. "I do not wish to be shot in this alley for conspiring."

Theo shook his head, scrubbed his face in frustration. "Right, then. Where is the Alchemist, Nina?" He was barely in control of the volume of his voice. "All that time you're spending with him, surely you've figured it out?"

My stomach turned. "I don't know," I said, working hard to keep my voice even. I'd been too distracted to come up with a stall tactic. I still had no idea what to say to Theo in order to protect him and persuade him at the same time.

Theo shook his head, laughed in disbelief. "And why exactly is that?"

"He isn't stupid, Theo. He'd suspect something if I pushed too hard right away. It would put us in danger."

"I'm in that hole every fucking day, Nina. You don't need to tell me about danger."

"And I have the House threatening my execution if I don't give them what they want," I spat, my temper getting the better of me. "You came here voluntarily, Theo. And you'll return to your esteemed position when this is all done."

Theo paled, taking obvious efforts to temper himself, and when he next spoke, it was in the same tone he'd had when we were teenagers and he was trying to placate whatever silly concern plagued me. "Nina, listen to me. I know the pressure must be insurmountable. But if we give Tanner the Alchemist, then we *all* go back to Belavere City. They'll forgive everything that came before this, Nina. *Everything.* You will be safe. You can finally start over."

I wondered if he meant that he and I could start over, that we could go back to the way we were.

"And all I have to do is murder a town full of people," I said. "You're willing for me to do that for you, aren't you?"

He stepped back like I'd struck him. "This isn't for me," he said. "Nina, it's for all of Belavere's Artisans. We can stop the war."

"By burying the other side."

"This isn't about Crafters at all, is it?" he said, voice rising. "This is about Colson."

My face heated. "Did you hear *anything* I just said?"

"You'll get us all killed. You do realize that?"

"Step back, Theo," Polly said suddenly, her hand on his chest, for the space between he and me had closed, and his hands still shook, and my throat felt riddled and blistered. "Enough of this. We have no time, Nina. There's news from the House of Lords."

I turned my eyes to her, my ire dissipating into dread. "News?"

She nodded. I heard Theo laugh bitterly, watched him turn his back on me and pace away. "You would have known sooner, but you were providing entertainment to the rebel leader of the Miners Union."

"*Enough*, Theo," Polly gritted out. She grabbed my shoulder and turned me toward her, until I looked at her and nothing else. "Tanner sent a scribble."

Fear like icy fingers gripped my spine. "What does it say?"

"Our time's up," Polly said, her eyes urgent. They shook in their sockets. She held out her hand, a piece of parchment tucked into her palm.

I took it warily, unfolded it.

The House moves to strike.
Provide safest routes to the heart for imminent attack.
Flee enemy territory.

I read it once, twice, the letters distorting and shifting. Polly had to grip my hand to retrieve my attention. "They're coming, Nina," she said. "The Lords' infantry. They'll invade the town. Take it all apart."

I shook my head. "The Alchemist," I uttered, looking to Theo for confirmation. "They wouldn't risk an attack without first securing the Alchemist."

"Evidently," Theo said darkly. "They're willing to take that chance."

My mind reeled. I read the words over and over, desperately searching for a way around them. "No. No, he wouldn't. There is nothing that matters more to Tanner than idium. Domelius Becker is too valuable."

"Which is *exactly* why he will now invade, Nina!" Theo nearly yelled. "Two years they've gone without an Alchemist. How long did you trust Tanner to wait? He's grown desperate. *You* were his last bid to find Becker, but even the prodigal earth Charmer has failed to turn out a single clue as to the man's whereabouts. He has no *choice* but to invade. To not do so would be to admit defeat to the Crafters." Theo's neck had become mottled in red; he heaved each breath, pulling it between his teeth. "And as we know, he will never concede defeat."

I shook my head, refuting his words beyond sense. "No."

"Nina—"

"I can find the Alchemist," I promised—whether to them or to myself, I wasn't sure.

"We've been trying to figure out his whereabouts for two years," Polly said weakly, strain written clearly across her face. "Patrick will never give him up."

"We've been given our new orders," Theo said.

"No!" This time, my voice rebounded dangerously off the bricks. It rattled up the pipes that snaked the building to the rooftops. It cracked open my chest and spilled out all the hope I'd precariously garnered.

I couldn't see this town razed. I couldn't forsake Rose Harrow and John Colson.

And I couldn't lose Patrick, whose heart I'd threaded mine with. Not after choosing him. Choosing here.

"Nina," Polly said gently. "We—"

"I'll find the Alchemist," I insisted.

"We can't." Polly shook her head. "There's no more time."

"We can go back to the city, Nina," Theo said, placating again. "My father will help you, I know he will. He'll pull strings for clemency."

"They won't come if there's no safe passage," I blurted out, clutching at final straws under duress. "They won't come unless you give them the route, Polly. You can hold them off."

"I can't," she said. "Not for long."

"They won't come unless they can find a way in," I said again, my voice surer this time, more confident. "There are no tracks, no roads, no canals. The surrounding hills are laden with land mines."

"There *is* a way in, Nina," she said quietly. "Right into the center. You created it yourself." There was no malevolence, no threat in her tone. Only sorrow. Resignation.

I cinched my eyes closed. Shook my head. What I thought was *They'll come here and shoot everyone, burn everything.* But what I said was, "If I can't give them the Alchemist, Tanner will have my mother killed."

"I won't let that happen," Theo said, eyes fervent. "You've built a tunnel for the Lords' infantry and it's their only way in. Tanner will see it as service enough—"

"*I'll find the Alchemist,*" I blustered. "If I find him, they needn't come, and thousands of innocent people won't need to die."

"Listen to yourself," Theo growled, pulling at his own hair. "These are the same people who would *shoot you* if they knew what you were. You can't do this."

"I can," I said, my voice shaking in unspent rage. "I *will* find him, and I'm not asking for your help, Theo. I'm only asking that you not stand in my way. If you have any lingering affection for me at all, then let me do this. *Please.*"

Perhaps it was cruel to press on that history, to use it against him.

But I was desperate.

Theo stared at me for a long time, tormented, it seemed, by whatever he saw in me. "A week," he said, pinching the bridge of his nose like he couldn't quite believe he was saying it. "We can hold them off for a week, and no longer."

Relief coursed through me. "Thank you," I breathed.

Theo shook his head slowly, watching the tremor in my fingers.

I clasped them tightly behind my back.

"You're very convincing with him," he said suddenly, his gaze disconnecting.

Something wretched cracked open in my chest. "I have to be. I—"

"You'll do what you must," he finished for me with a nod, already backing away. "And so will I." He turned his back, headed for the mouth of the alley and all those earthbound stars in the street.

"Theo?" Polly called to his back.

"One week," Theo said to the cobbles, and in the quiet it found its way back to us.

I waited an extra moment after he'd turned the corner, disappearing into the whorls of mist. Then I turned to Polly, took her hands in mine. "I need to ask you something," I said, and I knew how dangerous it was.

Her dark eyes pricked. She swallowed thickly and waited.

"The . . . *attachment* you have with Otto." Her fingers twitched in mine. "It's real, isn't it?"

She hid her face from me, her tone despondent when she said, "I know that it's pointless."

"It isn't," I said. "I know you don't wish to see him come to any harm. If the Lords' Army find their way into this town, the people here will stand and fight, Polly. They won't run to save themselves. They will all die."

Tears rimmed the crescents of her eyes. She blinked them back. "I know."

"They don't have to, Polly," I said, taking her shoulders in my hands now. "You can make sure they live."

She closed her eyes tightly. "Damn it," she said. "There is very little time. Do you understand that?"

"Yes. Can you hold them off?"

"I'll stall them," she said. "They know about the land mines. They won't be in a hurry to blow themselves up." She took my hand and squeezed it in hers. "But I don't have plans to die, Nina. This must work."

"It will," I vowed, but the words stuck to my insides.

"Then I'll help."

And then she disappeared as quickly as Theo had, skirting the corner and vanishing, leaving me with the fog of my breath and a mountainous dread taking hold.

I shivered all over. The missive in my palm was crinkled beyond repair.

I shredded it to pieces, until my fingers could no longer pluck apart the fibers. I trod over them as I stalked back through the alley, back to Main Street with its passing trolley and the lanterns. I shivered, heaving breath after breath of frosty air and listening to the sounds of the late hour. Drifting laughter and boot treads weaving their way back to their beds. All of Kenton's occupants at rest. No fear hammering their chests. No whistle in the distance. No battalions on the hills. No children in the alleys.

An insulated, condemned peace. Would it be on my shoulders if it shattered?

I pressed the back of my hand to my mouth and swallowed the sobs that erupted from my chest. Soon, Patrick would climb the stairs and knock at the door of number fifteen. If I asked him, he'd offer himself as a reprieve.

And I would offer the same. Forever, if I could. He could have whatever remained of me.

In return, there would be this one betrayal. Unavoidable. Necessary.

Somewhere hovering beneath the cloud line, an osprey squalled its warning. A lick of foreboding followed my footsteps all the way over the threshold of Colson & Sons, up its winding staircases and through the doorway of number fifteen.

I fabricated a new vault in my mind and locked away all that guilt and disgrace. It would have its time.

There came three knocks.

CHAPTER 52

PATRICK

Winter had seized Kenton overnight.

It stuck to the windows at dawn, curled into Patrick's collar as he dressed. Nina shivered in her sleep. Tonight, he'd ensure a fire was lit in the hearth.

It seemed to Patrick that she was uneasy in rest. Her body was curled into a spiral. Her eyelids were in flux. Whatever dreams played out beneath them carved creases in her forehead.

Contrarily, Patrick had rarely slept more peacefully. It reminded him vaguely of a time he'd swigged a vial of bad bluff in his adolescence and felt battered by some invisible gauntlet. It had knocked him unconscious into the next day, sleeping dreamlessly, but the waking was entirely different. He'd felt pommeled, flayed then. Today, he awoke in a mind he hardly recognized.

He leaned over the bed and pressed the pad of his thumb to her furrow, smoothing out the lines. As she came awake, he pressed his mouth to hers, felt her fingers thread into his hair in that way they had a tendency to do. "We've stolen enough hours," he murmured into her neck. "No more slothin', Scurry girl."

They were first to Margarite's Modern Ladies, their breath pulsing out in clouds as they let themselves into the shop.

Scottie and Otto followed quickly after, Otto balancing a cigarette between his lips and newsprint in his hands. He read something that made Scottie laugh. They greeted Patrick and Nina with shiny cheeks and high spirits.

"Far too early for such good moods," Patrick told them, despite the unlikely occurrence that he himself felt fifty pounds lighter than he could ever remember.

Scottie laughed, his great shoulders quivering. "Otto found an Artisan paper lyin' about Dunnitch last night," he said. "Got an interestin' headline."

"Dunnitch?" Nina queried. "You were in Dunnitch last night?"

"We had a trade arranged," Patrick answered, holding his hand out for Otto's paper. "Night is safest."

"A trade for what?" she pressed.

Otto didn't pause for even a beat. "Bit o' this, bit o' that," he said. "Sugar, salt, meat. You get the idea."

"And who handles these trades in Dunnitch?"

"Just some comrades of the Union," Scottie said.

Patrick unfolded the paper and quickly found the headline:

Miners Union Negotiate for Safe Return of Domelius Becker.

Patrick shook his head, a huff of mirth leaving him.

"What is it?" asked Nina.

"Just the House of Lords scramblin'," he said and offered her the newsprint. Beneath the headline was a rendition of Tanner, offering an address at his lord's lectern. Assuring a crowd, no doubt, that all was under control, that peace was imminent. That soon, the errant Crafters would give over their Alchemist, and idium would be restored to the dispensaries.

Otto chuckled heartily, clouds of smoke enveloping him. "Bunch o' old nutters."

"I take it no such negotiations are afoot?" Nina asked, her eyes rapidly tracking the lines of print.

Scottie tipped his head back and crowed.

"When the canals freeze over," Otto said. "Them lords say whatever they want to their news Scribblers. Bunch of fuckin' lies."

Nina seemed pensive. She smiled wanly. "They must be desperate."

Patrick nodded. "The tide's turnin'. They can feel it."

"Almost time to storm the castle," Otto said, rubbing his hands together. "Just need that pathway, miss."

Nina's smile weakened, and Patrick wondered if she judged these men their callousness, the slapdash way they spoke of mounting an attack against the House of Lords. He wouldn't blame her if she did. They had not lived in the castle as she had.

He wondered, in a deluge of sudden worry, what effect this was having on her. Could she live with it all, after it was done, knowing the part she'd played? Could she live with him, knowing he'd asked it of her?

But Nina dusted her hands together, then looked to Patrick. "Time's wasting," she said lightly. "Shall we?"

They waited for Gunner, Briggs, and Theo to arrive. It seemed all three were suffering last night's choices. Gunner and Briggs cursed and swigged black coffee from tin mugs. Theo's eyes were dark-rimmed and slitted. He looked at no one.

"Let's get this over with," Gunner growled, yawning widely, and down they all went.

The tunnel was, finally, clear of water. Whatever Theo had done to curb the seeping had held overnight. The floor was malleable but not sodden. The walls felt dry underhand. Patrick stayed with Nina at the corpus, shoveling loads of waste into mine carts as she carved.

He tried not to distract her while she worked, but it was a trial. Distraction was normally a requirement down here, when the walls and ceiling felt too close, the air sulfuric and clotted. Scottie was humming to himself by the waste chute Nina had created. Gunner and Briggs were speaking in foreign accents for entertainment while they framed the walls. Theodore appeared and disappeared with every cart that Patrick filled and pushed it away on its tracks. With each pass, his face grew more and more tempestuous. Patrick estimated how long it would take for the man to snap.

He could hardly blame Theodore his jealousy. If he had fumbled a woman like Nina Harrow, he'd likely walk about with a stuck jaw, too.

Patrick wondered how deep that bitterness went. Wars had been forged and finished in jealousy. Entire cities lay in the ruins of jilted hearts.

And jealous men made unpredictable allies. Theodore Shop ought to be watched closely.

Nina exhaled heavily at that moment, pressed her muddied fingers to her forehead.

Patrick went to her immediately. "Rest awhile," he urged her. "We've been down here for hours."

"It's all right," she answered, giving him a tight smile.

But he watched her hang her head, roll her neck, and his concern mounted. "I don't want you to push yourself if it's painful."

"It's a good pain," she said. "Like stretching a muscle."

"We've passed thirteen miles," Patrick told her. "I'd say we're somewhere between Dunnitch and Trent. It's far enough for today."

She sighed, yielding. "Will we walk back?"

"Unless you fancy skippin'."

She hit him lightly on the chest.

It took four hours to return. Tomorrow, he would let Nina rest. The journey through the tunnel would need to be made by mining cart as it lengthened.

As they walked, Nina peppered him with questions. She threw them over her shoulder every few minutes, and he answered them—about the Miners Union, the tunnels, the capture of the Alchemist.

"Last question, Scurry girl," Patrick said, placing a hand to her waist when she staggered sideways. "Then show me some mercy. I'm beggin'."

"I'm only curious," she said. "If I'm to be a member of the Miners Union, I should have the facts."

"The Miners Union, eh?" Patrick smirked. "Are you plannin' on joining the fight, then?"

"Whether I choose to fight or not, that shouldn't stop me from being a member."

Patrick smiled at the ease with which she said it, though the thought of Nina amid the fire of explosions made him ill. "I won't deny you, but you won't be going anywhere near the bullets and bayonets, darlin'. Just so we're clear."

She turned abruptly, leaving the others to walk on, already much farther ahead than them. "You underestimate me. I think I'd serve well in a battle."

Patrick rolled his eyes, braced his arms on either wall and looked down at her. "Have you ever fired a pistol?"

"I don't need one," was her answer, and dirt rose around her, began spiraling into a funnel. A diminutive windstorm.

"Show-off," he muttered, and she grinned, then let the dirt fall. "Keep walking," he told her gently, turning her by her shoulders.

"How much farther?"

Hours. "A short while."

She was dragging her feet already, exhaustion setting in. "If my knees give out, you'll be forced to carry me, I hope you realize."

"Ask me your final question," he prompted. Distraction was key. It delayed all kinds of mental voids.

She paused for a beat, then asked, "Why have I never caught wind of Domelius Becker in Kenton Hill?"

Patrick did not answer immediately. It seemed to him that her breath had shortened. "If he were in Kenton, you would've stumbled across him by now, Nina. There ain't many places to hide a man. No dungeons."

"I remember," she said. "How can you be sure he is kept safe, then? If he isn't where you can see him?"

Wariness fluttered to life. "That's two questions."

But Nina only gave an exasperated laugh. "You're not a very good walking companion."

"Choose a different subject matter," he said, "and you can keep prattlin'."

She looked at him over her shoulder. "I don't mean to pry."

"Then trust that what you don't know won't hurt you."

"But holding a man like Domelius Becker must be dangerous," she said now. "Surely he'd be better served as a trade."

A pulse of warning ran through him. "We've discussed this already," he said warily.

"We have," she said, and though her expression was neutral, Patrick couldn't help but detect a note of panic in her voice. Of urgency. "But I can't help but think it a surer course to save the hostages."

Ah. But of course she should be worried for her mother. Patrick sighed. "I promised I'd get her out, didn't I?"

"But if the Alchemist—"

"Enough." His tone was low, firm.

She appeared admonished, facing forward once more. For a while a restless silence stretched. "Is this how it is to be?" she asked, whisper-soft. Her shoulders drooped as though it took enormous effort to say it at all. "Secrets? Things I can't know?"

Patrick sighed. "This is how war works, Nina. We deal in secrets. The people in charge of keepin' 'em become targets." He thought of his father, locked away in a cell and holding his tongue while the Artisans thought of cruel ways to unravel it. "I won't make you a target."

She chuckled bitterly. "I've been a target since I was a girl, Patrick. I'd hardly know the difference."

A lick of violence ran the length of his spine. He imagined Nina in the hands of Lord Tanner. He imagined the things the House would do to acquire Nina, the weapon he could make of her.

And was that so different from what Patrick himself had done?

"Nina," he began, and he placed a hand to her shoulder to turn her, setting the lantern on the tunnel floor. Then he bent down to look into her face, to ensure their eyes were level, and she could see the sincerity with which he spoke. He swiped a finger across the freckles of her right cheek. There were times when he'd found himself staring at them, plotting their constellations. Her hands fisted his shirt at his chest.

Her lips parted invitingly. "Ask me how many there've been before you."

She seemed taken aback. Suspicious. "How many what? Women?"

He nodded, delighting in her shock.

She narrowed her eyes. "How many?"

He moved his lips an inch from hers. "None."

She blinked once, twice. "You're a rotten liar, Patrick Colson."

He caught her waist when she tried to turn away. "I'm not talkin' about women I've taken to *bed*. I'm talkin' about women I've—"

"Kidnapped?" Nina interjected, winding her arms around his neck. "Hog-tied and carried through a tunnel?"

"You got a smart fuckin' mouth." But she pressed that smart mouth to his, and he abruptly lost his train of thought.

"So why haven't these other women stuck around?" Nina continued, watching him carefully. "Was it the smoking? The whiskey? Did you drive them away?"

He dug his fingers into her waist so that she squirmed. "I never wanted any of 'em to stay. Partly because I never cared for anyone enough to try. But mostly I knew what I'd be tyin' 'em to. All those secrets. All those enemies. It isn't a life any woman wants, Nina. You should know that."

She watched him carefully, confusion marring her features. "But . . . you asked me to stay."

Patrick nodded. "I did. And I'm a selfish bastard to do it."

"Then why—"

"Because you've been stuck in my head for thirteen long years," he said. "And now that you're here, I can't bring it upon myself to see you leave." He lifted her then, clear off the floor, and her screeching laughter tinkled down the tunnel as he pressed his forehead to hers. "I'm in love with you, I'm afraid."

When Patrick was a boy, he and his brothers had stolen flares and lit them all at once. The gunpowder combusted into a million bolts of hot light. He saw it all again in Nina Harrow's eyes when he told her he loved her. "There might be things I can't tell you," he said. "There might be secrets. But I'll never lie to you, Nina. And I promise I'll love you as well as I can."

She was quiet and contemplative for a long moment, and then she grew sad. Her lips pressed together. "I . . . I want this to work."

His wretched heart soared. "Then it will. But I'm warnin' you. I won't be an easy man to love."

"Ah," she said, tightening her hold around his neck, her mouth hovering dangerously close to his. "But that's exactly the problem. You're entirely too easy to fall in love with."

If he ever forgot her face, and the way she looked at him just then, he'd loathe himself, so he didn't kiss her right away. Instead, he lingered. "Do you trust me, Nina?"

She nodded. "I do."

"Then there'll be trust between us, too. As well as love."

She exhaled and closed her eyes. "I hope so."

"Good enough," he said, and he kissed her as reverently as any man had ever kissed a woman, completely oblivious to the dark. Oblivious to Theodore, who waited twenty paces down the path, blending with the shadows, churning with rage.

CHAPTER 53

NINA

I had designs to return to bed when we finally stumbled back into Kenton Hill. The lanterns were beginning to blink to life overhead. Snowflakes fell lightly around us.

"We'll be attendin' First Frost, then?" Scottie asked.

My curiosity piqued. "What's First Frost?"

Gunner grinned. He threw a heavy arm around my shoulder, then Patrick's. "It's a party, darlin'. For the first day of winter!"

"It isn't winter for another several weeks."

"Aye, by the calendar perhaps, but then there's Idia's winter."

"Idia's winter?"

"When she first lets the frost stick to the ground," Patrick intoned. They were nearing Colson's, and even from a distance it seemed desolate.

I frowned. "Where is everyone?"

"At the market," came Theo's voice. He continued on to that darkened, lopsided building and all its mismatched shingles without a glance back.

Every muscle ached. My legs longed for reprieve and my stomach longed for sustenance.

I felt Patrick's eyes on me. "I'll take you home," he said. "Come on."

"Don't even think of it, brother," Gunner said, his face darkening. "You're not shirkin'. Not tonight."

Patrick stole Gunner's cap and slung it into a nearby coal bin. "I'm not in the mood to babysit a bunch of drunks tonight."

I watched conflicting emotions skitter across Patrick's face. His eyes slid to mine and held.

"That's beside the point. It's Dad's tradition, Pat," Gunner said to him then, having fished his cap out of the soot. "He'd never forgive you for missin' it. If I've gotta drag you—"

Patrick ignored him. "Nina, I can bring you home first, if you'd like? You're tired—"

"With no Sam to guard her door?" Gunner scoffed. "Everyone has the night off, Pat. No exceptions. Sorry, darlin'," Gunner said to me now. He did not appear the least bit sorry. "But you'll be comin' along as well."

I gave him a withering glare. "I don't need a minder."

"Ah, but you do," Gunner replied. Colson's was mere feet away, and my room beckoned me. "Can't be too careful, Nina. Not everyone is a friend."

I scoffed in exasperation. "You let Theo go up to his bed, didn't you?"

"And he knows better than to stay there," Gunner laughed. Briggs and Scottie joined him. "He's been dragged out of his room enough times. He'll be along. That boy can't stand dirt under his fingernails. No doubt he's washin' up and combin' his hair as we speak."

Scottie snickered. Briggs hid his grin. I narrowed my eyes at the trio.

"Enough," Patrick said on a heavy sigh. "Get going, boys. We'll be along."

Gunner pointed a dangerous finger an inch from Patrick's face. "No shirkin'."

"No shirkin'," Patrick rolled his eyes, then shoved Gunner's shoulder in the direction of lower Main Street. "Now, fuck off."

They receded into the dim, hands in pockets, shoulders bouncing off one another, thick laughter floating back to me and Patrick.

Patrick exhaled heavily. One hand crept to his pocket, blindly searching for cigarettes, but he came up empty. I tried to think of the last time

I'd seen him smoke and couldn't. "You're not gonna like what I'm about to say, Nina," he said, eyes marking the figures on the streets in their heavy coats. "But do you fancy comin' to a party with me?"

I thought of that soft bed above me, but if there was whiskey at this party, it might be good for loosening tongues, and Patrick surely wasn't the only keeper of secrets in this town. "Lead the way," I said, nodding down the street, my smile tight. "I should warn you, though. If there isn't anything there for me to eat I'll take a bite straight out of you."

He clicked his tongue. "Ah, don't make me promises like that if you can't keep 'em."

He wrapped an arm around my back to shield me from the cold. "What about Theo?" I asked, looking up at the lone orange light in a window high above.

"We'll see him at the market," Patrick said, and I wondered if I imagined the dark turn of his voice. "Of that, I have no doubt."

· · · · · ·

The market thrummed from a distance, light flooding from its mouth. Weak flurries chased children in squalls. There was a pig on a spit, roasting over hot coals, music drubbing the air. Patrick and I made our slow way toward it all, dirt-stained from head to toe. It garnered not a single second glance from any passersby.

I almost laughed to think of the difference time rendered. From the National Artisan House to a Kenton Hill barn. From ballgowns to chipboard floors. The comparison brought with it no ill feeling. I was warm and worn in a pleasing way. I was wrapped in the arms of a man who loved me. The speed of my blood made me suspect I loved him back. And if it weren't for that hourglass expending inside me, I thought I might be happy.

I took a moment to stare at the underside of his jaw, the blanket of stubble razing his cheeks, the fine slope of his nose, and the peak of his chin. "Look somewhere else, Nina. I'm only so strong."

I blushed.

Patrick collected plates of food at the door. Bread and corn and fatty pork, its juices swimming round the rim.

"Tell me, why is First Frost so important?"

Patrick grinned. "Mostly tradition. Winter used to be something these people feared. Back when the coal and wood were sent on trains to the city, whatever remained was exorbitantly priced. My father started this celebration the year Kenton took its first strike, and he promised we'd never have another dead winter. So far, the promise has held."

A dead winter. It had been a while since I'd heard the phrase. People in Scurry used to murmur it under their breath in the streets as the nights grew colder. The teachers would have us pray at our desks for a winter that was mild. A dead winter meant chilblains and watered-down soups and a cold in your chest like a long-fingered hand, snatching you away in the night. Not everyone woke the next morning.

No one had spoken of dead winters in Belavere City. I wondered if they knew what the term meant.

We were received warmly. A woman hugged me in thanks for saving her son. A swoop of little girls pulled on my dirty hands until I joined them in a skipping circle. They held me hostage for two songs before Gunner came to shoo them away. "Leave her be, you little blighters," he growled, and they scurried away laughing and shrieking.

He led me over to an old card table where the Colson inner circle held court. And by court, I mean Scottie pulled Donny off the center of the table before he could break it, Briggs argued loudly with a busty woman about an outstanding bet, and Sam tried valiantly to beat Otto in an arm wrestle while Polly laughed.

When Polly saw me approaching, she intercepted me from Patrick and Gunner both. "Let us ladies get a drink," she told them, then intertwined her arm with mine, leading me to the whiskey barrels along the far wall.

"Did you learn anything new today?" Polly asked beneath her breath. She retrieved a clean glass, filling it at the tap of a barrel.

The question brought reality walloping back. "Only that Becker isn't in Kenton Hill," I said, dropping my voice to less than a murmur as I moved in to get my own drink.

"Then where?" Polly replied. There was a desperate quality to her voice, though her expression was trained. "You need to ask him outright, Nina."

I closed my eyes briefly. "I'm trying." But it seemed any angle I tried, I failed, and my panic renewed.

Polly sighed. "Otto and Scottie brought crates in this morning from Dunnitch. Usually, the shipments are brought straight here to the market and some are left in the tunnels for safe keeping, but not these. These went right to the back of Colson's."

I frowned at her. "You think it's idium?"

"I don't know, but Dunnitch has the closest terranium mines. It would make sense to have the Alchemist there."

"And you're sure they brought them crated to Colson's?"

"I watched it from my window," she said, a hint of shame wheedling through. "Otto came to my room straight after. He told me where he'd traveled from."

I exhaled deeply. "I'll check the kitchens when it's safe."

Polly's hand gripped the underside of my arm then, squeezing it urgently. "Please, Nina. Don't wait. Every day makes the risk greater."

I shriveled. "I'm trying, Polly."

"That's not enough. There's too much at stake." Her eyes flickered back the way they'd come, to where I was sure Otto sat, waiting for her. "Please, try harder."

Polly returned to the card table without me, weaving through the crowd, leaving me to trail behind. By the time she reached Otto, she was smiling brightly again.

I tried to do the same.

Patrick was talking quietly with his mother as I returned. He kissed her on the cheek and she left, smiling tiredly at me before doing so.

"Is your mother all right?" I asked him, arriving at his side.

He put his drink on the table and nodded. "Just tired," he said. "Sit with me."

I went to draw out a seat at his side, but his hand closed around my wrist, and he pulled me gently into his lap, enveloped me. "That's not what I meant," he said into my ear.

I felt heat climbing my neck. "I'm a mess," I reminded him. "And I must smell awful."

"Like I give a shit," he murmured, one hand subtly caressing the curve of my arse, and I felt desire flare inside me.

"Teddy!" Gunner called suddenly, and I startled at the sight of Theo standing at the end of the table. He was newly dressed, his hair, indeed, neatly combed. He wore the expression of a man chewing on something sour.

His eyes swept over me in Patrick's lap, then Polly, who was sheltered under Otto's arm. He nodded, as though to himself, and rolled his jaw.

"You look sharp, Teddy boy!" Gunner drawled, hitting him heartily on the back. "Have a drink."

But it appeared Theo had already done so. He held up a glass with only dregs at its bottom. "I took the liberty," he explained, and downed the final swill.

Gunner eyed the cords in Theodore's neck in a hungry way. "You know what you need, Teddy? A woman. Or a man, if you're so inclined. Work out some o' that hum in your drum."

"Gunner," I reproached, tensing.

But Patrick squeezed my leg. "Let it be," he said very softly.

And was it my imagination, or did Patrick nod ever-so-slightly in Gunner's direction?

"What say you, Teddy? We can rent you a warm body for the night. My treat."

The other men laughed. Polly went rigid. Surreptitiously, Patrick maneuvered me onto the chair by his side.

"Whores and bluff," Theo nodded, staring into the depths of his glass. "Your favorite remedies, Gunner, are they not?"

The table quieted, surprised. I gathered it was unlike Theo to respond at all.

"Tell me, do you take the whore first, or the bluff? Can't imagine you can even keep yourself upright if you take the bluff first, let alone anything else."

Scottie, Briggs, and Donny hooted, but Gunner's cheeks had lost their pallor. His eyes flitted to Patrick and away.

"I heard your wife just walked out on you," Theodore continued. I wondered if the liquor had made him stupid. "My condolences. Was it the whores? Or did the bluff make you limp?"

Theodore had turned to face Gunner head on, as though welcoming that first punch. An invitation to swing back. He waited; the table held its collective breath. Patrick rose from his seat.

But Gunner only smiled. It was small at first, but then widened. Soon he was laughing heartily, his head thrown back. The others joined tenuously, and Gunner caught Theodore in a headlock, mussing his neatly combed hair. "We're all whores, Teddy," he barked, his good humor sending another wave of hysteria ricocheting down the table. "That should be your first lesson. Take my advice, don't ever let marriage enter your mind."

Gunner shunted Theo into a seat and passed him another drink, though his fingers wedged deeply into Theo's shoulder, and he sent a deliberate look down to Patrick, gauging his response.

I thought I saw Patrick shake his head.

It was a while longer before I realized I'd been holding my breath.

For a time, the night drew on with a forced sort of peace. The men continued their banter and drank a shocking amount of ale, but none so much as Theo, who refilled his pint twice as often. He offered nothing in the conversation but stared openly at me or Polly or Patrick. And though the group must have appeared chummy to anyone on the outside, it seemed to me a silent war was being waged.

Gunner made increasingly hostile jokes and slapped Theo on the back with more vigor than was necessary. Patrick waited with interminable patience, but not without tension, and Polly and I were silent, like children about to be punished. We traded glances. We were sitting on a ticking time bomb.

Pints kept arriving at the table. Every now and then, I drank one to dull the hostility in the air. I had now shifted myself out of Patrick's reach completely. It seemed Theodore marked my every move.

Donny was the only salve. He nattered incessantly with one anecdote or another, the stories growing more grandiose with the liquor. ". . . and then, to that man I said, 'I'll challenge you to a game of darts. If you win, I'll pay your tab. But if *I* win, I get to take your mother upstairs with me.' Now, I ain't ever seen his mother of course—"

"Lucky for him, you ain't ever seen a fuckin' bullseye, either," Otto yawned.

"I can throw darts as good as any," Donny slurred. "Just point me at the board."

Otto shook his head. "No way. I ain't makin' any bets with you tonight."

"Ah, come on. What about Gunner then?"

Gunner chuckled darkly. "Not a chance."

Donny pouted. "Teddy will throw darts with me, won't you, Teddy?"

Theodore's eyes were riddled red, his head wobbled on his neck as he turned to the call of his name. "What are we playing for?"

"How about this," Donny said, growing more animated. "If I win, you go wipe that fuckin' scowl off your face, save the rest of us from it. I can't even see, and I know it's there."

Otto and Gunner chortled into their drinks.

"All right," Theo said. "And if I win, I'll take your mother up to my room with me. How about it, Donny?"

A taut silence abruptly descended, and I thought the pint in Gunner's hand might splinter. His knuckles had turned white along the handle. The other men traded dark glances, their eyes swiveling back and forth between the Colson brothers. Patrick's stare, however, had solidified.

Donny, by contrast, was overjoyed. He bounced with excitement. "Ah, he's got spirit, Pat! See, I told you he didn't have a stick up his arse."

Theo's jaw ticked.

"Come on, then," Donny cajoled, standing in place. "Someone turn me round the right way."

Moments later, Donny was facing a corkboard tacked to the barn wall, his fist full of darts. The patrons had made a path, and those closest seemed strangely unconcerned, despite the drunken blind man holding sharp missiles he intended to throw.

The first three, shockingly, landed on the board, albeit with mediocre scores. "Let's have it then, Teddy," Donny said, and Theodore stepped forward.

His gait was very obviously unsteady. I'd lost count of the drinks he'd consumed. He didn't look at Donny as he readied himself before the dartboard. He stared at me, who stood against a beam to better see, and at Patrick, who hadn't bothered to stand at all. "I look forward to knowing Mrs. Colson a lot better," he said, and the whole barn held its collective breath, awaiting a rebuttal.

I stepped in. "Theo, stop it."

But he held up a silencing finger in my direction. "Just a friendly match between men, Nina."

Patrick said nothing. He picked up his drink, gestured for Theo to get on with it. "Throw your darts, Teddy."

Theodore's eyes flashed. He threw with violence. Two darts hit a twenty. One missed the board.

"How'd he do?" Donny questioned. "Someone tell me the score."

"Forty to twenty-one," a gruff voice called. "The swank leads."

The game continued, Theo throwing with middling results but Donny throwing worse. Twice he missed the board completely and once struck the wall an inch from someone's head.

"Sorry, sorry!" Donny hollered at the shriek of yet another woman. "Teddy! Do your worst."

Theodore took the darts from the board, but instead of taking his shot, he sauntered over to where I watched, the lip of his shoes dragging. "Blow on these for me, would you, Nina?" he asked, the words laced in poison. "For luck."

Well-versed as women often were with men and liquor, I knew better than to prod. Some of them turned into bulls, scoping for red. It was best not to move too quickly, not to say too much. Theo was fraying quickly. I pressed my lips firmly together, begged him silently to stop.

"Go on," he said, more forcefully now. "Blow."

And I felt Patrick stand from his seat, the chair scratching a path in the dust.

Quickly, I blew on the darts in Theodore's palm, a simple action made somehow degrading. And Theodore gave Patrick a satisfied smile. He held his stare. *See*, he seemed to say. *It hurts to watch, doesn't it?* He threw the darts in quick succession. Triple elevens and a bullseye. The onlookers clapped and caterwauled.

"She's quite the lucky charm, don't you think?" Theo said now, turning back to Patrick. He picked up another pint from the nearest table. "Willing, too. Always has been," he winked at me, but his sights quickly returned to Patrick, who remained standing, his hands in his pockets, face indecipherable.

Except for his eyes, which had turned glacial.

"Has she blown on anything of yours yet, Colson?" Theo continued, ignoring the blood in the air. "You need only ask her to."

A cold, sick hurt filled me. A thousand gentle touches and soft words from years past, now broken.

A hush followed Theo's rambling, broken only by the sound of Gunner's pistol falling heavily onto a tabletop. He regarded Theodore hungrily. "Just say the word, Pat."

But Patrick's head was tilted to me. His eyes trickled down to my hands—fisted and aching. "Take your turn, brother," he said evenly to Donny. He didn't spare Theo a glance. "One hundred and eighty to win it."

Theo grinned his drunken grin, but beneath it was a landscape of boiling anger. He barely paid attention to Donny's smirk, the way the man stumbled toward the dartboard, the lazy lift of his arm.

One, two, three, the darts flew, landing precisely where they needed to. Perfect triple twenties splitting the cork. A miraculous win.

The spectators cheered, slapping Donny's back. Patrick collected a pint. He stalked casually toward Theo, who backed away several steps, mouth agape. Patrick pushed the glass into Theo's chest. I did not miss the vigor with which it was done, or the way half the liquor slopped over Theo's clean shirt. "Have another," he told Theo. "It'll take the sting out of it."

"Fuck you," Theodore spat, so filled with unspent rage I feared he might implode. His fists shook. He breathed heavily through his teeth.

"Yeah," Patrick said slowly. "It'd feel good, wouldn't it? To take a swing? Don't ever seem to find the courage, though, do you, Teddy?"

Patrick set the glass on the table and leaned down to speak into Theo's ear. "I'll tell you what," he said. "I'll give you a free shot, right here in front of her. Show her you're a big man. Get it out of your system. But I don't promise to be in control of what happens after that."

The moment hung there, free for the taking, but it seemed Theo had finally had enough. With one last furious glare, he left with his tongue tucked into one cheek, with red ears and smoke fuming from his nostrils. He pushed through the crowd. I could just barely make out his dark hair quickly receding into the night.

And I followed.

I had to run to catch him. He kept up a frenetic pace down the lane. "Theo!" I called. And if he heard me he didn't show it. He passed the tea shop and turned a corner. "Theo, *wait*."

I caught his shoulder, and he turned so abruptly that I flinched.

"*What?*" he asked, swaying where he stood. "What do you want from me, Clarke?"

"*Harrow*," I said in frustration, breath collecting in short, sharp gusts.

"Ah, yes, the girl from Scurry." His eyes dragged over my sullied clothes and smudged face. He shook his head and said. "I barely recognize you."

"And I, you."

We stared at each other for a long time, both of us trying to piece back together a version of the other that had only existed before the world made us mean and full of fault.

"*You* left *me*," I told him, my voice heavy with old pain. "*You* broke us. And you may have come to regret it, but I do not owe you sympathy for whatever pain you feel now." I did not cry for him. I had purged him from my heart years ago. "If you want to hurt me, then—"

"Do you love him?" Theo asked, his voice quaked. "I heard you, in the tunnel. Have you honestly fallen in love with him?"

"I—I have a job to do," I said. "That's all."

But whatever Theo saw on my face told him otherwise. He nodded, laughed dryly, trembled. "He'll kill you, Nina," he told me. "And when the barrel of his pistol is pressed between your eyes, you'll wish you'd listened to me. You'll wish you'd never discarded what we had."

I remembered those last weeks in the Artisan school, clutching desperately to his fading promises while he did his best to ignore me. "We were only children, Theo. I hardly remember what we had." Blood pulsed in my ears. "But I bet you'll spend the rest of your life trying to forget."

I watched Theo's eyes bulge, watched a delicate puce climb his neck and mottle his face. I watched him kick a dustbin as he passed it and stalk away into the dark. I watched him until he became dim and distant.

I exhaled in a gust. Clutched my sides.

"Don't think any man could ever recover from that," said a voice, and I turned to find Patrick in his coat. He leaned against brick render, his arms crossed at the chest. "Might as well've run him through with a blade." It was said casually, but his eyes were assessing. I could feel them peeling back my layers.

My stomach fluttered. "You were listening?"

"Only to the finale," he said slowly. "I promise." He came toward me slowly, hiding his hands in his pockets. "You all right, Scurry girl?"

I nodded, somewhat weakly, and closed my eyes. "Will you take me back to Colson's?" Tears choked the column of my throat.

"Whatever you want, darlin'," he said. He lifted my hand and kissed my knuckles. "Always."

CHAPTER 54

NINA

I disentangled myself from Patrick's arms long before dawn.

The day had seemed endless and mottled, and though I'd spent much of it in Patrick's embrace, I could not ignore the sensation that I was shackled to a train track, a steam engine thundering closer and closer.

Find the Alchemist, I told myself. *Find him, and it will all be over.*

So, I did not sleep. While Colson & Sons curled in on itself, I rose in the frigid night.

I slipped through the unguarded door and descended the stairs. I made it to each landing with barely a creak.

The pub was dark and devoid. It was simple enough to tiptoe around its bar to the other side, to slip behind the counter and wrap my hand around the doorknob.

It would not turn. I tried uselessly once more before ceding. There must be a key somewhere. In Patrick's pocket, perhaps?

At that moment, the doorknob rattled of its own accord. It pulled inward. Light flooded my feet from within.

I shrunk sideways before it could open completely, sinking to the floor beneath the countertop, just in time for Tess Colson to appear.

She came into her bar slowly, rubbing her eyes. Already there was an apron around her waist. She coughed soundly into her fist, then wiped her mouth with a handkerchief. For a moment, she simply stood and caught her breath, her eyes closed. Then, she collected a tray of crockery on the counter before her and turned on her heel, carrying it back the way she'd come. I listened for a snick of a lock, but none followed.

When my heart had dislodged from my throat, I crawled out of my hiding place. I tentatively pressed my ear to the door and listened.

But there were no sounds on the other side of the door. No clashing of dishes. No belching boilers or shoes on the tiles. It seemed there was no presence at all. Either Tess had walked into the kitchen and ceased all movement, or she'd left via a back door. I decided to bet on the latter.

I pushed the door in on a fully lit kitchen. There was indeed a boiler, a stove, an industrial clay oven, but none were lit. The room was large and lined with counters. An ice chest dominated half of one wall, and along the other were wooden shelves, lined to the ceiling in corked amber bottles, sealed vials, jars, and, in some cases, unmarked cans.

Only it wasn't just one wall, but all of them.

And it wasn't just the walls, but the floor. Crate upon crate labeled DUNNITCH POULTRY, stacked in careful piles, blocking half the countertops.

And the substance within each container was ink-colored. It glinted threateningly from every corner.

Idium.

A stack of sealed crates waited by the back door, iron-branded on the exterior.

The door beside it suddenly opened again, and in came Tess. This time she was not laden in dishes, but with a cast-iron pot half her size. She froze at the sight of me.

"Nina," she said, stunned. Then slower: "What in God's name are you doin' down here?"

I tried to school my expression into one of polite surprise. I was still dressed in a nightgown. My feet were bare. I hope I looked as lost as I suddenly felt.

"I'm sorry," I said. "I couldn't sleep. I hoped I could find some tea? I didn't want to trouble anyone." I twisted my hands together in a show of contrition.

She sighed. Slowly, she set the pot on a countertop, then wiped her hands in her apron. "Left the goddamn door unlocked for one minute," she muttered, turning her eyes to the heavens.

"I apologize," I said. "I hadn't realized the kitchen was off-limits."

"And my dumbstruck son didn't think to mention it?"

I hesitated. I thought of the times Patrick had steered me away. "Not expressly."

"Hmm," she sighed, rubbing her forehead. "Well. No one comes in here but the spare few. I'm sure you've figured out why."

I looked again to all those mismatched bottles and canisters. Awed. A ready-made dispensary. "Is it idium?"

Tess Colson chuckled. "Wouldn't that be the day? Perhaps then my sons would be satisfied." She shook her head. "It's only bluff. The unsullied kind."

On closer inspection, it seemed she was right. "There's so much," I said redundantly.

"The brink needs medicine in droves," she explained. "We export it to the other towns."

"In exchange for food?" I deduced.

"Among other things. It's important you keep this to yourself, Nina. I suppose it'll be a test, if you like. No one should know where the stores are kept. Such information isn't safe."

"No," came a different voice. I whirled to see Patrick standing in the doorway, his expression drawn and colorless. His shirt was partially unbuttoned, untucked. "It surely ain't." He pulled the door closed behind him.

"You should've told her not to come in here, son," Tess reprimanded.

Patrick only looked at her briefly. "Excuse us a moment, Ma."

Tess gave him a look of warning, muttered under her breath, then left.

Patrick's eyes flickered back to me, and his were guarded but not angry. "How did you get in?"

"Your mother left the door unlocked," I answered. I was surprised to find my voice was a whisper. All my bravado had fled. "I was looking for tea."

He held my stare, and I was careful not to drop mine, though I wanted to.

He put his hands in his pockets, still wearing an indecipherable expression. "You might as well ask me your questions, Nina," he said. "I can see 'em burning up inside you."

I let my eyes skate over those shelves. "There's so much of it."

"That isn't a question."

I swallowed. "Why is it here?"

"Because I don't trust anyone else to look after it."

My teeth worried at my lip, my eyes looked over the crates stacked by the door, the ones Scottie and Otto had brought from Dunnitch.

And I almost came out and asked him. Almost.

Patrick rubbed his eyes tiredly, and without any preamble, he said, "Do you know why it is I don't sleep well?"

I shook my head.

"It started when I was twelve, after I got back from our siphonin' ceremony. First day I went underground, I came back up and didn't sleep a wink. Kept thinking about those tunnel walls and all the sounds they made. Felt like I couldn't breathe."

I took a step closer to him without meaning to.

"When I got older, it wasn't just the tunnels in my head, it was the other things, too. Fires, explosions, whistles. It all comes floodin' into my bed at night. I've learned to live with that. Learned to walk and work and sleep in all that noise.

"But recently," he said, his eyes resting on mine, "sleep has become easy. Quiet. All that noise in my head . . . I barely hear it."

I waited, breath catching.

"That's because of *you*. Do you understand?"

I nodded. Swallowed.

"But I woke up just now, and you weren't there, Nina. And I convinced myself that someone had taken you. Even as I was runnin' down those stairs, I imagined you were tied up in some hole, and a man held a blade to your throat and threatened to hurt you if you didn't name every one of my secrets. And *that* . . . that is a thought to keep me awake all night long." His stare was molten; I felt it heat up my skin. "Don't imagine that it's trust stopping me from tellin' you everything, Nina. There are certain men who would do terrible things to the people I love just to learn more about me. Don't ask me for answers I can't give, please. Let me have my sleep."

He seemed, suddenly, bone tired.

I looked my last to the walls of bluff, ceiling to floor. *That's enough for now*, I thought, and that train in my chest slowed. I told myself the collision was still some ways off. So I went to him and placed my hands on his chest. "Come on," I said. "There's still some night left."

CHAPTER 55

NINA

Patrick was gone before I woke again. There was a note on the night-stand that proclaimed I'd earned a day's rest.

Stay in bed, it said. *I'll return before sundown.*

A tempting offer, but despite the soreness of my muscles and the reluctance of my eyelids, I needed to find Polly and Theo.

Polly answered on the first knock and hurried me inside her room. Identical, for the most part, to mine, only with wallpaper of holly and thistle.

There was a frenzied look about her. I suspected she, too, had managed little sleep in the night.

"What did you find?" she asked in a hushed whisper. Her nails bit into my hands.

"We should fetch Theo first," I said, looking back at the door.

"He's already out. I knocked on his door not a minute ago, and he didn't answer. Tell me, what did you find?"

"Bluff," I said quietly. My eyes flickered to the walls as though they were made of paper, and could fall to expose us at any moment. "Stores of it. They must be bringing it in from Dunnitch."

Polly exhaled in a gust, released my hands. She glowed with relief. "Thank God," she breathed, wiping sweat from her forehead. "I just received this." From her pocket she pulled a freshly folded sheet of parchment and handed it to me. On it, a neat line of ink said *Attack imminent. Provide safest route urgently, as ordered by the House.*

"They're growing impatient," Polly breathed. "Nina, I must reply. If I don't, they'll assume I'm dead, or a traitor. That's the deal. I *always* reply."

"Tell them we have a lead on Domelius Becker," I said, hands shaking, the ink smudged beneath my fingers. "They'll wait."

Polly shook her head. "It would buy us a day or two. And it isn't true, is it? How do you plan to find him?"

I wrung my hands together. "What Scribbler crannies do you write to in Dunnitch?" I asked. "Is there anyone there that Patrick corresponds with regularly? *Think.*"

Polly screwed her eyes shut; she pushed her fists against them. "There are several," she groaned. "You cannot possibly search each address there."

"What *else* do you propose?" I asked, my own voice swelling.

Polly's lip quivered. "I—I can forge a scribble," though she seemed ill at the thought of even suggesting it. "I'll send a message to Patrick saying there's been some sort of trouble with the Alchemist, and that he should come. Then we can watch him."

I shook my head. "I can't just follow him. He'd notice."

"I don't see what other choice you have," she said. "I admit, it might not work."

"And if he leaves Kenton Hill without telling me? Or sends someone else?"

Polly sighed. "He'll ask me to send a scribble ahead of time, naming the time of the arrival and who should be arriving. I won't know who I'm sending it to, obviously, but if he intends to dispatch someone else, I'll know."

"And if he doesn't?"

"Then you and I are out of luck," Polly said quietly. "Along with the rest of the parish."

We stood there staring at each other, then at the sheet of parchment in her hand. "This is our last chance, Nina."

Panic swarmed in my chest. "Polly, it'll be all right."

She shook her head. "There are a million ways for this to go wrong," she mumbled, fear splitting the words. "This is suicidal."

I caught her hand to cease her pacing. "The House wants idium, Polly, that's all. We need only tell them where Becker is, and we'll have saved the entire town."

"And what, exactly, do we intend to do if the Colsons figure us out?" Tears rolled down Polly's cheeks, spilled over her lip. "Even if we run, we'll be hunted."

I wrapped my arms around her shoulders and felt her hang on to me. For a moment we stood there again, just like we had before the war began. "There's a way out of this," I said for the both of us. We who had found ourselves the playthings in a man's war game. "I promise you."

"And if there's not?"

And herein lay the truest test. "Then you'll need to choose your next course." I told her. "But I think I've had enough running for one lifetime."

She nodded, then went to a small rickety desk. She took a piece of parchment and shoved it into the pocket of my skirt. "Keep this hidden," she said. "And listen for my scribble."

"When will you write to Patrick?"

Polly grimaced. "He has a Scribbler's cranny in his mother's kitchen, but he won't check it until day's end. I'll wait until then."

I nodded.

"What of Theo?" Polly asked then, hands wringing. "I expect he'll burst through my door any moment, and demand that I give Tanner the route here."

I turned to the door in question. "I'll deal with Theo."

· · · · · ·

In the pub, Briggs and Scottie were swallowing coffee at an alarming rate, and Theo was nowhere to be seen. Their miner's overalls told me where they were headed.

"Is Theo visiting Margarite with us today?" I asked them.

"I bloody well hope so," Briggs asked, donning his cap. "We'll break under the Gyser River soon, and I don't much feel like drownin' in a hole."

"He isn't in his room." I frowned. "I thought I might find him here."

Scottie scowled. "Well, he must be waitin' with Margarite, then."

But Theodore wasn't waiting for them in the square, or inside the shop, or down the shaft.

"If Gunner finds that kid shirkin', he'll wring the poor bastard's neck," Briggs grunted when the lift doors clanged open.

"Perhaps he didn't hear you knockin' at his door, Nina," Scottie mused. "Must have one hell of a sore head this mornin'."

"That makes us a pair," Briggs grumbled.

I scowled down at the gaping darkness of the tunnel. I pictured Theo as he had been the night before, stumbling away into the night.

"Ain't much point in havin' you down here today, Nina," Scottie said. "We can't go no farther without hitting the edge of the Gyser. And we can't burrow beneath without Teddy to control the water."

"Go rest like Patty asked you to," Briggs suggested, loading the mining cart with timber logs. "And if you see Theo, give him a clip round the head."

I hurried alone back to Colson's, the route now memorized, slow-moving dread bubbling in my chest. I intended to knock on the door of number thirteen again, perhaps kick it in. But his expression from the previous night loomed in my mind, and I became sure I wouldn't find him there. I was suddenly horribly certain that I wouldn't find him anywhere.

Only feet from the stoop of Colson & Sons, I halted on the cobblestones. In the dim of the nearest alley, a shadow moved. A man stubbed a cigarette out under his boot, then shifted ever so slightly into the daylight.

"Theo?" I threw a panicked glance over my shoulder, but Kenton thrummed on as normal. The trolley rattled past, and amid the clamor, I hurried into the recess between buildings where he stood.

"Where have you been?" I hissed.

He looked wretched. His face had somehow elongated in the night. He was unshaven, drawn, eyes bloodshot.

"Are you all right?"

He scoffed weakly. "Just grand."

I glanced over my shoulder once more. We'd be easily seen here, without the cover of night. "Someone might see us."

"Then I won't keep you. Except to tell you goodbye."

The dread bubbled to its peak. "Theo—"

"In truth, I should have left last night," he continued. "But I've been delaying myself. I suppose I wanted to see you one last time."

A lingering tendril of guilt swirled in my stomach.

"I can't stand another day here, Nina." He closed his eyes briefly. "And they're coming for this place."

"Theo, I'm sorry," I blithered, snatching his sleeve when he tried to turn. "I'm sorry that I couldn't choose—"

"Don't," he interjected, his voice a gavel. And I saw that bright burning pain beneath the surface. "I do want to tell you that I'm sorry for what I did last night. The way I spoke about you."

I tried to take his hand, but he pulled it free. "Theo, you can't leave now. We've found the Alchemist. He's in *Dunnitch*."

He froze, and I thought I saw a spark, the cogs behind his eyes turning again. "Are you certain?"

"Yes." A lie, but one that would buy me time. "Polly and I will have his precise whereabouts within a matter of hours."

"And then what?" Theo asked. "You'll confront Tanner? Barter the Alchemist for your mother?"

"*Yes*," I said abruptly. "He'll make the trade, Patrick. There is nothing he cares about more than idium."

Theo nodded skeptically. "You might be right."

"I am."

"And then he'll send his soldiers into Dunnitch, and once they find Domelius Becker, the fire Charmers will leave it burning." Theo watched my expression carefully, saw the places where color bled away. "But that's better, isn't it?" he asked. "Something you're more comfortable with, I suppose. Better Dunnitch than Kenton Hill."

Bile slipped up my throat. He was right.

I'd been counting on the hope that another answer existed. Now, it seemed there was none that didn't end in bloodshed.

"You're slipping, Nina," Theo shook his head. "You should have seen this coming."

"These people don't deserve to die, Theo," I said weakly. "Tanner should be stopped."

"Why shouldn't it be the Miners Union instead?" Theo countered. "Or have you washed Patrick's hands clean of all that blood?"

"And how many have died in the mines?" I said, my temper sparking. "Did you ever know anyone who lost one of their limbs in a factory, Theo? Or ended up starving on the street? You never saw that toll before the strikes began." My voice was getting louder, the fire in my chest swarming. "You were in the city, always safe and fed. And I joined you up there in that ivory tower, in that *fucking* school."

But Theo seemed to brush me off. "So, Patrick truly managed it, then," he muttered. "And in record time."

"Managed *what*?" I hissed.

"To make a rebellion out of you" came the answer. "I wonder if it would've been different, if *we* could have been different, if I'd taken better care of you."

"We'd have ended just the same," I said. Because he was his father's son, and I was forged in the brink long before he knew me.

He did not answer. Instead, he put his hands in his pockets and looked out into Main Street. "Would you do me one last favor? And before you say no, just remember I've spent the last two years in this place, all for the promise of seeing you again."

I bit my tongue. "What's the favor?"

"Encourage the Colsons not to come looking for me," he said. "You're quite impressive when it comes to persuading them."

"How will you get out? It's dangerous, Theo."

"There's a tunnel that runs northeast," he said. "It's short, and the Colsons rarely travel it. It will get me far enough that I can find a boat."

"You . . . you won't—?"

"Alert the House that you've abandoned your duty?" he asked. "No, Nina. I won't get your mother killed. I'm not a monster."

Tears collected in the corners of my eyes as I nodded. "The tide of this war is turning," I warned. "Tanner can't hold the House for much longer."

"All the more reason for me to make myself scarce," Theo said dryly. "Can you guess who will take Tanner's place if he dies?"

Ice tripped down my spine, and he nodded his confirmation. "Lord Shop," he uttered with a cold, dead acceptance. "So I'd best return."

"Theo—"

"You think you know what you're doing," he said, already retreating down the alley. "But there will come a time, Nina, when you find yourself backed into a corner." He looked over his shoulder at me one last time. "And I'll be the only person left to free you."

CHAPTER 56

PATRICK

It took an entire day for Patrick to resolve that which had been left to wait.

Repairs to the eastern mine had begun, though he would need to consult Theo regarding the integrity of the soil and the water table beneath.

It was the water Charmer he sought now as night lengthened over Kenton. The first flurries of snow fell and evaporated before they touched the ground. Smoke curled from the coal bins and rooftops. The lanes were vacant at this hour, everyone retiring earlier to evade the cold.

Patrick whistled while he walked. He found he didn't so much mind the bite in the air. Kenton, at that moment, seemed a slow humming beauty. As a child he'd thought the same, even when it had been more mud and shit than cobbles.

He imagined Theodore would be in his room, licking his wounds. He wondered if the boy had rid himself of all those angry bees in his head, or if he remained as pent up as he'd been the day before. Patrick hoped the knock to his ego had set him straight.

The pub would have quieted by now, only the loneliest of patrons still hovering by the bar. Nina, he hoped, would be in her bed already. He wondered if she was yet asleep.

Thoughts of her carried him the rest of his journey, around bends and onto Main Street, within view of the hotel. He felt his chest lighten considerably at the sight of its amber windows. The day was finally at its close.

"Patty!" came a voice, followed by rapid footfalls. Patrick turned around to find Sam hurrying over the trolley tracks. One of his arms was raised. In the clutch of his fingers was a sealed piece of parchment.

"Been waitin' for you!" Sam greeted him, and he pressed the envelope into Patrick's hand. "The water Charmer asked me to give you this."

"Theodore?"

"Said it was important you get it tonight," Sam nodded. "Gave it to me outside the scrapyard."

Suspicion surged. "The scrapyard, you say?"

"Aye. Scottie says he weren't in the tunnels today, like he was s'posed to be. No one's seen him. Gunner and Donny are out lookin' for him now."

Patrick's stomach hollowed.

"Do you think he's taken off?" Sam asked, rocking lightly from heel to toe.

Patrick looked down at the envelope in his hand. It was sealed unevenly. "Thank you, Sam," he said. "Get out of the cold."

Sam nodded. "'Night, Pat." He shoved his hands deep into his pockets and strode away.

Patrick frowned at the letter for several moments before opening it. The lamps above offered an aura with which to see.

He recognized the bulletin immediately. He'd seen it a hundred times in towns all over Belavere Trench. A likeness of Nina, her aliases written above, the reward for her capture below.

It was old and faded. Its crease lines were deeply entrenched, as though the paper had been opened and refolded many times over. Perhaps carried in the pocket of someone who badly sought the person portrayed on it.

Along the borders was a frenzied ink scrawl.

Patrick read the message once, twice, a third time, his heart seizing in his chest with every pass.

Colson,

It isn't you she wants.

It's the Alchemist.

Long live Belavere.

His knuckles turned white.

But by the fourth pass, he was sure that the words were desperate, hysterical. The grand finale of a man turned inside-out by jealousy. Of course he would throw in one last wrench before departing.

The water Charmer was running. Sore hearts could fracture loyalties, and Patrick should have seen it coming. He cursed.

By now, Theodore could have taken a tunnel headed in three different directions. He would send Scottie, or Otto. They were the quickest underground. They'd bring him back one way or another. And if Theo had made it onto some distant train or narrow boat? Well, Patrick had enough contacts throughout the brink. Enough people who owed him a favor.

The boy knew of their plans. And they needed Theodore if they were to break through the Gyser. Even if Patrick had to drag him, Theodore Shop was coming back.

Patrick took his lighter from his pocket and considered burning Theodore's last words. The man was riddled through with jealousy. He'd say anything to come between them.

He let the flame hover just beneath a corner for a moment. Two moments.

But he didn't burn it.

He closed his eyes and saw Nina's likeness, watching him curiously. He thought of her mother, locked away in Belavere City. He thought of the strangled quality in Nina's voice when she'd begged him to just give up Domelius Becker, concede the Alchemist in exchange for their loved ones. Had she thought him callous, to dismiss the idea so thoroughly?

Nina trusted him. She had chosen him.

"She trusts me," he repeated, trying to let go of the rotten tendency in his gut that made him only ever see the world coldly, that made him believe the worst in people.

He crumpled the bulletin and shoved it into the breast pocket of his waistcoat, against his pounding heart.

It isn't you she wants.

It's the Alchemist.

It wasn't true. He refused to believe the worst in Nina Harrow.

He knew her.

He shook the idea from his mind and stalked into Colson's. He did not regard a single person as he rounded the bar, went through the kitchen and out the back door, his eyes on the little brown house in the courtyard.

Patrick entered his mother's kitchen, shucked off his coat, and let it drop to the floor. Tentatively, he pulled the blackened coin from his pocket and turned it over in his hand. The head of Lord Tanner on one side, a canary on the other.

For a long time, he simply stared at it, then he tossed it and let it fall into his palm. The canary glinted back at him.

He sighed deeply, shaking his head again. "I trust her," he mumbled to himself, then replaced the coin in his breast pocket.

He reached the Scribbler's cranny just as a piece of parchment from the top of the stack crinkled, ink appearing where there had been none.

Other scribbles from the day were waiting, but his eyes glued to the cursive now winding slowly across this latest one in a hand he did not recognize.

The lettering was slow. Deliberate. The words took an eternity to form.

But form they did, right before him, in punishing bold ink.

And every letter made him cold.

To the attention of Patrick Colson, with urgency.

Trouble with the Alchemist.

Please attend at earliest.

Patrick dropped into a chair. No name attached to the scribble.

It isn't you she wants. It's the Alchemist. He felt the words burn in his pocket.

And in his mind, walloping from some corner he'd bidden it into, came Nina's voice. *You wouldn't make the sacrifice? Not even to save your own men? Your own* father?

Slowly, as though it had lain dormant and waiting, a voice of reason rose its head. It berated him for being a fool.

He took the scribble and tucked it alongside Theodore's message, then left his mother's kitchen and carried his unwilling body back to the hotel, his eyes on the windows high above.

At the bar, Otto and Scottie sat talking softly. Both looked up at the sight of Patrick coming toward them.

"You all right, Pat?" Otto said, the man's warm features etching slowly in worry.

Patrick spoke in a voice not his own. "I need you tonight, boys. Urgent business."

· · · · · ·

Minutes later, Patrick arrived in front of room fifteen without remembering how he'd gotten there. But for the shake of muscle in his legs, he might have sprouted wings and flown.

He didn't go in immediately. Instead, he bottled the rage slowly brewing, creeping up his throat and filling his mouth. His vision blurred. The door distended. Beyond it, there would be Nina.

She loves me, Patrick told himself, over and over. He knew that, didn't he? Didn't it burn in her eyes when she looked at him?

He opened the door to a dark, tepid room. From the bed came deep, rhythmic breaths, hair strewn across a pillow, fathoms of perfect bare skin.

Nina rolled over as he descended beside her. Her eyelids fluttered open and she smiled. She curled into his side. All the lines of her pressed to all the lines of him. He let his fingers wonder down the curve of her waist. He felt her breaths lengthen, her languid heart beating reassuringly against him.

And already he felt the call of sleep. His body slackened immediately, expectantly. How easily she could spell him into stupor.

In an alternate world, far removed from this one, he could imagine how she might use that. How she might sneak out into the night like a wraith, knowing he'd been lured to sleep.

But now, in this room, it was unthinkable.

"Long day?" Nina murmured, and the sound of her voice was a vise.

He sighed. Closed his eyes. "There's been some trouble," he said. "I had to make some last-minute arrangements."

She tensed slightly in his arms. "Arrangements?"

"Mm hmm," he assented. And then he waited.

And for a moment it seemed as though she would say nothing more, and the knots in his chest began to unwind.

"What arrangements?" she asked. "What trouble?"

"Just some things the boys can take care of. I've asked Otto and Scottie to see to it." He opened his eyes to find her expression blank, her eyes unreadable in the dark. "Nothing to worry about."

She was quiet for a moment, and then she kissed him, warmth spreading from her lips into his, and he was instantly filled with the desire to press her back into that mattress, to taste the entire length of her.

Instead, he let her pull away. He listened as her breaths grew longer, slower.

He dreamed of walls closing in.

CHAPTER 57

NINA

Shortly after midnight, the parchment I'd folded and hidden in my sock crackled softly, and I woke on the cusp of a dream.

Patrick's lips were parted in sleep. I untangled my limbs from his with acute slowness, watching his face the entire time, ensuring it did not twitch.

I pulled the fold of parchment out inch by inch and unfolded it just the same—as though it were a trip wire. Polly's tiny scrawl now appeared.

Eastern tunnel. One hour.

I shuddered delicately.

The eastern tunnel led to Dorser, out to the seaways, not Dunnitch.

There are a million ways for this to go wrong, rang Polly's voice in my mind. I swallowed, looked back at Patrick one last time, then made myself stand. Dress. Patrick's pocket watch ticked down the hour.

When I finally slipped out of number fifteen, my belly rolled with sick.

Go back inside, the deepest parts of me begged. For several long moments I stood frozen, at war with myself. I even turned back and let my forehead rest against the paint. I traced the brass numbers one and five. I thought of every reason not to go.

But there was that train hurtling down the tracks toward me, and a reutterance of Polly's voice whispered *They're coming.*

You could tell him everything, I thought. *Tell him that Tanner won't attack*

Kenton Hill if he has his Alchemist. Patrick will make the trade to save this town. He'll listen. He loves you.

But telling him the truth would mean confessing myself an infiltrator. And would his love hold, if he knew why I'd come to Kenton Hill?

If not, would he take my life as routinely as the next traitor?

And so that was that. All the sand heaped the bottom of the hourglass.

I buttoned my coat to the throat, spared Sam's vacant seat a fleeting glance, and began the descent downstairs.

With every creak I was sure I'd be found out, that some door would swing open and catch me. I carried my boots in my hands, and yet still, it seemed every board was determined to creak beneath my feet.

The pub was quiet and silver with moonlight. I wove through the beams like a thief, as though the shadows would render me invisible. Isaiah barely lifted his head at my presence. He'd lowered it to the floor again before I'd made it to the door.

The air outside winded me. It sliced my throat, forced me to bury my nose in my coat collar, but I did not stop. I slid my boots on, tied the laces, coursed down the alleys of Main Street as quick as I dared, not crossing a single soul save the stray cats and vermin. Patrick's stolen pocket watch pressed tightly into the palm of my hand. The time read a quarter till the hour Polly had marked.

It wasn't a long journey to the eastern tunnel, and I was thankful I'd been there before. Left at the saddlers, then past the town houses, row after row; they were all black-windowed and silent. I tried not to think of anyone pulling their curtain aside to see a woman alone at an hour meant only for dark work.

I passed through identical brick veneers, moving mud away from the soles of my feet as I passed over gutters, and finally, finally, the hills spread out before me, and I could see the indentation on the hillside that would burrow into its depths, then fathoms below, all the way to the Alchemist.

There was no sign of Otto or Scottie, though I squinted through the dark for any sign of movement. Perhaps they were already partway down the tunnel, leaving me to follow quietly behind at a distance.

The yellow grass stalks were monochromatic in the night. The hill fell away behind me and it seemed as though this journey might not be so difficult. That I could simply slink away and be back before the sun threatened to rise. In the morning, I would have the exact location of Domelius Becker.

The pit entrance was small and vaulted with thick struts. It would be pitch-black inside, and I hadn't accounted for that. I would need to walk with either hand pressed to the walls and feel my way through. I shuddered and stepped into the gloom.

I felt my way along in the dark, ears straining for the echo of far-off footsteps. But there was nothing. Just uninterrupted black, dirt beneath my hands, Patrick's watch ticking its reproach.

I tripped and almost fell, my hand flying to my mouth to muffle the gasp.

And then a sound came.

Feet on the earth. Not the far-off kind I expected to hear. This was close. Discordant. I turned blindly in all directions and felt something touch my calf. The beginnings of a scream strangled me.

That something circled my ankles, sniffed at the hem of my skirt. Panted. And all the breath in my lungs released at once. I laughed, relieved. "Isaiah," I whispered, leaning carefully to feel for his scruff. He licked my hand. "What are you doing here?"

"Funny" came a wrathful voice. There was a click, and a light flared.

I backed into the wall hard, my head bouncing off the struts.

Patrick stood before me in the halo of his lighter. "I was about to ask you the same thing."

CHAPTER 58

NINA

It might as well have been a bullet.

Patrick stood there, just six feet away, his outline taking shape in the dark. And his expression was one I recognized—the same one he wore when I was first brought to Kenton Hill, the harder layers not yet pared.

And he stared at me as though I wasn't recognizable at all.

His hands were empty. He carried no gun.

Something primitive and base swelled. Survival, perhaps. My feet carried me toward him. "Patrick. Wait."

He watched my legs quake and stumble with keen discernment, as though that confirmed something for him. His eyes met mine from beneath his lashes, and they pierced as well as any blade. He didn't react when I fell into him, when my hands lay flat against his chest, then gripped the lapels of his coat. He only grew more rigid, staring down at my hands as though he no longer knew them. "Where are you goin', Nina?"

I thought of a thousand more lies in that moment. But none of them passed my lips.

"Yeah," he said. His breath fogged between us. "I can see all those stories passin' over your eyes. Which one are you gonna pick?" And beneath all that knife-sharp severity, there was pain; only for a moment, he let me glimpse how deep it ran. "You've got this last chance to give me the one that's true."

I didn't speak, and in the absence of my response, his eyes flared. The lighter clicked off, darkness collided, and his hand wrapped tightly around my wrist, began hauling me through the black, out, out, out, faster than my legs could move. I tripped and stumbled, until icy night air sluiced my cheeks and the stars glinted accusingly above.

My back was shoved up against the struts at the pit entrance, his face an inch from mine. "If you make me ask it once more, I'll fill in the answers myself," he said, voice barely controlled.

I inhaled once and said the only thing that could be said in that moment, my heart breaking the walls of its cage.

"I was following Otto and Scottie," I said, shutting my eyes. I didn't want to see the ripples of betrayal on his face.

"Tell me *all* of it," he said darkly. His hand gripped my jaw then, and he angled my face to his. "Open your eyes."

I did as I was bid, only to drown in ocean blue. Tears rolled over my cheeks, over his fingers.

"What are you looking for?" Patrick said, though I was sure he knew the answer. "Tell me."

"Domelius Becker," I yielded. "The Alchemist."

He dropped my chin abruptly, and the next breath he drew seemed to rattle. He turned his back to me. Took several paces into the moonlight and dug that coin from his coat. "You'll find Scottie and Otto in Hoaklin, tracking the whereabouts of your fellow Charmer," he said. "Despite what Otto told Polly, and what Polly told you."

Bile rose. "You . . . you knew? But how—"

"No," he said. "It ain't your turn to ask the questions, Nina." He turned to look at me, that coin appearing and turning over his knuckles. "What plans did you have for the Alchemist?"

He knew, I could hear it in his voice. But it seemed he needed me to admit it aloud, and I realized that while he seemed furious and hurt, perhaps he hadn't guessed the full depth of my treason. Perhaps he was looking for a way to excuse this transgression, for a way to save us.

"I was going to barter his whereabouts to the House of Lords." Tears slipped over my lips.

"For your mother," Patrick finished.

"Yes. And your father."

He paced in frustration from side to side, scrubbed his face with both hands. "I told you that wouldn't work," he said. "And you went behind my back anyway."

"I tried to ask you," I said. My voice broke. "To reason with you."

"And *I* asked for your trust," Patrick said, and he pinned me with a glare like steel. "I promised to free your mother another way."

"With a tunnel and a group of armed men?" I breathed. "And the risk of more deaths, including your own? Leveraging the Alchemist would negate *all* of that, Patrick!"

He closed his eyes. "It can't be done, Nina. I *told* you it couldn't."

"How can you say that?" My voice was pleading. "We could get back our families! And finally engage in a fair fight with the House. Does the need to control idium truly outweigh that?"

Patrick watched me, eyes boring in. "Nina, idium is *everything*," he said. "It is the key to this war. The House is useless without it."

"And you would forsake those you love for it?"

"Domelius Becker cannot be traded, Nina."

"*Why not?*" I demanded.

"Because he's *dead*."

I stilled. In the sky above, stars seemed to blink out of existence.

And Patrick watched me with unstifled torment. "You think I wouldn't have made that fuckin' trade myself if we had him?" he asked. "I'd do it a thousand times over, a million times if it could save my father. Your mother."

I stumbled back.

"You're two years too late, Nina." He looked to the sky. "I put a bullet in Domelius Becker the second he stepped foot in the brink, and I've regretted it every day since."

CHAPTER 59

PATRICK

Pieces of Nina's hair had become unclasped.

She'd forgotten gloves. A scarf. One boot remained untied. Her cheeks mottled in the cold, her knuckles reddened and cracked. She looked exactly as frayed as she sounded, and Patrick inwardly berated himself for not seeing it sooner—her enduring love for her mother, her desperation to save her.

Patrick wondered if Nina felt the quiet tremor in the earth. If she was aware of dust hovering inches above the ground at her feet. Or was she lost in that suspended state of disbelief?

She sagged, descended to her knees in the dirt. "He can't be dead," she insisted. "It isn't possible."

He wished he had told her sooner, even if it extinguished the last of her unreasonable hopes. Had he not trusted her, or had he done it to protect her, as he'd always told himself?

"Union fighters captured him in Belavere City," Patrick began, lowering himself to see her face, to ensure she heard him. "He was hiding in the basement of a lord. Our men brought him back here, and I killed him, just as my father had ordered me to." Patrick gritted his teeth, flexed his hands with the memory of it. "We buried his body in the hills. It was only afterward that I got word my father had been captured." He swallowed bitterly.

"Believe me, Nina. There is no one here who wishes it were otherwise more than I."

"No," she mumbled again, racked with tearless sobs.

Patrick knelt in front of her. "Nina. I promised you I'd save them, didn't I? Hey, look at me." He took her shoulders in his hands. Waited until her glossy eyes looked up at him. "I swear it, Nina. I'll get her out. But I need to know you won't do anything like this again. You have to promise me," he said firmly. "The Alchemist is dead."

"No."

He wanted to shake her. *"Yes."*

"He isn't dead . . . The bluff." And her eyes solidified on that which she had been so desperately searching for. "The bluff stores I saw. And the idium I took . . . How was it siphoned if not by Domelius Becker? He was the last Alchemist."

And this, Patrick knew, was always how secrets unraveled. Carefully woven fabrications unspooling one after the other.

"No," he uttered. "Not the last."

Her eyes narrowed at first, then widened as she understood.

"That title now resides with me."

Patrick took his coin from his pocket. It was heavier than the usual farthing, more darkly tinted than it should be. Black as terranium. He perched it on the edge of his thumb and flipped it in his practiced way. Only this time, the coin did not land. Instead, it hovered in midair, spun slowly as moonlight refracted off its inky surface.

Nina whispered in astonishment, "You're the Alchemist."

CHAPTER 60

NINA

Patrick stood and proffered a hand. "Walk with me."

I was too thrown to do anything but take it. My ears rang. Blood pounded behind my eyes. I barely registered the ground beneath my feet or Isaiah brushing against my calf.

I stared at the man beside me, part of him now unfamiliar. He waited for me to speak.

"I don't understand," I uttered. It was muted and waterlogged, as though I was sinking.

"Yes, you do" was his reply. Somehow, we'd arrived back at the laneways and town houses. Streetlights blinked off his irises. "You're too clever not to."

As he said it, there it was, the pieces connecting before me. I saw Patrick as he had been, thirteen years ago in that dusty courtyard. Two vials in one hand, and two in the other. *I was gonna be on that train home, one way or another.* I heard it again now. It clanged off the brick walls of the town houses. It chased the run of a copper pipe.

We didn't speak again until we stepped back inside Colson's. Isaiah retreated immediately to his bed. Patrick led me through the dim, behind the bar. His hand on the kitchen door seemed enough to unlock it. I heard the mechanism click with no key in sight.

Inside, the lamps were all out. Patrick went round to each one and pulled their strange cords and in increments, the hotel kitchen came aglow. Bottles and bottles of bluff winked from their shelves.

I nodded, to myself or perhaps to the hundreds of doses.

I almost smiled. Almost. "An Alchemist," I said.

"And an earth Charmer," he said.

I did smile then, and it was weak and disingenuous, and matched by Patrick, whose shoulders dropped so heavily I thought he might fold in on himself. "Didn't think the idium had worked at all, at first. I swallowed it, and it filled me up with all this light. But then there was nothin'. Seemed like I was unchanged. Wasn't until a few months later when my father took me to Dunnitch to meet with Union members. They had these displays of split terranium ore, the veins of idium already siphoned, and I felt a . . . a—"

"A frequency," I finished for him. "A hum."

He nodded. "I nicked one of the deposits off its shelf. Almost got away with it."

"But you were caught?" I asked.

"By my dad," he said. "He realized what I was long before I had a clue."

I stared around at all those shelves. "You made all this," I said. If I wasn't so wrung out, I might have marveled. "How did you learn?"

"Trial and error," Patrick answered.

"And you make idium for yourself?"

He nodded. "There is very little terranium left to be found. Bluff is more important for now. The brink has always suffered a shortage of it."

"And your father snuck into Belavere City, not in search of Lord Tanner, but in search of Domelius Becker."

"With the intention of havin' him killed," Patrick added.

I closed my eyes. "Making his son the only person in the Trench who can siphon both idium and bluff."

"Yes," Patrick said, and I felt every ounce of weight in it. The multitude of that remit. I wondered how any father could rest it all on their son's back. "Should've tossed that vial out the train window, shouldn't I?"

434

I knew that feeling well. "It seems this war has been won for quite some time. Only Tanner doesn't yet know it."

"Nor will he ever accept it."

"You can't be sure of that, Patrick," I said, stepping toward him. "Preserving Artisan mediums means everything to these people. Above all else, they'll want to ensure the continuation of tradition, of art, regardless of who heads the House."

"That's what we thought, too," Patrick said. He paused for a moment, his stare far-off and tormented. "Did you see what the Scribblers wrote in the newspapers, in the days after my father's alleged failed attack?"

I nodded. "It said they charged the House with dynamite in their trousers. That they were captured before they reached the courtyard."

"But my father didn't leave Kenton Hill with any dynamite. They weren't lookin' to blow anything up. They were to steal in and out quietly, with the Alchemist in tow. We were planning to kill Domelius Becker, send his branded arm back as a gift to the House, along with a message that I was now the last remaining Alchemist and a list of demands."

"But your father didn't come back," I said.

He shook his head. "Something went wrong. And then the headlines came, and I knew we'd fucked everything. Domelius Becker was dead, they had our chairman hostage, and it seemed only a matter of time before the Lords' Army came barrelin' over those hills. A man can only hold out so long beneath the whip. But they didn't come. And John Colson was never named in the newsprint. Nor was I." They sounded like thoughts that had cycled his mind many times over. "So, we know my father never gave up his name, nor my abilities, nor Kenton Hill." He swiped a hand over his face, rubbing his tired eyes. "They believe Domelius Becker is alive, and it's the only leverage we have left in this fight, because if they find me, then they have everythin'. The union, the idium, Kenton Hill—all of it will be theirs." He closed his eyes for a moment. "At least Kenton Hill is safe for now."

Not as safe as you think.

"So, I'm nailed to a corner, Scurry girl," he said now. "While there's still bluff floatin' around the brink, Tanner knows an Alchemist exists, and he thinks it's Domelius Becker. The second he starts thinking otherwise is the second I've lost that one advantage."

"But if he knew what you were—"

"If he knew what I was, there is *nothing* he wouldn't lay waste to in order to get to me," Patrick said assuredly. "Every week, another town is sacked. You've seen it."

I had. Fire Charmers smoking out buildings of occupants. Rivers contaminated and streams sullied in a perversion of water charming. Men, women, and children lined up on the streets and questioned.

"You're one of seven people who know the truth," Patrick said, moving off the counter he leaned on. "The other six, I've had a lifetime with. I know the insides of their heads better than my own. I'd bet all the lives of Kenton that they'd never betray me, never breathe a word of it to another. And now I'm tellin' you."

I shook my head. "Why?"

"Because I believe you were tellin' the truth when you said you want to be on this side," Patrick said. "Am I wrong?"

My legs were beginning to shake again. "No."

"But you love your mother," he said. "Enough to sneak out while I slept. Enough to lie to me."

I breathed once. Twice. Nodded.

He walked five paces, until he had my face in his grip again, staking me with the intensity of his stare. "You won't ever do that again. Do you understand me?"

And for a moment, I considered revealing it all—the day I was captured in Delfield and dragged back to Belavere City. The ultimatum Tanner had imparted, why I had come here. I wanted to purge it all and be done with it.

"I won't," I said.

· · · · · ·

If there was nothing left with which I was willing to barter peace, the infantry would come. And Kenton Hill would go up in smoke.

I would tell him all of it and hope he loved me enough not to kill me.

There was only one thing that stopped me. I was not the only Artisan in Kenton Hill.

I would warn Polly. Give her the chance to run, if she chose. It might save her life.

"I'm sorry," I whispered.

His grip loosened. He wiped the pad of his thumb over my bottom lip, as though he could erase its trembling.

"We'll find a way to finish the tunnel," he said. "I'll get your mother out, I swear it."

I closed my eyes and felt his fingers sliding into my hair. "And when I come home, I've got plans to marry you. Promise me you'll be waitin'."

Choked laughter escaped me. "What if I don't accept your proposal?" I asked. But my voice was hollow, lined in fear.

"You will." He seemed quite sure of it. "It'll be far grander than this one."

He seemed so filled with confidence—for a future still distorted, for his town, his plans. How I wished I could keep him blind to the missile headed for us.

He brushed my hair aside, pressed his mouth to mine. He kissed me so sweetly it was difficult to breathe.

I let myself drown in that moment, knowing it might be the last of its kind. I pictured yellow hills and black-spotted yarrow and Patrick offering a life with him, and I pretended there was nothing else. No idium, no lords, no Artisans or Crafters. I imagined I'd said yes to him as a girl and sat beside him on that train home, the years between then and now made simple and kind.

CHAPTER 61

PATRICK

In the night, Patrick's anger ebbed into the sheets. He watched her sleep and thought of the look on her face when she saw children on the street, when he chased her downhill, when she danced. He wanted to give her a lifetime of that.

He traced the burn marks on the inside of her wrist. Beneath it, he could just make out the Artisan brand, Idia's face refusing to be erased. Had it hurt, when she'd scorched away this version of herself?

She'd made a mistake. Hadn't he himself made plenty? He could forgive her this one error in judgment, this one deception. In some ways, he was responsible for it; he'd lied to her, too.

Nina Harrow had been in hiding most of her life, put through more than anyone deserved. And perhaps he was selfish for deciding she would be his—he, who could never bring her peace.

By dawn, his face was washed and clean-shaven. He was dressed but for his boots and pocket watch. He looked over to the bed, to Nina, still asleep. She was achingly beautiful.

Outside, duty beckoned, but he decided duty could wait a little longer. Instead, he pressed his lips to her exposed hip, tasted her skin with slow repose until she began to stir.

She came awake breathing his name, rolling toward him.

"Lie back," he told her.

And when she did, he leaned over her thighs and lavished her with his fingers and tongue, until his name wasn't just a murmur, but a cry. Until his clothes were once more discarded.

Until the troubles of the day seemed diminutive, hardly worth his time at all.

CHAPTER 62

NINA

Polly was in the post office at an early hour, sitting at her station. Her pieces of parchment lay haphazardly around her, their neat lines of ink appearing in rapid tandem.

But each piece stilled when she saw me, brazenly crossing the threshold alone.

"Nina," she said, standing and rounding the desk at once. She looked over her shoulder as though the policemen who once manned this square might come storming out of the walls. "Do you have news?"

"I have to speak with you."

She eyed the street-facing windows. "What of the Alchemist?" she asked beneath her breath. "Please, tell me you found him." Her eyes were bloodshot, and her teeth had reddened a spot on her lip.

I grimaced. I knew I could only give her a half-truth, and that it might break her. But at least afterward, I would be done with these deceptions. Already I felt less and less constricted.

"No," I told her. "Domelius Becker is dead."

Her face fell, her eyes becoming two fathomless pits, a slow wakening terror rearing in their depths.

"Polly, listen—"

"Then it's done," she whispered. "We're done for."

I nodded slowly, then steeled myself for my next words. "I have to tell him, Pol," I whispered. I looked over my shoulder as she did, the square beyond the windows empty. "I'm sorry. I'm doing it today—or tonight, if I must wait."

"Nina, you *can't*," she whispered, her voice catching with urgency. Her face had reanimated. She gripped my hands fiercely. "You'll *die*, Nina. *I'll* die."

"I don't believe that," I said, shaking my head, but tears were running freely down the slope of my nose. "Patrick loves me."

"He won't. Not once he knows, Nina. Loyalty is *everything* to these people. You don't know them as well as I do."

"I was raised by these people," came my retort, more biting than I had intended. "I grew up in a town full of them, remember?"

Polly looked like I'd knocked the wind out of her. She shook her head in dismay. "You truly believe that, don't you?"

I leveled her with a stare, the most empathetic I could conjure. "I do. And I believe Otto loves you as well."

She stiffened. Dropped my hands.

"Do you love him, too, Polly?" I asked. "Could you stand to see his home burned down to the ground by fire Charmers?"

She had begun to cry, tears cascading over the apples of her cheeks.

"No," she said. "I don't want that."

"Then there is no other choice," I said gently. "There are infantrymen coming this way. Patrick needs to know. I'm sure they can put up a fight."

"But they can't *win*," Polly said wanly. She shook her head at the tiles. I saw the toll of the past years finally colliding with her. "What use are guns against fire Charmers?"

I took her shoulders in my hands. "I'll bury them under piles of dirt if it comes to that," I said. "I'm telling him, Pol. I came to let you know, because . . . because I wouldn't fault you if you chose to run."

"Run?" she echoed. "Back to the House of Lords?"

"Yes. But if that's what you choose, then you should leave today.

Patrick is traveling to Baymouth. But he'll return before long, and when he does, I'll tell him they're coming, Pol. And I won't need to say who it was keeping Tanner informed. He'll piece it together."

Polly shook her head, swallowed a sob. "I don't know what to do."

"I hope you'll stay," I bid her. "Patrick will show us mercy. I know he will."

Polly looked at me once more, shook her head in doubt. "I hope so."

I hugged her tightly, briefly, then left her to her scribbles.

I walked into the square. Margarite's Modern Ladies, Seamstress Extraordinaire, bore up on the right, its windows still guarded by those faceless sentries. I exited the square through the brick arch and traveled down salt-dusted streets, counting grates, imagining the numbers that could be encased within. The hills rose in the distance, mined to holy hell with all manner of metal explosive.

They won't come close, I heard Patrick say.

Heard it all the way back to Colson & Sons.

· · · · · ●

With Theo gone, the Margarite crew was left to do nothing. Scottie and Otto seemed to have been unsuccessful in tracking him down. They lingered by the bar, turned about the pub restlessly, infuriated Tess Colson with every gathering minute. "Surely," she gritted out, "there is somethin' in this parish that begs your attention."

Briggs puffed on a cigarette and paced in tightening circles. "'Spose we could head down to the market, mind the queues for a bit."

"I'll come," Otto offered, tipping off the end of his stool. "Better than sittin' on me arse."

Scottie stretched with a yawn, reclining on his chair. "Might stick around, Mrs. Colson, if you don't—"

"Go home, Scottie," she interjected. "Pay a visit to your wife and your kids, for fuck's sake."

Scottie seemed more than a little cowed by the notion. But he stood and hiked up his sagging trousers. He nodded politely to Mrs. Colson, and then to me as he passed me at the door. "Mornin', miss," he grumbled.

With the departure of Briggs and Otto as well, it left only Gunner, Donny, and Tess. All three of them at the bar. All three suddenly focusing their attentions on me, standing by the door.

I paused in the motion of shaking slush from my hems. "What?" I asked. None of them blinked or shifted their gaze. I narrowed my eyes, suspicion dawning. "What is it?"

Tess Colson broke first. She muttered something beneath her breath that sounded like "Here we fuckin' go," then poured an absurdly large portion of whiskey into a waiting glass. "Come here, girl," she said. "Gunner, move over."

Gunner rolled his eyes. "Already, she's usurped us, Donny. Did you hear that?"

"I'm blind, not deaf."

"Shut up, you two," Tess snapped. And then to me, "Well, hurry up. We ain't got all day."

It may have just been the early hour, but she seemed wearier, older. Like the past fortnight had aged her terribly. She took a generous gulp of the whiskey she'd poured, then left the rest to me. I eyed it as I approached and took a tentative seat between Gunner and Donny.

Gunner leaned in, his eyes two slits of glinting humor. "Patty said he'd let the cat out." It was difficult to tell, but I thought he might be grinning beneath the matting of his beard.

I squirmed uncomfortably in my seat, well aware that Patrick was nowhere near.

"It seems my *son*," Tess said as though the word was tentative, "has chosen fit to tell you all the family secrets. Without runnin' the idea by the rest o' us, mind you." She took another tired sip of her whiskey and sighed. "Far be it from him to seek anyone's approval."

I swallowed thickly. It seemed safest to say nothing. At least until I could gauge their reaction to this news. Did they know Patrick had found me absconding down the eastern tunnel? How much had he told them?

"Quite a shock, was it?" Donny asked lightly. "Left you speechless, apparently."

Tess planted both elbows on the bar top and leaned in close to peer up into my face. "You should know, had Pat asked me my thoughts, I would have told him not to say a damn word," she said. "I'd have told him that, given your past, you'll likely find yourself a ship one day and he'll never see you again. I'd have told him that most romances between young men and pretty girls fizzle out, and that he'd be better to wait. To test your loyalty before givin' over all his confidence. But"—and here, she leaned away, breaking her spell over me—"here we are. And what's done can't be undone, can it?"

I blinked in quick succession, a rope of guilt cinching my insides. My mouth had gone dry. "If you mean to ask me if I can be trusted," I said carefully. "Then the answer is yes."

"That's the thing," Gunner said lowly. "What you say don't matter. It's what you *do*. Whether you take the information and run off with it."

"I'm staying," I said, far more boldly than I felt. "I'm not boarding some ship."

"Right you are," Tess Colson said gravely. "Because if you ever tried, darlin', we'd bring you back, dead or alive." She downed the last of her whiskey. "That's the thing about knowin' too much. It's dangerous."

The threat caused ire to prickle on my tongue. "I'd say threatening a Charmer of earth is rather dangerous, is it not?"

Movement from my left. Donny rising from his chair. From his waistcoat he drew a silver revolver, and I stumbled clumsily off my stool. Donny pointed the barrel away, out wide to the wall, and there was an earsplitting blast.

I jumped and covered my ears, my heart in my throat, blood pounding, and watched in astonishment as a bullet hovered an inch from the wall at which it had been aimed. Then, it turned of its own accord, followed the length of the room. It skirted the piano, the bay windows, swooped over Isaiah's head as he slept. It passed the door to the stairwell, the grandfather clock and gathered speed. It flew straight at me.

I closed my eyes before it could bury itself in my forehead, split my brain down its middle.

But there was no rupture. No pain. I opened my eyes again to see that bullet hanging again in the air, an inch from my nose.

"So's threatenin' a Smith of silver," said Donny. "Even a blind one."

A gust of air left me. The bullet clattered to the ground.

"Lord almighty, Donny," Gunner groaned. "Patty will fuckin' kill you for that."

I turned slowly to stare at the youngest Colson brother, who had resumed his seat. He shrugged. "It's important we all know where we stand, I think."

"Apologize to her, Don," Tess said gravely. "That was beyond the pale."

"I wasn't *actually* gonna shoot her," he argued, scowling. "I *like* her."

"*Donny.*"

"Fine. Apologies, Miss. It was right rude of me. I'd never really shoot you. Unless, of course, you ran your mouth all over yonder about my brother. Which is precisely why I thought it was a good idea to demonstrate—"

"I understand," I said, my voice thin. "If I betray your confidence, you'll kill me."

"Don't gotta be so harsh with her," Gunner said, shaking his head at his mother. "We owe her a lot of lives."

"We do," Tess Colson agreed. She stared at me intently. "And it leads me to thinkin' perhaps there's hope in all this." She leaned across the bar top and took my hands in hers. "He believes he loves you. So much so, that it worries me," she said. "Keeps me up at night. Because love makes men blind—"

"Oy!" Donny interjected.

"—and many a woman would see it as an opportunity to pull the wool over their eyes. I'm prayin' every night that you ain't one of them, Nina Harrow. Do you hear me?"

I nodded slowly, feeling as though I watched the scene play out from a distance, spools of guilt and dread twining together. "I love him," I said. It should've felt good to say, but it didn't.

Tess stretched the moment, discerning, calculating, and I waited with bated breath.

Then she smiled. "Welcome to the family, then."

Gunner held up his pint to me and downed his drink. "We're a wretched lot," he joked. "Try not to hold it against us." He stood and headed for the street.

I breathed in for what felt like the first time since stepping out of the cold. Then spun. "Wait!" I called to Gunner, just as his hand reached the doorknob. He looked back at me.

"If Patrick gave one brother idium, surely he gave some to the other?"

A grin and a wink in response.

"What is your medium?" I asked him.

"Copper," he said, tapping his one shining tooth. "How d'you think we made those bloody pipes and drums in the coal works?"

And then he disappeared out into the street, whistling a miner's song.

· · · · · ·

I spent the rest of the day in my room, wringing my hands, watching the trolley and wagons and horse carts from the window, following the cap of every man who passed in case it was Patrick, feeling as though the pin of a grenade had been pulled free and time was sprinting toward an impending explosion.

By nightfall, my fingernails were bitten all the way down, and I could hear that freight train bearing down upon me.

CHAPTER 63

PATRICK

Baymouth had kept him longer than anticipated, and Patrick walked back through the tunnels with his canary alone, troubled, thoughtful, forehead pinched to a keen ache.

The associate he'd been due to meet with had never shown. Patrick had waited for over an hour before finally deciding that the man must be dead, when a woman came in his place.

A woman completely disheveled, her housecoat badly stained in blood. Wisps of her hair stuck to her lips. "Your man's been shot," she said, her teeth bared in a grimace.

Patrick knew what she meant immediately. "A raid?"

"A bloodbath," the woman countered. "Yesterday. Fire Charmers and all. We barely got the children away in the tunnel."

His blood boiled. "How many dead?"

"A thousand at least," she'd said. "More by mornin'."

Patrick clenched his fists. "Tomorrow, I'll be waitin' here at this same hour. I'll bring as much bluff as can be carried for the injured."

"Heard a few of the Lords' men say they're headin' north," the woman said suddenly. "They might be comin' your way. If they show up, tell your lot to run," she said, her voice breaking. "There'll be no beatin' 'em."

Patrick had stared at her for a moment, at the ash and blood smeared across her right ear, at the tears shaking at the rims of her eyes.

"They won't get within a mile," he'd told her. "I'll be here tomorrow. Ensure someone meets me."

"And if you're not here?" she'd called after him, desperation cracking her voice.

"Then I'm dead." His words rebounded off the tunnel walls.

Now, he retraced the path back to Kenton. Baymouth was largely unguarded bar the artillery Kenton Hill had provided them with. They were surrounded by sea on one side, cornered on the cliffs. Easy to pick off. They'd been raided before and recovered. This latest desperate attempt by the House of Lords was not a prelude. And if it were, then they would find themselves with less limbs on the hills.

Kenton was safe. There was no way in but one.

And yet, Patrick's blood pounded. The gas bulbs began to blur as he passed them.

He ran like a boy bolting from his shadow.

But no matter how fast he moved through that tunnel, Kenton seemed no closer. And he was certain, though he couldn't see how it was possible, that through the walls he heard marching boots, the clack of artillery.

Miss Polly Prescott
To
RIGHT HONORABLE MASTER OF THE NATIONAL ARTISAN HOUSE
Lord Geoffry Tanner

My Lord,

I write this with the expectation that my remit in Kenton Hill be fulfilled, and that I seek safe return to Belavere City.

The Alchemist, Domelius Becker, is dead.

Passage into Kenton Hill can be found underground, using the map coordinates contained.

I urge the House of Lords to come to peace terms with the Union's members, who I believe will agree to quick surrender rather than see their parish and its civilians suffer.

Polly Prescott

CHAPTER 64

NINA

The window shuddered against my forehead.

I frowned at it, pressed my fingers to it as it shuddered again. It was minute. The smallest of disruptions. It wouldn't have woken any who slept in their beds, or indeed, any who did not at that moment have their face mashed to the glass.

Over Main Street, the lamps on their wires trembled.

I opened the window, impervious to the icy draught, leaned my head out as far as I dared, looked one way, and then the other.

In my years of hiding, I'd learned this—war had an air to it. I felt it now. Tasted the copper on my tongue before the blood flowed. Birds fled their gutter perches, swarmed into the night.

Too late, I thought. *Too fucking late.*

My heart stuttered. Patrick . . . where was he?

I strained my sights to the hills as though I might find him there, his men preparing a defense as the army marched over them.

But the hills were shrouded in darkness. No firelight or sparks flashed in the dark. The hills did not shake.

But Kenton did. The lanterns swung precariously now, with no wind to blow them.

Then, there was a burst of sound.

Not from the hills.

Not from the outside of Kenton, but from within.

Between the rooftops, an exquisite cloud of fire unfurled. A burgeoning sun.

I felt its heat even from this distance, heard the first screams swallow the air.

My stomach revolted. "No."

And then I ran. I flew down flights of stairs as the doors flung open, occupants within flooding out as I did, cascading down the landings and out the swinging door and through the pub.

I pushed out onto Main Street as a hundred others did. The men were half-dressed and armed with long-barreled guns, the women in nightgowns with children on both arms. Eyes wide with confusion swept to the dissipating cloud in the sky.

Finally, the siren whirred to life.

A large hand buckled my shoulder.

Gunner panted at my side, pulling a shirt over his head with one hand, a shotgun in his other. "Gas explosion," he said. "Go back inside." He yelled the same thing to those who stood gawking in the street.

"No," I said. Stopping him with my hand on his wrist. *"Listen."*

And then he heard what I did. The noises grew with alarming momentum. Eddies of glass breaking, a succession of short blasts, women screaming, the roar of fire.

And Gunner's face went slack. "Lord almighty," he breathed. His feet carried him forward as though of their own accord, toward all that glowing red. He gathered speed, and I chased him. "The Lords' Army!" I shouted to him. And he stopped as though he'd been shot.

"GET TO THE TUNNELS! THE BUNKERS!" he bellowed, his voice racketing up the brick facades and shaking the windows. "ALL THOSE ABLE WITH ME!" he roared. He threw the butt of his gun into every doorway he passed, barely pausing in his sprint. He pointed the barrel to the sky and fired it twice. Windows flew open all around, residents came screaming into the street.

"GET TO THE TUNNELS!" he shouted. "WE'RE UNDER ATTACK!"

The following moments would become murky in my memory. Just flashes of noise and frantic men and women with their wailing charges. Crafters disappeared through grates in the ground and threw all manner of weaponry onto the cobbles. Bullets rolled into the gutters. Red-faced men in their trunks and half-buttoned shirts sprinted to help. Women emerged from the swarm with guns slung over their shoulders.

And I moved with the current, watching the sky turn blood red.

They didn't stop until they reached a hidden alley to the square, the shadows protecting them. Gunner was at the spearhead. "Hold," he called back to the rest, and the message was passed down the line.

The rooftops of the square burned. Every window had burst with the force of the flames that billowed out. Glass splintered underfoot.

Only a handful of establishments remained untouched, and one of them was Margarite's Modern Ladies, Seamstress Extraordinaire.

Floods of army men spilled from its doors, tore toward the arch, filtering throughout the entire town. Only three stood still in the square, wearing long, ink-blue robes. A woman and two men, fire jumping from their hands into the air. A man nearby lay on his back, his skin blackened, a pistol discarded on the cobbles. Before him, a woman screamed. She wore a dressing robe. Her hair was still pinned into coils. She knelt beside him and sobbed.

A passing soldier in Artisan blue stepped out of his line. He lifted his gun in the woman's direction and fired.

Gunner turned. He found me with my back pressed to the brickwork and pushed men out of his way to approach me.

And then his hand closed around my throat, and my feet left the ground. His breath fogged my face and his eyes were wild.

I couldn't breathe. His fingers curled into the sides of my neck.

"*Did you do this?*" he seethed.

I tried to shake my head. My feet kicked wildly. "No."

"Where's my brother?" he demanded, voice quaking. He loosened his grip enough to let me fall, to let air flood my lungs again. "He didn't come back—"

A sudden volley of bullets. A racket of crumbling brick and clanging pipes. A man among the sea of infantrymen in the square pointed his rifle down into our shadows. He shouted for his comrades, gesturing wildly, eyes gleaming at the sight of us pressed between buildings.

"Fuck," Gunner said, and he gave me one last fleeting, murderous glance. "GO!" he bellowed. "OPEN FIRE!"

And the Crafters in the shadows flooded out, throwing their grenades and pointing their rifles into that sea of ink.

And Gunner turned back to me. He cocked his pistol.

"Gunner, no." My hands trembled as I rose them in surrender. "Let me *help*," I said. "I can stop this."

"That ain't for me to decide," he grunted, something mournful in his eyes, and the butt of his pistol collided with my temple.

I heard the cap of a grate sliding, Gunner's grunts as he lowered me into the bunker beneath. Felt the darkness surround me.

And then there was nothing at all.

CHAPTER 65

PATRICK

By the time Patrick climbed out of his pit high above, Kenton Hill was screaming.

People were scrambling up from below, running to the tunnels. He threw himself down the slope with sickening desperation, passing bawling children and people with babies in slings or on their backs.

The entire way, his heart remained in denial. It thumped a bid of *No. It isn't possible.*

It wasn't possible for the fire to come from within.

There was only one way in. It wasn't possible.

Unless . . .

Theodore, his mind concluded. Who else but him? The rich Artisan boy in love with the girl who'd discarded him for a miner.

Patrick clambered over the pickets and wove through familiar alleys. He jumped into the first grate he saw and pulled out a rifle and a box of bullets. He cut his knees on the drain edge as he climbed out, then bolted through the hordes running in the opposite direction to escape the town limits.

It took only minutes to reach the havoc. The closer he came to the heart of Kenton, the louder the destruction, the more cloying the smoke. He shot three men in Artisan navy before they could turn to see him streaking past.

He threw the full weight of his body into a soldier straddling a woman on the sidewalk, her sleeves ripped free of her shoulders. He pressed his pistol into his gut and fired.

The town square was somewhere ahead, and it all seemed engulfed from the sight of its rooftops. Just one more alleyway before the fray.

And Patrick would blast every one of them away. He'd have them eat their own fire.

From the dim of a narrow alley, Patrick threw his back against the brick wall and loaded his rifle. In the square, men lay on their faces. Their bodies, clad in navy or otherwise, were strewn everywhere. A circle of armed infantrymen stood in the center of the skirmish. They guarded three figures in long coats, fire in their palms. The Charmers sent streams of it into the town beyond.

Shirts caught fire and men ran, shrieking, only to fall on the bayonets of waiting Artisan soldiers.

Grenades detonated and sent both sides hurtling into the night, their stomachs and limbs and scalps torn from the rest of them.

The Crafters of Kenton Hill were holding the Lords' infantry in the square, keeping the fire Charmers from spreading their flames to the rest of the town, but they held them at bay by inches. More soldiers flooded from Margarite's doors, a seemingly endless reserve, and the Crafters were pushed back, allowing the fire Charmers and their ring of guards to expand outward. Within moments, they broke through, and jets of fire plumed into the air, alighting the shingles and gutters of every roof they touched. Soon, all of Kenton would be ablaze.

Where was Nina?

Was she safe?

What of his mother? Of Donny and Gunner?

The sound of pounding feet came from behind Patrick, and he turned and raised his rifle, hammer cocked, finger prepped.

"Wait!" said the voice, his face emerging from the shadow.

Theodore Shop stared at Patrick, his eyes wider than they'd ever been, his mouth slackened in shock.

He bore no weapon, just the same dirt-clad clothing he'd worn in the tunnels, his skin gritty with it. "I'm not with them," he said, raising his hands in surrender. "Pat—"

Patrick had the barrel at his forehead within a second, his forearm pinning Theodore to the wall at the throat.

"PATRICK! Wait! I only came back for Nina, I swear. I was worried you might have . . . that you might have hurt her. Sending you that note was stupid. I was angry—"

Patrick barely saw him through the film of red hazing his vision.

"Think about it, Patrick! Please! Why else would I return? Why would I risk it?"

Somewhere in the red mist, Patrick heard the sense.

"It wasn't me who let them in, Patrick! It couldn't have been. Not unless I had a Scribbler."

Or unless he *was* a Scribbler.

Which Theodore wasn't.

But Polly was.

"They're dying, Pat!"

He knew. He knew.

"The fire Charmers . . . if they get to the Coal Works, the entire place will blow. Do you hear me? All of Kenton will be gone."

Patrick's stomach bottomed. His arm against Theodore's throat loosened.

"I can help," Theodore said. "I can help you put them down."

Patrick's eyes flickered to Theodore's hands, then to the fire in his periphery.

"They'll have the Charmers surrounded by soldiers, Patrick. You can't take them on without me."

There was little time for deliberation, and Patrick well knew it. With an agonized growl, he released Theodore, only to take the scruff of the man's collar in his grasp. "Put them out," he bid Theodore, would have got down on his knees and begged him. "Put out the Charmers, and I won't shoot you right here."

Theodore nodded vigorously. "You can use the canals," Patrick told him. "Draw from whatever you can."

"Just point your gun at something navy," Theodore told him. "I know what to do."

Another figure moved into the alley. Patrick lifted his gun.

"Patty?" came Donny's voice. "I can help."

Patrick cursed. "No, Don. Not this time."

"I'm a much better shot," Donny said. "Hurry up. We ain't got time for chitchat."

Patrick looked out onto the square, at all his men, and with a deep ache, he turned his back on them. "We'll cut off the fire Charmers at the pass," he told Theodore. "Stay close. Some of the infantry found their way out of the square."

Patrick led them away, back into the maze of town houses. He cut over a canal, then another. Under a bridge and through the dusty courtyard of his old schoolteacher. This is how he'd once passed through Kenton Hill—on tumbling legs with a chest filled with fire, cutting corners and jumping pickets quicker than his feet could muster. Donny hardly slowed them. Patrick called warnings to him, but Donny had better ears than a hunting dog, and he'd run through these streets just as often as Patrick.

They only encountered two soldiers. They were sacking the narrow boats docked in the canals.

"Wait!" Theodore whispered, fear on his breath. But there was no time to wait. No time to mute their approach. Patrick kept on running. The first one to turn in Patrick's direction found a bullet between his eyes. "Dead ahead," Patrick called, and the next got two of Donny's in the chest. They toppled into the water.

Patrick ignored the fear that he'd be shot at any moment, that he'd topple just the same. "Hurry up!" he shouted to Theodore, whose breathing had grown ragged. Patrick thought he heard the man praying between inhales.

The Coal Works was ahead. In the distance, fire danced across tiles and disappeared down chimney flumes, trickling ever closer. Patrick broke into a sprint. Past the brewery, the metal scrap. Over the last canal crossing.

And there, at the end of the lane, came a flurry of movement, fire dancing in their midst. It leapt from roof to roof. The outlines of cloaked figures and armed soldiers became visible.

But the fire jumped ahead of them, bid by something faster than its own nature.

Patrick pictured those great copper drums waiting within the Coal Works. All that gas in the bellies of a hundred boilers. How big would the blast's radius be if it were all to combust?

Patrick became seized by something far greater than bravery, or any sense of responsibility.

He was gripped by fear. By the thought of losing his home completely. Every scrap of it blasted into oblivion.

"STOP!" he shouted madly, foolishly. They were three men on a road facing a group of twenty, thirty, and Patrick forgot himself, raised his gun.

Patrick heard the clack of many rifles lifted onto shoulders. Heard the blast of a barrel before he felt the bullet.

Pain shattered his left shoulder as he was thrown backward. The back of his head hit the cobbles, gun clattering beside him. Donny was suddenly over him, eyes ahead. His gun raised to defend them both.

But Theodore advanced. "Wait!" he shouted. "Don't shoot! I'm not Union!"

Patrick blinked up at him, tried to see and hear around the bursts of agony pulsing along his collarbone. He could see the underside of Theo's face, see the terror in his eyes.

"I'm an Artisan!" Theodore was saying now, shouting it. His hands were raised in surrender, the mark of Idia on his arm visible. "I'm an Artisan!"

"Theodore?" came a distant reply, a woman's voice. "Theodore Shop?"

Patrick rolled onto his side, a hiss of pain escaping him at the pull from his shoulder, but he squinted his eyes to see the brigade of fire Charmers and soldiers approaching them. Now a mere twenty feet away. At its head was a woman with tawny hair. "Is that you?"

"Tell me when to shoot, Pat," Donny murmured.

Another Charmer scoffed. This one was young, reedy. He cocked his chin with an air of importance. "Lord Shop's boy?" he said. "The disgraced son? Spare me."

"No, it's him, I'm quite sure," said the woman. "A water Charmer."

Theodore's eyes bounced between them, between all those guns. "I can prove it."

"And what would a water Charmer be doing all the way out here?" said the third fire Charmer, an older man. "Defected, have you?"

"No," said the woman. "Tanner sent him."

Something in Patrick fractured.

"An informant?" asked the young fire Charmer.

"One of them," said the woman, and that hole in Patrick ripped deeper. "Where is the earth Charmer, Mr. Shop? I was told explicitly to find her. That she would be here alongside you on this assignment."

Patrick turned his head in time to see Theodore's face. He waited for a frown, some display of confusion.

But Theodore nodded. His eyes flickered to Patrick for only a moment. "Yes," he said. "Though the earth Charmer is long gone. You won't find her."

Patrick didn't comprehend it. Refused to.

And yet there was that yawning abyss inside him, threatening to swallow him whole.

The woman grimaced. "Never mind. We have soldiers in every surrounding province. We'll round her up."

"What do you want with her?" Theodore asked, his eyes darting between them.

Pieces of Patrick broke away from the rest. He began to recall snippets of Nina's questions, her curiosity, the tunnel.

The woman frowned. "Lord Tanner will want to reward you both for your success."

Theodore hesitated. "Success?"

The woman frowned, suspicion dawning. "We received word from Polly Prescott that Domelius Becker was dead," she said carefully. "We've been ordered to find a man named Patrick Colson and bring him back to Belavere City."

Patrick stopped breathing. Stopped moving at all.

The fires coalesced, flourished.

"Why?" Theodore asked, looking to Patrick on the ground, true confusion marring the terror. "Why Patrick?"

The woman's eyes followed Theodore's. She looked to the ground, where Patrick lay strewn, bleeding, rapt in a turmoil she couldn't see. She looked back to Theodore with increasing wariness. "If you know where Colson is, you ought to tell us now, Mr. Shop. Or you'd be aiding the last Alchemist in the Trench."

Theodore's eyes widened. He swallowed.

Then, with horrible finality, he pointed one finger down to the ground where Patrick lay.

The woman's eyes lit up. "Take them all," she said.

And a ring of fire appeared, circling Theodore, Donny, and Patrick, its flames so tall Patrick could hardly see past them. He threw himself onto all fours, retrieved his gun. The heat made him pant wildly, made his eyes stream. Donny helped him stand, and Patrick tried to blink through the flames.

"Fuck," Donny cursed. His gun swinging wildly. "I can't hear shit with all this fire, Pat. Which way?"

But Patrick could hardly breathe, hardly see.

Suddenly, there was a shudder. A rapidly growing roar. Patrick looked over his shoulder in time to see a wall of water rising from the canal behind. It hurtled upward, impossibly tall. He heard suction as it was drawn from every possible corner, collecting into a giant murky wave over the Artisan forces. Its white cap teeming, tipping.

Patrick heard shouts, pounding feet.

Theodore grunted. "Brace yourself."

And Patrick had only enough time to cocoon his head in his arms before the water walloped down. It barreled over rooftops and thundered down walls. It came down onto the street with enough force to break bones, to crack skulls onto the pavement. It came down like a hand of god, crushing all beneath its palm.

But not over Theodore, Donny, or Patrick, who existed in their own dry cupola, curtained by deluge on every side.

When the water finished its colossal wave against doors and buildings and slid off gutters, it rushed back to the canals, carrying with it misshapen men and bent rifles. It left the roofs sagging, the Coal Works steaming, Theodore's hands and teeth shaking to holy hell.

Theodore watched those broken bodies become discarded on the cobbles or be sucked into the canals, eyes bulging. He looked at his hands, and Patrick wondered if he imagined them covered in blood.

"We need to hurry," Theodore said meekly, as though there wasn't enough breath in his lungs to draw from. "If they're looking for Nina, we need to find her first."

But Patrick lifted his working arm. He pointed his pistol directly at Theodore's mouth and watched as all color bled from the man's face.

"Patrick, I just saved your life."

"Tell me if it's true," he said simply. The words scratched at his throat and came out tattered. "Please . . . tell me. Did Tanner send her to me?"

Theodore's eyes fell to the gun, and then back onto Patrick. He seemed to be waning, just as Nina had after she'd saved Kenton Hill from an entire landslide. His energies were spent. "Tanner is the reason she came here," he said earnestly. "But she wanted to stay for *you*."

But there were only so many people on the continent who knew what he was and what he could do. Nina had sold him to Tanner.

Nina had brought hell to Kenton Hill.

He was a fool after all.

Patrick pulled the trigger, a terranium bullet firing from the barrel, coursing through air barriers toward Theo's teeth.

It stopped midair.

Theo recoiled away from the blast, his eyes screwed shut. It took him several moments to look through the slits of his eyes, to see the black bullet levitating before him.

"Why did you come back?" Patrick asked. "The truth, this time."

Theo shuddered delicately. "I was angry when I left you that letter," he said. "But by the time I reached the next town, I regretted it. I was worried you might hurt her, and I—I had to come back. Just to make sure—"

"That I hadn't shot her?" Patrick spat.

Theo eyed the bullet and nodded once.

"You love her," Patrick surmised.

And Theo nodded again.

"It's the only reason you're not dead now. You hear me?"

The man exhaled in a gust. The bullet kissed the bridge of his nose.

"You'll put out the rest of the fires," Patrick commanded. "It'll give me time to consider whether I shouldn't blast you away."

Theo swallowed. Nodded. "We should hurry."

Indeed. Kenton still burned. To the north, nearer to the square, the fires spread of their own accord, no longer compelled by anything but their own appetite.

Patrick collected his bullet, replaced it in the chamber, and grimaced against the pain in his shoulder. He collected the rifle from where it lay. "Come on," he said, running with Donny and Theodore in tow, back toward the sounds of rampant artillery. He collected the blossoming truth of it all and buried it deep. After all, it was likely that by night's end, both he and Theodore would lay dead. He'd be relieved from the knife in his middle.

She lied to you, sang a voice. *Outsmarted you. You were too stupid to see it.*

Patrick ran faster. He passed every familiar building like a comet.

And you can't even kill her for it, can you? taunted the voice.

CHAPTER 66

NINA

The bangs and blasts wrenched me from unconsciousness.

My neck tilted at an uncomfortable angle. A splintering pain pulsed behind my right eye. My back reclined over something solid and unforgiving—ration sacks. The confines of the bunker began to free themselves from the dark.

I was underground again. Beneath a grate, most likely.

I forced my reluctant hands to search along the gritty floor, forced my knees to crawl until I found a wall. My hands searched each crevice of mortar until they found a lantern. I pulled its cord and blinked against the sudden relief of light.

I was alone. And trapped. The bunker cover above was firmly in place. When I tried to push it away, it did not budge.

And beyond it, the fighting raged on. It shook the brickwork, shook the lantern in its sconce. And at every shot, I pictured Otto, Scottie, Briggs, Donny. I pictured Gunner. Patrick. They could all be dead. How long had I been unconscious?

With a grunt of frustration, I hit the timber that fortified the ceiling and was surprised when it shuddered in response.

The bunker cover turned an inch, and the timber shuddered some more.

I backed away in time for the cover to lift away completely, and the faces of two strangers hovered above, their eyes frenzied.

One of them had blood dribbling from his lip. Both wore the Artisan military insignia on their lapels.

"It's the earth Charmer!" one said. He had a Western accent, clipped and precise.

"Thank Idia," said the other. He even smiled.

And though I despised myself, I covered my ears against the noise and said, "Help me, please. My name is Nina Clarke."

· · · · · ●

The town square had turned into a smoldering mess. I blinked at the walls of smoke, tried to grasp the movement all around. It seemed the entire world was churning. Thousands of bodies colliding and melding and separating.

"Keep moving," commanded the soldier, voice at my ear. "We'll have you safely away into the tunnel, Miss Clarke. Keep your head down."

Death was everywhere. Another body hit the pavement every second. Bayonets sprouted through backs and necks and stomachs. A spray of bullets weaved through the navy uniforms.

I saw it unfolding in horrific slowness. Through the smoke, rooftops gave way.

The Crafters were losing.

"Hurry, miss!"

What use were shells and pistols and ticking mines against thousands of soldiers?

Kenton Hill couldn't win. It was plain to see. Somewhere in the chaos, I saw Gunner's arm swing wildly, a blade in his grasp. His eyes were deadened, his teeth gritted. I realized that he must have discerned, surely, that it was all hopeless.

But they would all keep fighting. The Miners Union would bleed themselves dry into the square to keep the Lords' Army from filtering outward for as long they could. They would place themselves in the way of these soldiers and their families, their neighbors, and give them time to run. Many would make it to the tunnels, to safety.

That was all they could hope for now.

I saw Gunner's head descend below the fray and let loose a sob. I prayed that Patrick was still in Baymouth, far away.

The doors to Margarite's materialized through the smoke, its windows shattered, the strange wooden mannequins riddled through.

"Get inside, miss," said the soldier at my back, his breath saturated in fear. In urgency. A stray bullet hit the last remaining window at our side.

But a different sound was growing. Something that quelled the booms and bangs of the square. It was enough to halt the scream of the artillery. I turned abruptly, as did every pair of eyes, and they each settled on a glinting wall of glass.

No, not glass. Water.

It grew and morphed into a monstrous mass above. Swallowing the rooftops to the south. Smothering the flames. Coursing closer at a tremendous speed.

And the men began to run. They ran to the perimeter of the square and curled their bodies like snails or else bashed at the confines that imprisoned them beneath this wave. It skirted the southern rooftops.

And I closed my eyes before the water hammered down.

For several manic moments, the only sound was a violent rush of water. It ripped the hand from my shoulder, knocked limbs in every direction. I was being carried, rolled, spun head over heel. I felt my bones strain against that which they collided with. And I only had enough sense to hold my breath. To shut my eyes.

I was discarded onto the cobbles. Limp, bruised, panting. The water dispersing supernaturally, as quickly as it had arrived.

I coughed among the cacophony of a thousand coughs, tried to make sense of that which had become senseless. I was dizzy. Displaced. There was a man lying across my stomach who I feared was dead. He did not flinch as I crawled out from under him. All around, soldiers and Crafters lifted their heads, peeled themselves off shop fronts and away from broken glass.

Through the square's brick arch, three figures emerged.

I could have distinguished them in less favorable conditions. Even in the night, amid the haze of steam, I knew these men.

Patrick. Theodore. Donny.

Theodore walked forward on legs that looked unwilling, exhausted, but it was Patrick that I watched. He stalked to the middle of the square, his shoulder blooming red. And he stood alone.

Then, horrifyingly, he held a pistol to his own head.

There was sudden movement from my left, a man standing. Gunner. "Patty," he called brokenly. Gunner held on to his stomach, where a wound bled profusely. He stumbled. "Patty, what're you—"

Patrick looked once to Gunner, and his face crumpled slightly, but he looked quickly away. With a thunderous voice, he bellowed, "I am Patrick Colson, the last remainin' Alchemist," and he pulled from his pocket a black rock, no bigger than his palm.

More men stirred. Many in navy uniform stood unsteadily. They raised their weapons.

But the terranium rock was instantly recognizable. So coveted in recent months. It stayed them. Patrick let the rock rise from his fingertips, let it float high above them all, and pulverized it. It turned to powder and fell to Patrick's feet.

The Lords' infantry seemed to pause collectively. Barrel ends wavered. Soldiers looked warily to one another.

Patrick did not lower the pistol from his head. "If you leave this town now, with no further fight, I will go with you willingly." His hand around the pistol tightened. "But if another bullet is fired at any man or woman of Kenton Hill, I will pull this trigger, and the water Charmer behind me will fill this entire square."

"No," I muttered, though I could not seem to fish oxygen from the air. I tried to rise to my feet, but there was a long cut on my thigh. It burned fiercely, and I stumbled. "NO!" I yelled.

And he heard it. He found me in that mess of bodies, fallen and battered. His eyes welled. His jaw pulsed.

And he shifted his eyes away again. *"Leave now,"* he said again. "And my soldiers will lay down their guns—"

"No, Pat!" Gunner shouted, blood seeping through his fingers.

"—and they will vacate this square."

"PATRICK!" I shouted.

"They will not try to stop you from taking me." His hand shook. His chest quaked. "But hear this! I will gladly shoot myself now if another of my own is struck down. Don't think I won't use this second to do it. Stand down."

There was confusion from soldier and Crafter both.

"STAND DOWN!" called Patrick, and he cocked the hammer.

A general with ranking stripes on his uniform moved forward slowly. He held his bayonet in one hand, its barrel skyward. His other hand was raised, placating. His eyes were pinned to Patrick. "Easy," he said, and then over his shoulder. *"Hold your fire."*

It seemed unnecessary. Every fighter was washed up. Half the ones still standing had lost their weapon or seemed unsure whether to point it at a man with a gun to his own head.

Otto had risen from the lot. He hobbled to Gunner's side, tried to pull him back.

"Direct your men to retreat," said the general to Patrick. "And I'll do the same."

My eyes were glued to that pistol at Patrick's temple. I felt suddenly, horribly sure that he meant what he said. That he'd rather shoot himself here than see the rest of Kenton Hill burn.

He'd rather give himself in to the Artisans.

"No," I whispered. Standing. Falling.

"All miners," Patrick called, and his voice wavered. He closed his eyes but kept the gun poised. "To the hills. To your families. Now."

It happened in painful increments. The surviving fighters of Kenton Hill rose. Some hoisted injured comrades over their shoulders. Others ran without looking back.

"GO!" Patrick bellowed to those more stubborn. "NOW!"

And perhaps they saw the desperation in his face. Perhaps they saw, then, this last gift Patrick had granted them. A thread of victory, the smallest of consolations. Patrick held the pistol steadfast. "Tell your men to get back into the fuckin' hole they came from," Patrick seethed. "Or you'll be tellin' Tanner it was all for naught."

The general gestured to his soldiers, a silent command. Slowly, they slunk back through the doors of Margarite's, their boots crunching over the glass. Warily, each retreated, miner and soldier, with red-rimmed eyes and blood on their hands. They took the wounded with them, and the square emptied. The Lords' Army dwindled to a small legion.

And I saw Theodore slink away, back into the shadows of the alley he'd come from, his eyes to the ground, as though he could not bear to meet anyone's gaze.

But Gunner refused to move. Otto remained at his side and was joined by Scottie, his eyebrow split, and Briggs, whose ear hung in bloody tatters, and Donny, who touched his forehead to Gunner's. Scottie laid down his weapon first. Then the rest. They peeled the rifle from Gunner's unwilling fingers, and the man let out a gut-wrenching yell.

I rose from the ground, then ran across the cobbles, unbalanced on my injured leg, past the general and all the way to Patrick, who did not react when I crushed myself to him, closing my arms around his middle.

I clutched him as a drowning person clutches a raft. I shook and shivered and dug my fingers in. I sobbed and thought they'd need a knife to cut me away.

I thought, *At least they'll take us both.*

But when I looked up into Patrick's face, he did not look back. He looked over me, away from me. The pistol remained at his temple and when he spoke, his voice was ice-cold. "Run," he said, and then, more brokenly. "Now."

And I didn't understand it, at first. Didn't recognize the hurt, the hatred. Not until his fingers curled over mine and ripped them harshly from his coat. He pushed me away. "Go," he said once more. "Theo will find you."

There was a resolve in his face, the one a convicted man wears as the noose pinches tight.

But I shook my head. "No," I said.

And I heard him curse as I turned my back. Heard him call to me as I took a step toward the general. "My name is Nina Clarke," I said loudly, and I watched recognition dawn as he took in the sight of me. "The earth Charmer."

"*Traitor!*" Gunner thundered, his eyes streaming. Scottie and Otto held him back at either side.

But the general nodded. Two soldiers came toward me. They grasped my upper arms.

"Lower the gun now, boy," the general called to Patrick. "Throw it to the ground."

I looked over my shoulder in time to see Patrick lift the pistol off his temple, only to point it directly at the general.

Several things happened at once.

The remaining soldiers raised their weapons.

A blade flashed in Gunner's hand.

And Patrick said, very clearly. "You'll take me alone and let the earth Charmer go."

The general looked from Patrick to me, his hands still raised. "We've orders to bring her back to the House of Lords," he said. "Alive."

"Then you'll be breaking those orders," Patrick said. "Now, tell your men to let her go."

The general seemed to deliberate for a long moment. Then, he sighed, and said, "I'll at least thank you for removing that pistol from your head."

And the gun was wrenched from Patrick's hand, as though something invisible pulled it. It fired once as Patrick tried to keep his grasp around its trigger, but the bullet only shattered a far-off window.

The pistol flew into the general's hand. He smiled at it. "We'll be taking you both," he said.

"No!" Gunner roared, and he made to lunge at the officer, but the blade in his hand turned on him, and the wound it made buckled him in half.

"Gunner!" Patrick shouted.

"Tell your men not to be foolish," the Smith said. "The fight's over."

CHAPTER 67

NINA

The soldiers tied our hands in front of us, walked us through Margarite's Modern Ladies, Seamstress Extraordinaire, over the wooden debris and into the storage room, where the trapdoor lay open and waiting.

I moved to the whim of the soldiers as if through a nightmare. My legs not my own, the gut-wrenching shouts of Gunner ringing out from the square. They grew weak quickly, and I imagined pints of blood slipping free, drawing the life from him.

Before I was lowered into the pit, the shouts ceased.

Patrick and I stood before the shaft and its pulleys to the tunnel we'd built together.

We were not lowered immediately. Before the soldiers could begin operating the pulleys, they were interrupted by feet staggering down the path. Three men came into view.

Two were soldiers, and between them was Theo, his face badly battered. His head lolled on his shoulders, unconscious.

"Found the water Charmer," one of the soldiers said. The rest of the navy blues cheered, slapped their comrades' backs as Theo was dumped into the shaft. "Let's see what his father has to say about that stunt, eh?"

The shaft lift sank down its fathoms, its joints clanking, metal screeching.

And as darkness fell, I couldn't see Patrick. But I could feel him beside me, his shoulder pressed to mine. I let it soothe me.

We'll find a way out, I thought. *I'll find us a way out.*

"Patrick," I said, not caring who heard me. But no answer followed.

Instead, I felt him shift suddenly. I felt the entire breadth of his weight shove me into the wall of the shaft. I felt his forearm push into the column of my throat.

The space filled with the shouts of men. I heard them scramble in the dark, trying to make sense of the movement, grasping blindly at Patrick's back.

I felt my eyes water and could hear my own blood pounding in my ears.

And his lips were at my ear. His speech was strangled, but I heard it clearly. "If there was ever a small part of you that loved me," he said. "Then you will sink this tunnel. Bury us all."

And then he was gone, pulled away by the soldiers at his back.

Oxygen rushed back into my lungs.

"Someone tie him up!"

The shaft clanked interminably downward.

There was a sharp thwack as a soldier struck Patrick with a baton.

And somewhere beneath us, cycling up the shaft, a canary sang.

ACKNOWLEDGMENTS

As I write this, my beloved first Alchemy book is still half a year away from its release, and already the support has been overwhelming. To the readers who've followed me from one book launch to the next, I'm indebted to you.

Ironically, this book came from failure. I had written another before it which failed to make any headway in the pitching process, and I was advised to pivot. Try something else. Come back to it later.

At the time, I very much wanted to dig my heels in. But as ideas tend to, I was railroaded by an underground network of tunnels and a woman who could start earthquakes. Nina Harrow decided that we would, indeed, pivot, and I was unable to think of anything else until this story was written.

Thanks must go to *Peaky Blinders*, *Six of Crows*, and my strange fascination with war history. *A Forbidden Alchemy* is a strange medley of weird imaginings inspired by these.

Amy A. Collins of Talcott Notch Literary, the best-looking agent I've ever met. If you were an Artisan, your medium would be earth. Thank you for moving mountains for me (ew, I hated that).

To the team at Saga Press, what to say other than thank you for giving this book such a warm home. Thank you for loving this story, and for your ceaseless efforts to give it life. Amara Hoshijo, roses for you forever. Thank you for championing Nina and Patrick.

To my found family, Hannah, Kaven, Amber, Samantha, and Maggie, my first ports of call for every miserable and amazing update. Thank you, always, for holding my hand, come what may.

ACKNOWLEDGMENTS

The McCallums: Mum, Dad, Alycia, and Teagan, my goal is always to make you proud. Thank you for being so weird and funny and loving (Dad, don't read this book, I'm not kidding this time).

Fifteen years ago I met my husband in a university lecture hall, and I've been infuriating him ever since. To Michael, my best friend, thank you for making it easy to do what I love. Thank you for loving me through it. The best parts of Patrick's character is based on your temperament and the way you care for those around you; quietly, and without much reward. I'll let you take the credit for him this time. I love you.

To those kids mentioned in the dedication, Zoe and Dean. I hope your Dad and I can give you a soft, gentle life. I hope you run wildly through it knowing we'll catch you. I hope you grow to realize the extent of our love for you.

Finally, to you, the reader. I hope you found solace in Kenton Hill before I burnt it all down. Sorry about that. I'll get to fixing it.

BELAVERE

Belavere City

Gilmore

Fenway

GYSER RIVER

Morland

Brimshire

Sommerland

Baymouth